DEATH IN PANAMA

To Janie,

I hope you enjoy it!

Bill

November 2017

Death in Panama is a work of fiction. Names, characters, places, and incidents are the products of the author's imagination or are used fictitiously. Any resemblance to actual events or to any person, living or dead, is entirely coincidental.

ISBN 978-0-9989703-0-1
eBook ISBN 978-0-9989703-1-8

www.williamhvenema.com

To all the men and women who are serving, or who have served, our country in the Armed Forces:

Thank you.

ACKNOWLEDGEMENTS AND DISCLAIMER

Death in Panama has been long in the making and influenced by many. Numerous friends and family members encouraged me along the way. In particular, however, I must thank my former law partner, Sherie Bush, who carefully read my manuscript with the eye of a perfectionist. I am blessed to call her my friend. I also owe a special thanks to Mr. Tom T. Hall for allowing me to quote his wonderful song, "Old Dogs, Children, and Watermelon Wine," in Chapter Seven. Finally, I must thank my wife, who patiently put up with my devotion to a project that she began to call my "mistress."

Because I served in the Army in Panama during the period described in this story, some readers might be tempted to conclude that this book is autobiographical or is, at least, loosely based on real people. Neither conclusion is correct. This book is entirely a work of fiction. Although some people who knew me during that period might think certain characters are based on real persons, they are not. Any similarity between the characters in this book and any real people, living or dead, is purely coincidental.

This book tells a fictional story that I hope the reader will find entertaining, thought-provoking, and perhaps even meaningful.

PROLOGUE

Sunday, December 19, 1982

THE OLDER MAN walked toward the young captain. He was elegantly attired in a dark blue pinstripe suit and a crisp white shirt despite the Panamanian heat. His tie was a red foulard; a matching pocket square puffed from his breast pocket. The Army captain—on his first assignment since graduating from medical school—hoped Dr. Gonzalez's medical acumen was equal to his appearance. They needed a miracle.

As they walked down the hall to the examining room where their patient was being treated, the captain briefed Dr. Gonzalez. "The parents brought their daughter in early this morning. She was lethargic. We examined her thoroughly and connected her to an IV, thinking she had acute bacterial diarrhea—like ninety percent of the kids we see."

They entered a small, windowless room away from the chaos of the emergency room examining bays. Dr. Gonzalez immediately removed his suit jacket and tie and draped them over a chair. The little girl was lying on an examining table, barely conscious. A nurse was stroking her matted, sweaty hair.

"Her breathing has been irregular all day," the captain explained. "She continued to be lethargic, so we intubated her."

The young captain looked at Dr. Gonzalez, seeking approval but got nothing. The elder doctor just continued to stare at the little girl. "I've never had to cut such a small trachea," he continued. Still no response. "She's been on the ventilator most of the day."

"That's good," said Dr. Gonzalez, finally nodding. "The oxygen will protect her brain if the blood supply has been compromised." He washed his hands and shoved them into the surgical gloves offered by the senior nurse. They snapped against his wrists. With great formality he turned and walked to the table, where he gave—first the nurse and then the patient—a practiced smile. "You don't look too good, Sweetie. I hope we can make you feel better soon." The little girl's glassy eyes stared up at him, her face expressionless.

"We've also kept her on an IV," said the captain. "When she presented, she couldn't keep any fluids down, and we were worried she'd dehydrate." The head nurse held a file folder in front of the captain and pointed to something. "Oh, yes, and she had a seizure that caused her to lose consciousness."

Dr. Gonzalez stopped his examination and stared straight ahead. "What time did this seizure occur?" he asked, squinting his eyes.

The captain turned to the nurse. "Thirteen thirty hours, sir."

"That's 1:30 p.m., Dr. Gonzalez," said the captain.

"You should have called me sooner," he sighed, shaking his head.

"We tried, several times…" Dr. Gonzalez abruptly stopped his examination, stood erect, shoulders back, and then turned to face the captain but said nothing. The young officer said nothing and avoided eye contact. After a few moments of silence, it was clear who was in charge, and Dr. Gonzalez turned back to his patient. He closely examined her neck and moved her head slightly from side to side. Taking a small penlight from his shirt pocket, he shined it into each eye. "Her pupils are dilated and respond sluggishly to light. Nurse, please make a note in her records." Turning to the captain, he added, "That is a bad sign. What is her blood pressure?"

"It's low, 78 over 40."

"What tests have you run?" asked Dr. Gonzalez—raising his eyebrows, as he looked over the top of his glasses, which had slid to the end of his nose.

"Just the usual tests we run when we suspect the patient has bacterial diarrhea. Cultures. Blood work."

"No CT scan?"

"No. There's only one scanner, so we have to request authorization because…"

"We need a CT scan immediately," said Dr. Gonzalez. "Nurse, please call Colonel Meacher. Tell him Dr. Gonzalez needs a CT scan on an infant female. Tell him it is urgent." He watched her scurry off and then turned back to the captain. "We need to have a CT scan to see if her brain is swelling. If it is, we need to know how much and where." He paused and shook his head. "I fear it might be too late."

"What else should I have done, Doctor?" asked the young captain—his voice now trembling slightly.

"Nothing, Capitain," he replied with a comforting half smile. "These things are very difficult to diagnose." He perused her medical records, which included only the treatment she had received that day. After ten minutes that seemed like an hour, the nurse returned with word that Colonel Meacher had approved the CT scan.

The nurses moved their patient onto a gurney and wheeled her, the IV bag, and the ventilator to the room where the CT scanner was located. The big, white doughnut-shaped machine was intimidating to most people. But this little girl was too sick to register any protest as the big machine clunked and whirred around her.

On his way back to the examining room, the captain stopped

by a break room and poured coffee into two Styrofoam cups. He took a sip. It was harsh and bitter. Probably been sitting there since this morning, but at least it's hot. He picked up a handful of sugar packets and the jar of powdered creamer and returned to the examining room.

"I wasn't sure how you take your coffee, Doctor, so I brought these."

"No time for that, Capitain. The scan confirmed that this child's brain is swelling. We must operate immediately to relieve the pressure. I need for you to obtain consent for surgery from her parents."

When the senior nurse offered the captain a consent form, he fumbled with the cups, causing him to spill hot coffee onto his bare arm. He flinched and set the cups on a counter.

"Quickly, Capitain. Tell them we are going to do a craniotomy. "

"I'm not sure that…"

"We have no choice, Capitain. This little girl will die if we do not operate. Get an operating room ready immediately."

The young captain froze. After a few moments, he turned to the head nurse, standing next to him like a coiled spring. "You heard him. Get OR One ready ASAP. Dr. Gonzalez, is there anything in particular you will need?"

"We will need to make burr holes, and we will pro'ly need to do a full craniotomy."

"Ensure that Dr. Gonzalez has a complete set of instruments. Get going." He turned back to Dr. Gonzalez, "I'll go talk to her parents."

"Hurry, Capitain. You will be assisting me."

After a few minutes, the captain rejoined Dr. Gonzalez. "I'm not sure the parents understand what's going on…"

"I will talk to them after the surgery," said Dr. Gonzalez. "Quickly, Capitain, change into scrubs and get washed up."

The two men walked into the operating room. Their little patient—still connected to the IV and ventilator—now had all manner of monitors and machines and tubes connected to her as well. Two nurses hovered over her, assisting the anesthesiologist, who was finishing his work. Within a few moments she was under.

"Shave her head," said Dr. Gonzalez. "Quickly, please." The head nurse—now in scrubs—stepped forward and with just a few strokes shaved the little girl's hair. Her movements were smooth, precise, efficient. She caught the hair in a towel, which she tossed into a receptacle and then washed the girl's head with an antiseptic soap that resembled strong tea.

The captain stared at the motionless child. Her eyes were closed, and tubes and monitoring lines were everywhere. The ventilator clicked and whirred as it methodically pumped air into her tiny lungs. It sounded so mechanical. And now, without hair, she looked even more fragile—a little shell of a person hanging on to life.

"First, we will make a burr hole," said Dr. Gonzalez, sounding like an instructor in medical school. He took a scalpel from the tray and made an incision in her scalp. Then he took a retractor and positioned it to hold back her scalp. "Cauterize those bleeders, Capitain." The captain's hands shook as he worked to stop the bleeding.

Dr. Gonzalez picked up a sharply pointed drill. He pulsed it a few times in the air to ensure it was working properly. The sound of the motor announced to everyone what was about to happen. He touched the slick, freshly shaved head and then pressed the bit against her cranium in the center of the incision he'd just made. As the bit dug into her skull, pieces of bone and tissue and blood splattered onto Dr. Gonzalez and the captain. Unfazed, he continued, "You must start with the sharp drill, and once the hole is large enough..." He stopped and picked up an instrument that resembled a carpenter's brace. "You switch to a blunt-ended burr hole bit to complete the drilling through the skull. This brace and bit minimizes the chance that you will penetrate the dura prematurely. You must be very careful at this stage. There... I've penetrated the dura." He looked intently at her skull. "*Mierda!* Just as I feared. Her brain is swelling."

The captain looked down and saw brain tissue oozing through the hole in her skull like toothpaste from a tube. For a moment, he forgot he was looking at the skull of a little girl.

Dr. Gonzalez continued his directions. "We must remove a portion of her skull immediately." The captain stood transfixed, staring down at the skull. "Capitain, listen to me! Assist me. Open her scalp to approximately six centimeters." The captain flinched and then tentatively picked up a scalpel and started to increase the incision. "I need more room, Capitain. I need to remove a portion of her skull. We must relieve the pressure immediately. If her brain herniates and swells downward, she will die. Do you understand? The areas of the brain that control her breathing and other functions will be compressed, and she will die. Do you understand me?"

The captain stared at the experienced surgeon's hand, as he used what looked like a small electric saw to make precise cuts into the girl's skull in the shape of a triangle. As he cut, her skull pressed upward, and more brain tissue seeped out.

"Nurse, I need some gauze on my brow," said Dr. Gonzalez. "This is terrible. Have you given her any steroids, Capitain?"

"No."

"Nurse, give her ten milligrams of dexamethasone," said Dr. Gonzalez. "Immediately. Let's see if we can slow down this edema."

The nurse left and quickly returned with a vial. She stared at the two doctors, awaiting instructions.

"Give her ten milligrams. Quickly."

"Should we remove more of her skull?" asked the captain.

"No. This is as much as we can remove without risking serious infection," said Dr. Gonzalez with more emotion in his voice than at any time since he arrived.

"What do we do now?" asked the captain.

"We wait. We wait to see if what we've done helps her."

"What if it's not enough?" asked the captain.

CHAPTER ONE

285 days *earlier*
Tuesday, March 9, 1982

ROBERT E. CLARK stepped out of the plane at Howard Air Force Base and was blinded by intense sunlight. It felt as if God had turned an interrogation lamp on him—the only thing missing was His booming voice and a burning bush. He reached for his sunglasses but stopped when his three-year-old began to squirm in the crook of his right arm. He grabbed the stair rail with his left hand, fearing he might stumble down the steps with her. At the bottom, he felt extreme heat rising from the tarmac and saw blurry waves as light refracted near its surface. Disoriented, he forgot to put on his cap and gave no thought to whether his wife had made it down the steps. He just wanted to get inside the terminal… fast. As he approached the open door, a rush of air-conditioned coolness helped him regain his composure.

"Welcome to Panama," came a Southern drawl from somewhere in the darkness. As Clark's eyes adjusted to the light inside, a wide, toothy grin appeared. It belonged to a tall, slim officer whose rather long, sun-bleached hair caused him to resemble a lifeguard dressed up in an Army officer's khaki uniform. "Hot as hell, isn't it?" he continued, without losing his grin. Then, extending his hand, "I'm Trip… Trip Stephens, your sponsor."

"Hell, yes, it's hot… Robert E. Clark," he said, shaking Trip's hand, "But my friends call me 'Clark.' How do people live in this shit?"

"You'll get used to it," Trip laughed, "You're a Southern boy, aren't you? Let's go get your stuff."

"I've gotta go to the bathroom," blurted a voice nearby, causing Clark to realize for the first time since leaving the plane that his normally talkative wife was behind him, also stunned by their new environment.

"I'm sorry, Sugar. I should've helped you down the steps." He turned to see his wife, cheeks flushed and drenched in sweat.

"I'm all right," she huffed, "but I do have to go to the bathroom."

"Trip, this is my wife, Janelle Clark. And this sweet little thing is Eloise, but we call her 'Ellie'." Ellie smiled at Trip with bright blue eyes and then tucked her face into her daddy's shoulder.

"Delighted to meet y'all."

Clark turned back to his wife. "Why don't you take Ellie and go find the 'facilities,' while Trip and I get the luggage?"

Although the Clark family had flown down from the States on what looked like a civilian passenger jet, the baggage-claim area bore no resemblance to a civilian airport. Instead of a circling carousel of suitcases, there was a pile of duffle bags, suitcases, and boxes thrown in the corner of the terminal. Although Clark had marked their bags with distinctive yellow tags, it took some time to locate all six, which he and Trip lugged to the curb outside the terminal.

Trip left to get his car and returned in a few minutes in a midnight blue, late model BMW 530 with tan leather interior. He jumped out to help Clark with the luggage but, upon opening the trunk, discovered he'd forgotten to unload his golf clubs. That meant three bags had to ride in the back seat, piled next to Clark and Ellie. Janelle sat in front with Trip.

As Trip drove down the palm-lined streets of Howard Air Force Base, Clark had no idea where he was headed. He knew Trip was taking them across the Panama Canal to Fort Clayton, where he would begin his career as an Army lawyer. He knew that, but he had no inkling of what was in store for him there. Everything he thought he knew about himself, his values, and the world around him was about to be challenged.

But at that moment those challenges were months away. He rode along in blissful ignorance of what was to come, excited about his future and captivated by the natural beauty around him. Red, pink, and yellow flowers formed splashes of vibrant colors against lush green foliage. Palm fronds on the trees lining the street swayed in the breeze against a brilliant blue sky. Crossing the Bridge of Americas, high above the water, they had a spectacular view of the Panama Canal and the Gulf of Panama. Two large, white cruise ships glistened in the sunlight, alongside two drab, box-like freighters, all waiting to enter the Miraflores Locks on their way to the Caribbean. Janelle turned around from the front seat and said, with wide eyes, "You know, Bobby, it's kinda like what Dorothy said: we're not in Georgia anymore."

A condescending smile crossed Trip's face, but it quickly disappeared when the traffic stalled and the grimy face of a small boy appeared outside the driver's side window. He held up a plastic bottle of gray water and a dirty rag, offering to clean the windshield. "Go away!" Trip shouted through the glass, waving his hand. The boy disappeared, and Trip proceeded through the thick traffic. "Sorry, Janelle. Sometimes you have to be rude to these people. Now, where were we? Oh yeah. Tell me about yourselves. Y'all are both from Georgia, right?"

"That's right," Janelle began, "Pemberton, Georgia, right outside Savannah. But, of course, most recently we've been at Fort

Hood and Athens and the JAG School. You know, Trip, Bobby and I have known each other our whole lives."

"Really?" The thin smile reappeared.

Janelle then proceeded to tell their entire life story to this person whom they'd just met. It wasn't the first time—she loved to talk about anything and everything to anybody. On their flight to Panama, she'd given the woman in the seat next to her a detailed account of their daughter's birth.

Her monologue continued. "We dated in high school. During Bobby's first year at West Point, I wrote him every day. Until he went off to school, the only time we were apart was when we went to church. My daddy and me are Baptists, and Bobby's family is all Methodist."

"You know how that goes in a small Southern town, Trip," Clark offered from the back seat, "most folks are Baptists or Methodists, although there isn't much difference—they're all pretty conservative. Folks used to say, 'Our churches are so conservative even the Episcopalians handle snakes.'"

Trip smiled again. "I'd say that's pretty conservative. There wasn't much talk of snakes in my church back home."

"Where are you from, Trip?" Janelle asked.

"Well, I guess you'd say I'm an Episcopalian from Jackson, Mississippi."

After a few moments of silence, Clark coughed and said, "Trip, I, uh, I meant no offense by that joke."

"Oh, none taken, Bobby. Or is it 'Clark'?"

"It's 'Clark.' Only Janelle and my family call me 'Bobby' anymore."

"Yeah, no offense taken, Clark. It's actually pretty funny because it's true—Episcopalians are a pretty formal bunch." Trip paused, seeming to collect his thoughts. "My family's been in Mississippi forever..." His voice trailed off as if he'd lost his train of thought—or decided not to continue. After a few moments, he began again, "Y'all will soon find out that Panama is *a lot* different from the States. I suppose it's the hot weather that makes people a little crazy. It's a fascinating place, though. By the way, do either of y'all play golf?"

Before Clark could say anything, Janelle answered, "No, Trip, Bobby doesn't play any sports. All he does is work. He's been that way his whole life. In high school all he did was work and study, work and study. He didn't know how to have fun."

Clark squirmed in the back seat, causing one of the suitcases to slide in Ellie's direction. After shoving it back into place, he said, through clenched teeth, "Well, I knew I needed to be prepared for West Point."

"You worked like a mad man there, too," she said, turning to the back seat. "Didn't you say you only slept five hours a night?" She paused when she saw the look on his face and softened her tone. "Bobby, you know everybody in Pemberton was proud of you." Smiling, she turned back to Trip. "When we thought about West Point, Trip, we thought about the men carved on Stone Mountain—Robert E. Lee, Stonewall Jackson, Jeff Davis. For one of our boys to be going to their school was a big deal."

"The truth is, Trip, none of them thought I'd make it."

"Well, you never made the football team. You didn't play any sports."

"I don't think Trip is interested in my lack of athletic ability, Janelle," Clark said with a forced smile.

"Well, you remember when Stanley Griffin came back home from the Air Force Academy when we were seniors. And he'd been the captain of the football team and class president his senior year. People thought if he couldn't make it…"

"But you obviously did make it through West Point," Trip interjected. "That must've been tough. And you must've done pretty well—you were a FLEP, weren't you? If I remember correctly,

13

aren't there only twenty-five officers out of hundreds of applicants who get selected for the Funded Legal Education Program?"

"Yeah. That's right. Then I went to law school at the University of Georgia. Where'd you go, Trip?"

"Ole Miss," he sighed. "It's a family tradition: my father and grandfather both went there. If I ever have a son, I'm sure they'll expect him to go there, too. 'Hotty Toddy, Gosh almighty,' and all that…" Trip smiled, but not like a loyal Ole Miss Rebel. After a few moments, he continued, "So, after law school you went to the JAG School in Charlottesville?"

"That's right."

"We had a number of FLEPs in my basic class," Trip offered. "Most of them were West Point graduates. We used to watch them in classes like 'Introduction to Map Reading.' They were bored out of their minds. But they said the training we had on the Uniform Code of Military Justice was much better than what they'd had at West Point or the basic courses in their original branches."

"I'd agree with that," Clark replied. "In fact, I decided to become a JAG, in part, because nobody in my unit, including my company commander, seemed to know how to use the UCMJ to deal with all the BS."

"What do you mean?"

Janelle interrupted. "Are there any malls down here, Trip?"

"Huh? Uh, yeah, but you'll find they aren't like the ones back home. Mostly cheap junk. The good shopping is in downtown Panama City. I've found some fine linens and jewelry that were very reasonably priced."

"I was trying to answer Trip's question, Janelle. Trip, you asked what I meant about all the BS. I was referring to what I found when I got to my platoon. Vietnam had been over less than a year, and the Army was exhausted. We had more dirt bags than good soldiers, more high-school dropouts than high-school graduates. And nobody seemed to know how to use the Uniform

Code of Military Justice to get rid of the bad apples. One of my troops even pulled a knife on me. When I told my company commander about it, he just asked me if the guy lunged at me. Can you believe that? What difference should that make?"

"It sounds like you want to be a prosecutor."

"Absolutely."

"Well, we'll have to see what Colonel Allen has to say about that," Trip replied, in a way that suggested there was something important he wasn't saying.

For a moment Clark considered asking him to explain but decided to play it safe. "So, Allen is a full colonel?"

"No. Lieutenant colonel. That's what's authorized for this SJA slot."

"What's an SJA?" Janelle asked, indicating that she was paying attention.

"It's the staff judge advocate," Clark explained from the back seat. "He's the head lawyer in Panama."

Trip turned off the road and pulled up in front of a dreary pink stucco building with a terra cotta tile roof. The mold on the outside walls gave a hint of what they'd discover inside. "This is it," he announced. "The visiting officers' quarters. Unfortunately, y'all will have to stay here for a while. We couldn't put you in for quarters, because you have to do that yourself when you in-process. It isn't too bad, though. At least it's air conditioned, and the food is pretty good."

The oppressive Panamanian heat greeted them again when they got out of the car. Janelle took Ellie inside to get cool, while Clark and Trip hauled in the luggage. They had barely exchanged "goodbyes" when Janelle started whispering her list of complaints.

"Trip was right about the air conditioning, but it's really too cool. Do you smell that? It smells like cigarettes and mold at the same time. Ellie should *not* be breathing that stuff."

"We don't have any choice, Janelle. There's no other place to stay." She gave him a sullen look, as he turned to approach the registration desk.

Without looking up, the plump woman seated behind the counter mumbled, "How lon' you gonna stay here?"

"We just arrived from Charleston. Here's a copy of my orders," Clark said, pushing the document across the counter.

"I don' nee' to see no orders. Captain Stephens tol' me you gonna be here until you ge' into quarters. Did he tell you how lon'?"

"No."

"Well, you gonna be in Room 215. I's a nice room."

"Is there anyone to help us with our bags?"

The clerk looked up for the first time. "No, you gotta tha' yourself, and you can' leave dem here. You nee' to hurry i' you wanna eat, 'cause the restauran' gonna close' in t'irty minutes, an' we go' no room service."

Great. Welcome to Panama. Turning toward Janelle, Clark was going to suggest that she take Ellie to their room, but she was already on the way. It took him three trips to get all six bags to the room. They held everything the Clark family would have until their furniture, dishes, and other household goods arrived. Because the VOQ was old—and because modern comforts like elevators were low on the Army's priority list—Clark had to lug the suitcases up narrow stairs two at a time. He felt like a rookie, going through some sort of initiation or rite of passage.

*

The next morning Clark got up early to start "in-processing," an Army term for running all over the installation, clutching reams of paper, and waiting for a clerk to take a copy of your orders and stamp your in-processing checklist with a rubber stamp. Army bureaucracy at its finest. Fortunately, Trip drove Clark around post, so the process went more quickly than it had on his previous assignments.

As Clark walked into the orderly room of Headquarters Company—the last stop on his inprocessing checklist—he had a flash of *déjà vu*. The smell of musty files, the gray steel desks and chairs, the bulletin board with its neatly arranged documents that no one ever read—all of it brought back memories of his time as a line officer. This company was different, though, because it was not a line unit. It was, instead, the repository for everyone who was assigned to the headquarters staff, and it reminded Clark that he had become what soldiers derisively call a REMF—a rear echelon motherfucker. Still, this was the headquarters company of an infantry brigade, so it was more spit-and-polish than most.

He was completing the last of several forms when the clerk yelled to the company commander. "Sir, the new JAG officer is signing in. I think you're gonna want to meet him."

The company commander emerged from his office, and Clark immediately thought of one of his grandmother's sayings: "he had a grin on his face like a mule eatin' briars." Some might have even called it a "shit-eatin'" grin, although this soldier looked like an infantryman from the top of his crew-cut head to the toes of his spit-shined boots. He was fit and trim and appeared to be about the same age as Clark.

His grin grew to a broad smile, and his eyes widened. "You've got a Ranger Tab," he said, referring to the patch Clark proudly wore on the upper left sleeve of his uniform, signifying that he'd graduated from the Army's toughest school. "You're a JAG, and you've got a muther-fuckin' Ranger Tab." Then, looking down at Clark's orders, his eyes got even bigger. "And your middle name is Elmer! Pleased to meet you," he said, extending his hand. "I'm Elmer T. Jackson."

At that moment, Captain Elmer T. Jackson and Captain Robert Elmer Clark bonded for good.

"Yeah, it was my grandfather's name," Clark replied, "But I usually just use Robert E. Clark. Uh, no offense, Elmer, but I've always been teased about my middle name."

"Are... you... kidding?" Elmer said the words slowly and deliberately, emphasizing his mock disbelief. Then, the grin reappeared. "It's a great name. What other name allows you to walk up to a gorgeous woman in a bar and say, 'Hi, my name is Elmer. I'm all outta glue, but I can still stick to you.'" He paused and stared at Clark with an expectant look.

"That really works for you, huh?"

"Like a charm. Every time."

As Clark later learned, Elmer wasn't kidding. His boyish grin and aw-shucks charm made "Elmer" the most well-known name on post, especially among the attractive Panamanian secretaries who worked in the headquarters offices.

Clark was pleased with himself as he settled into Trip's BMW to head to the JAG Office. It had been a good morning. He had arrived.

CHAPTER TWO

THEY PULLED UP to a four-story building on Fort Clayton. Originally a barracks, it had been recently converted into offices. Like the VOQ, it was stucco with a terra cotta tile roof, although it had been painted white during its renovation, giving it a bit more dignity than the Visiting Officers' Quarters. It had something resembling awnings made of terra cotta tiles, which encircled each floor just above the windows. These "awnings" were designed to keep out Panama's torrential rain, back when there was no air conditioning and windows had to remain open during storms. They made the building look like an overly ornamented layer cake. But even more bizarre was the presence of a liquor store on the first floor. The JAG Offices were on the third and fourth floors, which meant that soldiers coming to meet with their defense counsel had to pass by the place where they bought their Jack Daniels, Bacardi, and beer—a weird juxtaposition.

The first person Trip took Clark to meet was their boss, Lieutenant Colonel John Allen, the Staff Judge Advocate. Allen was a decorated Vietnam veteran and had been an Infantry company commander until he was seriously wounded and forced to change branches. Trip knocked on Colonel Allen's door, and a voice said, "Come in."

Clark walked to the front of the colonel's desk, assumed the position of attention, and saluted. "Captain Clark, reporting for duty, sir."

Colonel Allen smirked and returned a half-hearted salute. "Relax, Clark. Sit down." Clark turned to see Trip lounging on the couch with his arm stretched across the back and his legs crossed. Allen came around from behind his desk and sat down in a chair across from the two captains. He was short—no more than five feet, five inches—and very thin, especially his wrists. His face was gaunt, with deep creases and a yellowish-gray complexion. His eyes had droopy, heavy lids and puffy gray bags beneath them. A big scar ran across his left forearm, and the fingers of his left hand were stained from having held countless cigarettes. His hand shook slightly, as if he had a mild case of palsy, which caused the cigarette it held to bobble until he put it between his lips and took a long draw. He exhaled and tapped the ashes into an ashtray on the coffee table. "Well, Trip, are you getting Clark, here, squared away with his in-processing?"

"We are. In fact, I think we're finished. Isn't that right, Clark?"

"Yes, sir," said Clark, redirecting his answer to Colonel Allen. "Thanks to Trip, I finished in-processing this morning. I'm just waiting on quarters."

"Tell me about yourself, Clark." Allen took another long draw on his cigarette, leaned back in his chair, and crossed his legs.

"Well, sir, I'm a FLEP..." As soon as he said the words, Clark realized it was an incredibly stupid way to start a conversation with his new boss.

"Yes, I know that. The Funded Legal Education Program." Allen's smirk indicated that another comment was coming. "Isn't that the West Point higher education program?" Allen and Trip looked at each other and grinned like schoolboys.

"Well, sir, there were a number of grads among the FLEPs in my JAG Basic Class, but we had some ROTC types as well."

Clark didn't help himself by using the term "grads," which is what West Point graduates call their fellow alumni.

"Do you think you West Pointers need to rescue the JAG Corps?" asked Colonel Allen. Trip snickered under his breath.

"No, sir, not at all," Clark blurted out—perhaps a bit too loudly. "It was an honor to have been accepted into the program. I'm proud to be wearing JAG brass." Trying to recover, he attempted to change the subject. "Have you decided on a slot for me, sir?"

"Well, what are you interested in doing?"

"I'd like to be a prosecutor, sir."

Allen took his cigarette out and slowly exhaled. His mouth morphed into a condescending grin. "That's what Trip, here, wants to do, too. All you boys want to be prosecutors, and yet the most important work that JAGs do deals with administrative law."

That comment reminded Clark that someone had told him Allen had never been a prosecutor and had spent his last tour of duty in the Pentagon doing—of course—administrative law.

"Yes, sir," said Clark, leaning forward, "but I thought administrative law matters were handled by more experienced lawyers." And then, with all the sincerity he could muster, he added, "Being a rookie JAG, I was hoping to cut my teeth as a prosecutor."

Allen studied him for a moment. "Well, Clark, it just so happens I have a slot for you in the Trial Counsel Section." From the corner of his eye, Clark saw Trip sit up straight and uncross his legs. "We'll talk about the details later." Allen stood up, signaling the meeting was over. "Trip, why don't you show Clark where his office will be?" Allen said something about wanting to meet "the wife," which made it clear that he was ready for them to leave.

Trip was seething. He barely slowed down to say, as he was leaving the front office, "You can get some lunch at the NCO Club next door. I have to meet someone. I'll be back later."

The NCO Club? Clark was stunned. The only time he'd been

to an NCO Club was when he was a platoon leader and his sergeants took him to "Bring-Your-Boss Night." But he was hungry, having started the day with no breakfast, so he walked over. Not expecting much, he was surprised to find that, unlike the VOQ, the NCO Club was well appointed, with new carpet, wooden furniture, and table clothes. There was even a waitress. He ordered lunch and sat down, ready to relax after a hectic morning and mostly sleepless night.

"You must be Captain Clark," said a tall, tanned, lanky major with an obvious Texas twang.

"Yes, sir," Clark replied as he stood up, "I'm Robert E. Clark, the new JAG."

"Well, I'm Jacob Darst, the Senior Defense Counsel. But you can call me Jake. Why don't you join us for lunch?" He motioned to a table across the room, where a stunning, light-skinned, black enlisted soldier was seated.

As they approached the table, Major Darst continued his introductions. "Captain Clark, this is Specialist Belinda Weeks. She's been my right hand since I got down here. Couldn't have done my job without her. I'm gonna miss her." Darst smiled at her like a proud parent.

"Pleased to meet you Specialist," Clark said, extending his hand.

"Most folks just call me 'Belinda,' Captain, but I'll answer to just about anything." There was a hint of a Panamanian accent in her voice. And as she stood and shook Clark's hand, he felt the soft, delicate hand of a woman, not that of a soldier in an Infantry unit. She appeared to be in her mid-twenties and had an alluring smile and a sexy way about her, which few women could pull off while wearing an Army uniform. For a few awkward seconds, Clark stared at her but said nothing. She caught him looking and smiled. Not only was she beautiful, she smelled like a woman—fresh and delicate. But then he caught himself: What was he doing? He was a married man and a father.

"Belinda's mom is Panamanian," explained Major Darst, "so she's got lots of family down here."

"I grew up in Panama for the most part. My dad was in the Army, but he and my mom got divorced when I was five. So my mom and I moved back here to be close to her family."

"That's interesting," said Clark, sounding and looking like an awestruck teenager at a high school dance. "You grew up here, but you're in the U.S. Army. So, I, uh, guess you speak Spanish."

"*Jo hablo español muy bien.*"

"*Si*, uh, *yo comprendo*," Clark said. Since the only Spanish he knew had come from high-school language class and ordering dinner at a Tex-Mex restaurant outside Fort Hood, he decided to forego any further attempt.

Major Darst picked up the conversation again. "So, I hear that Trip is getting you in-processed."

"Yes, sir. He's been taking me around."

"You can go easy on that 'sir' stuff, Clark. We don't stand on formality too much down here. We focus on getting the job done." Darst smiled to show that he wasn't trying to be critical. "Has Colonel Allen told you where he's going to slot you?"

"As a matter of fact, he has. He said he's going to assign me to the Trial Counsel Section."

Darst grinned and raised his eyebrows. "How'd Trip take that news?"

"Not very well, I'm afraid. I think he's pissed. Any idea why?"

"Well, Trip's been eyeing that slot for himself. He's been stuck in the Legal Assistance Section for over a year—writing wills, powers of attorney. You know, doing all that family law crap. He's ready to get out of there."

"Can't say that I blame him."

Darst lowered his voice. "Yeah, but what he doesn't know is

that Colonel Allen has other plans for him anyway. I'm moving over to become the Chief of Military Justice, and Trip is going to take my place as Senior Defense Counsel. Colonel Allen thinks you'll be a good trial counsel because you've had experience as a line officer. He told me we need somebody who speaks the language of these battalion commanders, most of whom think we're a bunch of pussies."

Clark glanced at Belinda, who gave no indication she'd been offended.

"He likes your Airborne wings and Ranger Tab, too. Says they'll give you credibility with these grunts we support."

"Really?"

"Yeah. I think it's bullshit, myself. Sorry, Belinda. What really matters is that you understand your clients' needs. And Allen is right about that. Trip doesn't have a clue."

"Why's that?"

"You don't know about him? He comes from 'old money' in Mississippi. His name is actually A. Clifton Stephens, III. His grandfather was a U.S. Senator, and his father is a sitting federal judge. Basically, he's a spoiled little rich boy. The only reason he's in the Army is to pad his political résumé. Rumor has it he wants to be governor of Mississippi someday and then run for the Senate like his grand-daddy. He wants to make a name for himself as an Army crime fighter." Darst grinned and shook his head. "He's not going to be happy when he finds out he's the next Senior Defense Counsel."

"Well, I hope this doesn't put us at odds."

"Don't worry about it. He's young. He'll get over it." Turning to Specialist Weeks, he added, "Won't he, Belinda?"

She gave Darst a knowing smile, and Clark was again struck by her beauty. But he also wondered whether she and Major Darst might be sharing something to which he wasn't privy. After the waiter brought their lunches, the conversation tapered off. When they finished, Belinda excused herself, saying she needed to get back to the office. As she was leaving, Major Darst asked Clark to stay for a few minutes to talk.

"Tell me about yourself, Clark. Where'd you come from?"

"Pemberton, Georgia, a small town near Savannah."

"Let me guess. You went to a small high school, where only a handful of the kids went on to college. After high school, most of them settled into life in your little town, just like their fathers and mothers before them, working on the family farm, getting a job at the mill, or as a secretary, clerk, or mechanic. Have I got it about right?"

"I think you've been readin' my mail."

"And, let's see, a lot of them got married right after high school and had a couple of kids before they were halfway through their twenties. But you knew you wanted something more, although you weren't sure what."

Clark stared at him like a kid in front of a carnival magician. "How'd you know all that?"

"Because I've learned to read people, Clark. You're the product of a small Southern town. It's predictable. If you want to be an effective trial counsel, you've got to learn to read people. I knew a little bit about you and sort of guessed at the rest."

"What about you, Major Darst? Where'd you grow up?"

"Well, I guess you'd say I'm an Army brat, Clark. My dad was career Army. He retired about ten years ago as a master sergeant."

"You must have seen a lot of the world."

"Just Panama. Dad's a Texan. He either took short tours overseas and left us with relatives in Texas or found a way to be assigned to a post in Texas. So, I spent a lot of time in small towns, too."

"Your dad must have been proud to see you follow in his footsteps."

"Not really. He didn't care. I joined the Army out of necessity. I went to community college and then night law school to save

25

money, so I wasn't marketable to the big-city law firms. They're all about pedigree—you know, where you went to school and all that. I couldn't find a civilian job, so I joined the Army as a JAG."

Clark didn't respond. Instead, he steered the discussion to their experiences in the Army and asked him about life in Panama. After about twenty minutes, Darst said he needed to leave for an appointment. They said good-bye, and Clark headed back to the JAG Office.

He hoped Colonel Allen had broken the news to Trip about being named Senior Defense Counsel and that his sponsor was in a better mood. Unfortunately, he had, and he wasn't. After taking Clark on the obligatory tour of the building, Trip deposited him in his assigned office and said he'd be back around 4:30 p.m.

No other lawyers were around, so Clark busied himself with settling in, learning how to use the telephone system, and chatting with the civilian secretaries. His personal office, though small, was private. (Even colonels in the Pentagon had to share offices). What's more, it had an incredible view of the Panama Canal. Massive ships appeared to be sliding through the grass on their way to the Pacific Ocean. He turned the desk ninety degrees from the door, so he could look sideways out the window. That commotion attracted the attention of another officer.

"Hi, my name's Suzanne Watkins," said a rather homely captain in athletic attire and running shoes, standing in his doorway. She had a distinctly Midwestern accent, wore no make-up or anything else that could be construed as feminine, and was flushed and sweaty. "You must be Clark. I didn't see you come in. I just got back from a run." She extended her hand—also sweaty—which Clark reluctantly shook. As he introduced himself, he slipped his hand into his pocket and wiped it on the inside.

Introductions over, she began: "I heard you were assigned to the trial counsel slot. Trip thought he was going to get it, but he said he's going to be a defense counsel. Have you heard much about the Criminal Law Section? We don't have a Chief of Military Justice, so we're not exactly a well-oiled machine. Have you met Major Darst?" He's a real pain-in-the-ass to deal with." Clark tried not to smirk. "You know, Lieutenant Colonel Allen doesn't know anything about criminal law, so we pretty much run our own show."

Clark concluded Suzanne was one of those people who feel compelled to convince those around her that she was always "in-the-know." He let her continue without interruption until she paused long enough for Clark to ask, "How many cases have you tried so far?"

"Well, uh,..." She paused, looked down to the right, and then back at Clark. "I've been assisting the former Chief of Military Justice, Major Eastman, who left for a new assignment in the States last week. So, I haven't, uh, exactly tried a case by myself yet."

"Oh, I see."

"But I'm sure I'll be handling one on the next trial calendar."

"Do you have any idea who the next Chief of Military Justice will be?" Clark asked.

Trying to appear confident and regain her superior status as the officer with more time on post than the new guy in front of her, she announced, with great conviction, "I'm certain Lieutenant Colonel Allen will select Captain Thompson from the Administrative Law Section. He's had a lot of experience, and we could use his leadership. And, Lieutenant Colonel Allen really likes him."

"When are we going to find out?" Clark asked, probing to see if there was a limit to her unwarranted self-assurance.

"Lieutenant Colonel Allen is supposed to announce it sometime this week."

"By the way, Suzanne, most folks just say 'colonel' in casual conversation," Clark said with a smile. "You'll sound less like a newbie if you adopt that practice." Suzanne looked back at him blankly. She may have had more time in Panama, but he had a lot more time in the Army.

"Are you ready to go?" asked Trip, suddenly appearing in the doorway.

"Hi, Trip." Suzanne said, smiling and stroking her fingers through her hair. "How's it going?" She sounded like a sorority girl, pathetically flirting with a boy who would never ask her out.

"I'm all right, Suzanne, but I've got to get Clark back to the VOQ." He turned to Clark. "Are you ready?" Clark nodded. As they walked out of the office, and were beyond Suzanne's earshot, Trip turned and said, "Congratulations on getting the trial counsel slot." He no longer sounded annoyed. "Would you like to grab a drink before we head to the VOQ? I'd like to talk to you about my new assignment as well as yours."

"Sure."

"Good. I'll take you to Mother's Inn."

CHAPTER THREE

MOTHER'S INN WAS a concrete-block building situated in the middle of a group of athletic fields. The origin of the name was lost to time long before Clark arrived in Panama. As the principal watering hole for young officers on Fort Clayton, it had seen its share of rowdiness, so it was—of necessity—a durable structure. Its windows were painted over and wire gratings had been screwed to the outside of each. The gratings prevented anyone from breaking in—or getting out, for that matter. But then, things like fire codes were more like suggestions than rules in Panama, even among Americans.

As they pulled up, Clark noticed a black, highly polished Harley-Davidson motorcycle parked by the front door. It was unadorned with side compartments or any other accoutrements—just a sleek, no-nonsense street bike. "That's Elmer's," Trip explained. "I've heard he's here almost every night."

They walked through the door into what appeared to be a Texas roadhouse. Merle Haggard was blaring from the jukebox, singing "The Green Green Grass of Home." A smoky, gray-blue haze hung in the air. And the room was packed with noisy young officers wearing fatigue uniforms. The floor was concrete, and the walls were the other side of the concrete blocks, adorned with nothing other than white paint. What served as the "bar" resembled the Formica counter of a tired fast-food restaurant, devoid of bar stools or anything reminiscent of a cozy tavern. Tables made of rough lumber were scattered around the room, surrounded by folding chairs—functional furniture for a bunch of rowdy, beer-drinking lieutenants and captains.

In a far corner of the room, Elmer was holding court with a bunch of lieutenants who were hanging on his every word. He appeared to be in the midst of telling a "war story," though not the kind one normally thinks of. This was, after all, the early 1980s. The Army had not seen combat since the Vietnam War ended five years earlier, so none of these junior officers had combat experience. *These* war stories were more like fairy tales, except they didn't start with "once upon a time." They started with "no shit, there I was…" And they typically concerned something that had happened during training, not courage under fire. Their only common thread was that the storyteller played the starring role.

Elmer looked up and noticed Clark and Trip walking toward him. "My favorite JAG officer," he boomed. The lieutenants stood up and made way for the two captains who'd stolen their mentor's attention.

Clark cringed, fearing Elmer was about to reveal his middle name to everyone present. But before he or Elmer could say anything, Trip's ego intervened. "Thanks, Elmer, I'm fond of you, too."

At least six empty long-neck bottles were lined up in front of Elmer, and the fingers of his right hand were wrapped around a half-full seventh. His left hand held a cigarette. And in that regard he was not alone. The numerous smokers in the room were the source of the gray-blue haze. Despite what appeared to be a substantial consumption of beer, Elmer was in complete control. Clark and Trip sat down, and Elmer motioned for the waitress to come over. The presence of three captains—including two JAGs—was too much for the Infantry lieutenants. They paid their respects and moved to another table, beers and cigarettes in hand.

"I hope we didn't intrude on your party, Elmer," said Clark.

"Them? Oh, hell no, I was just telling them about how important it is to be a good platoon leader and what their men expect from them. I can do that almost any night."

The waitress arrived. She was slim. No. She was skinny, black, and—to put it delicately—rather unattractive, with the hint of a scowl on her face.

"These guys need a drink, Sweetie."

"What'll it be," she asked, with no indication of a Panamanian accent.

"A beer is fine for me," said Clark, pointing to the bottles lined up in front of Elmer.

Trip began speaking without looking at the waitress. "I'd like a G&T, with Tanqueray, an extra twist of lime, and a tall glass." The words spilled out of his mouth quickly and perfunctorily, as though he'd made that request a thousand times before.

"Huh? Tanquer... what?"

In a slow and condescending voice Trip repeated his request. "A gin and tonic with extra lime, in a tall glass. I prefer Tanqueray gin."

"Yeah. I'll tell the bartender," she said, rolling her eyes as she turned and walked away.

Clark smiled. Trip would be lucky if that "extra twist of lime" wasn't, instead, a globule of the waitress's spit.

"Trip, I think your tastes are a little too sophisticated for Mother's," offered Elmer.

"Well, she ought to be able to handle a simple request like that."

The waitress returned. "Bartender say he only have cokes, beer, and Jack Daniel. If you want anythin' else, you need to go to the officers' club at Fort Amador." She stared at Trip and waited for his answer.

"Oh... well, uh, I'll have... I'll have the same as them." Trip motioned to Elmer and Clark.

31

"Thanks, Sweetie," Elmer said with a wink. He rocked onto the back legs of his chair and flashed her a big smile.

Clark turned to him and said, "Elmer, we didn't have much time to talk this morning. Tell me about yourself."

Elmer took a long draw on his cigarette, exhaled, and looked Clark directly in the eye. "Well, Clark, I'm an Infantry officer, plain and simple. That's what I am, and that's all I ever wanna be. There's no finer profession in the world."

"What'd you do before the Army?"

"Damn, Clark, that was a long time ago. Let's see… I went to college for a while…"

Sensing some common ground, Clark followed up. "Really? Where?"

"You won't believe it, if I tell you." A devilish smile appeared just as Elmer sipped his beer.

"Texas A&M? North Georgia?"

The waitress sat a beer in front of Trip and handed a fresh one to Elmer. She smiled at Elmer and said, "This one on the house."

Elmer smiled back and then turned back to Clark. "Oral Roberts University." He paused with a twinkle in his eye and waited for a reaction. "Kinda incongruous, wouldn't you say?" He said the word "incongruous" as if he were pronouncing it in vocabulary class.

"You're shittin' me."

"Yeah. No shit. I was a Bible-thumper with the best of them."

"That's hard to believe."

"Now, why is that, Clark? Has my reputation preceded me?" Elmer's shit-eatin' grin was in overdrive. "Actually, I didn't last long at Oral Roberts. The administration decided that I adhered too much to Proverbs 14:30." Elmer raised his chin as he quoted the scripture. "'A relaxed attitude lengthens a man's life.'" He took a long draw on his cigarette, and then—as he exhaled—said, "They thought I was a little too relaxed."

"You're kiddin' us, right?" Trip finally piped in.

"No. It's the truth."

Clark sensed the need to change the subject again. "What made you join the Army, Elmer?"

His expression became very serious—and not in a mocking way, as if he were setting up for a joke. "Well, I was lookin' for somethin' honest and genuine, and I think I've found it." The grin was gone. He was obviously making a serious point.

What a refreshing change from the cynics in law school, Clark thought. The conversation soon turned to lighter subjects, such as the attractive secretaries in Building 101 and the ceviche at the Balboa Yacht Club. After a few more rounds, Clark felt sufficiently lubricated to broach a touchy subject with Trip. "I guess you're excited about being named Senior Defense Counsel."

"So you're going over to the other side?" Elmer interjected. "I think that's great!" He put almost too much emphasis on the last word. The grinning and bravura were back. "Now, you'll get to see cases from a totally different perspective."

After the substance of Elmer's comment sunk in, Clark's expression revealed his confusion. "You tried cases before, Trip?"

"You know what? I've had enough of this beer," Trip replied. "Elmer, can you get that waitress to bring us three shots of Jack Daniels?"

"Sure, as long as you're buying." Elmer motioned to the waitress and held up three fingers. Trip said nothing and stared blankly at the lieutenants gabbing away at the next table. When the waitress arrived with the shots, Elmer and Clark exchanged an awkward smile. She set them in the middle of the table and walked away without saying anything.

Trip tossed back his shot and then said, "Yeah, Clark. I was a trial counsel for about a year, before I was transferred to Legal Assistance. And, yeah, I am ready to get back into the courtroom."

Something bad must have happened, because trial counsel

usually remained in the job for an entire tour, unless they started losing cases. Fishing for more information, Clark continued, "Must've been tough to leave something you enjoy doing."

That comment hung in the air for what seemed like five minutes before Trip muttered, "It wasn't my choice." He paused, appearing to ponder what to say next. "Let's just say that I didn't see eye to eye with Major Eastman, the former Chief of Justice. And Eastman had the SJA's ear."

"Colonel Allen's?"

"No. His predecessor's. Allen is a reasonable man."

Trip's comments were puzzling. Why would Colonel Allen assign Trip to the position of Senior Defense Counsel after he'd lost his job as a trial counsel? Was he trying to help him? Or was he looking for an ineffective defense counsel?

Elmer injected himself into the conversation again, "You know, Trip, I never thought Eastman was worth a shit." He paused for a moment and then—sounding like a locker-room smart aleck—teased, "So, you two boys might be going at each other before too long. That should be interesting."

"Well, I hope not," Clark said quickly.

"We might, Clark," said Trip. "But I know each of us will strive to keep things professional."

Searching for a response—and finding none that didn't sound trite—Clark decided to change the subject again. "You know, Trip, I need to be heading back to the VOQ. My family's been stuck there all day by themselves."

Trip and Elmer both chuckled. "Where do you plan on taking them, Clark?" Elmer asked. "The main officers' club is on Fort Amador. You're sittin' in the only place to go on Fort Clayton. You wanna bring 'em here?"

"Probably not. But maybe they miss my company," Clark replied with a smirk. "Anyway, I do need to get going."

On the way back to the VOQ, Trip began what bordered on

an interrogation. He was serious and seemed to be sorting out their respective roles. Then he changed the subject to the man they'd just left.

"So, what did you think of Elmer?" Trip asked.

"He's a character, all right. That business about Oral Roberts University was a shocker, wasn't it?"

"He's got some strange habits, which I'm sure he didn't pick up there."

"What do you mean? The smoking and beer drinking?"

"No. Worse than that." Trip drove along for almost a minute with a smirk on his face and then said, "You know that black waitress back there? The one who'd never heard of a G&T?" Clark nodded. "Well, Elmer's screwing her."

"You've got to be kidding me. How do you know that?"

"Hell, everybody knows. That's why he was so protective of her. And she's not the only one. He screws waitresses and secretaries all over post."

"I can't believe it," said Clark. "I've heard some wild stories about Panama, but that's crazy."

"Yeah. It's hard to believe. As black as she is. And she's married to a master sergeant."

What? Clark's head was spinning. Elmer was committing adultery with an enlisted man's wife? And she isn't the least bit attractive. Even if Elmer was "hard up," she wasn't worth risking his career. After a few moments, Clark broke his stunned silence. "Elmer could get court-martialed for that, couldn't he?"

"In theory. But if they started with him, they'd have a long list to prosecute. Elmer whores around with some of the most powerful officers on post. They're all doing it." Trip then added another shocker. "And to think he's married to a sweet woman and has three little girls."

"Elmer's married?" Now, Clark was disappointed as well as stunned.

As they pulled up to the VOQ, Clark thanked Trip for carting him around, got out of the car, and told him he'd catch a shuttle bus to the office the next day. As Trip pulled away, Clark stood for a while in the warm, thick night air, accented by the faint smell of burning grass in the distance. As he soon learned, that distinctive smell marked the Dry Season, whose balmy, breezy weather would linger for only a few more weeks.

He trudged up the stairs to Room 215 and fumbled for his key. He could hear the faint sounds of scurrying in the room as he unlocked the door. But instead of being greeted with a hug and a kiss when he walked through the door, he caught an icy stare from Janelle and a puzzled look from Ellie. Before he could even set down his briefcase, the icy stare found a voice.

"Where have you been?" Her words were like fingernails on a chalkboard. She pronounced the last word as if it were spelled "bin."

"Where do you think I've *bin*, Janelle? I've *bin* in-processing."

"Don't start with me, Bobby. You smell like beer and cigarettes. I'd say you've beeeeen in a bar." She delivered the last sentence like the "ah ha" moment in a preacher's sermon. Clark hated that self-righteous sanctimony.

"It's not what you think. Trip wanted to grab a beer after work and talk, and so we went to Mother's Inn."

"Mother's Inn?"

"It's the Officers' Club Annex on Fort Clayton. My company commander was there too."

"Why do you care about him? You don't work for him, do you?"

"No, Janelle. But he does sign my leave form, doesn't he? He takes care of all sorts of admin stuff that affects you and me and my career. Besides, it's only 8:00."

"We had to eat in the cafeteria downstairs again. Trip is full

36

of it. That food is terrible. Ellie ate almost nothin'. We can't live like this, Bobby."

"It's only temporary, Janelle. You know that."

"When are we gonna get housin', and where?"

"I don't know. That's all the in-processing I have left to do." He was too tired to put up with her whining. He just wanted the conversation to be over. "I'm hungry. I'm going to get something from the vending machine downstairs. Do you want anything?" No answer. He grabbed his keys and walked toward the door.

"Be quiet when you come back. We might be asleep."

CHAPTER FOUR

FERDINAND DE LESSEPS, the Frenchman who built the Suez Canal in the nineteenth century, attempted to repeat his success across the Isthmus of Panama. Unfortunately, his visits were always during the Dry Season, causing him to grossly underestimate the challenges brought by the Rainy Season: water-saturated hillsides (which caused recurrent landslides) and death from malaria and yellow fever. In the end, de Lesseps's attempt to connect the Atlantic and Pacific was a dismal failure.

Panama's Dry Season seduced Clark as well. Its balmy breezes and spectacular sunsets made the early evening hours a magical time. After two long months in Room 215 of the VOQ, his family moved into quarters, the best feature of which was a terrace with a spectacular western view. Almost every evening, he sat on the terrace before dinner, sipped a cold drink, and enjoyed the majesty of creation. As the sun slipped below the horizon, the sky became awash with colors. Yellows, oranges, and purples swirled together like paint on a child's watercolor. Flowers bloomed everywhere, which gave the breeze a captivating fragrance. Surely, Clark thought, the God who made such a beautiful place must love us.

Yet it wasn't the Garden of Eden. Although the climate was forgiving (no one ever froze to death in Panama), and the jungle, streams, and oceans had bountiful sources of food, Panama was scarred by poverty unlike anything Clark had ever seen. People lived in shacks. In many areas raw sewage ran in open ditches or simply lay on the ground. The shanty town that he passed on his way to work each day had been cruelly dubbed "Hollywood" by the Americans. It was anything but. He saw toddlers with grimy faces, blankly staring back at him, many wearing nothing more than a dirty T-shirt. Most were barefoot as they walked in the filth that surrounded them. Disease and death were commonplace and somehow more poignant because they existed alongside the relative wealth of the Americans living nearby.

Even worse was Panama's rigid social structure. Clark had read about Latin American oligarchies in school, but until he spent time living in one, he didn't understand their complex consequences. Hope never takes root, so it never has a chance to blossom. A person born into poverty remains there. Escape is virtually impossible, without using brute—and often illegal—force. Poor Panamanians toiled away at menial tasks simply to survive. They knew "the system" was stacked against them.

In contrast to the residents of Hollywood were the Panamanian elite, who owned everything that was worth anything. To be successful in Panama, one needed connections—preferably bloodline connections—with the members of the elite families. Wealthy Panamanians would say that something could be obtained or accomplished because "my cousin works for this government agency" or "my brother-in-law owns so and so." No legitimate business could be started without dealing with one or more of them, none of whom were prepared to provide the benefits of their status without receiving significant compensation in return. That meant little profit for those who actually did the work and took the risks. Consequently, the poor focused on making enough money to go from one day to the next.

A socio-economic system in which the vast majority of

people have no hope is a sad thing to observe, regardless of the natural beauty that surrounds it. And societies like that don't change unless their cultures change. In the case of Panama, there had been little change for hundreds of years. Its poverty, and the oligarchy that perpetuated it, shaped the country's culture significantly. Other forces did as well, of course. Its history of Spanish occupation, its former existence as part of Columbia, and the dominating presence of the United States during the building and subsequent operation of the Canal all combined to create a country that had much to commend it but also—regrettably—much to condemn it.

Clark's first encounter with the darker side of Panamanian culture came when his car arrived from the States. Because Trip was Clark's sponsor, he offered to take him to the holding lot when his car finally arrived. On the way over, he offered some advice. "Clark, you need to put a five-dollar bill in the ashtray before you take your car to be inspected."

"Why?"

"Because it'll ensure that it passes the Panamanian safety inspection."

"I don't understand. It's a 1981 Chevy Nova. It's practically brand new. The tires aren't even ready to be rotated yet."

"You don't get what I'm sayin', Clark. It ain't about the condition of the car." Trip paused for a moment and then pivoted from his good-ole-boy routine and said, plainly, "The guy inspecting the car is expecting a tip."

"Well, it sounds like a bribe to me."

"I guess you could look at it that way, but I prefer to think of it as a tip for efficiently getting the inspection completed."

"Well, I'm not paying a bribe. That's illegal, and it's wrong."

"Suit yourself."

When they arrived at the Navy lot where the car was being kept, Clark made a quick visual inspection and then went inside the office to complete the necessary paperwork. As he handed the last form to the Navy civilian employee (another Panamanian in a coveted American job), the clerk said, "You gotta ge' your Panamanian safety inspection righ' away. Otherwise, dey gonna close, and den dere's a holiday. So, you better hurry."

Clark thought it best not to ask about the five-dollar-bill-in-the-ashtray business. After getting the directions to where the safety inspections were conducted, he went back outside and yelled across the lot to Trip, telling him that he'd meet him back at the office. Trip just smiled, waved, and drove away.

The Panamanian vehicle inspection facility was located on Albrook Air Force Station, which had been the U.S. Air Force base in Panama before the construction of Howard Air Force Base about twenty years earlier. Clark walked into the office not knowing what to expect. The first thing he noticed was that it didn't appear to have been updated since Panama took it over. It was a dingy green color, in dire need of fresh paint. A wooden counter stretched the length of the right side of the room and across the back. Taped to the front of the counter were hand-printed signs in English, directing applicants where to go. Behind the counter there were at least a dozen attractive, young Panamanian women wearing non-military uniforms and lots of make-up. He had a flashback of Specialist Weeks and her sexy smile. How did Panamanian women manage to look so sexy in mundane uniforms? As he made his way through each stop, the routine was the same: the young woman at that station took a copy of his military orders and then stamped a red seal on his Panamanian form. Panamanians love the pseudo-officiality of rubber stamps. Finally, after about thirty minutes, and almost a dozen red seals on his form, Clark proceeded outside for the actual vehicle inspection.

A short fellow in military uniform took Clark's form and keys, hopped into the Nova, and drove away. A few minutes later, he returned and handed Clark another form. "Your car need' to have dese thin's fix'. You can use dis form for one week only. So, you need to get the car fix' and bring i' back for another inspection."

"For what? This car is almost brand new," Clark snapped.

"Sir," he replied, now sounding like a Georgia State Trooper with a Spanish accent, "You must ge' the car repair' within a week and bring i' back here." He handed Clark the form and walked away.

Trip had been right. It was a shakedown, plain and simple. Clark was so annoyed that for a split second he contemplated burning rubber as he left the lot. Fortunately, discretion prevailed, since Panamanian police were everywhere. When he got back to the JAG Office, he bumped into Trip in the hallway outside the Staff Judge Advocate's Office.

"Well, Dudley Do-Right, how'd it go?"

"Just like you said, Trip. And that's bullshit! It's a goddamn bribe."

"Better watch that language in the office," Trip cautioned in a fake whisper that was loud enough to be heard by those nearby.

"Yeah... sorry. The worst of it is that I've got to waste money at the garage and then go back and do the stupid process all over again for nothing. It's a complete waste of time."

"You don't have to do all that, Clark." Condescension dripped from Trip's voice. "Just listen to me this time. All you have to do is wait a few days, take the car back, and leave ten dollars in the ashtray."

"I thought you said it was five."

"That was before you pissed them off."

Three days later, Clark took the car back, having done nothing but wash it. The same short guy took the keys and drove away. When he returned, he handed Clark the form stamped "PASSED" in red. As he got in his car to drive away, Clark looked down at the empty ashtray. Was it a bribe, or was it a tip? Who knows? All he knew was that it was a product of a dysfunctional culture.

Somehow, that inspector had gotten himself into a position with a little authority, and he was using it to get what he could. Clark's irritation lasted for a long time, but after he'd learned more about how hard it was for the poor to get ahead in Panama, he decided he couldn't blame the inspector after all.

*

The American ex-patriots who lived in Panama and worked for the Canal Commission were known as "Zonians," after the Panama Canal Zone, where they all lived. The Canal Zone had been created in 1903, when the United States signed the Hay-Bunau Varilla Treaty and began its attempt to conquer the isthmus that had defeated the French. The Zone consisted of the Canal itself and the land extending for roughly five miles on either side. In other words, it cut through the heart of Panama. To most Panamanians, it was emblematic of U.S. imperialism. To Zonians, it was sovereign U.S. territory. President Jimmy Carter changed everything in 1977 when he signed a treaty with Panamanian President Omar Torrijos, in which the United States promised to begin a process of turning over the Canal and the Canal Zone to Panama. That process was completed in 1999.

But before Carter and his treaty, Zonians had a good life. In a way, the Canal Zone was an experiment in socialism—and, some would say, a very successful one. Everything was provided: housing, healthcare, schools, recreation facilities, cars. Panamanian manual labor was cheap, which enabled Zonians to live in shaded, orderly neighborhoods, where Panamanian maids and gardeners took care of menial chores, leaving the Zonians with lots of leisure time in a country where there was much to do with leisure time. There were swimming pools and tennis courts in every neighborhood. Community centers offered music lessons, sports programs, dances, and all manner of clubs. The housing, schools, hospitals, and recreation facilities were all outstanding because everything—every aspect of Zonian life—was subsidized by the revenues the Canal generated. In many respects, life in the Canal Zone was better than in the United States.

Zonians didn't mind being in a socialist system. Far from feeling trapped in an Orwellian experiment, they were, more than anything, content. Just as dispirited poor Panamanians were an example of the adverse effects of oligarchy, Zonians were the product of a socialist system that had plenty of other people's money to spend. Many of them demonstrated little initiative and often behaved liked spoiled children. They even joked about it among themselves, as in: "How many Zonians does it take to change a light bulb? Two. One to call the Canal Zone Electrical Shop and another to have his maid make the drinks."

The easy life and sense of entitlement fostered a dark side of Zonian culture: many Zonians treated Panamanians—especially black Panamanians—horribly. Not all Zonians were that way, of course. But Clark was shocked by bigoted behavior in the Canal Zone in the 1980s that was as bad as anything he'd seen growing up in Pemberton, Georgia, in the 1950s and 60s. Racial slurs were commonplace, and Panamanians were often treated no better than serfs.

Sadly, Zonian prejudice had its roots in a caste system that extended back to the time when Americans were constructing the Canal. The unskilled black laborers—who, for the most part, had been brought to Panama from Barbados, Martinique, and other Caribbean islands—were paid in Panamanian silver balboas, while the skilled—mostly white—American workers were paid in gold-backed U.S. dollars. That distinction was continued through other aspects of life in the Canal Zone. "Gold towns," where Americans lived, had the best schools and recreational facilities. "Silver towns," where the mostly black manual laborers lived, were better than the neighborhoods where poor Panamanians lived, but were a far cry from the gold towns. Segregation was the order of the day, and vestiges of it were still apparent when Clark arrived.

Not long after the incident involving his car's safety inspection, Clark came face-to-face with Zonian bigotry. After a particularly hectic week as the new guy in the office, he decided to take Janelle and Ellie to dinner at The Happy Buddha, a Chinese restaurant recommended by one of his colleagues. It was located in Panama's version of a strip mall, a short drive from Fort Clayton's back gate. After they had settled into their seats near the back of the restaurant, a waiter came by and, in Spanish, asked for their drink orders. Clark stumbled through an answer in Spanish, which was apparently incorrect. The waiter smiled and replied in perfect English, "Sir, if I understood you correctly, you would like a Balboa beer and the lady would like a glass of white zinfandel. I can also bring some fresh orange juice for this beautiful young lady," he said, gesturing in Ellie's direction.

"Uh, yeah. Thanks," Clark replied. The waiter soon returned with their drinks and took their dinner order. Before long they were enjoying their sweet-and-sour pork.

A few minutes later, they heard a commotion at the front of the restaurant. Two couples, who appeared to be American, had entered the restaurant and were talking loudly among themselves in English. The hostess escorted them to a table next to the Clark family. None of the new arrivals looked their way or acknowledged their presence. They just kept talking and laughing loudly. They were dressed in clothes that were at least twenty years out-of-date and appeared to have been worn that long. One of the women had bleached hair arranged in a 60s-style bouffant. She was overloaded with inexpensive costume jewelry and smelled as if she'd been marinating in cheap perfume all afternoon.

A different waiter approached their table. He was younger than the Clarks' waiter and appeared to be a bit nervous. He asked, in Spanish, if he could take their drink order.

The woman behind the cloud of cheap perfume spoke. "Don't you speak English?"

"*No, señora*. I don't speak too goo' English."

Staring at the young man with an exasperated look, she spewed, "Well, get me someone who speaks English. I've lived in the Zone for forty years. I haven't learned any Spanish yet, and I don't intend to start tonight."

The young man dropped his head and walked away. Soon, the older waiter who had waited on the Clarks approached the odorous Zonian and said—in English—and with the grace of an English butler, "I'm sorry there has been an inconvenience here. May I take your drink order? It's on the house."

"That's more like it," said the cloud of perfume.

Clark couldn't believe what he was hearing. Was this how Americans treated the citizens of their host country? Although he knew he should have said something, he didn't. He sat there with his wife and daughter—in silence—and finished his sweet-and-sour pork.

CHAPTER FIVE

THE RAINY SEASON arrived in May, and the weather changed. Gone were the beautiful azure skies and breezy, sunlit days that had come one after another. Almost overnight, the sky took on a hazy, white appearance, and each and every day it rained. Although the afternoon thunderstorms were torrential, they didn't last long. Temperatures remained in the 80s, so the air was thick and moist, wilting fresh uniforms within minutes. The daily showers made the countryside even more lush and green than in the Dry Season and cleaned the air and the streets, making everything smell fresh—at least for a couple of hours.

The Rainy Season also brought some of the problems that had plagued the builders of the Canal almost a century before. Instead of landslides, there were flooded streets and impassable bridges. Every stream filled to capacity. Worst of all, mold grew everywhere, even on the underside of the roof decking on the carports, which turned black and required weekly cleaning.

On a Tuesday, after the Rainy Season had been in full swing for a about a month, Clark was working late. Although he hadn't been assigned a case yet, each day felt like his first day at West Point—a mix of unrelenting stress and anxiety. For some reason, Major Darst was still working as the Senior Defense Counsel, and Trip was still assigned to the Legal Assistance Section. Without a mentor to guide him, Clark struggled to learn the many facets of his new job. Each day he was plagued by the weight of the responsibilities entrusted to him and his feelings of inadequacy. He dealt with the situation the way he always had: he dug in and worked harder than everyone else. On this particular Tuesday he left his office around 9:30 p.m., completely exhausted.

By the time he got home, Janelle and Ellie were in bed. Finding no dinner on the stove or in the refrigerator, he grabbed a beer and some pretzels and settled down on the couch to watch the Armed Forces Network. He heard restless sounds coming from Ellie's room, so he lowered the volume of the TV. At some point, he fell asleep.

"Bobby, get up." Janelle was bent over him, shaking him.

"Leave me alone. I'm exhausted."

"It's the baby."

"You take care of her. I have to go to work in the morning."

"I said get up," she barked. He looked up at her. "This is serious." She glared back at him with a look he'd never seen, which must have triggered a shot of adrenalin, because he was instantly awake.

She got nose-to-nose: "We need to go to the hospital now!"

"Is it that serious? It's 2:30 in the morning. What's wrong with her?"

"I don't know, but she's not right."

Janelle was holding Ellie in her arms, so Clark stood up to get a better look at her in the dim light. Although she appeared to have been crying and looked sweaty and sleepy, she didn't look like she needed to go to the hospital. But it was obvious that Janelle was not going to change her mind, so he headed to the bathroom, splashed cold water on his face, and combed his hair. As he headed out the back door, he saw that Janelle and Ellie were waiting for him in the car, with the motor running. Janelle was in the front passenger seat, and Ellie was perched high in her car seat in the back.

They rode through the darkness in silence. The only sounds were those made by the tires on the rough pavement and the rush of air outside the open windows. Clark looked at Ellie in the rear-view mirror, her hair dancing in the breeze coming through the windows. The cool night air seemed to comfort her, although she didn't smile. Her expression was flat, and her eyes were glassy.

Their destination was Gorgas Hospital, named for William C. Gorgas, the Army doctor who had been the chief sanitary officer during the construction of the Panama Canal. The hospital was located off the installation, on the edge of downtown Panama City near *La Commandancia*, the headquarters of General Manuel Norreiga. They got to the neighborhood where the hospital was located around 3:15 a.m. No one was on the sidewalks, and only a few cars were on the streets. Most of the stores were dark. Clark felt as if he had driven into a *film noir* movie from the 1940s. When they finally arrived at the emergency room entrance, he stopped and quickly got out.

As he unbuckled Ellie from her car seat, he turned to Janelle and said, "We'll probably have to deal with some desk sergeant, so I'll take her and get checked in. You park the car." He ran inside, cradling his listless daughter in his arms. As soon as he entered the door, a nurse looked at Ellie, snatched her from his arms, and ran down the hall. He was so stunned that he was still standing in the same spot with a blank look on his face when Janelle arrived.

"Where is she?"

"I don't know."

"What do you mean you don't know?"

"They took her down the hall," he said, pointing. Janelle burst into tears and took off running with Clark close behind. A nurse stepped into the hallway and directed them into one of the examining rooms. As they entered, they saw their little girl lying on a gurney. The room was dark, except for one light over the gurney. Two female nurses in white uniforms were working on her. One was holding her still, while the other was trying to insert an intravenous needle. Ellie stared at them from the gurney, lost and afraid, but so weak she didn't even whimper.

"Stay back until we get this IV in her," barked one of the nurses, without making eye contact.

Janelle continued to sob, and Clark could feel his own emotions start to bubble up. He tried not to cry and after a few moments was able to regain his composure. "What's going on?" he asked, trying to sound like an Army captain, instead of a scared father.

The nurse who had told them to stay back—and who looked and sounded like an Army drill sergeant—replied, "You let this go too far. This child is dehydrated. She might lose her kidneys. Don't you know that diarrhea can kill a child?"

Janelle's sobbing became a torrent, and she fell to her knees. Clark felt like shit. His emotions were confused and running full speed on a collision course with the reality he was facing. He was furious that Janelle had not dealt with this crisis sooner but thanked God she had a mother's sixth sense. He looked at her, as she cried uncontrollably on her knees, and prayed it wasn't too late. He thought about all those times when, as new parents, they'd anguished over every detail related to their little girl—how much she weighed, how long she was, how much she drank, what she ate, whether she had cloth or disposable diapers, whether she had a diaper rash, whether she pooped, the length of her nap, the inoculations required for travel to Panama, and on and on. Now, however, they were dealing with something far more serious. He helped Janelle to her feet, held her close, and told her it was going to be all right, although he had no idea whether that was true.

When they approached the gurney, the drill-sergeant-nurse barked again, "You folks wait outside. I'll come get you in a minute."

"I'm not going anywhere," said Janelle, looking so steely-eyed that no one—not even this veteran nurse—would dare to cross her. The nurse apparently saw the situation the same way Clark did, or maybe she'd seen that same look on another mother's face, or maybe she was a mother herself. Something caused her to change. She huffed and pointed to some chairs in the corner of the room.

"We're going to draw some blood to check her kidney function," she said. Clark and Janelle didn't watch, though they heard Ellie cry out as the needle was inserted. After a few minutes, the younger nurse left in a hurry, carrying a vial of blood, and they were able to see their little girl, who was now strapped to the gurney. She stared at them with the same mournful expression they'd seen when they entered the room. The older nurse moved around the gurney tending to her little patient. Clark moved his head from side to side, trying to loosen the increasing tension in his neck. He had no idea what the nurse was doing. And the grave expression on her face only increased his anxiety. Repeatedly, she examined the suspended bag of fluid and took Ellie's temperature and pulse. How serious was her condition to warrant so much attention?

Clark noticed a clock hung high on the wall to his right. It was hard to see it in the dim light near the ceiling, but it appeared to be broken—the hands didn't seem to move. Grass grew faster. His mind began to wander. How in the hell had he wound up in this place? Why had he brought his daughter to this disease-ridden garbage-dump of a country? Why hadn't Janelle called him? If his baby died, would the Army transport her body back... No! He couldn't think about that. He should resign from the Army and take his family back to Pemberton. His stomach was in knots, and his entire body was hot. Sweat dripped from his hands and formed a puddle on the linoleum floor.

After what seemed like several hours, a doctor arrived, looking down at a document he held in his hands. He had a military haircut, although a white lab coat obscured his uniform and any indication of his rank. He didn't speak and went straight to the gurney. After examining Ellie's eyes, he held her hands and feet and looked at the top of her head. He opened her mouth and looked inside with a small penlight, all the while smiling and saying soothing words to her and stroking the side of her face. She was so lethargic she didn't react to this stranger's probes. Finally, he turned to her parents.

"When did she have her last wet diaper?"

"Late this afternoon," Janelle replied, "about four o'clock."

"Have you been giving her fluids?"

"I tried to give her Pedialyte, but she wouldn't drink it."

"That was the right thing to do. But if she wouldn't take it, you should have brought her in sooner."

Janelle began to sob again and put her face in her hands.

"Now, now," said the doctor in a soothing voice, "listen to me. I think she's going to be all right." The sweetest words ever spoken. "But we'll need to keep her connected to an IV for a few days to ensure she has plenty of fluids while she's getting over the diarrhea."

"Doctor, we didn't know... ," Clark began.

"You're new to Panama, right Captain?" Clark nodded like a schoolboy. "Down here, we have a very serious problem with bacterial diarrhea in young children. Cases are not always easy to detect. For now, though, you need to watch her. Next time, at the first sign of trouble, give her some of the medicine that we'll give you. If that doesn't fix the problem within twenty-four hours, then you need to bring her in."

"I understand," said Clark. "Thank you." Janelle nodded in silence.

After the doctor left, the senior nurse said, "One of you can stay with your daughter in her room tonight."

"I will," Clark said immediately. Turning to Janelle, he asked, "Do you think you can make it home by yourself?"

"Of course. But don't you leave her for one second. And I want to be back here first thing in the morning, regardless of when visiting hours begin." She stared in the direction of the nurse.

"That won't be a problem."

Clark put his hands on Janelle's shoulders and looked at her intently as she wiped her tears with a tissue. "She's going to be all right, Janelle." Janelle nodded but said nothing. "Would you do something for me? Before you come tomorrow, would you please call the office and explain that I won't be coming in for a few days?" Again, she nodded but said nothing.

For the rest of the week, they took turns sitting by Ellie's bedside. The first night was the worst for Clark. He was tired but no longer sleepy. He hadn't eaten much of anything since breakfast, but he wasn't interested in food. Why hadn't he gotten home on time? Maybe he would have seen that something was wrong with her. What if she lost one or—heaven forbid—both of her kidneys? Thank goodness Janelle had grasped the seriousness of the situation. He felt that he'd done a terrible job of taking care of his precious little girl. That night, on his knees next to her bed, he begged God to forgive him and to restore her health.

CHAPTER SIX

A LITTLE OVER a week after that horrible night at Gorgas Hospital, Ellie regained her strength and was again a bundle of energy. She took full advantage of Panama's perpetual summer and played in the backyard almost every day. There were no other children her age nearby, so she played by herself, with Janelle watching from the kitchen window as she skipped and jumped and danced around their small backyard like a fairy princess. She sang "Old MacDonald Had a Farm" at the top of her lungs and talked to her imaginary friend, "John." Sometimes, she appeared to have heated arguments with him, raising her voice and waving her arms.

Early one afternoon, while studying one of the many manuals concerning how courts-martial are to be conducted, Clark received a telephone call from a hysterical Janelle. "I wanna go home!" She was sobbing uncontrollably. "I can't live in a place like this."

"What's the matter, Sugar?"

"Your daughter..." Janelle began inhaling and exhaling rapidly, as if she was trying to catch her breath and talk at the same time.

"What? What's wrong with her?" Clark almost screamed into the phone.

"...was almost eaten by a monster!" she finally finished.

"What? What are you talking about?"

"She was playin' in the backyard, and I was watchin' her through the window and then all of a sudden she froze."

"Is she all right?"

"Yes, she's cryin', but she's all right now. But I wanna go home."

"What happened?"

"I'm trying to tell you. Just give me a minute. She's all right now, 'cause she's inside. She was lookin' at something in front of her in the backyard that I couldn't see. And when I moved to get a better look, I saw it."

"What? A snake?"

"No. It was a giant lizard, at least four feet long."

"Like an alligator?"

"No, not that big. Just let me tell you. When I saw it, I went tearin' out the back door, screamin' at the top of my lungs. I must've scared it because it ran up that big palm tree."

"That's it? Thank God."

"What do you mean 'That's it'?" She was no longer panting—she was annoyed.

"I mean what you saw was an iguana. There's one that lives in the tree in the backyard. He's harmless. Panamanian kids catch them for pets."

"Well, I don't care, Bobby. I'm not lettin' her ever go back outside. It's not safe." She paused for a few moments to collect herself. "This place is awful. We just need to go home."

"Okay, Janelle. But can we just talk about this tonight? I need to get back to work."

"It's always work, idn't it?" She hung up.

The iguana call was one of many he received from Janelle during their first few months in Panama. Although that call was somewhat understandable, since she'd never seen an iguana, most of her calls were not. She called about everything from the washing machine not working, to the drainage ditch in the back-yard flooding, to the neighbor's dog relieving himself on the lawn. Clark began to wonder whether she could make it as an Army wife. She seemed to be incapable of handling *anything* by herself, and she complained constantly. There were times he thought his head was going to explode. He tried to remind himself that she was adjusting to a new environment, just as he was adjusting to a new job in a new career field.

*

Captain Suzanne Watkins, whom Clark had met on his first day, was unlike any woman he'd ever known. He decided she must be from Michigan or Ohio or someplace up North. She had a thick Midwestern accent that made her sound like she spoke more through her nose than her mouth. She wasn't much to look at, with a big nose and a bunch of curly hair that resembled a light brown Afro. Her lips were big and thick and, it seemed, con-stantly pursed, as if she was about to spit. And, she was seriously overweight for an Army officer. Nevertheless, Clark had to admit that she worked hard at being an Army officer, as well as a lawyer.

The first real legal task assigned to Clark was to review the record of a court-martial that had taken place before he arrived in Panama. The Manual for Courts-Martial provided that the "con-vening authority," meaning the commander who "convenes" the court-martial, could set aside a conviction or reduce a sentence, in the same way a civilian governor can grant clemency or a pardon. Clark was tasked with preparing the report that would be submit-ted to the convening authority for consideration prior to making his final decision. He knew that Colonel Allen and the Command-ing General would be reading what he wrote, which caused his hands to sweat so much that the notes on his legal pad smeared and the paper wrinkled as if someone had set a cold drink on it.

"Whatcha doin'?" Suzanne was standing in the door of his office, hot and sweaty, cheeks flushed.

"I'm working on the post-trial review of the Smith and Dunbar trial."

"Oh. Well, I just got back from a run."

Clark could tell she wanted to talk. "Good for you," he said, continuing to look down at his work and hoping she would go away.

The tactic didn't work. She kept talking. "Yeah, it sure was hot out there. They said it was only supposed to be 89, but with the humidity it felt more like 100. I'm still sweating."

"Well, Suzanne, it is the middle of the day. And we are in the tropics."

"I've got no other time to do it, Clark." Feeling the need to explain, she continued, "I got out of shape during law school. Between school work and my job, I just didn't have time to work out. So now I have to do remedial Physical Training until I pass the stupid PT test. I can do the pushups and sit-ups; I just can't finish that stupid two-mile run in less than 24 minutes."

Never passed a PT Test? The Army was desperate.

"I don't suppose I could talk you into running with me."

"In the middle of the day? I don't think so, Suzanne. Didn't Kipling say something about 'only mad dogs and Englishmen go out in the midday sun'?"

"What?" Her eyebrows arched.

"I'm teasing, Suzanne. Have you thought about running in the morning?"

She shrugged her shoulders, ignoring his suggestion, and continued her chitchat. "So, you're working on the Smith and Dunbar case. That's the one about the two guys who murdered a Panamanian taxi driver, isn't it?"

"Yes, and it's awful. They stabbed the poor guy twenty-seven times with a pair of scissors. And you know what they got?"

"It wasn't much I heard."

"Twenty-six dollars. Twenty-six dollars for killing the poor guy." He sighed and looked at her. "Somehow, it seems more depraved that they murdered him for only twenty-six dollars."

"Why? Would it be different if they'd gotten thousands of dollars?"

"I don't know, Suzanne. It's just sick. You should see the photographs…" Clark reached for the file folder.

"No, no. I'm not interested in looking at those now. I've got my own trial to prepare for." Her voice trailed off as she headed back to her office.

Clark looked at the photographs again. The victim was old and gray and thin. A close up of his face showed that at least one stab wound had penetrated his right cheek and ripped it open. The hole was so big Clark could see the old man's yellowed teeth. There were photographs of puncture wounds on his hands and forearms. Defensive wounds. The old man had fought hard for those few dollars. As Clark pored over the photographs and read the trial transcript, he found himself rocking in place and tugging at his uniform shirt as if all of a sudden it didn't fit. He kept thinking about how the crime had taken place in the community where his family now lived. He'd never seen anything like it in Pemberton, Georgia. At Fort Hood he'd seen the results of a bar fight—a few black eyes and some bruises. Never anything like this. The savagery of this attack and the pitiful amount of money the murderers got somehow suggested that the old man's life wasn't worth very much. It was depressing.

Clark continued to review the record of trial over the next few days, while Suzanne stayed in her office, preparing for the first court-martial she would handle by herself. It involved the possession of marijuana, a common offense in Panama. Soldiers could buy weed on almost any street corner downtown. There were even different grades: Panama Red, Panama Gold, El Jefe. It was too much temptation for young men away from home, with extra money and free time.

On Friday afternoon, Clark decided to give Suzanne a return visit.

"How's it going?"

"What?" She looked up from her desk.

"Your trial. Are you ready?"

A broad smile crossed her face. "Oh, yeah, I'm ready, all right. I've looked at every relevant case, and I've studied all the related provisions of the UCMJ and the Manual for Courts-Martial. I'm going to annihilate him." She drew out the word "annihilate" for emphasis.

"Well, remember, you're going up against Major Darst."

"I'm not intimidated by him," she shot back.

"He's tried a lot of cases, Suzanne."

"Yeah, but this case is open and shut. I'm going to nail this guy."

"Okay. Well… let me know if I can help."

The trial session began the following week, and as it turned out, Suzanne's case was the only one being tried, which was unusual. During breaks in the proceedings, she would stride quickly past Clark's office, although her gait reflected anxiety, not confidence, and her face was pale and drawn. It certainly didn't appear that she was "annihilating" Major Darst. If she had known then that Major Darst would soon become her direct supervisor, she would have had a complete nervous breakdown.

Anxious to see a real court-martial, Clark slipped into the back of the courtroom as Suzanne was finishing her presentation of evidence. The case wasn't particularly noteworthy, so there were only a few other people in the visitor's gallery. Suzanne spotted Clark and gave him a look an older sister might give a pesty younger brother.

It soon became apparent that Suzanne had made a huge error.

Like a lot of inexperienced lawyers, she thought that admitting physical evidence is simple. In fact, it is not. If an attorney fails to carefully consider each necessary step, the results can be disastrous. Suzanne had successfully admitted into evidence a brown paper bag containing some dried vegetable matter. The investigating officer had brought it to trial and testified concerning its chain of custody. In other words, no one had had an opportunity to tamper with the evidence from the time it was seized from the accused until it was produced at trial. Where she stumbled was in failing to get the lab report admitted. When his turn came, Major Darst pounced.

"Your Honor, the defense moves for a finding of not guilty." Darst's voice sounded strong and confident.

The judge excused the members of the court-martial, the equivalent of the jury in a civilian trial. "What is the basis for your motion, Major Darst?"

"Your Honor, the government has only proven that the accused had a paper bag of vegetable matter in his possession. There is no evidence that said vegetable matter was, in fact, marijuana or any other illegal substance."

"What do you have to say in response, Captain Watkins?"

"The government disagrees, Your Honor."

"Well, I assume that. The question is: Why do you disagree with what Major Darst said?"

Suzanne shuffled some papers on her table, as if she was looking for something—an answer, perhaps. She turned and stared at Clark with imploring eyes. Her cheeks were flushed. Red blotches were forming on her neck.

"Captain Watkins?"

She turned back to the judge. "Your Honor, it is… it is obvious that this vegetable matter is marijuana. Marijuana can be found everywhere in Panama."

"Yes, Captain Watkins, but what evidence do you have that

this particular specimen of dried and crumpled vegetable matter is, in fact, marijuana?"

"It looks like marijuana, Your Honor."

Major Darst and his client sat motionless at the defense table, eyes to the front, fixed on the judge.

The judge pressed her. "Are you planning to be a witness, Captain Watkins? Are you an expert? Did you conduct a lab test on the material?"

"I'm not an expert, Your Honor, but we do have a lab report..."

Major Darst stood up. Suzanne stopped in mid-sentence, and both she and the judge looked at him. "The defense objects to the admission of the lab report, Your Honor. There has been no authentication of that lab report. And, as far as we know, the government is unable to authenticate it."

"Captain Watkins?"

"Your Honor, I... I request that the defense stipulate to the admissibility of the lab report."

"Captain Watkins!" The judge was clearly perturbed. "Do you have anything further?"

"No, Your Honor."

"Court will be in recess." The judge banged his gavel and was out the door behind the bench in what seemed like a single movement.

Suzanne went back to her office, and Clark went back to work on his post-trial review. Although the walls of their offices were supposed to be sound proof, Clark could hear her crying next door. Was it his place to console her? He was the new guy, after all. And anyway, crying was no way for an Army officer or a lawyer to behave. But then he considered that it could have been him in that courtroom with an unauthenticated lab report. After a few minutes, he decided to check on her. He knocked.

"Suzanne?"

"What?"

"May I come in?"

"Of course."

She was seated behind her desk in her Class A green uniform. Unlike most JAGs with no prior military experience, her insignia and patches were in perfect order, and all of her brass was polished. Her eyes were red, though, and she had a tissue in her hand. "So, you want to come in here and gloat as I go down in flames?"

"No, Suzanne, no. I want to help. Is there anything I can do?"

"What could I possibly do at this point? I can't believe I didn't get that stupid lab report authenticated."

"There's a lot to think about, Suzanne. What about asking the judge for a recess?"

"That's just it. I have no clue who to contact to get the stupid thing authenticated. It'll be even worse if I come back empty-handed after a recess."

They sat in silence for only a couple of minutes, before there was a knock on the door. "The judge is ready to reconvene, ma'am." Suzanne dried her eyes, stood up, and smoothed her uniform. She took a deep breath and seemed to regain her composure. Together, they walked to the courtroom, and Suzanne resumed her place at the counsel table. Clark sat in the back.

The military judge re-entered, and everyone stood up. "This court is now in session." He banged the gavel and turned to address the members of the court-martial. "I want to thank the members of the court-martial for your time and attention to this matter. You are now excused." Clark knew that was a bad sign. It meant the judge didn't need them.

After the members left, the judge continued, "The court finds that the government has failed to introduce *prima facie* evidence of the crime with which the accused has been charged and, therefore, grants the defense motion for a finding of not guilty." He leveled his gaze at Suzanne. "Captain Watkins, you are obviously an intelligent woman. You must, however, meticulously prepare your evidence. That is your responsibility, and you failed to fulfill it. This court is adjourned." The judge's gavel sounded again, and it was over.

At that moment, Major Darst showed that he was a professional and a gentleman. He walked over to Suzanne, extended his hand, and said something to her that Clark couldn't hear. His client sat at the defense table with a big smile plastered across his face. He knew he'd just dodged a bullet.

Suzanne turned to walk out of the courtroom, looking as if she'd been kicked in the stomach. The swagger of the week before was all gone, and Clark genuinely felt sorry for her. The judge was right, though. As the prosecutor, Suzanne had to prove beyond a reasonable doubt that the vegetable matter was marijuana. She had offered no evidence to support that conclusion—not even the expert opinion of the arresting officer, based on his years of experience.

Anxious to get home and tell Janelle all about having seen his first real court-martial, Clark left work early. "Honey, I'm home," he yelled as he came in the back door. Dishes were piled up in the sink and on the counter, along with an open box of Cheerios and a carton of milk.

"I'm in the bedroom," she called from the back of the quarters.

As he walked through the dining room, he noticed toys strewn all over the living room. It looked like the aftermath of a kids' play group. Maybe John and some of his imaginary friends had joined Ellie for a tea party.

"Man, did I have an interesting day," he said as he walked into the room. Janelle was folding clothes from a pile on the bed.

"Well, that's great, Bobby. I did, too, if you can call washing clothes and taking care of a baby interesting. I'm gonna have to have some help."

"What do you want me to do? I still have reading to do tonight."

"I'm not talkin' about you. I'm talkin' about a maid."

"A maid? You want to hire a maid? Do you have any idea what that would cost?"

"Yes, I do. Angela has a maid, and she pays her $110 per month, plus room and board."

"Who's Angela?"

"The neighbor across the street. Her husband's name is Roy. He's a captain, too. They just moved in a little over a week ago. He's a helicopter pilot over at Howard."

"I thought you said you were busy all day. So when were you talking to the neighbor?"

"Don't be a smart ass. I need help, and it's only $110 a month. That's not a lot of money."

"Not a lot of money? What are you talking about? It's almost as much as our car payment." He was annoyed whenever she used the word "only" in front of a dollar amount. What did she know about earning money? Her father had found her job after job, and she promptly quit each one. She always had some sort of excuse: "they don't assign the work fairly… so-and-so was rude to me… I don't understand what they're doing." The last one was her favorite. She used it so much Clark began to believe she really didn't understand anything.

Sensing Clark's growing annoyance, Janelle smiled and changed the subject. "Let's go somewhere. I've been stuck in here all day."

"Have you forgotten we have a daughter?"

"Angela and Roy can watch her for a couple of hours."

"You've got to be kidding. We don't know anything about them."

"No, *you* don't know anything about them, Bobby. I do. While you've been payin' attention to nothing but your career and totally ignorin' your family, I've made a point of meetin' our neighbors. Angela and Roy are good people. And, they have an eight-year-old little girl. Her name is Elizabeth, but they call her Libby."

"Oh, yeah, you're a real hero, Janelle. Your life is so tough.

While I've been busting my butt to learn a new job, you've been chatting with the neighbors. How can I compete with that?"

"Well, I *do* take care of our daughter and this house. But I guess you don't consider that a job." She glared at him for a moment and then continued, "Why do you always have to be so sarcastic and hateful? I just want to get out of here for a while." Tears began to well-up in her eyes.

He looked at her and realized he had overreacted. "You're right, Sugar. I'm sorry. Let me get changed, and we'll go." She followed him into the bedroom. "How'd you meet the neighbors, anyway?"

"They're on our party line."

"Party line? You mean where you pick up the phone, and you can hear someone else talking? I thought those things went out in the 1960s."

"Not down here."

"So, if they pick up, they can hear us when we're on the phone?"

"Not all the time but sometimes. It was kinda funny how Angela and I met. We were both tryin' to make a call at the same time. If we're goin', Bobby, we need to get goin', or they won't want to keep her."

*

And life went on. Day in and day out, Janelle wanted this, and then she wanted that. The Army-issued dryer is too old and doesn't dry properly… the clothes at the Post Exchange are not in style… they don't have her line of makeup, so she has to go to a shop downtown to get it. And on and on. It seemed to Clark that the focus of her life was always the same: what she wanted. She had no interest in hearing about his new job or learning about the fascinating country that was now their home. All of that was too complicated, and she just didn't "understand." He found himself spending more time at the office and Mother's Inn.

Colonel Allen finally announced that Major Darst would

assume the role of Chief of Military Justice and that Trip would become the Senior Defense Counsel. Although Suzanne was upset when she found out that the guy who'd just embarrassed her in court was going to be her boss, she quickly got over it. Like Clark, she was glad to have someone with whom to discuss things. She and Clark soon learned the value of Darst's experience and good judgment.

He was wrong about one thing, though. It turned out that Clark's experience as a platoon leader *had* given him the ability to understand the needs of their "clients"—the commanders of the line units—far better than most young JAGs. He knew instinctively what they needed, which was not always what they asked for. One of the battalion commanders he supported provided a case in point.

"Judge, Colonel Bednar, here." The voice on the phone was that of Lieutenant Colonel David T. Bednar, commander of one of the infantry battalions on Fort Clayton. (When he used the term "Judge" in this way, it was to show respect for the lawyer advising him. Otherwise, he would have said "Captain" or "Clark.")

"What can I do for you, sir?"

"I've got a scumbag that I need to get in jail by sundown."

"Damn, sir, what's the scumbag's name? What'd he do?"

"He's a goddamn doper named Ramirez. I'm sick of dopers screwing up my troops. I care about my boys, Judge, and I don't want shitbirds like Ramirez getting them involved with drugs. There are way too many dopers on Fort Clayton. We need to get rid of 'em."

"What evidence have you got, sir?" Clark wanted to get to the heart of the matter before Bednar hung up, thinking he'd communicated enough.

"We found drug paraphernalia in the trunk of his car. No drugs with it, but the drug dog alerted on it."

"What kind of paraphernalia, sir?"

"Hell, I don't know. Bongs and roach clips and shit."

"If there's drug residue on it, then we'll have a case. Be sure the MPs take control of the paraphernalia and anything else they found, so we'll have a good chain of custody."

"Are you listening to me, Captain Clark? I want to put the little bastard in jail!"

"Is he a flight risk, sir?"

"Hell, I don't know. He's a doper, and I want him gone."

"Understood, sir. But if we put him in jail without showing he's a flight risk, the magistrate will just let him out. You could confine him to the barracks…"

"You goddamn JAGs. I want the motherfucker gone, Captain."

"Yes, sir. Why don't we move him to the headquarters company administrative hold platoon, which is across the Isthmus, and start administratively processing his discharge from the Army? That's the fastest way to get him out of your unit and keep him out. In the meantime, if we get sufficient evidence on his possession of drugs, we can still court-martial him."

A knot tightened in Clark's stomach as he waited for Bednar's response. Although Bednar had made it clear that he wanted Ramirez out of his unit immediately, it didn't sound like there was any evidence that Ramirez was a flight risk. If they put him in pretrial confinement, the magistrate would probably release him, and Bednar would look like a fool. The administrative discharge procedure, which wais used to discharge soldiers whose duty performance was substandard, was a good alternative to a court-martial until the evidence against Ramirez could be evaluated. The standard of proof was lower than in a court-martial, and it would get Ramirez out of Bednar's unit. Clark was taking a gamble, though, and was counting on Ramirez actually being a "shitbird," so that he could show a pattern of misconduct that would justify discharging him from the Army.

After a painfully long silence, Bednar grumbled, "You think that's the best way to get him out of my unit?"

"Yes, sir, I do."

"Well, get on with it, then."

Clark wasn't sure how that telephone call had gone until the next day, when he had an unexpected visitor at his office.

"Clark, where'd you learn how to handle a sonofabitch like Bednar?"

Colonel Allen was making a rare appearance in the Criminal Law Section. "He called me just now to tell me that you took care of some dirt bag named Ramirez. Said you'd done a good job and understood what he needed."

Clark stood up, surprised. Why had the SJA come to his office? Why hadn't he summoned him to come downstairs? Did he want Major Darst to overhear him? Although it was all a bit strange, Clark was pleased that his senior rater had gone out of his way to praise him within earshot of his immediate rater. Not only could Major Darst hear Colonel Allen's announcement, so could Suzanne. No sooner had Allen left than she was in Clark's office with the door closed.

"What was that all about?" From the look on her face, it was clear she wasn't about to say "congratulations."

"Oh, just a call I had with Colonel Bednar yesterday concerning one of his soldiers."

"Bednar is a male chauvinist pig," she seethed. "I've tried to explain things to him in the past and found him to be too dumb to grasp basic concepts of criminal law."

"That's funny, Suzanne. I didn't have that problem with him." Why was she on her "high horse"? Had she already forgotten that she had recently missed another "basic concept of criminal law"—the one about a prosecutor having to present evidence that a green leafy substance was, in fact, marijuana?

"*You* wouldn't have a problem," she continued. "The Army is full of male chauvinists, and they all stick together."

"Come on, Suzanne. Do you really believe that?"

She dropped her head and grinned. "Well, no. But Bednar is still a pig."

"Duly noted."

CHAPTER SEVEN

"WHAT ARE YOU doing on Sunday?"

Clark looked up from his work to see Major Darst standing in the doorway. "Uh, nothing, I guess," Clark stammered back. Clark hoped his boss wasn't going to ask him to come into the office on Sunday to work. But that didn't make any sense—they weren't that busy. Was he going to invite Clark to go to church with him? Clark should have said something about going to church—that would have pleased his mother anyway. Instead, he just sat there and waited for Major Darst to continue.

"You want to go fishing?"

Well, so much for trying to figure out Major Darst in advance. "Sure. I'd love to, sir, but I don't have any gear."

"Don't worry about that. I have all you'll need. Meet me in the parking lot outside the office. That's as good a place as any. Be there at 0600 hours."

"Thanks, sir. I look forward to it. Do I need a fishing license or anything? Can I bring anything?"

"A fishing license? In Panama? Just bring yourself and sunscreen. And wear a hat." He turned and walked away.

And, of course, no sooner had he left than Suzanne appeared.

"What was that all about?"

"Nothing. Just talking about the weekend. How's your PT coming along?"

"It's okay. So, you and Darst are doing something this weekend?"

"Yeah. It's no big deal. He just asked me to go fishing." Clark looked down at his work and hoped she would go away. She didn't. He could sense that she was pacing around his office. He looked up to see her scrutinizing his West Point diploma.

"You must be special. I've been here for over a year, and he's never asked me to go fishing."

"You like to fish?"

She turned to face him, satisfied that she'd started a conversation. "Well, I've never actually fished, but he still could've invited me."

"You've never fished, but you think he should have invited you?"

"Well…"

"And, he used to be the Senior Defense Counsel, Suzanne. Don't you think that would've been a conflict of interest?"

"I guess so," she mumbled. "Well, have fun. And, by the way, you better know how to fish."

"What do you mean by that?"

"You don't know about Darst and fishing?"

The way she asked the question was designed to show—once again—that she possessed some superior knowledge and thus a superior position, simply because she'd been in Panama longer than he had. Nevertheless, he was curious.

"No. I'm afraid I don't."

"He's some sort of professional fisherman."

"That doesn't make any sense, Suzanne. He's an Army officer. I'm sure it's just his hobby."

"Well, maybe it's a hobby, but he takes it *very* seriously. And you know, Clark, there's a fine line between a hobby and mental illness."

He smiled at her. That was pretty funny.

"Wait until you see his boat," she continued, "He parked his trailer in the parking lot one day when he was going to the liquor store downstairs. It's like one of those you see on TV fishing shows. He might not be a professional, but he's competed in tournaments, and he writes articles for fishing magazines."

Suzanne's explanation indicated that she spent far too much time studying the personal lives of her colleagues. How did she find out such stuff anyway?

"Thanks for the info, Suzanne, but I really need to get back to work." He looked down at his papers again. After a long silence, she realized he wasn't interested in bantering back and forth about their boss. She walked away, mumbling something he couldn't understand.

The workday ended, and Clark headed home to tell Janelle about the invitation from Major Darst. He walked through the back door calling for her but heard instead the voice of Juanita, the maid Janelle had hired. Nita, as she was called, was twenty-five years old and as cute as a head cheerleader, with a sweet smile, big brown eyes, and a shapely figure. In short, a doll. More important, though, she took good care of his daughter. Nita came into the kitchen with Ellie on her hip, and he could see that the baby had been crying.

"What's wrong?" he asked.

"Nothin', Señor Clark. She jus' a li'l cranky 'cause she wan' her mommy."

"Where is she?"

"Señora Clark tol' me she nee' to go downtown for some bidness. She sai' she woul' be back before you go' home from work."

"Business my foot!"

"I sorry, Señor Clark."

"No… no, Nita. I'm not upset with you. I'm sorry. I should

not have raised my voice. I'm not upset with you." He smiled to reassure her.

"Let me get you a beer, Señor Clark. Go res' on the sofa,"

"You know what, Nita? That sounds like a great idea. It's been a long week." That girl was going to make some man a great wife. Why wasn't she already married? At twenty-five, she was a bit old by Panamanian standards to still be single. Maybe she was trying to find a G.I. to marry and get her out of poverty. It wouldn't be the first time a beautiful young woman had that plan.

He took Ellie from her, went into the living room, and sat down on the couch. His daughter quickly squirmed out of his arms and ran to her bedroom, saying she wanted to show him something.

He leaned back on the couch, and his thoughts turned again to Janelle. She'd become a shopaholic who'd rather prowl the stores in downtown Panama than spend time with their daughter. In fact, she was beginning to behave like an addict. When they were growing up in Pemberton, a trip to Atlanta would have intimidated her. Now, she ventured into all parts of Panama City, with its narrow, dirty streets and shops run by folks who didn't look or sound like the folks back home. He couldn't understand what was going on with her. Was she unhappy? Bored?

As he bent over and started to unlace his boots, Nita emerged from the kitchen with his beer.

"Señor Clark, le' me help you wid tha'. Sit back and relax," she said. She handed him the beer, knelt in front of him, and started taking off his boots.

Damn, was this woman for real? What a sweetheart. He had to catch himself from staring at her cleavage, which was ample and on full display as she knelt in front of him. A couple of times her breasts brushed against his leg. Was she doing that on purpose? She looked up at him and smiled. He sipped the beer and smiled back.

The back door opened, and an exasperated voice yelled, "Nita, where are you? I need your help." It was Janelle. Nita jumped up and scurried to the kitchen.

As soon as she entered the living room and saw Clark on the couch, boots off and beer-in-hand, she snarled, "How long have you been home?" There was no hi-honey-how-was-your-day.

"Long enough to know that you've been goofing off and spending our hard-earned money again."

"What makes you think you know what I've been doin'?" She stared at him for a few moments. "It just so happens I was downtown buyin' Christmas gifts."

At that point Ellie came running into the room, clutching a doll and yelling, "Mommy's home. Mommy's home."

"Since when do you buy Christmas gifts months in advance?" Clark asked, almost shouting. He knew he was in no danger of losing this argument. She never thought ahead. Her idea of long-range planning was: What's for lunch?

"Would you lower your voice? Your daughter is standing right here. Just so you know… I bought this linen tablecloth and napkins for your mother." She pulled them out of one of the shopping bags.

They didn't look anything like what his mother would use. They were far too ornate, and Janelle knew it. She'd been to his house many times when they were growing up. He looked at her and then the linens but said nothing. He just got down on the floor and started playing with Ellie and the doll she'd brought to show him.

As the rest of the evening wore on, there was no real interaction between them. Although Janelle acted annoyed when he told her he was going fishing on Sunday, he knew she really didn't care.

Saturday was full of chores around the house, including washing the car and cleaning the mold off the underside of the carport roof, all of which Clark did by himself. Nita left at noon, and shortly afterwards, Janelle announced that she was taking Ellie to the neighborhood pool, although she didn't ask Clark to join them. Her white, two-piece swimsuit, though modest, revealed her shapely figure, and for a fleeting moment he felt like the teenager who couldn't stop thinking about her. He started to insist on joining them, but changed his mind, and instead watched as she walked down the street, holding their daughter's hand. Her long, lean legs were as graceful as a ballerina's. She looked just as beautiful as the day they were married. Why couldn't they get along?

On Saturday evening, he partook of one of the great benefits of living in Panama. He sat on his terrace and watched a gorgeous sunset, while sipping a cocktail and smoking a Cuban cigar. He'd become a big fan of cigars after discovering how good the Cubans were. They were beautifully made, with few blemishes on the wrapper leaf, and they smoked smoothly, yielding fine, pale-gray ashes. They smelled and tasted great. And, surprisingly, Janelle didn't mind, as long as he smoked them outside. Alone.

Sunday morning arrived, and Clark was out the door by 5:15, even though it took only twenty minutes to get to his office. Major Darst had not yet arrived when Clark pulled into the lot and parked his car in what he knew would be a shaded spot later in the day. He got out so that he could soak up the peace and beauty of the time and place. It was so different during the week, when he was rushing in and out of the building and there were dozens of other people around. At this hour it was so quiet and still. The sun had yet to make its appearance in full, so it wasn't hot. A warm breeze swayed the palm branches in the dim morning light and carried the fragrance of the violet wisteria and yellow angel's trumpet that bordered the parking lot. He could hear birds twittering in the distance as the sun began to peek over the horizon. Panama was truly a beautiful place.

Before long, he heard Major Darst's truck pulling up. It was a big, late-model, white Ford pickup truck, complete with a Texas-style grill guard. And sure enough, just as Suzanne had described, it was pulling a trailer carrying a black and red boat with glittering silver accents. It looked like the ones on *Bill Dance Outdoors*, a fishing show that Clark and his dad used to watch every Saturday. He estimated that Major Darst must have had at least two years' of a captain's pay invested in his truck and boat. Clark worried that he might look foolish. He'd never fished on such an expensive rig. Most of the time, he and his buddies fished from the shoreline. His father used to say they were "just drowning worms."

"Morning, sir," he said as he climbed in the truck.

"Okay, Clark, let's get one thing straight. I don't want to hear any of that 'sir' stuff today. We're fishing and having fun."

"Yes, sir. I mean, uh, yeah, let's catch some fish." He then tried to show his appreciation for Major Darst's invitation. "I'd be happy to buy the minnows." Clark had heard they were the bait of choice when fishing in the Canal.

Major Darst turned to him and said solemnly, "We're not going coon fishing, Clark."

Clark was stunned. First, Trip's comment about the waitress at Mother's Inn, and then the Zonian at The Happy Buddha restaurant. Now, this. Surely Trip and Major Darst had been to race relations classes. Clark certainly had. There had been hours of training at West Point, in his Armor Basic Class, and at the JAG School. The Army was doing its best to eradicate racism from its ranks and had made it clear that racist remarks were no longer a laughing matter. Why were things so different in Panama?

"Uh, no offense, Major Darst. I guess I'm just not used to fishing with such fancy equipment."

"None taken. And at least for today, Clark, do me a favor and call me 'Jake.' By the way, that was a joke about the 'coon fishing.' Don't black folks in Georgia always fish with live bait?" Clark smiled but said nothing. That explanation didn't make his boss's attempt at humor acceptable, but he wasn't about to cor-rect him.

Before long, they arrived at the Gamboa boat ramp. Clark noticed a group of young boys—maybe eight to ten years old, barefoot, dirty, with tattered T-shirts hanging on their skinny frames. Some had long kitchen knives in their hands. "What's with all these kids?" he asked.

"They're slicky boys," Jake replied.

"Slicky boys? What the heck is that?" As soon as he asked the question, Clark realized that he sounded like an overly curious kid on a field trip.

"They're 'slick,' because they're slick enough to sell ice to Eskimos. They hang around here because they'll clean fish for a modest fee."

"That's good," Clark replied, remembering the many times he'd cleaned crappie in the backyard and wound up smelling like fish for hours. "You know, back home most folks would freak out to see young boys with knives, hanging around unsupervised."

"Well, Clark, these kids don't get to play Little League. They're working to survive."

Of course. Another naïve comment from the young captain. Clark said nothing in response but contemplated how differ-ent his own childhood had been: lazy summer days swimming, fishing, playing baseball, watching old movies on TV when it rained—no worries, except when his father made him help in the garden or cut the grass. He never had to be concerned about where his next meal might come from or where he was going to sleep that night.

Jake backed his trailer down the boat ramp, and the boat slipped into the water. Clark waded in and held the bowline while Jake parked the truck. Jake trotted back, climbed into the boat, and started the motor. After it had warmed up a few minutes, they were off, gliding across the smooth water of Lake Gatun in the early morning light. Unlike most of Panama City, which was dirty, smelly, and scarred by poverty, Lake Gatun was a piece of heaven. There was almost no development around the lake—nothing around them but beautiful jungle vegetation; clear, clean water; and a brilliant, blue cloudless sky.

Jake semi-shouted over the roar of his outboard motor, "You West Point guys should be real proud of this Canal." He grinned at Clark.

"How's that?"

"Well, Teddy Roosevelt sent a bunch of West Point engineers down here to finish the Canal because everybody else had quit. He knew they wouldn't quit."

"That's the way it goes, I guess." Clark smiled at Jake's attempt at small talk.

"Yeah. They were pretty practical, too. The French had wanted to make a sea-level canal but had no plan for dealing with the Chagres River, which crossed their proposed path for the Canal. The Americans knew that the river had to be dealt with. So, they dammed it up and formed what was, at the time, the largest man-made lake in the world. It's a fine example of American ingenuity." Jake stopped talking for a minute and looked around to see if there were any other boats in the area to watch out for. Then he started again. "Making a big lake wasn't an 'elegant' solution, but it got the job done." Jake said the word "elegant" with a hint of disdain in voice. "Anyway," he continued, "they gave us a great lake to fish."

Clark noticed a series of red buoys—each extending about eight feet above the water—with white numbers painted on two sides and lights on the top of some of them. He assumed they were used to mark the channel of the Canal. When they reached number 75, Jake steered a hard right and pulled back into a cove. The sun was up by this time, although it was not yet hot—just muggy. Jake slowed the boat to a troll, squinted his eyes, and scanned the water. He sensed something and throttled all the way back. "This is it."

Somehow the pros just know.

"Toss out that anchor, Clark. I think we'll be here for a while."

Clark knew enough about boating and fishing to know that you don't "toss" the anchor, because it will scare away the fish. He slowly lowered the anchor into the water, looked up at Jake, and saw him grinning at him.

As Clark looked at all of Jake's expensive gear, he reminisced about his fishing buddies back home, some of whom were black. If Jake had seen them, he would have said for sure they were "coon fishing." They took their catch home to eat. And, they *always* used live bait.

"Clark, here's a rod and reel for you." Jake handed him the most expensive rig he'd ever held. "I assume you know how to use one of these."

"Sure."

"You see those flowers floating on the water near the bank? See if you can cast your lure just this side of them. Then, count to three and slowly reel it in."

"Okay. I can do that," he replied, knowing that casting was one of his strong suits. He made a few casts but got no bites.

The two men sat in silence for a long while, listening to the birds and hearing the occasional fish breaching the surface of the water in pursuit of a bug—or perhaps for the sheer fun of it. All of a sudden, Clark heard a roar that sounded as if a lion had jumped into the boat with them.

"What the fuck was that!" he yelled, as he jumped up and looked around like a kid who'd just been spooked on Halloween.

"Did it scare you, Ranger boy?" Jake asked, laughing so hard he could barely get the words out.

"Have you got a speaker in the boat or something? What the hell was that?"

"It's a howler monkey, Clark. They're all over the place out here. We probably got in his space."

Clark looked up into the jungle and at first saw nothing but some birds fluttering, as if they were startled, too. Then, he saw a black monkey swing from one treetop to the next. It stared at him with a pouty expression. "There he is," he said, pointing, "your co-conspirator."

"Yeah, that's him," Jake smiled, "But forget about him. Let's catch some fish. He's not gonna bother us."

And catch fish they did. As the morning wore on, the fish started to bite as fast as they could get lines in the water. They pulled in one after another that were definite "keepers." Jake didn't seem to mind that Clark wanted to keep the big ones. Maybe at heart he was a country boy, too.

When the sun got higher in the sky, Jake deployed a canopy. "You'd better get under here," Jake said. "Your face is getting pretty red. Did you put on sunscreen?"

"No, I forgot. I thought this hat would be enough."

"Not down here." Jake pulled a tube from a compartment near the steering wheel and tossed it to him. "Put this on. Wanna beer?"

It wasn't even noon yet. But then, this was Panama, and it was hot. "Sure," Clark replied.

One beer led to another and another, and the fish kept biting. It was the most fun he'd had in a long time. At one point, the frenzied pace slowed a bit, and Jake brought out some sandwiches for lunch. They were the pre-packaged kind you buy at the commissary, not homemade. But when you eat outdoors, everything tastes good.

"Does your wife like Panama?" Jake asked between bites, uncharacteristically venturing beyond small talk and work.

"Honestly?" Clark stared at him until he realized he was ready for the answer. "She likes it just fine. She's got a maid and doesn't do a damn thing but shop."

"Does she come from a wealthy family?"

"Hell, no. She was spoiled, though. After her momma died, her daddy spoiled her rotten. She's his only child, and he worships her like she's some sort of idol, although he'd never admit it. Oh, he can quote you Bible scriptures about idols, all right, but he doesn't have a clue what they mean."

"That doesn't sound too good, Clark. You need to be careful she doesn't go crazy down here spending money. That's what my wife did."

That bombshell stunned Clark to silence: he'd never heard anything about Jake being married. Not knowing how to respond, he just sat there. Jake sensed what he was feeling and cut to the chase.

"We divorced a little over a year ago. She went nuts down here. All she ever did was go shopping and watch that stupid soap opera *General Hospital*. She actually started thinking that real people behave that way. We'd get into an argument, and she'd start sounding like one of those puffed-up melodramatic characters—like she was reading from the script of one of the episodes. I think that's part of the reason we fell apart."

"Yeah. My wife watches that stupid show, too. Do women really think most people sit around all day talking about their relationships and acting all melodramatic about everything?"

"They do when they've got nothing else to do. You know, if you watch enough of that crap, it's gotta affect the way you think."

"How long were you married, Jake?"

"Ten years. But we didn't have any kids, so we worked things out pretty quick. Frankly, I'm glad she's gone. My life is much better now. How long have you and Janelle been together?"

"Basically, forever."

"Forever's a long time. Just one kid?"

"Yeah, it is a long time. And, uh, yes, just one little girl, Ellie."

Jake paused. "I guess I sound like a jerk talking bad about my ex, don't I?"

"No. Not at all."

"Maybe I'm old fashioned, but I think this women's lib crap has screwed things up. Look at Watkins. She has no business being in the Army. I suppose if she wants to be a lawyer that's fine, but she's a sorry example of an Army officer. She hasn't even passed a PT test yet, for chrissake."

Clark couldn't believe Jake was being so frank about their colleague, who also happened to be Jake's subordinate and Clark's peer. But again, he said nothing.

"Like I said," Jake continued, "I guess I'm just a jerk."

"No. I, uh, I don't think you're a jerk," Clark replied. "You're entitled to your opinion." He hesitated for a moment. "And you're probably right. Suzanne doesn't seem to be much of an Army officer."

"Right. And she's not shaping up to be much of a lawyer either. She was pathetic in the case she tried against me." Jake let that comment hang in the air for a while and then continued, "I wanted to talk to you about that, Clark. I want you to be co-counsel on the assault case she was assigned last week."

"She's not going to like that," Clark blurted out, perhaps a bit too quickly. (Several beers had eroded the filter in his brain.) "She thinks she's the experienced one."

"Well, she can think that all she wants. She's not," Jake replied. His manner was matter-of-fact, not disdainful. "I guess we can save her pride by telling her that I'm breaking you in." He then stared at Clark and said with unusual intensity, "But you be sure that case is prepared for trial and that you get a conviction. Drugs are one thing, but that little sonofabitch assaulted his fellow soldier with a broken bottle over nothing." Jake stopped, took a breath, and exhaled, obviously having let off some steam. "Well, enough of that crap. What were we talking about?"

"Women."

"Yeah, women. They're a pain in the ass, aren't they?" Jake smiled.

"I couldn't agree more," Clark replied as he sipped his beer.

"Have you heard that old Tom T. Hall song 'Old Dogs and Children and Watermelon Wine'?" Jake asked.

"Yeah. That's a good one. What made you think of that?"

Jake's eyes lit up, and then he said, "Well, there's a line in there that goes:

Ain't but three things in this world
that's worth a solitary dime,
But old dogs and children and watermelon wine...

Then, the next line goes:

Women think about themselves,
when men-folk ain't around.

"Boy, ain't that the truth," Clark replied, with a big, beer-drinker's grin.

Jake was rolling now. "A man told me the other day that dogs are better than wives."

"He's obviously been listening to Tom T. Hall," Clark quipped.

"Yeah. He said if you don't believe me, lock 'em both in your garage. Then, come back about an hour later and open the door. See which one's happy to see you."

Clark almost fell out of the boat laughing. Jake was acting more like Clark's big brother than his boss. The time passed; the fish continued to bite; and the beer continued to be cold. Most of the conversation was small talk about Panama and the Army, although as they became more "lubricated" with beer, they both got philosophical.

"I wish my wife was more like my mom," Clark lamented at one point.

"I couldn't agree more," Jake said. "What's wrong with a wife taking care of her husband the way our moms did? Would it kill them to have dinner ready when we get home and to look presentable, instead of like they just crawled out of bed?"

"My dad's arrival at home each night was an event," said Clark. "My mom would scurry around, make sure that the house looked nice and that she looked nice, too, and that dinner was ready. No matter what was going on, she always greeted my dad with a smile and a kiss," he said wistfully, without directing the comment to Jake. After a few moments, he looked at Jake and brought it current. "My wife has never done any of that stuff. Now that we have a maid, she's usually not even home when I get there, unless I'm late. And the maid does all the cooking. All my wife does is watch TV and shop. She's not even interested in playing with Ellie."

"Well, Clark, I doubt if you could have ever found a woman like your mom. Women's lib has ruined 'em all."

"Not down here. These Panamanian women appreciate their men."

"Yeah, but could you take one back home to Georgia?" Jake asked, again sounding like a big brother.

"I guess you're right. Hey, you got a bite."

CHAPTER EIGHT

AS THEY PULLED up to the boat dock at Gamboa, the sun was beginning to get low in the sky. It had been a glorious day. The natural beauty of Panama was stunning, and the fishing was unlike anything Clark had ever experienced. Their catch filled the bottom five inches of the cooler. Perhaps he shouldn't have insisted on keeping so many.

He looked at Jake, who was head down, stowing some of the gear. "I sure hope we didn't wreck the environment by keeping all these fish."

"This is Panama, Clark, don't worry about it." When Clark didn't respond, Jake turned and looked at him. The expression on Clark's face must have betrayed what he was thinking. "I was kidding, Clark. The peacock bass population in Lake Gatun is out of control. They're not indigenous to Lake Gatun. The Panamanians want us to catch as many as we can to try to restore some ecological balance."

"Oh, that's good to hear. I was beginning to feel a little guilty." Potential environmental issue resolved, there remained a looming practical problem. "How in the hell are we going to clean all these fish?" Clark asked. "It'd be a sin to waste such a catch."

"We aren't going to," replied Jake, with an emphasis on the word "we" that gave Clark a sinking feeling—taking the luster off the day and stirring memories of backyard duties that drew every cat in the neighborhood. "Why are you looking so glum? The slicky boys will clean 'em, remember? They'll be finished in no time. Motion for them to come get the cooler."

Clark waved to the largest of the slicky boys, a skinny, barefoot kid, wearing a T-shirt with a smiley face on it and carrying a gleaming, eight-inch butcher knife. He came over, picked up the heavy cooler, and carried it to where the other boys were gathered. Clark returned to helping Jake get the boat on the trailer, pull it out of the water, and stow the gear in the compartments in the floor. Jake seemed to have a particular place for each piece of gear. He removed the lures from each rod and put them in little drawers and then snapped each rod into brackets underneath the floor. They had just finished when the boy reappeared with the cooler.

"Seventy-five fish," he announced in surprisingly good English.

Clark couldn't believe it. In less than fifteen minutes, the kid and his pint-sized crew had cleaned that entire cooler of fish. He wished he'd seen them in action. They hadn't just cut off the heads and scaled the fish. They had filleted them and removed the bones and skin—leaving nothing but beautiful white meat, ready for the skillet.

"Let's each give the head kid five bucks," Jake suggested. "That includes a pretty good tip over the going rate, and he'll take care of the other boys."

"Ten dollars for cleaning that many fish? Isn't that a little low?"

"This ain't the Atlanta suburbs, Clark. The going rate would be around seven fifty. They probably think we're patsies."

Clark paid the boy and loaded the cooler in the boat. As he hopped down, a man walked up wearing a faded Texas A&M T-shirt and a ridiculous-looking straw hat that had probably been purchased from a sidewalk vendor in Panama City. Three younger men were with him.

"Been fishin', boys?"

"We caught a few, colonel," replied Jake.

Clark just smiled and let Jake, his senior, do the talking.

"Yeah. You gotta be queer not to catch fish in this lake," boomed the man. He seemed confident that no one within ear-shot would be offended by that comment—that is, if he cared. He was clearly playing to his audience of younger companions, who snickered like schoolboys.

They would be surprised to learn how many gays are serving alongside them. They just don't see them. While Clark was stationed at Fort Hood, he had seen his platoon sergeant—who Clark felt was the best non-commissioned officer in the unit— outside a gay bar in Austin holding hands with another man. Later, the sergeant asked him to keep that information to himself. He did.

The Army's official policy at that time stated unequivocally that homosexuality was incompatible with military service, so gays kept quiet about their personal lives for fear of being discharged. And, they knew that most soldiers agreed with this big-mouth by the boat.

Jake just smiled and nodded at the man with the funny hat. To his credit, Jake was trying to avoid going down the road of gay bashing. When the party left, Clark couldn't wait to ask, "Who were those guys, Jake?"

"You don't know?"

"No."

"I thought you two gung-ho boys were tight," Jake teased. "That was your buddy, Lieutenant Colonel David T. Bednar, and three of his junior officers."

"That was Bednar? I thought his voice sounded familiar. I mean… I've talked to him on the phone, but I've never actually met him. He doesn't look anything like I expected."

"Yeah. That's Bednar. And you want to know what's really

crazy?" Clark nodded. "His wife is smokin' hot. She used to be a model or something. Rumor has it she was in *Playboy*, but I've never seen any proof." Darst squinted his eyes and shook his head. "Bednar must have some attraction that escapes the male eye."

So that was Bednar. Maybe Suzanne was right: he did appear to be a bit of a pig.

Jake checked the tie-downs on the boat, and then the two men climbed into Jake's truck and headed back to the parking lot where Clark had left his car. It had been, without a doubt, Clark's best day in Panama. What's more, he'd gotten the feeling that Jake was pleased that he'd been assigned to his team.

Jake surprised Clark when he said didn't want any of the fish. "I just catch 'em; I don't eat 'em. Just bring the cooler to work on Monday." As Jake drove away, Clark loaded their catch into his trunk and headed home.

*

"Oh, Señor Clark, wha' beau'iful fish!" Nita exclaimed when he showed her the contents of the cooler. "You wan' me to fix some tonigh'?" Although it was still her day off, she seemed excited about cooking them.

"Sure," Clark replied. "Why don't you cook enough for us and freeze the rest? If there's not enough room in the freezer, then put some in the refrigerator, and we'll give them to the neighbors tomorrow." He was happy that Nita wanted to cook because he knew she would create something delicious.

"You got some sun," Janelle observed as she walked into the kitchen. "And it looks like you had a good day."

"Yeah. A great day, as a matter of fact. The best fishing I've ever done. And there's a lot to tell you about. Do you want to have a drink while Nita's cooking?"

"Sure. I'll fix them," Janelle replied. "You go get one of your cigars, and I'll meet you on the terrace."

When she didn't have any real work to do, Janelle could be a very agreeable person. She soon appeared with the drinks and a big smile on her face. "I've got something funny to tell you about Nita," she said in a hushed voice. "Today, I asked her what kind of cleaning supplies she needed, and she looked at me with a straight face and said, 'just some penis oil.'"

"Penis oil?" Clark whispered in disbelief.

"Yeah. I asked her, 'What did you say?' And she looked scared. I finally figured out that she was trying to say 'Pine-Sol.' I never laughed so hard in my life."

They both laughed again at Nita's expense, although Clark hoped she hadn't overheard them. Then he and Janelle sat for a while in silence, enjoying the warm evening breeze. After a few minutes, he began telling her about the events of the day with Jake, the howler monkey, how fast the fish were biting, and—most important—what Jake had told him about being co-counsel to Suzanne during the next trial term. Janelle rose up in her chair and stared at him, squinting her eyes and fretting her brow above her nose. "So why is he wantin' you to be in charge?"

Janelle's response annoyed him and put a damper on the mood. "I'm not going to be 'in charge,' Janelle. Jake just thinks that I could help Suzanne with an important trial and learn the ropes of trying a case at the same time. It's actually quite a compliment."

"I guess. So why can't Suzanne do her own work?"

"That's not the point. She does do her own work. She's just not getting it."

"Why do you always get so testy with me?"

He took a deep breath and exhaled, as if trying to calm down. Then he smiled at her. Realizing she was still perturbed, he continued, "I'm sorry, Janelle. I didn't mean to be testy. I just think this is going to be a big opportunity for me. It's my first chance to try a real case. And it's one that Jake is really concerned about. I just thought you'd be more excited for me."

"Well, it sounds to me like you boys go on your fishin' trip and drink your beer and then come back and say that the only woman in the office can't do her job without your help."

Where did that come from? Janelle sounded like a redneck who'd been reading *Cosmopolitan*.

"She's not the only woman, Janelle."

"Well, she's the only woman trial counsel. Didn't you say that bein' trial counsel was the best job in the JAG Office?" That question indicated that perhaps Janelle actually did listen to him on occasion.

"Why are you so concerned about Suzanne? I'm trying to tell you about a big opportunity for me."

"I guess so," she replied, half closing her eyes in a condescending way, as if she had a keener insight into the situation than he did. "But remember, Suzanne was the only one of your so-called colleagues who visited us when Ellie was in the hospital. I like her. And another thing: why is Major Darst now all of a sudden 'Jake'?"

"He was just trying to have a nice relaxing day fishing. I'm not gonna call him that at the office."

"I'm sure."

Seeing that the conversation was going nowhere, Clark changed the subject and started talking about the enticing aromas emanating from the kitchen.

"Nita's a great cook, isn't she?"

"I suppose," Janelle replied, again with her eyes half-closed.

"Are you kidding? She's a great cook."

"She might be a good cook, but I seriously question her judgment."

"Question her judgment? What are you talking about? Did she mess up something with Ellie?"

"No. Just listen to me for a minute. I paid her on Saturday before she left, and then she showed up today, askin' if it was all right to come home early and eat dinner here because she'd run out of money."

"Run out of money?"

"Yeah. She spent her entire two-weeks' salary on clothes, make-up, and goin' to some bar last night." At this point Janelle had more than a hint of moral superiority in her voice. "She didn't save a dime."

"Save? What do you know about saving? And what in the hell is she gonna save for? It's not like there's any opportunity for somebody like her to get ahead in this country—that is, unless she marries somebody."

The last comment must have struck too close to home: Janelle glared at him for a moment, then cocked her head, turned away, and said, "Well, I still think she's foolish."

"Well, if you think she's foolish, then we have no business allowing her to watch our daughter."

"Don't be a smartass. You know what I mean. Stop playin' lawyer for a minute."

Sensing that the conversation had taken a decidedly wrong turn, Clark changed his tone. "I don't 'play' a lawyer, Sugar. I *am* a lawyer." He smiled.

Unfortunately, his attempt at peace-keeping fell flat. Why was Janelle so insensitive toward Nita? Was she jealous of Nita's beauty and centerfold figure? But that didn't make any sense. Janelle was attractive and only a few years older than Nita. And, she had a husband and a beautiful baby girl. How could she be jealous of Nita?

"*Señor y Señora*, the dinner is ready," came a sweet voice from the kitchen. The three of them sat down at the table on the terrace to one of the best fish dinners Clark had ever tasted. Fresh and good. Nita had also made papas fritas, the Panamanian version of french fries, that were perfect: cooked on the inside and golden-brown crispy on the outside. To top things off she had made a salad with her homemade, one-of-a-kind dressing. Although the cuisine was distinctly Panamanian, the meal was no less memorable than those his mother had prepared following a day of fishing with his buddies.

After they finished, Nita started to clear the table, when Janelle stopped her. "Nita, sit down. I want to talk to you." Still smiling—and clearly not reading Señora's mood—Nita took a seat across from Janelle. "You're going to have to do a better job of managing your money. How did you spend it all so fast? I just paid you yesterday."

Nita's lips started to quiver.

"That's really her business, don't you think?" Clark interjected.

"Not if she has to come home early and eat dinner at our expense on Sunday night."

"Well, she did cook it, didn't she? And the fish were free. What's your problem?"

"Go on into the kitchen, Nita," Janelle commanded. "I'll talk to you later."

After Nita was inside, Clark asked in a hushed voice, "What is wrong with you? Does it make you feel important to talk to her that way? You and I used to talk about how some folks back home treated blacks. We said we would never be like that, remember? Just now, you sounded exactly like them."

"Nita's not black."

"Now who's being a smartass? You sounded just like old Mrs. Dupree back in Pemberton. You remember how she talked to her maid Mrs. Johnson like she was a child, instead of a grown woman who was raising children of her own. We even talked about how disrespectful she was to Mrs. Johnson. And now you go and do the same thing to Nita."

"Nita's not as old as Mrs. Johnson."

"Do you really think that makes any difference? Do you remember us talking about the people who went to church twice on Sunday and came out with their bigotry intact? Do you want to be like them?"

"I'm not gonna sit here and let you insult me. I don't think I'm a bigot."

"Well then stop acting like one. The Bible says we should love one another and whatever we do for one of the least, we do for Him. Or something like that." Clark stared at her for a long time but got no response. She looked the other way, as if she were studying something in the neighbor's yard.

"I hear Ellie crying," she said. "I need to check on her."

*

The days passed, and the trial term grew closer. Almost every day, Suzanne and Clark worked late at the office preparing the cases, especially the aggravated assault case that Major Darst had mentioned during the fishing trip.

"Clark, I want you to pick up the judge at the airport." Major Darst strode into Clark's office and thrust some papers in his direction. "He's not flying into Howard: he's coming into Torrijos. Here's the information on his flight."

The judge was being flown in from the United States because the units in Panama didn't have enough cases to justify a full-time judge.

"Yes, sir. Shouldn't I take Trip with me, so he doesn't think we're trying to get in good with the judge?"

"I guess... You can offer, but I'll be surprised if he goes." Darst's voice trailed off as he walked back to his office.

Trip proved Major Darst wrong—he did want to go. Since Darst had told Clark to pick up the judge, they went to the airport in Clark's Nova, although Clark would have preferred to ride in Trip's BMW. The judge was flying into Omar Torrijos International, the civilian airport named in honor of the Panamanian leader who negotiated the treaty with President Jimmy Carter. To get to there, Clark and Trip had to drive about forty-five minutes from Fort Clayton over a bumpy, two-lane road that was clogged with all manner of buses, cars, trucks, and overloaded, under-powered motorcycles. Along the way, they passed an array of Panamanian society: street walkers, poor kids begging for money, roadside vendors selling soft drinks from makeshift stands. And then a country club, where chubby golfers were driving carts around a manicured course, in stark contrast to their immediate surroundings.

When Clark and Trip arrived at the terminal, the judge's flight from the U.S. had not yet arrived. The paperwork provided by Major Darst indicated that they should be expecting Major Jeffrey Knowles, currently assigned to Fort Benning, Georgia. Knowles was "promotable" to lieutenant colonel, meaning that his promotion had been approved and he was merely awaiting his turn. Neither Clark nor Trip had ever heard of Major Knowles, although Clark felt that the judge's assignment was a good omen because Fort Benning—home of the Infantry Branch and the Army's Airborne and Ranger Schools—was known to be a no-nonsense military installation where self-discipline is almost a religion. He hoped that Knowles shared that view and would take a dim view of one soldier assaulting another. And, his impending promotion to lieutenant colonel meant that he was an experienced JAG.

Though he was in civilian clothes, the judge was easy to spot among the crowd of passengers making their way through the terminal. He had short-cropped hair and pale skin, and his attire was straight out of the Post Exchange—nothing stylish, just white-bread, Middle America. Trip took the lead and stepped forward to greet the major and introduce Clark.

After exchanging a few pleasantries, the judge got right to the point: "Have you guys ever heard of the Davila Inn?" Clark's stomach turned. This was not a good sign. Instead of talking about how he wanted to organize the trial term and process the cases they had to try, the judge was asking about a notorious strip club in downtown Panama City.

Because the Isthmus of Panama is literally at the crossroads of the Western Hemisphere, it had been visited by sailors from around the world for centuries. Because of the strategic importance of the Canal, a U.S. Army augmented brigade had been stationed there for decades. Consequently, the "oldest profession" was practiced extensively in the city. Although the downstairs of the Davila Inn was a nightclub with strippers, the real action—it was rumored—took place upstairs. Clark had no interest in going there, but before he could say anything, Trip responded, "Sure, judge. You wanna go?"

"Well, I've heard a lot about it," the judge replied with a timid smile.

Yeah. And I know what you've heard, too, thought Clark. Now, I'm not going to be able to spend the rest of the evening playing Candyland with Ellie. Of course, Trip doesn't care. He goes home to an empty apartment.

"Well, let's go, then," said Trip, turning on his country-boy routine in an apparent attempt to bond with the judge.

"You'll have to tell me how to get there, Trip," Clark replied. "I've never been."

"Hell, Clark, you know where it is. It's right below Gorgas Hospital."

The Davila Inn was obvious to anyone who drove by the area. Trip was correct: it was at the bottom of the hill below Gorgas Hospital. And, it was difficult to overlook. A large neon sign with pink lights was above the door, and every evening a flock of young women in spike heels and sexy outfits gathered on the sidewalk outside, leaving little doubt about what went on inside. Clark pulled up in front of the club, let his passengers get out, and then drove away looking for a place to park on the street.

Walking along the sidewalk from his car to the club, he was propositioned three times by attractive Panamanian girls who emerged from the shadows and promised to do all manner of things to "rock his world." He declined.

The inside of the club was typical of most Panamanian bars: the air conditioning was turned down too low, and a faint musty smell hung in the air, along with a blue haze of cigarette smoke reminiscent of Mother's Inn. Beer bottles were everywhere. Drunken Panamanians and Norteamericanos were gathered at tables around the room, gawking at beautiful young women, in various states of dress and undress. A half-naked girl was on the stage, gyrating to Rod Stewart singing "Da Ya Think I'm Sexy?" which was blasting over the sound system. All in all, it was a pretty decadent scene. By the time Clark found the judge and Trip, they already had beers and seemed to be enjoying themselves.

"Get you a beer, Clark, and lighten up," yelled Trip over the music. "I would have ordered you one but thought you might be drinking Shirley Temples again."

That's right, Trip, anything to make yourself look like the cool one, thought Clark. He bought a beer and nursed it for the rest of the evening, while telling one beautiful girl after another that he didn't want a "date."

Ignoring Trip and Clark, the judge sat and stared at the naked girls with a foolish look on his face, while downing one beer after another. At one point—much to Trip's amusement—he asked one of the girls for a table dance. When he offered his hand to help her step up on the table, Clark noticed he wasn't wearing a wedding ring. Was he single or had he removed it for the trip? Clark was worried the evening would never end and became even more worried when the judge began to slur his words. How would he explain delivering a drunk major to the Visiting Officers' Quarters? And how late would they hold his room? The judge wasn't staying at the musty pink stucco building on Fort Clayton. He was going to Fort Amador, where the VOQ for senior officers was located, and each room had a stocked bar. Finally, the judge said, "Let's go."

As they walked to Clark's car, the major, now unsteady on his feet, balanced himself between the two captains. Clark and Trip exchanged glances, but Trip just smiled as if to say: "don't worry, we can handle this." But what came next challenged even Trip's confidence. Approaching them with a slinky walk that exuded sex was a slender, yet voluptuous, creature, wearing spike heels, an extremely tight, low-cut, red dress, excessive but expertly applied make up, and what appeared to be a blonde wig. When the distance between them began to close, the smell of cheap perfume was so strong it overpowered the foul smells of the city. Suddenly, this person reached over, grabbed the judge in the groin, and whispered, in a deep, sultry voice, "Are you boys looking to have a good time?"

That was too much even for Trip, who quickly responded, "No!" as he hustled the judge along to Clark's car. The judge, on the other hand, seemed to enjoy the encounter: he had a smile on his face that was still there when the two captains deposited him in his room at the VOQ, along with his suitcase and briefcase.

After they got back into Clark's car, they drove toward home in silence for at least five minutes before Trip finally said, "So, I think we should promise each other that we will never tell the judge or anyone else that he just had his balls fondled on the side-walk in downtown Panama City by a guy dressed up like a girl."

They burst into laughter that continued until their eyes began to water. When they stopped long enough to catch their breath, only a few seconds would pass before they'd start again. Fits and starts of laughter continued until Clark dropped Trip off at his car and headed for home.

CHAPTER NINE

"I WANT TO go ahead with the motion *in limine* in the Rodriguez case," Clark said, as he stood in the door of Captain Suzanne Watkins's office.

"Why?" she asked, although her tone suggested she really didn't want to discuss the matter.

"Because I want the judge to rule—before the trial gets underway and without the members of the court-martial being present—on whether Trip may ask questions about the epithet in the presence of the members."

"We talked about this, Clark," she replied, using her best I-am-the-veteran demeanor. "I know this is your first trial and that you want to do a good job and all, but if there's a motion *in limine* to be made, it's made by the defense."

"Why? That's not what the Manual for Courts-Martial says."

Now she made no attempt to hide her irritation. "Because that's the way it's done," she replied, her cheeks now flushed.

"I don't see why we shouldn't make it. You know Trip is going to try to bring up the bad blood between the accused and the victim. And you know that their prior dealings are irrelevant. The members of the court-martial shouldn't hear that evidence. The fact that the victim is a jerk and had a previous verbal altercation with the accused doesn't excuse the assault. Don't you think that testimony about the epithet would prejudice their decision?"

"You'll make us look like fools," she said, the pitch of her voice rising in a way that suggested she was resigned to the fact that he wasn't going to take "no" for an answer. "I'm sure Trip already thinks you're a fool for giving him notice of the motion."

"I don't care. Rodriguez attacked Johnson with a broken beer bottle. The fact that Johnson had called him a 'spic' is irrelevant."

"It shows provocation."

"Provocation doesn't excuse an aggravated assault, Suzanne. It might be relevant for sentencing but not for the case-in-chief. And remember, he called him that almost a week before the assault." Clark studied her, waiting to see if she found his argument persuasive. Sensing she was still unconvinced, he pressed further, "You know that if the members of the court-martial hear that crap, they'll hold it against the victim, and we'll have difficulty getting a conviction. Hell, I'd be surprised if a majority of the members of the court-martial aren't Hispanic enlisted soldiers. Once they hear the testimony about the epithet, the trial's over."

"Okay, fine. Go for it," she said, dismissively waving her hand as if to indicate he was excused.

Clark left without saying anything further. Although her air of superiority annoyed him, he wasn't going to let that get in the way of doing the best job he could. He wanted to show Major Darst that his confidence in him was justified. He spent the rest of the day in the law library, researching every case he could find that had any connection with the suppression of irrelevant evidence. Back and forth he went to the shelves, searching for relevant cases. The process was slow and tedious, but in the end he was satisfied that Trip would be unable to surprise him. He was confident that the law was on his side.

At supper that night he didn't interact much with Janelle or Ellie. Janelle couldn't understand why he was so anxious, even after he tried to explain the significance of the hearing the next day. He ate quickly, said he had work to do, and spent the rest of the evening going over his notes. He wanted to ensure he was ready. Tomorrow was a big day, his debut as a real lawyer. He awoke the next morning with a knot in his stomach, having slept very little. The tension of appearing as counsel in a courtroom for the very first time—especially when he was making a motion that his co-counsel disagreed with—was almost paralyzing. If he failed, he'd be hearing "I told you so" forever.

As he drove to the office, he tried to calm his nerves by recalling stressful situations that he'd overcome in the past: being hazed by upper classmen at West Point, jumping out of airplanes at 1250 feet, rappelling down ice-covered cliffs, leading a night patrol through snake-infested swamps. If he was able to do those things, surely he could handle the stress of presenting a case in court. Thousands of JAGs had done it before. They were no better than he was. Were they?

That mental pep talk seemed to work. Clark arrived at the office in a confident mood, ready to meet whatever challenges he might face in the courtroom. But when he walked into Suzanne's office, he was stunned by her appearance. Gone was the cocky co-counsel who had glibly told him to make his motion *in limine*. Her face was ghostly pale, and she was visibly shaking. "Suzanne, are you all right?"

"I don't feel too well," she whispered.

"Do you want me to handle the trial by myself?" he asked with as much sympathy as he could muster.

"I'll be all right," she replied, though her voice belied her statement.

Should he tell her to use his technique and think about past experiences in which she had overcome her fears? Not knowing enough about her background, he decided to give her a pep talk instead. "Look, Suzanne, we're in this together. We can do this.

We're gonna get this guy. The evidence is clear. We're going to nail him." Clark stopped. He was starting to sound like his Little League coach.

"I'm just afraid we're going to lose." Suzanne stared at him with red, moistened eyes, although tears were not yet streaming. Her thick lips were quivering.

"Come on, Suzanne, we haven't even begun yet. This guy is guilty, and we're going to get him convicted. Dry your eyes and let's go."

They gathered their papers and walked into the courtroom, which was adjacent to their offices. Although Clark had been in this courtroom many times before, it felt different this time... foreboding... especially when he passed through the swinging gate that separated the public gallery from the arena in which he would soon be tested.

The courtroom had no windows, preventing those inside from being distracted by what was going on outside. The walls were a pale green, and the floor a gray linoleum. There were two tables in front of the judge's bench, which was elevated. The defense table was on the left, and the government table was on the right. Behind the two tables was a railing that ran parallel to the way the counsel tables were positioned and separated them from the public gallery. The gallery had rows of benches like pews in a church. Another railing, running perpendicular to the government table, was on the right side of the room. It separated the area where the members of the court-martial would sit. The only light in the room came from fluorescent ceiling fixtures, which gave the room a cold and sterile atmosphere. In fact, if the judge's bench, counsel tables, and railings were removed, it could have passed for an empty ward at Gorgas Hospital.

The Army has guidelines for everything, including how a court-martial should be conducted. There is a manual that includes a script, with parts for the prosecutor, defense counsel, and judge. It's designed to cover the reading of the charges and other preliminary matters quickly. After Suzanne, Trip, and Major Knowles finished the first portion of the script, the judge turned to Clark. "I have before me a notice that trial counsel would like to make a motion *in limine*." Although he sounded authoritative and professional—nothing like the redneck party boy at Davila Inn—there was a hint of irritation in his voice as he looked down and sorted papers on the bench. Looking back up, he directed his gaze at Trip. "Because it is a motion to suppress evidence, it must be considered prior to the accused entering his plea. Does the defense have any objection to proceeding at this time?"

Clark's mind was racing, and his hands were sweating. The judge's demeanor suggested that he was annoyed that Clark, as the prosecutor, had filed the motion. Maybe Suzanne was right. Maybe he was over-doing it.

After what seemed like an eternity, he heard Trip say, "No, Your Honor. The defense has no objection to proceeding."

"Captain Clark, the floor is yours."

Clark took a deep breath. "May it please the court, Your Honor," he said with as much confidence as he could summon. "The government seeks a ruling from Your Honor, concerning the admissibility of certain evidence of prior communications between the victim, Specialist Johnson, and the accused, Specialist Rodriguez. The government believes that the evidence is irrelevant and that the defense should not be allowed to elicit this irrelevant information in the presence of the members of the court-martial."

Clark went on to explain the evidence and why allowing witnesses to testify that they had heard the victim call the accused a "spic" would be improper. He made several other points and cited a number of appellate court opinions, photocopies of which he handed to the judge and to Trip. He sat down, held his breath, and hoped he hadn't screwed up.

Trip rose to challenge the motion. Much to Clark's surprise, he seemed to be winging it. He rambled a bit and then said something about "*res gestae.*"

The judge interrupted him. "Counselor, *res gestae* is not a part of the jurisprudence of military courts-martial. Moreover, when used in civilian trials it concerns an exception to the hearsay rule, not the relevance of evidence. Accordingly, it has no application to the government's motion to suppress this evidence. Is that all, Captain Stephens?"

"The defense has nothing further, Your Honor." Trip had no idea that he'd just gone down in flames.

Clark stood up, prepared to respond to Trip's arguments.

"What do you want?" the judge asked.

"Rebuttal, Your Honor?"

"A word to the wise, Counselor: when you've just won, sit down and shut up."

"Yes, sir," Clark replied, so stunned that he lapsed into the language of the Army, rather than that of the courtroom—saying "sir," instead of "Your Honor."

The judge turned to the court reporter, grinned, and said, "I know when the record is summarized." No verbatim transcript meant he could safely make what some might consider an unprofessional comment without it becoming a part of the record of trial. He then continued, "I hereby grant the government's motion *in limine...*"

Clark didn't hear anything after those glorious words. He'd just won his first motion in his first real trial. When he emerged from his fog, he heard the judge say, "Court will be in recess for thirty minutes." And then the gavel came down, and it was over—his first actual trial court session.

Trip huddled with his client, probably explaining to him what had just happened. Suzanne and Clark collected their files and papers and returned to her office. She flopped down in the chair behind her desk, looked at Clark, and beamed. "Well, you did it, Counselor," she said with a grin. "I didn't think you could do it, but you did. Now, we gotta win this darn thing. Are you ready?"

"I think so," Clark replied. "We have three witnesses who saw Rodriguez come after Johnson with a broken beer bottle. I don't know how the panel could view that any other way than that he assaulted Johnson."

"What about intent?" she asked, sounding like a student, instead of the lead trial counsel.

"The statements from the witnesses indicate that Rodriguez was not playing around. He was mad, and he was coming after Johnson. I think that's enough, don't you?"

"I hope so."

"You're going to handle the direct examination of our witnesses, and I'm going to handle the cross-examination of the defense witnesses and do the closing argument, right?"

"That's the plan," she said with a confident nod.

They returned to the courtroom, and Suzanne handled the procedural steps to empanel the members of the court-martial. When she and Trip finished, there were seven members on the court-martial panel, five of whom appeared to be Hispanic. Then, the "case-in-chief"—the actual trial—began. Suzanne did a professional job of questioning their witnesses. She had thoroughly prepared each witness in advance because she knew all too well that a lot can go wrong between preparation and trial.

To Clark's surprise, Trip didn't cross-examine any of the government's witnesses. Each time the judge asked him if he wanted to cross-examine, his response was the same: "The defense waives cross-examination of this witness." He seemed to be oblivious to the evidence that was stacking up against his client. After Suzanne finished presenting all of their witnesses, Trip made a weak motion for a finding of not guilty, arguing that the government's evidence was insufficient to sustain a conviction of the offense of aggravated assault. Remembering the judge's earlier admonition, Clark made only a few points in his rebuttal to Trip's motion and then sat down. The judge denied Trip's motion, without even leaving the bench to deliberate.

To Clark's further surprise, Trip stood and said that the defense had nothing further: in other words, he wasn't putting on any witnesses, not even Rodriguez. Maybe Elmer was right. Maybe Trip was lazy, or maybe he just wasn't too bright.

When Trip sat down, the judge asked Clark and Suzanne if they were ready to make closing arguments, since the government normally goes first and then has the opportunity to rebut the closing arguments of the defense. When Clark told the judge that the government waived closing argument but reserved rebuttal, Suzanne started to fidget and looked nervous. Not wanting the members of the court-martial to see her reaction, Clark whispered to her that he knew what he was doing. He had concluded that there was little chance they were going to lose this trial and sensed that the judge and the members of the court-martial were ready to get it over with.

Trip made a weak closing argument, which Clark easily rebutted. After both sides finished, the judge excused the members to the deliberation room. They took less than thirty minutes to return with a verdict of guilty. Clark was ecstatic. He had just won his first case. With the help of Suzanne, of course.

Next came the sentencing phase of the trial, where the members of the court-martial heard evidence relevant to their decision on punishment, as well as defense evidence in "extenuation and mitigation." As Clark and Suzanne expected, Trip called several witnesses who each said—in four different ways—that Johnson had called Rodriguez a "spic." When the members of the court-martial returned from the deliberation room, the senior member announced Rodriguez's sentence: reduction to private E-1, forfeiture of all pay and allowances for one month, and confinement for thirty days.

That was a light sentence for an aggravated assault conviction. The members of the court-martial had probably decided the victim had it coming. But if Clark had lost his motion *in limine*— and the members had heard about the "spic" comment during the case-in-chief, instead of during the sentencing phase—he and Suzanne might have lost the case entirely.

But Clark didn't lose the motion, and they didn't lose the case. More important, though, he helped put a bad guy in jail— at least for a little while. It felt good.

After the judge left the courtroom, Suzanne graciously walked over to shake Trip's hand—the same way Major Darst had approached her when she went down to defeat in her marijuana case. Since she was the lead counsel, Clark held back and let her enjoy that little ceremony as the victor. Walking out of the courtroom, he almost bumped into Elmer, who was wearing his trademark grin. "Congratulations, Counselor, you kicked butt. Bednar's gonna be real happy. Rodriguez is a shit bird. He needs to go to jail."

"Suzanne was lead counsel, Elmer."

"Watkins? Please. She couldn't convict Charles Manson. Your motion is what won it. You did great, buddy."

"Well, I don't know about that." For some reason, Clark felt awkward and embarrassed by Elmer's praise. He was proud of his first victory, but even he knew it wasn't that big of a deal.

Clark and Elmer were still standing in the back of the courtroom when Suzanne and Trip walked by, deep in conversation. "Good job, Counselor," Elmer said to Suzanne. She smiled.

"Yes. It was a good job, wasn't it, Elmer?" Trip interjected. "She did a fantastic job, don't you think?"

"Absolutely."

After they left, Elmer turned to Clark and, with a devilish grin and twinkle in his eye, said, "Let's go celebrate."

"Why did you say that to Watkins?"

"The compliment? Because she needs cheering up, Clark. Anyone who watched the trial knows that you won it with your motion. Even she knows that. Trip just said that bullshit about Watkins because he doesn't want *you* to get confident. He doesn't want you to think you can beat him. It's psychological bullshit."

"You really think that?" Clark asked, thinking Elmer might now be bullshitting him.

"Yes, I do. But forget that. I want you to meet a buddy of mine who's an agent with the Criminal Investigation Division." At that point, a big Hispanic guy who'd been standing nearby walked up. He was probably six feet four inches tall and weighed well over 230 pounds. "Meet Jaime Hernandez, the best damn CID agent in Panama," said Elmer.

"Nice to meet you," Clark said, extending his hand.

"Nice to mee' you, too, sir. You di' a goo' job. We nee' more trial counsel like you," said Agent Hernandez, with a deep baritone voice and a thick Panamanian accent.

"Thanks, but I'm still a newbie."

"Newbie, or no', sir, you di' a good job."

"Where do you guys want to go?" Clark asked, "Mother's?"

"Hell, no," said Elmer. "We're going to take you to a special Panamanian place."

"It's not the Davila Inn, is it? I've been there and have no desire to go back."

"No, Clark. That place is a dump. Trust us. You're gonna love this place," said Elmer, with an even more devilish grin than usual.

Clark called Janelle and told her about the results of the trial. After saying "good for Suzanne," she launched into an account of the trials and tribulations of shopping in the commissary and taking care of a three-year-old little girl. Clark could tell she really wasn't interested in his role in their little triumph, so he told her that he and Elmer were going to have a drink to celebrate and he'd be home later. She replied that she was going to play Bingo at the Officers' Club with some girlfriends and then hung up.

She really didn't care if he came home, as long as she was entertained in some fashion. She used to be so interested in what he was doing. Now he was just a distraction from whatever it was *she* was doing, even if it was something as insignificant as combing her hair.

"Let's all go in your car, Jaime, if that's okay," Elmer suggested.

"Fine wid me."

Elmer explained that Jaime was not only a CID agent, he was also half Panamanian. Since they were going to be driving in downtown Panama City, it made sense to have him behind the wheel, especially if they were stopped by a member of the Guardia National.

Clark deposited his files and papers in his office and then followed Jaime and Elmer downstairs to Jaime's car. Jaime and Elmer got in front seat, Clark in the back seat. Soon, they were winding their way through the city's busy streets. Clark was glad that Elmer had "volunteered" Jaime and that he wasn't driving.

"I don't know how you guys drive down here, Jaime," Clark observed. "Panamanians act like the lines on the road are just suggestions. They don't pay attention to them at all."

"No shit," said Elmer.

Jaime just chuckled. "You ge' use' to i'."

Finally, they pulled into a dark, gravel parking lot, surrounded by an eight-foot concrete-block wall. As he got out of the car and looked around, Clark saw no evidence of a night club. The entrance was marked with a dim light bulb over a window-less door.

"Is this it?" he asked in disbelief.

"Yep," Elmer said with a grin. "Wait 'til you see inside."

As they entered, Jaime was greeted by a stunning hostess in a short, tight black dress, who led them to a table in the corner. The room was dark, the music soft. It reminded Clark of a nightclub scene in a 1940s movie. As his eyes adjusted to the low light, he noticed that at most tables there were one or two smartly attired, middle-aged men chatting with several beautiful young women, each of whom was wearing an elegant cocktail dress. Although most people were smoking, the place smelled fresh.

"What is this place?" whispered Clark.

"Club Iguana, my friend," said Elmer, "the best little whorehouse in Panama."

"A whorehouse? No, Elmer, I can't stay here. Get me outta here."

Elmer stared at Clark in disbelief and then whispered, "Okay, okay, but Jaime wants to get laid first. His wife is pissed off at him because he won't take leave and take her to Puerto Rico. She's cut off the nookie for almost a month. We gotta give him a minute."

Sensing he was about to be branded a wimp, Clark replied with a grin, "Just 'a minute'?"

Elmer chuckled. "We'll get you outta here soon, Putty Butt."

"I don't want to spoil his fun, Elmer, but I'm a married man. I can't stay here."

"So am I, Clark. What's the big deal? This is Panama. What goes on off post, stays off post."

Elmer grabbed Jaime's arm and explained that Clark wanted to leave. Jaime offered to take them to another club, come back to Club Iguana alone, and then pick them up later. Sensing that Clark was still concerned, Elmer assured him that they could take a cab home if need be. Problem solved, they piled back into Jaime's car and headed to one of the swanky hotels in the Punta Patilla region of Panama City. Jaime dropped them off and pulled away quickly.

Clark and Elmer walked through the hotel bar into a disco, which was more like what Clark had expected initially. It was full of fashionable, affluent-looking young people, all of whom seemed to be having a good time, even though it was a Wednesday night.

Music was booming out of speakers in the ceiling that were pointed down at the dance floor, so dancers not only heard the music, they felt it. Elmer and Clark found a quieter corner, ordered two beers from the waitress, and sat back to enjoy the scenery.

Elmer took a long swig on his Balboa beer. "You did a heck of a job, today, Clark. No bullshit."

"Thanks, man. I appreciate that."

"No, seriously, Clark, the prosecutors down here have screwed up one case after another. Those of us who have dirt bags to get rid of have gotten pissed because a lot of them have walked away when they should've been convicted. When they come back to their units, they're cocky little assholes—worse than before their trials. It's nice to finally see an aggressive prosecutor."

"Just tryin' to do my job," Clark said, as he sipped on his beer.

Just then, Clark caught a glimpse of a familiar face in the flash of the dance-floor lights. "Don't look now, Elmer, but I think Specialist Weeks is in the corner behind you with a couple of burly Panamanian guys."

"Who?" Elmer obviously hadn't heard him. Everyone knew he never forgot a pretty face.

"Weeks. You know, the defense counsel clerk. And she's with two big Panamanian dudes."

When the lights flashed into the corner again, they both spotted Weeks, except this time she was looking straight at them, although she didn't smile or otherwise acknowledge their presence. Her expression was blank, as if she didn't know them. "She's acting strange, isn't she?" Elmer observed. He turned back to face Clark. "Well, forget her. Let's look at the eye candy."

A few minutes later, Clark looked in the corner again. Weeks and the two guys were gone. Elmer and Clark drank a few more beers. Around 9:45 p.m. Jaime showed up with a big smile on his face.

"So, you had a good time, I see," teased Elmer.

"Frickin' amazin.' Dis chica was abou' nineteen an' look' like a cen'erfold. Much better dan the one you ha' las' time. An' dis one did i' all. She…"

"Don't say anymore," Elmer interrupted. "I don't wanna know. You're just makin' me envious." Despite Elmer's sham request, Jaime continued.

Elmer may have been envious, but Clark was disgusted: two married guys talking about Jaime's sexual exploits as if he'd just bagged a trophy buck. How could they be so cavalier about their marriage vows? What kind of men were they to frequent a place like Club Iguana? And, they weren't even having affairs—they were screwing whores, which somehow seemed worse. Clark sat in silent judgment, while Jaime described his encounter in great detail.

"Guys, I hate to spoil your fun, but I've got to get home," Clark finally interjected. "I might've won my trial today, but I still have to go to work tomorrow."

Elmer insisted on paying the bill, and then they left.

As they swerved through the streets of Panama City, heading home, Clark started thinking about his first day in court. But all the beer he'd consumed and the late hour made his eyelids heavy. Suddenly, Jaime yelled, "Wha' the fuck is tha'?"

Clark sat up. Bright light was streaming through the back window. Someone was tailing them, not four feet off Jaime's rear bumper. Clark turned to look behind them. It was dark, and the headlights made it hard to see, but it appeared to be a white Ford truck like Major Darst's.

Wham! The truck slammed the rear bumper of Jaime's car. "Fuck! Tha' son o' a bi'ch tryin' to run us off the road!"

Fortunately, Jaime was not only a good driver, he also knew the streets of Panama. Making one quick turn and then another, he soon lost the truck. He pulled his car to the curb and stopped.

The three men sat in silence for a few moments, and then Jaime asked, "Wha' the hell jus' happen?"

"I have no fuckin' idea," said Elmer.

"Me either," Clark added.

"Somebody tryin' to sen' us a message," said Jaime ominously.

"A message?" Clark asked.

"Do you think Weeks had something to do with it?" asked Elmer.

Jaime's expression immediately changed. "Weeks was at tha' club?"

"Yeah, she was there with a couple of big Panamanian guys," said Clark. "Is Weeks in some kind of trouble?"

Jaime stared at him, and then he looked at Elmer. "Shoul' I tell him?"

"You might as well. He's not stupid. He'll figure it out eventually anyway."

Jaime looked back at Clark with a grave expression on his face. There was no hint of the party boy with whom he'd celebrated less than a half hour before. Jaime swallowed and then said, "Captain Clark, dis is very confidential, but Specialist Weeks is the target o' an investigation. We thin' she involve wid drug suppliers in Panama. Dey know who I am, and dey now know who you are. I thin' dey were sendin' us a message."

"You're kidding, right? I'm the new guy, and you're coming up with a bullshit story to scare me, right?"

"No, Captain Clark, dis is serious," said Jaime. "You can' tell nobody, includin' Major Dars'."

"I can't tell Major Darst that his former clerk is the target of a criminal investigation? Are you kidding? He's my boss. And, he's the Chief of Military Justice."

"No. We're not sure ye' if Dars' involve or not. We lookin' a' him, too."

"You've got to be shittin' me," Clark said. "Darst is a straight-up guy."

"Well, his ex-wife ran up a lo' a bills," said Jaime. "We thin' tha' Dars' and Weeks migh' be workin' wid Panamanian drug suppliers. Dey pay goo'. An' Dars' spen' a lot o' money, too. You seen the boat he ha'? Clark said nothing but wondered whether Jaime knew he'd been on that boat. "Major Dars' and Weeks saw all the criminal investigation reports when dey trying cases. Weeks know who I am, 'cause I testify in cases. She pro'ly saw you tonight a' tha' club. If she thin' you saw her wid the Panamanian guys, den dey migh' thin' tha' you could ID them. Tha's why dey givin' us some-thin' to remember besides seein' dem in the club wid Weeks."

Jaime started his car and headed back to Fort Clayton. The three men rode in silence. Clark couldn't decide whether to tell them that he thought the truck might have been Major Darst's. Whether it was a conscious decision to protect Darst or some sort of mental inertia, he kept quiet. Good Lord, how screwed up is this place?

CHAPTER TEN

ON THE FIRST Sunday morning following the Rodriguez trial, Clark and Janelle decided to have coffee on the terrace of their quarters and enjoy the beautiful weather that was so typical of Panama. The sky was clear and blue, with only wisps of clouds floating high above. Their terrace was shaded by some tall trees, one of which was home to the iguana that had approached Ellie and, in the process, terrified Janelle. The shade, coupled with a gentle breeze, made it comfortable to sit outside, despite the hot sun. God's beautiful creation was on full display, and Clark convinced himself that it was all right to enjoy it on his terrace, rather than worship Him in His church. Deep down, though, he knew that wasn't a good reason for skipping church, but on this Sunday morning it was good enough.

He and Janelle had attended the Protestant service on post several times, but it was nothing like their churches back home— pretty plain vanilla, so as to appeal to a wide audience with different religious backgrounds. The chaplain seemed like a nice enough guy but more of an Army officer than a preacher. All in all, it just didn't feel like church, so neither Clark nor Janelle was very motivated to go.

Clark was trying to peruse the Sunday newspaper and catch up on the news, which he'd been unable to do during the week because of the Rodriguez court-martial. He was reading an article about some Egyptians who were accused of conspiring to overthrow the government. Most of them were members of Al Jihad, an Islamic fundamentalist group bent on turning Egypt into an Islamic state. Normally, an article like that would have held Clark's interest, but on that morning he couldn't focus. He kept thinking about his relationship with his wife. They seemed to argue all the time about how much money she spent, the hours he worked, and whatever else popped up during the day. Their first year of marriage had been so different, and as he recalled those days, he was reminded of a passage of poetry he'd read back then.

"Do you remember what we did with that book that Paul gave us as a wedding gift?"

"Book? What book?" Janelle asked from behind her three-month old copy of *People* magazine with Scott Baio on the cover.

"You know," he answered, repeating each word with separate emphasis. "The book Paul gave us as a wedding gift. It came in a special box."

"Who are you talking about?" She dropped the magazine in her lap, now engaged solely out of curiosity.

"My sister's friend Paul. You remember, he had that gold Camaro. He gave us a fancy book in a slipcase as a wedding gift."

"Oh that. I think it's on one of the shelves in the living room," she said, giving no indication that she had any interest in why he was asking about a present they'd received six years before.

Clark went to the living room and found the book: *The Prophet* by Khalil Gibran. He flipped to the section on marriage and read the following passage:

Aye, you shall be together even in the silent memory of God.

But let there be spaces in your togetherness,

And let the winds of the heavens dance between you.

115

Love one another but make not a bond of love:

Let it rather be a moving sea between the shores of your souls.

"Listen to this," he said, as he stepped back onto the terrace and tried to engage her in conversation. He read the passage aloud. "What do you think it means?"

"I have no idea. It sounds like somethin' out of Proverbs in the King James Bible. I never understood much of that."

He tried again. "Do you think the author is saying married couples should be free to have relationships with others, in order to 'let the winds of the heavens dance between'?"

"What are you talkin' about?" Suddenly, she was engaged and eyeing Clark suspiciously.

"I'm talking about marriage, Janelle. Do you think there is a 'bond' of matrimony? Or, is there supposed to be space between a married couple?"

"Are you talking about foolin' around? I've heard there's a lot of that going on down here."

"No." Clark's irritation was apparent. He looked up in the trees and saw the infamous iguana lounging on a branch, staring back at him with a mocking sneer. For a moment, he considered pointing him out to Janelle. But he didn't. He just stared back until the animal scurried further up the tree.

"Bobby, are you listening to me? It sounds like you're talking about foolin' around. And in case you're wonderin', I don't believe in that 'open marriage' stuff. It's not right."

"That's not what I'm talking about. I'm just trying to talk about marriage in general. But you know what? Just forget I said anything."

"Well, what were you talking about?" she pressed.

He paused for a moment, trying to decide whether he really wanted to continue the conversation. "I was talking about the nature of the spirituality of marriage," he explained in a calm voice. He looked at her intently to see if there was a glimmer of understanding or any hope of having a deeper discussion.

"I feel like spirituality has to do with God, not relations between people," she replied before returning to her magazine. They sat in silence for a couple of minutes. "That poor Debby Boone. She is so talented. The *New York Times* trashed her in a review of her Broadway show, and now they've closed it." She dropped the magazine and made eye contact for emphasis. "I bet they did it just because she and her father are such good Christians."

"I'm trying to have a serious conversation, and you want to talk about Debby Boone?"

"There's no need to get testy with me. You always get testy with me."

"Okay, let's just forget it," he said as pleasantly as he could. It was no use. He should just try to be nice. "Why don't I get us some fresh coffee?" He picked up their mugs and went to the kitchen.

When he returned with the coffee, she was still absorbed in her magazine. He sat down and re-read Gibran's passage on marriage several more times. She was right about one thing: it was hard to understand how husbands could so easily ignore their vows—how good guys like Elmer and Jaime could be so cavalier about the commitments they had made. It was clear that Gibran wasn't writing about that kind of openness in marriage. Maybe their marriages were based on the convenience a wife affords a man when it comes to taking care of household chores, as well as bedroom activities. It was also clear that neither Elmer nor Jaime acted like he had much of a spiritual bond with his wife. But, he had to admit, he didn't either.

Clark recalled how his parents would sit on the back porch, watching the sun go down and enjoying each other's company without saying a word. They never bickered the way he and his wife had just now. He longed for that kind of marriage. After several minutes, he broke the silence. "I think I'm gonna go to the PX and call home."

"What for?"

"I haven't talked to Momma and Daddy in a while. I just want to check in with them. You wanna call your daddy, too?" He knew he needed to invite her along but secretly hoped she'd say "no."

"No. Ellie's still sleeping, and I don't want to wake her up. I had a hard time gettin' her to sleep last night. Besides, Daddy's not home. I got a letter from him on Wednesday. He said he was gonna go fishin' in Savannah this weekend with some of his buddies."

"Okay. Well, I won't be long."

At the Post Exchange Clark had to wait in line to use the phone. Back then, long distance calls to the United States were expensive—around $3.50 per minute—so most people bought minutes in advance, to get a discount, although it was still expensive. When it was finally his turn, he keyed in the code and dialed his parents' number.

"Hello."

"Momma, is that you?"

"No, it's your big sister, dummy." Darlene had always loved to tease him.

"Where's Momma and Daddy?"

"They're driving back from Atlanta. I'm over here doin' a little house cleanin'."

"Atlanta? What's that all about?"

"Oh, I don't know." Darlene's voice sounded strange. He knew something was up, because she would have known why they'd driven all the way to Atlanta. But she didn't give him time to ask anything more. "What brings you to call?"

"I need someone to talk to."

"Awww, does Bobby need his mommy?"

"No, this is serious, Darlene."

"Oh, I'm sorry, Bobby." Her voice softened, which made her sound even more like his mother. "I was just kiddin'. Do you wanna talk to me?"

He thought for a moment and then blurted out, "I'm worried about my marriage."

"What's wrong?"

"Well, we sure as hell don't have a relationship like yours."

"Oh, don't kid yourself, Bobby. Frank plays golf every Saturday, and I mean *every* Saturday. And then he leaves his nasty golf shoes on the porch, thinking I'm supposed to clean 'em, I suppose."

"I'm serious, Darlene. It's worse than that."

"Well, we have our days, too, Bobby. And remember, marriages take work."

"I don't feel any bond with her anymore. It's like we're roommates. I'm working like a crazy man at my job, and when I come home I have to pay all the bills and take care of things around the house. She doesn't do anything. She has a maid who does all the housework and cooking. All she does is shop downtown, watch TV, and lounge around the pool."

"She's got a maid?"

"Yeah, they're not very expensive down here." He paused to collect his thoughts. "You'd think that she'd take advantage of all her free time, but she doesn't do anything constructive. She doesn't even spend time with Ellie. All her time is free time, and she wastes it."

"Does she like to garden? Frank and I planted a vegetable garden at Momma's. We had all sorts of fresh vegetables and wound up canning fifteen quarts of pickled okra. It was a lot of work, but we had fun with it. And we did it together."

"She doesn't know how to do any of that. She doesn't know

how to do anything. All she does is spend money and read stupid gossip magazines."

"Well, maybe she could go back to school and finish her degree."

"Finish? Darlene, she never got started. I've already wasted I-don't-know-how-much money on courses she never finished."

"You say she doesn't spend time with Ellie?"

"No. I'm the one who taught her how to count and say her ABCs. And the maid is teaching her Spanish."

"Spanish? That's something." The line was silent for a few moments, and then she asked softly, "Do you think y'all are headed for a divorce?"

"I hope not. You know what the Bible says about divorce."

"Well, what are you thinkin'?"

"I'm thinking I've committed my life to the wrong person. I'm never gonna have the kind of marriage that Momma and Daddy have or like you and Frank have." He realized he was beginning to sound desperate, so he took a breath and slowed down. "Momma and Daddy always act like partners."

"Well, that's because they are partners. But it takes two committed people to make a marriage work, Bobby."

"I think about all the stuff Momma and Daddy have been through: the war, startin' a family, droughts, the time you wrecked the car. No matter what they're facin', they face it together. Whatever joys they have, they share. Whatever challenges they have, they tackle together."

"Daddy never has been one to show affection, though. And he's stubborn. He didn't talk to me for a month after that stupid car wreck. And it wasn't my fault."

"Darlene, you know that's just Daddy's personality. We never have doubted that he loves Momma and us, have we? Don't you remember how he used to say if somebody told him that Momma had murdered somebody he'd figure the guy deserved killin'."

She laughed. "You're right about that. He certainly loves our momma."

"When I got married, Daddy was my role model. I wanted my marriage to be like his and Momma's. But it's not working out like that at all. Or like yours."

"Things aren't all bad, Bobby. You've got a beautiful baby girl."

"That's true. She's unbelievable. The other day I caught her trying to teach one of her dolls Spanish. She'd say '*hola.*' That means 'hello.'" He was quiet for a moment as he reflected on what he'd just said. "It seems like only yesterday she started talking, and then I see her pointing to a glass of water and saying 'Agua'... 'Agua' over and over again. She looked kinda upset that her doll wasn't gettin' it. And she still gives me that look—the look I saw the first moment our eyes met. She'd just been born, and the nurse put her under one of those heat lights in the delivery room. She looked up at me, and I looked down at her. I am convinced she knew I was her daddy. From then on, she's had me."

"That's sweet, Bobby. When are we gonna get to see her again?"

"That's another reason I can't get divorced. I don't want to be away from her. I'm not gonna be a weekend dad. You know, Barry and some of the other guys have gotten divorced."

She interrupted, "Are you talkin' about those boys you used to run with?"

"Yeah. They told me it was hell takin' their little ones back to their mommas on Sunday night. They almost start cryin' talkin' about it. And they're tough country boys, Darlene." He paused for a few moments and then continued, "And for me, it would be even worse. I have no idea where the Army might assign me next. Can you imagine how it would be if I was in Korea and Ellie was in Pemberton?"

"I see what you mean. Well, you need to try to work with her, Bobby."

"You're right." He paused. He recalled how things were when

he was a cadet and had to use a calling card to call his wife—then his girlfriend—back in Pemberton. She was anxious to hear from him then, and they didn't just talk about what was in *People* magazine.

"Hey, are you still there?"

"Yeah. I'm sorry. You're right. She does have some good qualities. She's not hard to live with. Barry said that when he was married his wife nagged him all the time and was never happy with anything. He said she complained every time he wanted to go huntin' or fishin' or watch a ballgame on TV."

"She doesn't bother you like that, does she?"

"No. But that's what I mean. As long as she doesn't have any responsibilities, she's easy to get along with and lets me do whatever I want."

"Well, that counts for something, doesn't it?"

"I guess. But it probably just means she doesn't care whether I'm around or not."

"Come on, now. Don't be so negative. Does she still sing for you and Ellie? She always had such a beautiful voice."

"No. She hasn't done that in a long time. But, you're right. I shouldn't be so negative. Listen, Darlene. I'd better let you go. I'm gonna run out of minutes. Tell Momma and Daddy I said 'hi,' and give Momma a hug for me."

"Okay. You take care of yourself, Bobby. We love you."

Driving home, he reflected on what a sweet woman his sister was. Frank didn't know how good he had it. He also thought about those sermons he'd heard growing up, preaching that divorce is a sin. He knew he wasn't a particularly devout Christian. In fact, Barry used to say they were "shitty Christians." He was right: neither of them did a very good job of following the scriptures, but they did try. Clark knew that fooling around the way Elmer and Jaime were doing was *way* out of line. He also knew he didn't want to be separated from his daughter. No matter how he looked at it, he was stuck with his wife. So, he vowed on that Sunday morning to do the right thing and make the best of the situation from then on. He would be a good father and a faithful husband. He'd try to avoid any rancor at home and focus on his career, which, by any measure, required a lot of work.

His thoughts turned to the office, and he started to mentally make a "to-do" list for the next day.

CHAPTER ELEVEN

"PRETTY DAMN CREATIVE, Clark," boomed a voice outside the doorway of his office. It was Colonel Allen, speaking so as to be heard by everyone down the hall, including Major Darst. Clark looked up from the "to-do" list on his desk and stood up.

"Thank you, sir, but I'm afraid I don't know what you're talking about."

"Your motion, Clark," Allen replied with a big grin. "That was a good piece of lawyering. Colonel Bednar called me just now. He's really pleased."

Although he liked the compliment, Clark knew the only reason Allen had come to his office was that Colonel Bednar—a pain in the ass to everyone on the general staff—had called the SJA with something nice to say. Colonel Allen couldn't even pronounce "*in limine.*"

"Thank you, sir, but I had a lot of help from Captain Watkins and Major Darst." He made sure his voice was loud enough to be heard up and down the hall.

"Take the compliment, Clark. Enjoy it. Bednar doesn't give out many. You made us look good to the command. Good job." Allen smiled and walked away as quickly as he'd appeared.

That was odd. Allen didn't even speak to Major Darst before he left. And why had he come to Clark's office and not Major

Darst's? Darst was the section leader and Clark's immediate supervisor. But before he could think much more about it, Suzanne was seated in front of him.

"Well, you just got big kudos from the boss," she smirked. "I guess our motion *in limine* was a good idea."

"I guess so." Clark didn't look up from his papers.

"Yeah. You're the fair-haired boy, now," she continued, with a hint of irritation in her voice.

"For now, maybe, but you know how those things can change, Suzanne. After all, you were lead counsel."

"Yeah. Well, tell that to Allen. And to Bednar, for that matter."

Clark looked up. "Push that door closed, would you?" She gave Clark a funny look but complied. "Colonel Allen might still be in the outer office," he explained.

"Oh. Yeah."

"Look, Suzanne, you know Allen doesn't understand what we accomplished with that one motion. Remember, for most of his career he's been dealing with admin law."

"Right. And Bednar is *so* appreciative of the contribution made by women in the Army."

"Come on, Suzanne, Allen only came up here because Bednar called him. And we know you have your own opinion of him."

"Who?"

"Bednar."

"Well, yeah, but it's still nice to get a compliment from the boss."

"I can't argue with that, and I'm not saying it's fair." He looked at her to gauge her reaction. She gave only a half smile. "I wonder if Darst will say anything to us. I'm sure *he* understands what we accomplished."

"I don't know. He's been acting strange lately." She sighed and got up to leave. Opening the door, she entered the hall without looking and almost collided with Major Darst himself.

"Don't you have work to do?" Darst snapped.

"Uh… yes… yes, sir. I was just, uh, talking with Clark about the fishing trip you guys had."

"Well, might I suggest you do that on your own time?"

"Yes, sir."

Darst walked to the outer office, and Suzanne turned back to look at Clark with a puzzled look. When Darst returned, he was silent and somber as he walked down the hall to his office. He shut the door and stayed there until 5:00 p.m., at which time his door opened, and he left the office without even saying goodbye to anyone.

In the days that followed, Major Darst became increasingly distant and rarely spoke to Clark or Suzanne. Clark couldn't bring himself to believe that his mentor was the one behind the wheel of the white pickup on that night in downtown Panama or that he might actually be implicated in some sort of criminal activity with his former clerk. That was not the man he'd gone fishing with. But he had to admit that Suzanne was right: almost overnight Major Darst's behavior had become very strange. Clark recalled how serious Jaime had looked when he told him that Weeks and Darst were being investigated. Was Major Darst beginning to feel that investigation closing in? Clark didn't want to contemplate the answer to that question. Major Darst had been a good boss and an outstanding JAG officer and would surely make it to full colonel—and maybe even to general officer. It was sad to think that his career might come to an ignominious end.

If Major Darst were relieved of his duties, who would replace him? Despite Clark's concern for his mentor, he couldn't help but wonder. Clark hadn't been a JAG for as long as Suzanne or Trip, but he had been an Army officer longer than either of them, and he had been promoted to captain before they had. Would that seniority, coupled with his recent success at trial, be enough to cause the SJA to consider him for the Chief of Military Justice slot? That would be something, especially since the Chief of Military Justice was normally a major. Holding that job as a captain would look great on his record. His daydream ended abruptly when it dawned on him that he would be profiting at Major Darst's expense.

Several weeks passed. The next trial term was fast approaching. And Clark had become more and more anxious about Major Darst's situation and whether he should confront him with what Jaime had said about the investigation of Specialist Weeks—and him. On a Thursday afternoon he decided it was time. He knocked on Major Darst's door.

"Come in."

"Sir, have you got a minute?"

"Not really, Clark. Is this about the trial term?"

"Uh, no sir, it's about…"

"Well, then let it keep until after the trial term."

"Yes, sir."

Clark retreated to his office like a scolded puppy. He knew he should have said something, but he couldn't bring himself to do it. Despite his boss's peculiar behavior, Clark respected him, and he didn't want to risk destroying his relationship with the best mentor he'd ever had. And yet, he knew he needed to do something. It was hard to deny that Darst's behavior suggested something was wrong. He decided to talk it over with Elmer.

"What are you doing tonight?" he asked, when he finally got through a succession of clerks to the Headquarters Company Commander.

"Nothin', Counselor. What's up?"

"I need to talk to you about some stuff."

"Okay. Wanna meet at Mother's?"

"Sure. How about 1730 hours?"

"Sounds good. Like the sound of that military time, Clark, especially coming from a JAG weenie." Clark could almost hear Elmer's shit-eatin' grin through the phone line.

For the rest of the day, Clark contemplated how to broach the subject of Major Darst with Elmer. He kept pondering the same questions. How could he continue to work—as a prosecutor—for a guy who's the subject of a criminal investigation? Was he being disloyal to Major Darst for not telling him about it?

When Clark pulled into the parking lot at Mother's Inn, Elmer's motorcycle was parked in its usual spot. As he walked in the door, he smelled a mixture of cigarette smoke, stale beer, and popcorn. Country music was booming out of the jukebox, and Elmer was holding forth in his usual spot—a beer in one hand, a cigarette in the other. Judging from the empties in front of him on the table, he'd been there a while. As usual, three fresh-faced lieutenants were sitting around him, hanging on his every word.

"Evenin', fellas," Clark said as he walked up. Because he'd been there a few times—and because Elmer had run his mouth about the JAG with the "muther-fuckin' Ranger Tab"—Clark's reputation preceded him, so this time the lieutenants didn't scatter. They now saw Clark as a soldier, not some egghead lawyer who knew nothing about the real Army.

The members of Elmer's entourage were picking at a large bowl of popcorn, around which they had arranged at least a dozen empty beer bottles. One of them, who looked like he'd only recently started shaving, stood up and approached Clark. "Sir, Captain Jackson said you used to be a Cav Officer."

"That's right. That's what I did before I went to law school."

"Where'd you serve, sir?"

"I had a platoon at Fort Hood."

"Clank clank, I'm a tank." The young man grinned, trying to be chummy after consuming more than a few beers.

Anxious to cut off that chatter and get down to the business of talking with Elmer, Clark responded curtly, "No, son, I was a Cavalry Officer in a Cav squadron. We had Sheridans, not tanks."

That dismissive comment would probably ensure that the

lieutenants would not consider him to be one of the "good guys." But he couldn't worry about that now. Elmer looked at him and sensed that it was time to get rid of his entourage.

"Gentlemen, Captain Clark and I have some pressing business to discuss. Would you please excuse us?" Elmer was able to use courtly language in a mocking sort of way that made him downright charming. They smiled, grabbed their beers and the popcorn, and moved to another table.

Elmer more or less owned this corner of Mother's Inn. It was his throne room. When he was holding court with a group of lieutenants or having a conference with someone, no one bothered him. And that was good, because what Clark wanted to talk about was extremely sensitive.

"What's happening with Darst?" Clark asked before taking a sip of the beer that Elmer had ordered for him.

"You get straight to the point, don't you Counselor? I thought you were comin' here because you enjoyed my company and glittering conversation."

"Stop messing with me, Elmer. You know what I want to talk about. I'm going crazy trying to work for a guy who's being investigated." Clark then downed most of his beer in one swallow.

Elmer's smile went away, and he said, quietly, "Yeah. I understand. The problem is: I don't know any more than what Jaime told us that night. I hear about a lot of stuff, Clark, but that investigation is top secret." He said the last two words with special emphasis. "I haven't heard anything."

"I guess I should have figured it would be conducted on a need-to-know basis. What do you think, Elmer? Do you think Darst is mixed up with Weeks?" Clark's anxiety was apparent. He fidgeted in his seat, finished his beer, and ordered another.

"It wouldn't surprise me," Elmer replied.

"Really? Why do you say that?" Clark took a long swig of his second beer.

"Have you seen Weeks? That's a fine lookin' piece of ass."

"Damn, Elmer, is that all you ever think about?"

"Hey, it's what makes the world go 'round, Counselor." His trademark grin was back on full display. "And remember, they were working alone together when he was going through his divorce. A man's pretty vulnerable at a time like that."

"I doubt they are—or were—romantically involved." Clark gulped most of his second beer and then looked intently at Elmer. "Do you think Jaime would tell me anything more about the investigation?" Clark paused for a few moments to let Elmer ponder that question. When he didn't answer, Clark asked, "Would Jaime tell you anything?"

"Look, Clark, I think Jaime went out on a limb by telling us what he told us the night that S.O.B. in the truck almost ran us off the road. I think he said more than he intended because of the alcohol and the excitement of the evening, especially the chase. I even asked him about Darst the next day and got nothing." Elmer cocked his head and looked at Clark. "Man, you are obviously wigged out. You'd better slow down on those beers, especially if you haven't had anything to eat."

"That wasn't just any truck, Elmer. I think it was Major Darst's truck."

"What? What are you talking about? I thought he drove some piece-of-shit Corolla."

The grin was gone. No more joking about pieces of ass.

"The Corolla is what his wife used to drive. Now he drives that car to work. But when I went fishing with him a while back, he pulled his boat with a brand-new, white Ford truck that looked just like the one that chased us that night."

"Damn," said Elmer, looking down and then staring back at Clark. "You think Darst was trying to do us in?"

"I don't know. But that truck looked a lot like his." Clark took a swig of beer and stared back at Elmer. "Do you think

Weeks could have borrowed it? Maybe she was driving." As soon as the words were out of his mouth, Clark realized it sounded like a lame attempt to cling to a version of events that would relieve him of any obligation to come forward.

"Hell, I don't know, Clark. You're the one who works for the guy every day. And you're the one who's seen his truck." Elmer looked down at the table. His eyebrows scrunched together, and he looked back at Clark with an intense blue-eyed stare. "I do think you need to tell Jaime about it." Elmer was serious in a way that Clark had not seen before. There was no grin, no boyish charm. He was somber, as if contemplating the ramifications of being in the middle of a shitstorm involving two officers in his unit.

"I can't tell Jaime that it was Darst's truck." Clark said the words slowly and firmly.

"Why not? Because you're his boy?"

Elmer had assumed an entirely different demeanor, and Clark didn't like the insinuation that he wasn't prepared to do the right thing.

"I'm just not sure about the truck, dammit, and I don't want the CID getting any more interested in Darst if I'm wrong." He looked at Elmer to see if there was any indication that he agreed. Nothing. So he changed course. "Why don't I tell Darst about seeing Weeks that night with those Panamanians, and see how he reacts? If he looks guilty or acts evasive, then I'll tell Jaime."

"So, now you're the investigator?"

"Let me try it, Elmer. The man has never done anything to indicate he would be involved in any kind of crime. Furthermore, there are probably a lot of trucks like that one in Panama."

"Sure, Clark, look around the next time you're in downtown Panama. I'm sure you'll see a lot of big ole white pickup trucks. They stand out against the beat up old Ladas and Toyotas."

Clark knew Elmer was right: in Panama, a new, white American pickup truck was as rare as an overcoat.

Elmer continued, "Do what you need to do, Clark. But whatever you do, you need to do it quick. And, if you aren't one hundred percent sure that Darst isn't involved, then you need to go to Jaime. If you don't want to, then tell me, and I'll do it."

Clark felt he'd reached a reasonable compromise. "Okay. I'll tell him about seeing Weeks at the nightclub and see how he reacts." Clark paused and looked at his friend. "Let's change the subject, Elmer. This crap is depressing the shit out of me."

For several minutes, they sat and stared at their beers, and then Clark broke the silence. "I gotta hit the head. Where is it?"

"Over there." Elmer pointed to a hallway near the entrance.

Clark got up—a bit unsteady—and almost stumbled over a folding chair as he made his way to the latrine. When he returned, he'd combed his hair and seemed to have composed himself. Elmer's grin was back. "We can't do anything about this shit tonight, can we?"

"Right. So, let's talk about something enjoyable." Clark was smiling now, but his speech was slurred.

"No," said Elmer. "First, you're gonna do shots with me."

"Are you kidding? I've had too much already, and I've got to work tomorrow."

"Bullshit. You're a pussy if you don't." Elmer motioned to the waitress, who scurried over to their table. He whispered something to her, and a few minutes later she arrived with what appeared to be three shots of Jack Daniels for each of them. "Thanks sweetheart." Elmer winked at her; she smiled back and then walked away. "Cheers, Counselor: to secrets and pickup trucks." He downed one shot after another, finishing all three before Clark had finished one. He then insisted that Clark catch up, but the best Clark could manage was one and a half. Elmer looked at him, and his eyes widened. "Have I told you about the new secretary in the personnel office? A fine piece of ass if ever I saw one."

"Man, Elmer, you are a horn dog. What about your wife?" The question came out of Clark's mouth before he considered how Elmer might receive it. The subject had been on his mind for a long time, and the filter that kept him from saying stupid things was temporarily disengaged, courtesy of Balboa beer and Jack Daniels.

"What about her?" Elmer asked, without seeming to be upset.

Clark knew he couldn't just leave his question hanging out there, so he plowed ahead. "Well, Trip told me you had a sweet wife and three little girls."

"Well, Trip doesn't know shit. First of all, those are her daughters, not mine. The first one was born because she got knocked up in high school. The second two are from her worthless ex-husband who never pays child support." Elmer paused and stared at Clark with his piercing blue eyes. He continued slowly. "I met her at the O-Club at Fort Benning after I'd finished OCS, which was around the time of her divorce. She was sweet then, but not now. And, she needs to lose about a hunnerd pounds."

Clark could see that he should've kept his mouth shut. The shots hadn't brought out the best of Elmer's personality.

"Listen, man, I wasn't trying to be judgmental…"

"Yes you were," Elmer shot back, "And you know it."

That comment hung in the air for a while. "You're right, Elmer. It's none of my business."

"That's right. It is none of your business." He said each word separately for emphasis.

After what seemed like ten minutes, Elmer finally broke the silence. "Forget it, man. I don't hold grudges. Life's too short." He looked at Clark, smiled, and then added, "Let's just forget it."

The conversation then turned to lighter subjects. Elmer recounted his observations of every girl that he'd seen during the prior week. Clark listened half-heartedly. His mind was focused on how he would raise the subject of Specialist Weeks and the truck with Major Darst.

Fortunately, Janelle and Ellie were asleep by the time he got home. He brushed his teeth and gargled so that his breath wouldn't betray where he'd been. He quietly slipped into bed but didn't sleep much.

He rose early the next morning and went straight to the office. His head was pounding, so he made a pot of coffee and then sat and stared into his mug, as if he might find the answer there—his version of reading tea leaves. If he handled this situation incorrectly, it would probably destroy the good relationship he had with his boss. On the other hand, now that Elmer knew about Major Darst's truck, he could also be guilty of dereliction of duty for not coming forward with important information about a criminal investigation. There was no clear-cut way to proceed. He decided he had to approach Major Darst.

Around 7:45 a.m., Major Darst arrived. As was his habit of late, he passed Clark's office on the way to his without saying a word. Clark decided that it was now or never. Suzanne had wisely shifted her daily workouts from noon to early morning, which meant he could talk to Major Darst without raising her suspicion. Darst's door was open for a change. "Sir, could I speak to you for a minute?"

"When you start like that, Clark, I know it's not going to be good. Is this what you wanted to talk about yesterday? Come in. What's up?" Like yesterday, he was abrupt, although this time it was with a weary voice.

"Well, sir, it's kind of a sensitive subject," Clark began, as he stepped into the office and closed the door. "After the Rodriguez trial, Captain Jackson took me downtown to celebrate."

Major Darst looked up from his desk. "You're not going to tell me you got a DUI in Panama, are you?"

"Oh, no sir, nothing like that. We went to one of the night-clubs in the Punta Patilla area. I'll get the name of it from Elmer, if it's important. Anyway, we saw Specialist Weeks."

"Well, yeah, Clark, you do remember she's half Panamanian? She grew up in the city. She goes there all the time. What's the problem?"

He looked carefully at Major Darst's face, trying to detect whether he was nervous or being dissembling. No sign of guilt or anxiety.

"Yes, sir, I understand that, but she was with two big shady-looking Panamanian guys, and she didn't even acknowledge our presence, other than staring at us."

"I'm not sure what you're getting at, Clark. Did you expect her to come over and talk to you? She was off duty, having a good time."

"Oh, no, sir. We didn't expect her to pay respects."

This was the critical juncture. Should he tell him about the car chase? Should he tell him it looked like his truck? Clark didn't know what to do, so he decided to wait.

"It's just that these two guys looked pretty rough," he said finally.

"Well, so what, Clark? Belinda has a lot of relatives in Pan-ama. Maybe they were her cousins, or maybe she was on a date with one of them and the other guy was his buddy. Not everyone down here looks like they're from South Georgia."

"Well, it didn't look like a date, sir. These guys looked mean."

"You're not seriously suggesting that I confront Belinda because you saw her hanging out with two guys who you thought looked 'mean'?"

"No, sir, I'm not trying to borrow trouble. It's just that the whole situation looked suspicious. She didn't appear to be inter-acting with them as if she were on a date. She…"

"Look, Clark, you haven't been doing this job long enough

for me to be comfortable relying on your gut instincts. Maybe at some point but not yet."

That comment stung a bit, but Clark still wasn't ready to tell him about the car chase. He decided to shut up and try to avoid looking annoyed. The veteran trial counsel wasn't fooled and took a different turn.

"Did you guys study psychology at West Point?" Darst asked.

"Yes, sir. We took a semester of it."

"Psychology was one of my favorite subjects," Major Darst continued. "I remember one lesson in particular. It was about perception. The professor had all of us look at a picture on an overhead slide and then turned off the projector and asked us to write about what we'd seen. About half of the class wrote about a young woman, and the other half wrote about an old woman. We'd all seen the same picture, but we had interpreted it very differently. Did you ever see the picture I'm talking about?"

"I don't believe I have, sir."

Major Darst then reached into his desk, pulled out a tattered piece of paper, and handed it to Clark. It had this picture on it:

"You see the tight-lipped old lady looking down and to the left?" Major Darst paused for a moment, while Clark looked at the paper. "Now, look again. Do you see the young lady looking away, with a dark necklace around her neck? Do you see how the old lady's mouth could be the young lady's necklace? When I first looked at it, I saw the old lady, but my buddy saw the young one. We quietly argued about it in the back of the room, until the professor explained that that was the point of the exercise."

"Yes, sir," Clark answered. "Now that you explain it, I can see how somebody could see the picture a couple of different ways, but I'm not sure what you're getting at."

"What it shows, Clark, is that you have to be careful when drawing conclusions about what you *think* you see. You need to examine all the evidence carefully before you draw any firm conclusions. People can see the same thing and yet draw very different conclusions. You have to factor that in." Major Darst sounded like a college professor. He stared at Clark for a long time with an expression that once again looked like the man Clark had gone fishing with. "As a prosecutor, you have to get at the truth."

Clark sat in silence a few moments, trying to absorb what his boss had just said. Then he decided it was time to leave. "Okay, sir. Thanks. You've given me a lot to think about." He stood up, handed the paper back, and left.

After stopping to get some more coffee, he returned to his office to think about what had just happened. His mind was flooded with questions. How was he going to explain this to Elmer? Was Major Darst blowing smoke? Was his story about the college professor and the picture for real? Or, was he simply trying to plant seeds of doubt? Why would he have that old picture in his desk, anyway? Had he used that same speech on someone else? Maybe in a trial? Was he spinning the facts to suit his needs, which was a skill he used so effectively in the courtroom? Clark couldn't tell. He needed to think about it some more.

CHAPTER TWELVE

CLARK AWOKE THE next day after another night of fitful sleep and repeated his steps from the previous morning. He went to the JAG Office early, made a pot of coffee, and sat in his office thinking about whether he should tell Major Darst about the car chase. His strategy of telling Darst about the behavior of Specialist Weeks in the nightclub and then assessing his reaction, hadn't worked at all.

Clark's musings were interrupted by the sound of Major Darst's voice. "Clear your schedule for this afternoon, Clark. We're going to the CID Office at 1300 hours and will be there the rest of the day." Darst was standing in the doorway, briefcase in hand and a grave look on his face. "When Watkins gets here, tell her to do the same."

Before Clark could ask what was up, Darst was down the hall, in his office, door closed. Clark's head began to spin again with questions. Is Major Darst going to confront the CID about investigating him? Does he even know about the investigation? Does the CID know we're coming? Have I waited too long to tell Jaime about seeing Major Darst's truck? Should I contact Jaime now? Clark struggled to think clearly about the situation and concluded only that he couldn't conclude anything, so he did nothing. Before long, Suzanne arrived, her face still flushed from her morning run.

"Major Darst said to clear your schedule for this afternoon. We're going over to the CID Office at 1300 hours."

"Really? What's up?" she asked, screwing her face into a puzzled look.

"I don't know. Haven't you gone over there before?"

"No. I don't even know where the CID Office is." Wearing the same puzzled look, she walked to her office, mumbling something Clark couldn't understand.

For the rest of the morning, Clark couldn't stop speculating about what would happen that afternoon. He tried to focus on answering the growing pile of phone messages on his desk. As things turned out, Colonel Allen had been right about one thing: when commanders discovered that Clark had prior experience as a line officer, they preferred to talk to him rather than Suzanne. Sometimes they called about matters that didn't even involve legal issues, much less criminal law. He got calls about how to deal with superiors who weren't good leaders, how to motivate troops when their assigned tasks seemed meaningless, how to avoid becoming discouraged. They trusted him, and it felt good. Calling on his experience as a platoon leader, as well as his legal education and training, he tried hard to give them practical advice, rather than a regurgitation of what was in the Army manuals and legal treatises.

Around 11:45, Suzanne appeared in Clark's doorway and asked if he wanted to go to lunch, which she'd never asked before. Given the circumstances, he decided to go. She drove to the mess hall, where they lined up with other soldiers in the cafeteria line. Suzanne was picky about what she put on her plate, opting for salad and vegetables, rather than a cheeseburger and fries, which was Clark's selection. After they went through the line, she told Clark to follow her. As they wound their way through the mess hall, several officers greeted Captain Clark. Captain Watkins, on the other hand, seemed to be anonymous. Finally, they arrived at a small table in a corner by itself.

"Whew," she said as she sat down. She looked at Clark as if she might have been perturbed by his relative celebrity but said nothing about it. "This is a good place to talk. Captain Jackson usually has this spot," she said with an air that suggested she thought she was some sort of VIP.

Suzanne obviously didn't know that company commanders who are responsible for mess halls usually have a "regular" table, and although there is no rule about reserving it, most folks honor that prerogative. Fortunately, Elmer had gone fishing, so it didn't matter.

Before Clark took his first sip of Coke, she started. "What do you think this visit to the CID Office is for?" she asked, bubbling with childish enthusiasm. It was as if she thought some big melodrama was about to unfold and she was going to play a starring role.

Trying to keep a poker face in order to hide his true concerns about the meeting, Clark looked down and swirled a french fry in a pool of ketchup on his plate. Without looking up, he mumbled, "I have no idea."

"Well, it must be something big," she continued. "I've never heard of going to the CID Office for a meeting. Maybe they're going to charge Bednar with being a male chauvinist pig."

"Very funny," Clark replied, still staring at his plate.

Suzanne proceeded to prattle on about this subject and that, the only common thread being that she was the centerpiece of each topic. Clark contributed nothing to the conversation, but he didn't need to. Suzanne seemed to be interested only in hearing the sound of her own voice—like a radio that worked on transmit only. Clark finished eating first, thanks to a habit he'd picked up in the Army: soldiers always seem to be in a hurry to get back to whatever it was they were doing before they stopped to eat.

"Suzanne, we need to watch the time." he said, looking at his watch. "It's 12:20. We don't want to be late." Because of her monologue, she'd barely eaten anything. Nevertheless, she jumped up, ready to go.

Clark could feel a knot forming in his stomach as they drove back to the JAG Office to rendezvous with Major Darst. Upon arriving, they discovered he had already left, and Suzanne panicked.

"Dammit! We're in trouble now! I don't even know where the CID Office is!" She must have been nervous, because she never cursed.

"Calm down, Suzanne. I've already looked it up. We can go in my car. Grab your stuff, and let's go."

On the way to the CID Office, Suzanne regained her composure and resumed her lunchtime monologue, which continued until they arrived at the CID Office about twenty minutes later. As they pulled up, Clark saw Major Darst's Corolla in the parking lot and checked his watch. It was 12:50—ten minutes to spare. They walked up to the back door and were greeted by an enlisted soldier who was obviously waiting for them. He escorted them down a long hallway to a conference room.

The room had no windows. A standard-issue, gray metal table took up most of the space. Fluorescent lights hung from the ceiling and glowed with a dim, white light. The walls were bare and, although painted white, looked dingy, as if time and the events they had witnessed had made them tired. Maybe the somber gloom of the place was intentional, since it was probably where the CID agents interrogated suspects.

Seated along one side of the table were Jaime Hernandez and two other men who Clark presumed were CID agents. Each of them wore a blank expression. Major Darst sat opposite them with a pile of files in front of him. His head was down, and he was intently scrutinizing a document. It appeared that the meeting had been underway for some time—several half-empty Styrofoam coffee cups were on the table. It did not, however, appear to be an interrogation of the major. When Darst heard them come in, he looked up and motioned for Clark and Suzanne to sit next to him. Clark's stomach tightened.

"Guys, I thought we should meet here because we have something very sensitive to discuss," Major Darst began.

The knot took another twist as Clark waited for the next sentence.

"There's been a homicide on Fort Clayton."

What? That's what this meeting is about? Clark's thoughts jumbled into chaos. He needed to focus. Obviously, this was important.

"Since it occurred on post," Major Darst continued, "the CID will investigate, and we'll have jurisdiction to prosecute, if the perpetrator turns out to be a soldier, which we have reason to believe it might. Agent Robinson is going to brief us on what we have so far."

The man seated to Jaime's right was a black man, who appeared to be approximately the same age as Jaime. He picked up a document in front of him and cleared his throat.

"The victim is a thirteen-month old Hispanic female…"

Robinson continued to speak in a deep, monotone voice, but Clark couldn't focus. He couldn't believe a baby had been killed on post. Who would do such a terrible thing? An innocent little girl.

"The victim's mother brought the child…"

He sounds so stoic, Clark thought.

"…to the emergency room of Gorgas Hospital, complaining that she was groggy and would not wake up. The child was examined by Captain David Pearlman, a U.S. Army doctor, who brought in Dr. Roberto Gonzalez, a Panamanian civilian neurologist who is on staff at Gorgas Hospital. Dr. Gonzalez determined that the child was suffering from acute brain, uh, eda-ma, uh, eh-dee-mr."

Robinson struggled over, and then mispronounced, the word "edema." At that point, Clark didn't realize how familiar he was going to become with that strange word, which means excess fluid in tissue.

"Dr. Gonzalez pronounced the child dead at 1525 hours on Sunday, 19 December 1982."

He paused to refer to his notes. The room was as quiet as a church during silent prayer.

While Agent Robinson was looking for something in one of the folders, Major Darst turned and said, "Clark, they're going to do an autopsy of the victim at 1700 hours at Gorgas Hospital. I want you to be there."

"Yes, sir. But I'm not sure what I'm supposed to do."

"You don't need to do anything except keep your mouth shut and listen. Take careful notes about what you see and hear. Agent Hernandez will be there, too, right Jaime?"

"Yes, sir, Major Dars'. I' done dese thin's before," Jaime replied. "Dey no' pleasant, bu' we nee' to be dere to learn wha' we can."

Turning back to Clark and Suzanne, Major Darst continued, "Guys, I don't need to tell you how important this case is. Colonel Allen has made a preliminary report to the CG, but he'll want to be kept up to date on the investigation. Homicides are bad enough, but a dead baby is horrible."

Major Darst then paused and stared at the floor. Clark saw his jaw clench, and then he turned to his two captains again. "You might get asked about this case when people find out about it. Keep your mouths shut. Don't say anything to anyone other than those of us involved." He gave Suzanne a hard look but said nothing.

Clark had never seen his boss like this—totally in command

of the situation. The major's confidence comforted his two captains, who were still stunned by what they had just heard. The CID agents around the table gave no indication that they were the least bit concerned about Major Darst taking the lead in what was bound to be a very important case. Maybe the investigation of Major Darst was over, or maybe they were just going to keep their eyes on him while he handled this case and let the investigation run its course. Clark couldn't make sense of it all. Now, however, he knew he needed to keep his thoughts focused on that poor little girl.

"The CID is in charge of this investigation," said Major Darst, with a degree of emphasis that Clark hadn't heard before. "We are here to help them. And, we've got to be ready to try this case if and when the time comes. So, keep your eyes and ears open."

"What do you want me to do?" Suzanne asked.

She'd been so quiet since they arrived that Clark had forgotten she was sitting next to him.

"I want you to go back to the JAG Office and start researching shaken-baby cases. That's what we think this is. Isn't that right, Agent Robinson?" Major Darst turned to look at the agent who was still thumbing through his notes.

"Yes, sir, that's right," replied Robinson.

Turning back to Suzanne, Darst resumed his explanation. "At this point, it appears that someone shook that little girl violently, causing her brain to rattle around inside of her skull. It became bruised and swollen and ultimately killed her. So, I want you to find out everything you can about that kind of homicide case."

Suzanne nodded quickly but said nothing. Was Major Darst sending Clark to the autopsy because he was a good lawyer or because he thought Suzanne was too emotional to handle it?

Agent Robinson finished going through his notes and then looked up and asked, "Do you gentlemen have any questions?"

Clark glanced at Suzanne, who gave no indication that she

had taken offense. Had Robinson used the word "gentlemen" purely out of habit? Surely he intended no disrespect to Suzanne. Clark turned back to Robinson. "I have a question, Agent Robinson." All eyes turned in his direction.

"What's her name?"

Robinson stared at Clark for a moment and then, almost in a whisper, replied, "Lydia Mendoza."

The room was quiet again for a few moments, as if they were all paying their respects to little Lydia Mendoza.

Major Darst refocused the group. "Okay, guys, grab your stuff. Let's get back to the office. We've got work to do."

On the drive back, neither Clark nor Suzanne said a word. They were beginning to understand the reality of the tasks ahead. This wasn't a television drama or a movie, or a mock trial in law school. It was the real thing. Lydia Mendoza's short life had been ended by someone, and now they were part of the team trying to bring that person to justice.

When they got back, Clark headed to the library to look for anything he could find that might provide some guidance on autopsy procedures. He was surprised to find a book on forensic pathology, which he reviewed as carefully as he could in the time available. Although the photographs were horrible, they were only images on a page, an inadequate preparation for what he was about to witness.

As he pulled into the hospital parking lot, he had a *déjà vu* moment, recalling the night he and Janelle had brought Ellie to this place. Now, he was here for someone else's little girl under very different circumstances. He knew that what he was about to see would be unlike anything he'd ever experienced. He felt sick and didn't want to go inside. Finally, he took a deep breath, got out of his car, and slowly walked toward the entrance.

He was able to find the room where the autopsy was to be

conducted primarily because big, hulking Jaime Hernandez was standing in the hallway, waiting to go in.

"Man, I'm not looking forward to this, Jaime," Clark sighed as he walked up.

"Don' worry abou' i', sir. You' be fine. Elmer sai' you di' all tha' Ranger shi' an' stuff, and so, you ha' mental discipline. You jus' gotta use your mental discipline."

"Yeah, but this is different, Jaime."

They chatted for a few minutes, and just as Clark got up enough nerve to ask Jaime about the investigation of Major Darst, a Medical Corps captain appeared in a starched white lab coat. The coat had no rank insignia on it but above the right breast pocket was embroidered "CPT Jonathan P. Smith, M.D." Most Army doctors just pinned on a name tag.

"Gentlemen, please follow me. The medical examiner is about to begin the autopsy." The captain's demeanor was overly formal. He made a sweeping gesture with his arm as he pointed the way to the examining room.

Jaime and Clark followed him down a corridor to a room that was well off the main hallway, probably selected to avoid having an unsuspecting patient wander in. The captain directed them to sit in some chairs on an elevated platform located along the wall of the right side of the room, not more than ten feet from the examining table. The room was freezing cold, which Clark later learned is standard procedure, and it smelled like it had been washed down with hydrogen peroxide. The bright light over the table made the entire scene surreal.

Lydia Mendoza lay there nude, looking like a doll whose owner had taken off her clothes and left her on the table, instead of putting her back into the toy box.

The medical examiner carefully studied every square inch of her body, especially her head, which had been shaved. He measured the circumference of her head and the length of her limbs.

As he worked, he dictated what he observed into a microphone and instructed a photographer to capture various images. Clark thought he heard him say "her eyes are hemorrhaged," but he wasn't close enought to hear well, and the examiner was speaking quickly, in an English monotone but with a thick Panamanian accent. Clark sat quietly and hoped he would be able to get a transcript of the dictation and copies of the photographs.

After about twenty minutes, the examiner stepped back from the table and spoke to an assistant, although Clark couldn't hear what he said. The procedure then became even more surreal. The examiner began to dissect Lydia, as if she were a biology lab project. Reaching under the table, he came out with what appeared to be an electric saw—a miniature of the kind carpenters use to cut plywood. He flipped the switch, and the blade began to whine. As he lowered it into the little skull in several places, the sound modulated into a disgusting low pitch as the blade cut into her flesh and bone. He removed a piece of the skull, revealing her brain, which looked like something from a butcher's display case.

Clark couldn't bear to think he was looking at a child, someone's precious little daughter. Unable to watch any more of the grisly process, he looked away and hoped that Jaime, who seemed to be taking everything in, didn't notice his reaction and would—without any help from him—ensure that everything was done properly. After what seemed like an eternity but was actually only a little over two hours, the medical examiner announced that his examination was finished. Clark jumped up and exited the room as quickly as he could.

He ran down the hallway, looking for a water fountain and found one a good distance from the morbid scene he'd just left. He gulped the cold water, as if it would remedy the awful, hot feeling that welled up inside of him. When he felt someone's hand on his shoulder, he looked up to see Jaime smiling at him. It wasn't a sarcastic smile, as if Clark was about to become the butt of a joke. Instead, it was comforting.

"Are you okay, Capitain Clark?" Jaime asked without a hint of condescension. "Why don' we sit down over here. Your face i' white like a ghos'."

They walked over to a bench and sat in silence for a few minutes. Through a window looking out over the Bay of Panama below, they could see the sun setting. As usual, the colors were magnificent, and as was so often the case in Panama, Clark was struck by the beauty of it. But when he looked below the horizon, he could see the Davila Inn and the brightly colored clothes of the hookers gathered in front, waiting for the evening's work to begin. The wind was blowing litter along the sidewalk, and the street was crowded with cars and buses. His thoughts turned to the purpose of this visit to Gorgas. Why did God make that beautiful child in the first place, only to allow her to be murdered thirteen months later? How did that fit into His grand cosmic plan?

After a few minutes, Jaime spoke. "Sir, autopsies are a'ways har', bu' the firs' one is the wors'. The firs' one I saw was a prostitute in Vietnam. She couldn't have been more dan sixteen year' old. It was sick." Jaime sounded like a big brother, not a CID agent. "A'ter a while, you learn to be like the docs. They don' ge' emotional. They jus' make i' all bidness."

Clark nodded. "It's just so hard to understand how someone could hurt a child." He could hear his voice getting wobbly and decided to shut up.

"I saw a lot o' crazy shi' in Vietnam, Capitain Clark. I saw one of my buddies impaled on a two-foot spike from a booby trap. He wasn't t'ree feet in front of me. The Cong were sick fucks. So, I go' use' to seein' crazy shi'. Nothin' surprises me anymore. Bu' you gotta stay focus' or you'll miss somethin'."

They sat in silence for a few more moments. Clark thought

again about asking Jaime about the investigation of Major Darst but couldn't bring himself to do it.

"I think I want to go home," Clark said. "When do you think we'll get the medical examiner's report?"

"Pro'ly by Friday the 28th."

"Did you see any problems with the autopsy?"

"No, sir. I thin' i' was pretty goo'. Dey di' X-rays and every-thin' before the autopsy started. I thin' we gonna ge' a good repor'. Why don' you go home?"

"I think I will. I'll talk to you tomorrow." Clark stood up and headed for the exit.

He struggled just to drive home. All of his energy was gone. He'd never witnessed anything like what he'd just seen. Despite the brutal training he'd endured in the early part of his military career, he realized he wasn't that tough after all. The autopsy was the real thing, not training, not pictures in a book, and it was awful. He felt nauseated as he recalled the images that were now seared into his brain. Feeling that he was about to vomit, he stopped his car several times, with no result. Finally, he pulled into his driveway.

As he walked through the back door, he heard a familiar lit-tle voice.

"Daddy's home! Daddy's home!"

Never had those words been more welcome. Ellie ran up to him and threw her arms around his legs.

"Daddy, I nee' tell you something," she said with a serious look that seemed out of place on her sweet little face. "If you see a 'nake, don' pick it up," she said sternly, while pointing an admon-ishing finger in his face.

"Okay, Sweetie. I won't," he replied, though he had no clue what she was talking about.

His expression revealed his confusion, prompting Janelle to explain that a public service announcement on television advised viewers (and especially children): "if you see a *snake,* don't pick it up." Barely three years old, and already she wanted to ensure that her daddy was safe.

After dinner, he read her a bedtime story and then went to bed himself, completely exhausted. He hadn't slept well for several days, and the experience of the autopsy had left him emotionally drained. He consciously tried *not* to think about the investigation of Major Darst or Lydia Mendoza or the autopsy and, instead, focused on the image of the adorable little face he'd just kissed goodnight.

CHAPTER THIRTEEN

CLARK AWOKE THE next morning to captivating aromas emanating from the kitchen. Normally, he didn't eat breakfast, but this morning he'd overslept, and Nita was already at work creating one of her spectacular meals. He looked at the clock: 7:45 a.m. He should have already been on the way to the office. He jumped out of bed and dashed to the shower. Trying to shave quickly, he managed to cut himself three times and had to use pieces of toilet paper to blot the blood on his face and neck. He put on his uniform, grabbed his briefcase, and headed for the back door.

"Bobby, slow down a minute." Janelle was sitting at the dining room table in her bathrobe, drinking a cup of coffee.

"Why didn't you wake me up? I am way late."

"You seem like you had a bad day yesterday. It was almost 8:30 when you got home, and you tossed and turned all night. They'll understand if you're not there right at 8:00. Besides, Nita's made a real good breakfast. What happened to your face? How on earth did you do that? Sit down and enjoy this breakfast. You need to stop bleedin' anyway." She half laughed at him.

Although Janelle hadn't lifted a finger to help prepare the meal, Clark knew she was right. Besides, it presented an opportunity to explain to her what was going on with the Mendoza case.

"Look," he said, which by now she knew was the word he

used to precede something important or serious or both, "I need to tell you something, but you've got to swear to me that you won't repeat it to anyone." He turned and looked to ensure that Nita was still occupied in the kitchen.

Janelle set down her mug and leaned forward. "What's goin' on?" she whispered.

"I'm involved in a murder investigation."

"A murder?" Her voice elevated in pitch but not volume. He could see she was shocked. "Who?" she asked, wide-eyed.

"A little girl on Fort Clayton. But listen, you've got to promise me you won't tell anyone anything."

"I won't." She glared at him, now annoyed.

"We both know you like to talk."

"Are you goin' to tell me about it or what?"

"I had to witness the autopsy yesterday. That's why I was so late getting home."

"Why were you witnessin' the autopsy?" She emphasized the word "you" as if his participation made no sense.

"To make sure they did it correctly."

"What do you know about that stuff?"

"I did go to law school, you know. I have studied criminal law and the rules of evidence."

"Well, I've just never heard you talk about that stuff, that's all."

She wasn't impressed. He had wanted to tell her about what a gut-wrenching experience it had been, but when she acted the way she did, he changed his mind. It wasn't the first time she had shown little interest in—or respect for—his work, not to mention his education. She was right about one thing, though: it would have been a shame to miss the breakfast that Nita had prepared. It was unbelievably good—freshly squeezed orange juice, sausage, and *arepas*, a flatbread made of corn and topped with eggs and cheese.

He finished quickly and headed out the door without

attempting any further explanation of the events of the previous day. He wanted to get to the office and start writing his report about the autopsy while the experience was still fresh in his mind. When he finally sat down to write, however, the words didn't come. After struggling for more than an hour to compose a coherent description of what he'd seen and heard, he decided he needed help.

"Jaime? Captain Clark here. Do you have a minute?"

"Yes, sir. I' jus' typin' my report abou' the autopsy. Wha' you nee'?"

Quickly changing course from what he had originally intended, he asked, "Do you have an extra typewriter I could use?"

"Typewriter?" Jaime was perplexed.

"Yeah. I thought I might come over there to type up my report of the autopsy, so that we could compare notes while we're doing it."

"Don' your secretary type i' fo' you?"

"Well, actually, I haven't finished writing it. I figured I'd do that while I typed it up."

"Okay, well, sure sir, come on over." Although puzzled by Clark's request, Jaime was, as always, accommodating. Clark put the few notes he'd prepared in his briefcase and headed for the outer office.

"Where are you going?" Suzanne asked, as he passed her door.

"CID."

"Well, Major Darst wants to have an all-hands meeting today at 1500 hours to see where we are on the Mendoza case. I've got some great stuff. In one case, the court even ruled..." Her voice trailed off as Clark walked down the hall toward the outer office.

"Okay. I'll be back before then," he shouted over his shoulder. He wanted to avoid getting stuck in a conversation with Suzanne that might disclose why he was going to the CID Office. On the drive over, he considered how he would address the issue with

Jaime. He didn't want to look like somebody who didn't know what he was doing, but he also knew he needed Jaime's help.

"Goo' mornin', sir," said Jaime, greeting him with a smile at the security entrance. "Le's go to the conference room."

Clark followed Jaime to the same room where they'd met the day before. He sat down and got out his notes. Seeing what he was doing, Jaime said, "Sir, I don' thin' you nee' to write anythin'. We gonna ge' the medical examiner's repor', and I gonna write a report, too. I don' thin' we missed anythin'."

Jaime sat down, stared at him for an uncomfortably long time, and smiled, "You nee' to try dis case, Capitain Clark."

"What? What are you talking about? This is a murder case. I'm sure Major Darst will try it himself."

"Yeah." Jaime paused and looked at the floor and then looked straight at Clark. "Well, we still no' sure abou' Major Dars'. We thin' he migh' be involve' wid Specialist Weeks."

"You think she's trafficking? And she's got Major Darst involved with that? Is that it?"

"No, sir. We thin' she involve' wid drug traffickin', bu' we thin' Major Dars' involve wid her." He emphasized the word "her" and then paused again. "We thin' he' screwin' her."

"You've got to be kidding. Major Darst wouldn't have a relationship with Weeks. She's enlisted."

"Tha's the leas' o' his problems, Capitain Clark. We thin' she workin' wid some o' the drug lords in Panama. She feedin' dem information, so dey know who dey can use to brin' drugs on pos' an' when an' how. She' coul' be in a lo' o' trouble."

"Why do you suspect that Major Darst is having... having relations with her?" Clark chose his words carefully, trying to avoid sounding like the town gossip.

"'Cause dey work together for a lon' time. She a good lookin' woman, and he' divorced."

"That's not very much to go on, Jaime," said Clark, feeling obliged to defend his boss.

"And, a man fittin' his description ha' been photographed comin' an' goin' from her apartmen'. Look a' dese." He pulled some 8 X 10 color photographs from an envelope and slid them across the table. They were grainy and taken in poor lighting conditions, but the man in them could have been Major Darst in civilian clothes, and the black woman who greeted him could have been Specialist Weeks.

"Shit. That sucks," said Clark as he looked at the photographs.

"Yeah. It sucks. He would no' only be guilty o' fraternization, he migh' also be tellin' her stuff he shouldn' abou' our investigations. Remember, she' still work for the defense counsel, Capitain Stephens."

"So, Major Darst is still a target of investigation?"

"Yeah. We still lookin' a' him, bu' he no' an official suspec' yet." Again, Jaime looked at Clark for a few moments and smiled. "Tha' why I thin' you should try to ge' dis case."

"That's out of my control, Jaime. Unless you guys make Major Darst an official suspect, he'll be trying the case. Besides, you saw me at the autopsy. I'm not sure I'm ready for this."

"You ready, Captain Clark. Mos' guys don' like autopsies, especially the firs' one."

"Maybe, Jaime, but I've only tried one case so far, and this is a murder case for crying out loud."

"Bu' you di' a damn good job. I been watchin' trial counsel for a lon' time, Captain Clark. Most o' the time dey take our investigation reports an' jus' repeat wha' we write as questions. Dey don' thin' abou' wha' they doin'. You' not like that. An' Agen' Robinson heard all abou' it."

"Agent Robinson heard about what? Me trying the Rodriguez case?"

"Yeah. I came back an' tol' him we go' a prosecutor wid some

155

balls." Jaime recounted that statement with a smile and a familiar gesture.

"So why is Robinson somebody you report to?"

"'Cause he' the head o' the CID Office in Panama, Captain Clark. You don' know abou' him? He' a stud. He commanded an MP company in Vietnam durin' the Tet Offensive. He go' a Silver Star."

"I didn't know."

"Yeah, an' the Army screwe' him over a'ter we pull out o' Nam. See, he wa' an enlisted guy an' dey ma'e him an officer in the field. He wa' a hot shi' and go' promoted fas', bu' a'ter the war was over, dey pu' him back to master sergean', 'cause he didn' have a college degree. Dey did tha' to a lo' a guys tha' go' battlefield commission'. When the war was over, dey didn' need dem, so dey pu' dem back to dey permanen' rank."

"That stinks." How humiliating it must have been for Robinson, having been a company commander—a captain's job—to move back to master sergeant.

"Well, he show dem," Jaime continued. "He finish' his degree an' go' two masters degrees: one in criminal justice and one in bidness admin'stration. Den, he become a warrant officer an' a CID agen'. He still a hot shit."

"I take it he's a good guy to work for?"

"Yeah," said Jaime, "Bu' he' a hard ass." Jaime then paused as if to consider what to say next. "Captain Clark, you know me. I don' give a shi' who a guy is foolin' aroun' wid. You know Elmer like to fool' aroun'."

"So I've heard."

"An' a'ter the other nigh', you know I like a trip on the wil' side, too." Jaime smiled.

"Yeah, I get it."

"Well, for some reason, Agen' Robinson i' really pissed tha'

Major Dars' migh' be screwin' Weeks. Di' you see how he was a tigh' ass in tha' meeting we ha'?"

"I thought that was just his personality."

"No. He' usually a nice guy. I thin' he migh' be jealous. I don' know. But he' no' gonna drop dis thin' wid Major Dars'. So, I thin' he woul' tell General Kraus tha' you shoul' try the case." Jaime paused again. "You know a homicide case can make a JAG officer's career."

"Oh, I get that, all right. I just don't know if I'm ready."

"Believe me, Captain Clark, you ready. The whole CID office will help you convic' the son o' a bi'ch tha' kill tha' lil' girl."

"Do you have any leads?"

"Better dan tha'. We go' the S.O.B."

"What? You have a suspect? How did it happen so fast?"

"'Cause the baby stayin' wid dis enlisted guy. The baby's mom i' his sister-in-law."

"Wait," said Clark, holding up both hands. "Let me get this straight. The victim and the victim's mother..." He stopped. He was doing the same thing Agent Robinson had done. Starting over, he asked, "Lydia Mendoza and her mother were staying with an enlisted guy on Fort Clayton who was the mother's brother-in-law?"

"Tha's righ'."

"So, where was he living?"

"Oh, he ha' quarters on For' Clayton. He' married wid kids. Hi' wife i' the mother's sister."

"So, what's his sister-in-law doing in Panama?"

"Dey all Panamanians, Captain Clark. The enlisted guy is Specialist Raul Gomez. He' half Panamanian. Hi' wife's sister was livin' in a shi' hole downtown, and so, she tol' her to move in wid dem."

"Wasn't it crowded?"

"Yeah, bu' better dan a shi' hole."

"I still don't get the Panamanian connection." As soon as he said the words, Clark realized it was a dumb comment. He was surrounded by people who were half Panamanian—Weeks and Jaime to name two.

"Soldiers ha' been down here a lon' time, Capitain Clark. An' Panamanian women are hot. So, wha' happens, happens, and you whine up wid kids wid Panamanian mothers and American fathers. Sometime, dey good dads, like mine. Sometime, dey shits, like Weeks's dad."

"You know Weeks that well?"

"I know lo's o' girls like Weeks. Dey grow up wid a Panamanian mamma, but dey still half American. Dey learn English an' fi' in. Ot'er dan basic trainin' an' advance' individual training, Weeks spen' her whole Army career in Panama. She wa' a legal clerk, an' den she move over to Trial Defense Service. She been dere for a while, even before Major Dars' got dere."

Clark stared at Jaime for a while, trying to absorb all that he'd just said. "This is all a little overwhelming, Jaime. If I understand you correctly, the CID thinks Major Darst is having an affair with Specialist Weeks, and so, you guys want me to try a murder case, even though I've only tried one case. Is that right?"

"Righ'."

"At this point, Jaime, I can't do anything to affect the assignment of the case. So I think I just need to keep doing my job, keep my mouth shut, and see what happens. I have a meeting with Major Darst this afternoon at 3:00 o'clock. Should I tell him about the suspect?"

"No' ye'. We gotta pick the guy up an' interrogate him. Don' say nothin' ye'. I keep you posted on wha' happens. Bu', thin' abou' wha' I said, Capitain Clark. You coul' try dis case."

"Thanks for the vote of confidence, Jaime. You've given me a lot to think about." Clark paused and considered what Jaime had said. "Well, I'd better get back to the JAG Office."

"Okay, sir. I keep you posted."

As Clark left the CID Office, he was struck by what a beautiful day it was. He rolled down all the windows in his car and let the wind blow through. He attempted to consider whether he could handle the Mendoza case, but his thoughts soon turned to how his assignment was unfolding. Everyone in Panama seemed to be screwed up. Either they were opportunists, like Trip; or neurotic, like Suzanne; or they screwed around on their wives, like just about every married man in Panama. And then, this news about Major Darst. Even though he wasn't married, he had no business having an affair with an enlisted person—especially one who was working for him at the time. And he damn sure had no business continuing an affair with the defense counsel's clerk, after he became the Chief of Military Justice.

Was it possible that Major Darst was actually having an affair with Specialist Weeks? It would explain why he'd been acting so strangely lately, as the investigation of Weeks was heating up, and why he came up with excuses when Clark told him about seeing Weeks in the nightclub that night in Punta Patilla and why they were so chummy that first day at the NCO Club.

Rather than head straight back to work, Clark decided to stop at home for lunch. The memory of Nita's breakfast was still fresh. It turned out to be a good decision. Nita greeted him with her beautiful smile and made him a fantastic lunch. As an added bonus, he had Ellie all to himself because Janelle was on one of her many shopping excursions downtown.

CHAPTER FOURTEEN

BACK AT THE Criminal Law Section, Suzanne pounced on Clark as soon as he walked in. "What were you doing at the CID Office all morning? Are you ready for the all-hands meeting with Major Darst? I heard that the CID agents are coming, too. Did they tell you that?" She fired off each question in quick succession, leaving no time for Clark to even attempt an answer. He brushed past her, sat down at his desk, and pulled his papers out of his briefcase. Suzanne was right behind him. "So, what's going on? Are you pissed at me, or something?"

"No, Suzanne, I'm not pissed at you. It's just that you've got diarrhea of the mouth. I can't get a word in edgewise."

"I'm just trying to be a team player, Clark."

"Well, slow down then. Wait for someone to answer your question before you ask another one."

She stared at him, and her eyes became glassy. She turned and walked away.

"Look, Suzanne, I'm sorry." He got out of his chair and followed her. "I've got a lot on my mind. Wait a minute, will you?" Although she was in the hallway, he could see her wipe her eyes. "I didn't mean to be short with you."

"Okay."

"No, really, Suzanne. I'm sorry." He then told her about the autopsy of Lydia Mendoza, how Agent Hernandez had said he thought it went well, and that they should get a good report from him and from the medical examiner. He intentionally did not mention that the CID had a suspect they were about to interrogate.

The moment he paused, Suzanne launched into a monologue about all the research she'd done, which Clark had to admit was pretty impressive. She'd read every military case that had anything to do with child abuse, not just shaken-baby cases. And, she told him that she knew a civilian prosecutor back in the States who was going to send her some materials on how to try a shaken-baby case. Although she was irritating at times, Suzanne clearly knew how to work hard.

When the time for the all-hands meeting arrived, Clark and Suzanne made their way to the conference room together. Major Darst was already there, as were Jaime and Agent Robinson. Darst began. "There've been some developments, guys. Agent Hernandez has arranged to meet the victim's mother this afternoon. She lives in downtown Panama."

Apparently, the CID agents had not told Major Darst that they had a suspect or that Lydia Mendoza had been living with the suspect in government quarters. Were they keeping critical information from the man at the head of the table, because they really didn't trust him?

Darst cleared his throat, indicating he had more to say. "Clark, I want you to accompany Agent Hernandez when he interviews the victim's mother. He's leaving from this meeting to go there."

"Yes, sir."

Out of the corner of his eye, Clark could see Suzanne squirming beside him.

"Sir, I have a question," she said finally.

Darst turned toward her.

"Clark went to the autopsy yesterday, and now he's going to

the interview of the victim's mother." Suzanne stopped and stared at him.

"Your point, Captain Watkins?" His question was obviously rhetorical because everyone in the room understood her point.

"Well, when am I going to get to do something? I've been in this job a lot longer than he has," she said, gesturing in Clark's direction.

"Did you really want to see them cut that baby apart, Suzanne? And do you really want to venture into a rough part of downtown?" Darst turned to Jaime and said, "No offense, Agent Hernandez. I'm sure she'd be in safe hands with you. I just don't think there's any need to call attention to things. Sending a young Anglo woman to that part of town doesn't sound like a smart thing to do. Specialist Weeks and I went down there one time, and even she—a black Panamanian—was uncomfortable. Do you agree with my assessment, Agent Hernandez?"

Jaime and Agent Robinson stared at Major Darst when he mentioned Weeks. It took Jaime a few moments to compose himself. "Mos' definitely, sir. I' woul' no' be smar'."

"I'm not slighting you, Suzanne," said Major Darst, turning back to her direction. "In fact, I want you to brief these gentlemen on the work you've done so far."

Suzanne's countenance changed immediately. She was pleased to be center stage. In excruciating detail she described each case she'd read and included her opinion on why they were relevant to the Lydia Mendoza case. Her briefing was premature, of course, and of little use to the CID agents, and yet Major Darst let her go on and on. Was he placating her? Clark recalled how Darst had said her performance in the courtroom was "pathetic." Had he changed his mind about her abilities?

When Suzanne finally finished, Jaime was ready to go. "Capitain Clark, why don' you ride wid me? I know where dis Mendoza lady live'."

"Sounds good to me."

Major Darst wasn't the only one who thought downtown Panama wasn't safe. Clark was happy to be riding with Jaime. Not only was Jaime half Panamanian and a big guy (a characteristic he'd obviously inherited from his American father, since few Panamanians are very big), he was also armed.

They got into Jaime's car and drove to one of the poorest communities Clark had ever seen. Jaime was right: it was a "shit hole." The street was narrow and, though paved, seemed to be in a losing battle with potholes, each of which was filled with fetid muddy water. The buildings were multi-story apartments that blocked Panama's sun and ocean breezes, and everything was dirty: the buildings, the windows, the clothes people were wearing, even the clothes on the lines strung between the buildings. And the smell was awful. It reminded Clark of when their septic tank backed up, and he and his father had to dig it out. The smell on this street was even worse. It nauseated him. But worst of all were the children. They were everywhere. Their tattered T-shirts and shorts were little more than dirty rags, tragically juxtaposed against their smiling sweet faces. Few of them had on shoes as they ran through the filth and muddy water. There was no telling what diseases they were being exposed to.

"Dis is the place," Jaime said, as he parked in front of a building that appeared to be abandoned.

They got out of the car and were swarmed by little boys, staring at them, and holding out their hands. They were chattering in Spanish, laughing, and pushing and shoving each other. Jaime advised Clark to ignore them, but he couldn't help but look at them and think about how their lives were already determined. They were in this neighborhood now, and it was very likely that they would still be here—or in a similar situation—when they died. It was depressing, and yet they seemed happy. They ran around like kids on a playground back home.

Jaime yelled up the stairs to announce their arrival. He explained later that strangers were not welcome and could be greeted by having a heavy object dropped on their heads. A young Panamanian woman was waiting in the doorway of one of the apartments when they reached the third floor. Unlike everything else around, she was clean, although her clothes were worn and frayed. And she was pretty, despite a few acne pimples on her nose and forehead. Jaime said something to her in Spanish, and she let them in.

The apartment was small but appeared to be relatively clean. The windows were frosted glass and cranked open, like the jalousie windows on sun porches back home, although these had no screens. They were open, and the smells and noise of the street below poured in. In the center of the living room was a table with four unmatched chairs. A solitary light bulb hung from the ceiling. A "boom box" on a nearby shelf was blaring salsa music; Jaime motioned for her to turn it off.

All of them sat down, and Jaime started to speak. His demeanor was stern and authoritative and showed no sign of the friendly smiling person Clark had come to know.

"Señorita Mendoza, Capitain Clark is the *fiscal, comprende?*" he asked, using Spanglish, which Clark often heard in Panama. The "fiscales" were the prosecutors—individuals who were feared by almost everyone in Panama, especially the poor. Jaime continued, "We nee' to speak in English, 'cause Capitain Clark don' speak Spanish. Aw right?"

She nodded, and Jaime pulled out a tablet and got ready to take notes.

"Firs' of all, we wanna say tha' we' very sorry abou' your baby. We wanna fin' who di' dis and prosecute him. You understan'?"

Her dark eyes widened and became glassy, and she nodded quickly again. Jaime began his interview by taking down information about her. Her name was Carmen Mendoza, and she was eighteen years old. She said that the building they were in was her current address. It was her parents' apartment, but they were at work. When Jaime pressed her, she admitted that her parents had kicked her out when they found out she was pregnant, and she had lived with her sister and brother-in-law after that. She moved back in with her parents only after Lydia died. The father of her baby was a soldier in her brother-in-law's company whom she had dated several times. When Jaime asked her about Lydia, her eyes welled up with tears, which began to stream down her brown cheeks, wetting her entire face. Clark's heart went out to her. Here was a young mother who had nothing but her little girl, and now she was gone.

As she started to cry, Jaime softened. He said something in Spanish and then continued, "Look, Carmen, I know dis is har', bu' you gotta help us."

She nodded again in silence.

"As I say, I know dis is har', bu' I nee' to as' you 'bout the day Lydia go' sick. Wha' happen tha' day?"

Carmen's accent was even worse than Jaime's. That, combined with her sobbing, made it difficult to understand her. Clark gathered that her daughter had stayed with Raul, her brother-in-law, while she had gone out with the baby's father in the hope of convincing him to marry her or to at least acknowledge that the child was his. Raul had been alone with Lydia because Carmen's sister had gone to visit her aunt and had taken all of their children with her. When Carmen got home from her date that night, Lydia was asleep, and Raul reported that everything had been fine. Jaime pressed her, and she repeated that Raul had said that nothing out of the ordinary had happened.

"When di' you firs' realize somethin' was wrong wid Lydia?"

Through a new stream of tears, Carmen explained that the next morning Lydia wouldn't wake up. She seemed groggy and wouldn't eat anything. That's when Carmen became concerned and made Raul take them to Gorgas Hospital. But why had Gorgas treated someone with no apparent connection to the Army? They must have thought Carmen was Raul's wife instead of his sister-in-law. Or maybe Raul convinced the nurses that Lydia was the daughter of a soldier. In any event, Carmen didn't know much about what they had done to her little girl. She and Raul had waited in the waiting room all day, until Dr. Gonzalez brought them the terrible news that little Lydia was dead. When Carmen got to that part of the story, she started sobbing uncontrollably.

Jaime put his arm around her and said, "I's gonna be okay, Carmen. Trus' me. We gonna fine out wha' happen. I's gonna be okay." He told her he'd be in contact again and that he and Clark would let themselves out.

Clark practically fell into the front seat of Jaime's car. "Is it always this bad, Jaime?"

"Yeah. Bu' now I know we go' the righ' guy. I' ha' to be Raul. He was alone wid the baby. The medical examiner said i' was a 'classic'—his wor', 'classic'—shaken baby case. Raul mus' have done i'."

Clark didn't say much on the drive back. Although Jaime's analysis made sense, Clark was afraid he might be jumping to conclusions. There was a lot more evidence to consider. And even though Carmen appeared to be grieving, she might be lying. Figuring this one out would be tough, since there were no eyewitnesses. All of the evidence so far was circumstantial. Despite all that, Jaime appeared to have made up his mind that Raul was guilty.

By the time they got back to the JAG Office it was almost dark. Clark thanked Jaime for driving and said good-bye, but could barely get out of the car and into his. For the second day in a row, he felt completely drained.

CHAPTER FIFTEEN

THE NEXT MORNING, Clark wanted to get to his office early to start finalizing his notes from the meeting with Carmen Mendoza. He felt he could think more clearly before the phones started ringing and people began to chatter up and down the hall. He left his quarters before sunrise, but when he pulled into the office parking lot and got out of the car, he realized that he'd left his briefcase at home. He'd been so tired the previous evening that he hadn't put it in its normal place. When he got back to his quarters, he left the car running and hurried to the back door. Nita was already in the kitchen.

"Goo' mornin', Señor Clark. You wan' some breakfas'?"

"No, Nita. I forgot my damn briefcase." Her smile disappeared, and she looked frightened.

"I's righ' here, Señor Clark."

"Nita, I'm sorry. I'm not mad at you. It's my fault." He took the briefcase from her and smiled apologetically. "I just got in too big of a hurry this morning. I wish I could stay for breakfast, but I can't."

"Take this, Señor Clark. You nee' somethin'." She handed him a warm empanada, wrapped in a napkin.

"Thanks, Nita. You're right. I probably do need this." He dashed out the door and sped off.

By the time he got back to the JAG Office, the clerks were already at work at their desks. After greeting them, he poured a cup of coffee, went to his office, and closed the door. As he sat at his desk, eating the warm empanada, he gazed out the window and watched a ship enter the Miraflores Locks. During Jaime's interview of Carmen Mendoza the previous day, she had seemed so sweet and sincere. But then he reminded himself: When it came to something as important as a homicide case, he could not allow himself to be swayed by emotions. He had to make sure they examined all the evidence. It was the evidence that would reveal whether Jaime was correct—that Raul killed his niece—or whether there was another explanation for Lydia Mendoza's death. He finished his empanada and headed to the latrine to wash his hands. But when he opened his door, he almost ran into Major Darst.

"I was just coming to see you. How'd it go yesterday?"

"Uh, it, uh, went well, sir," Clark stammered. "Jaime seems to know what he's doing. I think the fact that he's half Panamanian made things go a lot better."

"Good. Let me see your notes when you finish them." Darst's face was stern and somber. He turned, walked down the hall to his office, and closed the door.

Clark's mind began to race. What is going on with him? He's not the same man I went fishing with just a few weeks ago. He no longer smiles. His conversations—if you can call them that—are short and abrupt, just like this one. And if Agent Robinson is right, he could be in a lot of trouble. If he is, maybe I *could* try the Lydia Mendoza case. But would the SJA let me try it, or would he bring in an experienced prosecutor from the States? Clark's mental speculations was interrupted by Suzanne's voice.

"So, how did Boy Wonder do yesterday?" Clark looked up to see her standing in the door with a smirk on her face. Before he could answer, she was seated across from him, staring at him as if she was waiting for a report.

"It went okay," he answered, without looking up, which was his not-so-effective technique for getting rid of her.

"What's the mother like? Is she going to be a good witness? Did she cry? How old is she? Is she pretty?"

"You're doing it again, Suzanne."

"Doing what?"

"Do you not realize you run strings of questions together without giving the person you are talking to a chance to respond?"

"Sorry. You're right," she replied, with no hint that she'd taken offense. "I just know this case is going to be big. We need to think about everything. Most JAGs never get to work on a homicide case."

Why was she so enthusiastic? Had she forgotten a little girl was dead? She should have witnessed the autopsy. That little girl looked just like Ellie, lying on that table as if she were asleep. And then, the rest of it. So gruesome. The sound of that saw. Why did Darst have him attend anyway? He should have known he had nothing to contribute.

"Clark, did you hear me?" Suzanne was now staring at him. "Major Darst is yelling for you." Clark jumped up, leaving Suzanne sitting in front of his desk, and hurried down the hall.

"Yes, sir?" he asked, as he entered Darst's office.

"The SJA wants to see you downstairs."

"What's up, sir?"

Darst stared at him with a blank look. "I have no idea. He just said for you to post down there ASAP."

"Will do." Clark headed back his office without saying anything further. Now his mind was racing. Was the investigation of Major Darst finally coming to a head? Why else would the SJA summon him to his office without explaining anything to Darst? Clark's hands started to sweat, and he began to get that queasy feeling in his stomach. He stopped by the latrine to check his appearance before going downstairs.

"Major Darst said you wanted to see me, sir."

"Yeah, Clark. Come in and sit down." Colonel Allen had a grave look on his face and avoided direct eye contact. Clark sat in the chair immediately in front of the SJA's desk and waited for what seemed like an eternity.

Colonel Allen took a draw on his cigarette and crushed it out in an ashtray on his desk. "I've got some bad news, Clark," he began and then paused. "It's about your dad."

"My dad, sir?" The gears of his brain ground, as his thoughts shifted from Panama to Pemberton. His heart sank.

"Yeah. Your dad is sick, and we've been notified by the Red Cross that you should go home."

"What?" Clark's jaw slackened and his eyes narrowed.

"We've been notified that he has a serious medical condition—serious enough that his doctors advised him to have you come home."

Clark was stunned to silence. His father was only sixty-two, the picture of health. As he regained focus, he realized that Colonel Allen was still talking.

"Go down to Headquarters Company and see Captain Jackson. Here's your DA 31, which the Air Force will want to see." He pushed a request-for-leave form across his desk. "Good luck, Clark." Allen then went back to his papers, and Clark assumed that was his cue to leave. He got up—still in shock—and walked out. He was halfway up the stairs before he realized that he'd left the SJA without saying anything—something junior officers shouldn't do—though at this point he didn't care. Of course, Suzanne was in his office again before he could even sit down.

"What'd the SJA want?"

"I've got to go home," he said, staring in her direction but not making eye contact.

"Is something wrong with Ellie again?" Suzanne actually sounded sincere.

"No. I've gotta go to the States. My dad is sick. His doctors said I needed to get there soon."

"Oh, I'm so sorry, Clark. Is there anything I can do?"

"I don't know, Suzanne. I'm still trying make sense of it all."

Major Darst appeared at the door. "Clark, I overheard what you said." His voice was warm—something Clark hadn't heard in a while. "I'm really sorry. You should get over to Howard Air Force Base ASAP. You might be able to catch the flight today. You know you've got to sign out first, though."

"Yes, sir. I was going to give you my notes about the inter-view of Carmen Mendoza…"

"Don't worry about that, now, Clark. There's plenty of time for that. Get over to Headquarters Company. I'll call your wife and explain what's going on."

Clark looked around his office in a daze, thinking there was something he was supposed to take with him. Major Darst and Suzanne stared at him in silence.

Suzanne spoke first. "Get going, Clark. You heard Major Darst. We've got things covered here."

She actually sounded nice. Or was she really just happy that he would be out of the way? She would be Major Darst's principal assistant for the Mendoza case while he was away. But there was no time for such thoughts now.

Clark drove to Headquarters Company and barged into the orderly room. "I need to see Captain Jackson right away."

His entrance startled the clerk at the front desk who looked up and asked, "Can I tell him what it's about, sir?"

"No. Tell him Captain Clark is here, and…" Before Clark could finish, Elmer emerged from his office.

"What's going on, Counselor?"

"It's my dad, Elmer. I gotta get home." Clark's voice

telegraphed his concern, and he was afraid that to all within ear-shot he sounded like a scared little boy.

"Come to my office." Elmer threw his arm around his shoulder and ushered him back.

"I've got this DA 31…"

"Yeah, let me have that." Elmer took the form from him and handed it to the clerk. "Get this processed immediately."

As they entered Elmer's office, Clark persisted, "Major Darst said I should get to Howard ASAP."

"Yeah, but he doesn't know what I know." Elmer sat down behind his desk, picked up the phone, and dialed a number from memory. "Hey, Sweetie, this is Elmer. Captain Clark is here, and he needs to get on the next plane to Charleston. It's an emergency. Can you take care of that for me, please? It would mean a lot." He then paused while he listened to her answer. "Good. How soon does he need to be there? Ninety minutes?"

Elmer turned to him. "Can you be there in ninety minutes?"

"Yeah. I… I think so."

"He'll be there, Sweetie. Put him on the manifest. That's right. Captain Robert Elmer Clark. Yeah, 'Elmer,' that's his name, too. Thanks, Sweetie. I owe you. You're a sweetheart. I'll see you soon." Elmer hung up the phone, looked at Clark, and said, "Get going."

Clark jumped up and headed for the door. For all of Elmer's bullshit and flirting and carrying on with everything in a skirt, he could damn sure get things done fast. Clark raced back to his quarters and was surprised to find Janelle in their bedroom packing his suitcase.

"I guess Major Darst called you." She didn't look up. "Did he tell you what it's all about?"

"Yes. He was pretty blunt about it. He said you get to go home, but the Army won't send me and Ellie with you. So you get to see your family, but I don't get to see mine."

The way she said the word "you" sounded like she thought he'd been awarded some sort of undeserved status, and she was annoyed. Clark couldn't believe what he was hearing. His father was seriously ill—serious enough to call him home—and she was mad because she couldn't go, too.

"Janelle, you know we can't afford to buy two tickets at the last minute, and the Army will only cover my travel."

"Well, I would like to see my daddy, too, you know. I've been down here just as long as you have."

"That's not what this is about, Janelle. Daddy's sick. Besides, if we could afford to buy tickets for you and Ellie, I would. We just can't."

"Well, I just don't understand…" She didn't look up or say anything else, while she continued to throw things into his suitcase.

"I don't have a lot of time, Janelle. Just close it up. Whatever I don't have, I'll get at home. I've got to change my uniform."

He quickly changed and started to leave, but stopped and picked up Ellie to give her a kiss.

"Where you going now, Daddy?"

"Daddy has to go see Papa. He's not feeling well."

"I sorry. Tell him to get all better." She strung out the word "all" in her sweet little voice.

"Okay, Sweetheart, I'll be sure to tell him."

He said a quick goodbye to Nita, who gave him a comforting smile and a hug. Janelle said nothing as he drove to Howard Air Force Base. Her eyes stayed fixed on the road ahead. Clark wanted to say something to her but was too hurt by her failure to appreciate the gravity of the situation, so he drove along in silence. When they arrived at the terminal, Clark unloaded his suitcase and turned to say something to her, but she spoke first.

"I'm not gonna park and come in with you. You don't have much time, anyway." She then gave him a perfunctory kiss on the cheek and got into the driver's side of the car. "Tell everybody I said, 'Hi,'" she said as she sped away.

Clark stood on the curb and watched her drive away. "Tell everybody I said 'Hi'?" Is she completely clueless? I'm going home because my dad's life could be hanging in the balance, and she says to tell everyone "Hi"? He didn't know what was going on with his father, and all his wife seemed to care about was getting a free trip home. What was that country song Major Darst mentioned? Something about how women think only about themselves when men weren't around. Well I *am* around, he thought, and she doesn't give a shit about me. He felt an indescribable emptiness in the pit of his stomach.

Clark didn't remember much of anything about the seven-hour flight to Charleston. He was in a fog, although the opportunity he might be losing by going home kept creeping into his thoughts. He worried that by the time he got back to Panama, it would be too late. The trial might even be over by then, and he would have blown his chance. But each time he had such thoughts, he felt ashamed. This was his dad for chrissake. And here he was worried about a damn case.

There was a Red Cross worker waiting for Clark when he arrived in Charleston. Bald, in his early fifties, and wearing an armband with the Red Cross emblem on it, he seemed to know immediately who Captain Robert E. Clark was. He walked up to Clark and greeted him with gentleness. "I'm Bob Jenkins, Captain Clark. I'm sorry about the circumstances that have brought you home."

Bob told Clark to follow him to the Red Cross office, which was a small room with more desks and file cabinets in it than it could reasonably accommodate. "You'll need a rental car to get to Pemberton, won't you?" Bob Jenkins had clearly been down this road before and knew what he was doing.

"Uh, yeah, I guess," Clark mumbled, blinking his eyes so slowly they were barely open.

Bob picked up the phone and dialed the rental car company to make the arrangements. After he finished, he turned to the exhausted young captain. "Captain Clark, listen to me. Private White will take you to get your rental car. They'll give you a preferred rate. Here's some coffee. You need to drink it and stay awake. If you get sleepy, pull off the road and take a nap. You don't want to compound your parents' troubles."

The guy was a pro. He knew exactly what to do. Clark, on the other hand, didn't have a clue. He hadn't slept much on the plane, and his emotions were running all over the place. He followed Private Julius White—who ironically happened to be black—down the hall and outside to a military sedan. Neither of them said a word until they arrived at the rental car office. Clark got out of the car, told Private White thanks, and walked into the dimly lit office. He was surprised that the clerk was friendly, considering that it was late at night and this was a time when the memories of Vietnam were still fresh and the military was not held in high regard. Clark finished the paperwork, found his rental car, and collapsed into the driver's seat. He paused to orient himself and focus on what he needed to do, then started the car and drove off into the night.

Fortunately, he knew the way home from Charleston and didn't need a map. Despite Bob Jenkins's concerns, Clark had no trouble staying awake. He started to worry, and he was angry. Why had his wife acted so selfishly? How could his father be so sick? Lydia Mendoza, his father, his marriage—they all became a tangled knot in his brain. He would catch himself thinking about the murder case, instead of the events that had brought him home, and he would feel ashamed. Then he would pray out loud like a child, asking God to fix whatever was wrong with his father. But he knew that God isn't Santa Claus. Life and death are a lot more complicated than that.

He crossed into Georgia from South Carolina and found himself on the familiar roads of his childhood. Somewhere, deep within his psyche, there were brain cells that directed him, without demanding any conscious thought, as he wound his way along the dark country roads. When he got to the bridge over the Ogeechee River, he recalled the time he and Barry had jumped off it—the stupidest thing he'd ever done. Other memories began to surface—images of his life in Pemberton, though they were faded and blurry.

When he got closer to home and the situation that awaited him there, the reality of what he was about to encounter began to dominate his thoughts. How sick was his father that they would call Clark home? Could it really be that he might pass? He'd fought in World War II, for crying out loud. He could do anything. He fixed a clogged toilet with a garden hose while house guests were waiting to use the bathroom. He hot-wired the car when Clark locked the keys in the trunk and they were miles from nowhere. And he took care of his family no matter what problems came their way. He was an amazing man: strong, decisive, in control.

Tears formed in Clark's eyes, and he began to cry. He cried hard for miles without thinking about anything. At some point the tears stopped and Clark composed himself again. He reflected on what kind of man his father was.

More than anything his father was wise. He always seemed to know what to do at the critical time. He always knew what was important. Silly things didn't distract him. His guideposts were things that mattered. Clark always knew that taking care of their family was the most important thing in his father's life. He had been the guardian who enabled them to live without fear. Clark should've told him that a long time ago.

Unfortunately, Clark had inherited only his father's appearance. He was educated, all right, but he wasn't wise like his father. And he certainly didn't have the wisdom produced by sixty-two years of life experience. Now, the person to whom Clark had always looked for guidance needed him, and he didn't feel up to the task. The knot in his stomach tightened.

Finally, Clark saw the yard light that illuminated his parents' little ranch-style house, one of many built in the 1950s and 60s, after the men who had defeated tyranny abroad came home and started families, trying to enjoy a little of the American dream they'd fought for. He turned into the driveway and heard the familiar sounds of gravel crunching beneath the tires and Brandy, his yellow Lab, barking so loudly he was afraid she'd wake the neighbors. As he stepped from the car, she instantly knew who he was and started wagging her tail. The backdoor light came on and silhouetted his mother in its glow. He walked toward her and heard her tired, sweet voice call out, "Is that you, Bobby? Thank God you're home."

CHAPTER SIXTEEN

"DADDY'S ASLEEP," HIS mother whispered as Clark stepped into the kitchen, holding the screen door behind him to keep it from slamming it. The only light on was the one over the sink.

"He's here? I thought he'd be in the hospital."

She looked down, and her lips began to quiver. "Let's talk about it in the mornin'. It's late, and I'm too tired to talk about it now."

Clark's worst fears were realized. They had sent his father home because there was nothing else they could do for him. At that moment, though, he was too exhausted to fully comprehend the gravity of the situation. He was on autopilot.

They walked silently through the kitchen and into the living room, where Clark counted four photographs of himself in uniform and noticed that his West Point saber was mounted on a wooden plaque above the fireplace. Clearly, his parents were proud of their boy. He'd forgotten that his house had a certain smell, partly the lingering aroma of years of his mother's cooking, partly her Mr. Clean, which she mopped the floors with every Saturday morning. It was familiar… comforting.

As they went down the hall to the bedrooms, Clark saw that a light was on in his sister's old room. He recalled how Darlene would sit in there at her vanity table—curlers in her hair the size of orange juice cans—putting on make-up for what seemed like hours. She almost always made them have to rush to church. But she wasn't in there now. His mother was. The door to his parents' bedroom was closed, but Clark could still hear his father snoring the way he had heard him so many times before.

Clark kissed his mother good night and went into his old room, which looked pretty much the same as it did years ago when he'd left for the Academy. The same blue chenille bedspreads were on his twin beds, and his high school diploma was still hanging in the same spot. The lamp on his nightstand featured a pointing bird-dog statue as the base; the shade was one he'd decorated in a project at Boy Scout camp. His mother had given him the lamp for his fourteenth birthday, telling him the dog looked like Brandy. He smiled when he remembered how—as an earnest fourteen-year old—he'd tried to explain to her that Brandy was a Labrador, not a bird dog. Too tired to wash up, he took off his clothes, switched off the light, and climbed into bed in his underwear. Momma would not have approved. She had always insisted on pajamas. He was asleep before he could think very much about the bad news he'd just received.

He awoke the next morning to the familiar aromas of his mother's kitchen. They were different from the ones that Nita produced, and they rekindled fond memories that made his mouth water. He could hear his mother bustling around and knew that she was making her special biscuits because her boy was home. He got up, got dressed, and shaved and washed up before heading to the kitchen.

"You want some coffee, Sweetie?"

"Yes, ma'am, I'll get it." She still used an old-fashioned percolator, even though most everyone used drip coffee makers. She said Daddy thinks her coffee tastes better. The kitchen looked the same as it had when he left for West Point: avocado green appliances and harvest gold walls. The ruffled, tie-back curtains with birds printed on them had hung on the window over the sink for years. Although his mother kept things spotless, she didn't care too much about updating the style. The weather was unusually warm for early spring, so the back door was open. Wood thrushes were singing in the pecan trees.

Clark sat down at the table and studied her. She looked the same as she had for years. Already dressed and ready for a trip downtown, hair and make-up perfect, she was the picture of a Southern lady. He waited to see if she would continue the conversation from the night before. She didn't. Instead, she just stared into the mixing bowl and virtually attacked the dough with a wooden spoon.

He walked over to her and put his arms around her waist from behind. "It's gonna be okay, Momma."

"No it's not, Bobby. Your daddy's in bad shape." Tears welled up in her eyes and rolled down her cheeks. Turning around, she hugged him tightly.

"What am I gonna do?" she sobbed into his shoulder.

"God's gonna take care of you, Momma." The response was automatic, not thoughtful.

She pulled away and looked at him through her tears. "Really? God's gonna take care of me? Is God gonna pay the bills and fix the roof when it leaks… hold my hand when I take a walk or hold me at night when I'm scared?"

Clark just stared at her. Her face bore a painful expression that he'd never seen before, not even when her parents died. He just looked at her and tried not to cry. She wiped her tears with her handkerchief.

"I'm sure my face is a mess. Let me go fix it, and then I'll get this breakfast finished. I bet you haven't had a good meal in a while." She left and returned in a few minutes looking as pretty as she always did. After finishing the biscuits and putting them in the oven, she sat down at the table with her coffee, having composed herself a bit. "I'm embarrassed, Sugar. I haven't asked you about Ellie or Panama or anything."

"That's okay, Momma. Things are going all right. Ellie's learned her ABCs."

"That's wonderful, Sweetheart." Her blue eyes sparkled, and she smiled.

"I'm real proud of her. And Panama. What can I say? It's real different, Momma. It takes a lot of getting used to. But I like it. It's real pretty, except for the poverty. And I like my job."

"Well, that's good to hear, Sugar."

Clark stopped talking and looked at her to see if she would talk about the sensitive subject that had brought him home. She was still smiling. "Tell me about Daddy, Momma."

Her smile disappeared and the sparkle left her eyes, but she didn't cry. "Well, son, he's got colon cancer. The doctors at Emory Hospital in Atlanta treated him with chemotherapy, but his condition didn't improve. He's in bad shape. In fact, his doctors don't know how he's survived as long as he has." She looked at him with a forced smile. "I think he's been waitin' for you to get home."

"Why didn't y'all tell me, Momma?"

"Well, everything happened so fast after we went to see the specialist in Atlanta. And, your daddy said not to say anything to you. He didn't want to worry you. He knew you were workin' hard at bein' a lawyer and all. And, you know your daddy: he figured he was gonna beat it." She stopped, and her eyes welled up with tears again. "I think he now knows he's not."

Those words hung in the air for a long time. Clark didn't want to comment. He didn't want to say anything that would affirm that conclusion. Instead, he said nothing and clung to the hope she was wrong.

"He's takin' morphine for the pain, and so, he sleeps a lot. But he said he wanted to talk to you as soon as you got home. So, when he wakes up, we'll go in there. But, Bobby, you need to be ready. He looks terrible. And remember, he dudn't need to see that in the look on your face. Don't let his last memory of you be a pained look." Clark nodded his head but said nothing.

They finished breakfast and sat and drank their coffee, while his mother told him all the news from their little town. At one point she got excited. "Larry Gray—you know Larry and Betty that we play bridge with?"

"Yes, ma'am."

"Well, he's been elected to the Georgia House of Representatives." She was smiling again. "You know, he ran two times before and lost." Clark nodded. "Well, this time he won by a big margin. We're all so proud of him. He deserves it."

"That wonderful, Momma. He's a fine man."

Suddenly, she perked up as if she'd heard something. His mother had always had a sixth sense, especially when it came to the ones she loved. If any of them were sick, she knew it before they did. If any of them awoke in the night with a fever, they saw her hovering over them with a cool washcloth. God had certainly blessed him with great parents.

"I think I heard your daddy stirrin'." She jumped up and headed down the hall, then returned with a strained look on her face. "He's awake. Why don't you go in there and say hello and see how he does?"

Clark got up and walked down the hall, not knowing what to expect. When he entered the bedroom, he could hardly see his father because it was so dark. As his eyes adjusted, he could see his father propped up in bed, swollen from the chemotherapy and bald. He didn't look like himself at all—that is, until he smiled.

"Hi, son. Come over here and give your daddy a hug."

As Clark leaned over to hug him, he smelled that awful hospital smell, so foreign to his father. He remembered when he was a child, watching his mother gently inhale as she tenderly held his father's shirts against her face. Her eyes would sparkle, and she would say "your daddy always smells like the woods." That was not the case now. If not for his father's smile and tired voice, Clark wouldn't even have recognized him.

"How's it goin', Daddy?" As soon as he asked the question, he realized how stupid it was. But his father didn't flinch.

"It's goin' great, Bobby. I've got a ways to go, but I'm ready to take it on."

If anything, his father was tough. Despite his response, Clark could tell that he understood his situation. That comment was solely for Clark's benefit.

"Sit down here and tell me about what's goin' on with you. How's my granddaughter? We sure miss y'all. And tell me all about Panama." He tried to sound as enthusiastic as his tired body would allow.

Clark pulled a chair close to the bed. "Well, we're all doing fine, Daddy. Like I told Momma, Ellie's already learned her ABCs."

"Really?"

"Yes, sir. I'm real proud of her. As for Panama… Well, Daddy, it's a strange place. It's beautiful and all, but they've got some strange ways of thinkin'." Clark looked at his father with raised eyebrows, and his father smiled.

"I think I know what you mean, son. You be careful and stay away from that stuff."

"Yes, sir. I will." Not wanting to discuss the crazy culture of Panama with his father, Clark changed the subject. "I've got a good boss. He's a Texan and a fine lawyer. He and I went fishin' on Lake Gatun, and Daddy, you wouldn't believe what we caught. Almost a hundred fish."

"No kiddin'?"

"Yes, sir. And he's got a boat like the one on *Bill Dance Outdoors*."

"Really? Sounds like a lot of fun."

"Yes, sir. It was incredible. I think it's spoiled me from fishin' back here, though."

His father smiled again but then coughed into a tissue. "Tell me about your job, son. Are you enjoyin' bein' a lawyer?"

"Yes, sir. In fact, I'm working on a murder case right now."

"A murder case?"

"Yes, sir. It was a little girl who got shaken to death." Clark stopped and looked at his father, trying to discern whether he was following him and seemed interested. He looked back at Clark with eyes that still had a hint of sparkle. He had always been eager to hear what his son was doing. Clark continued. "In fact, Daddy, I had to go to the autopsy. It was awful."

Immediately, his father's face took on a totally different countenance—solemn and strained, as if he was remembering something horrible. Neither man said anything for a few moments. "The Army can put you in some tough situations, can't it, son?"

"Yes, sir, it can."

His father then did something he had never done before: he started to reminisce about World War II. When Clark was a Cavalry platoon leader at Fort Hood, one of his sergeants, a Vietnam veteran, had told him that if someone talked a lot about their war experiences, it meant they actually hadn't seen much action. Those who had seen action didn't want to talk about it. His father was definitely in the latter category: he had come home determined to put the war behind him. So this conversation was a first. It was as if, after so many years, his father wanted to create a record for their family before he passed. He talked about his unit's preparations in England, about his unethical company commander, about his tank driver—all of it recounted in his father's humble, matter-of-fact way.

"You know, son, I haven't talked to those men in almost forty years, and yet I owe them my life. You and your sister wouldn't even be here if they hadn't done their jobs because I wouldn't have made it out of Germany."

"War is a terrible thing, isn't it, Daddy?"

"You can't imagine, son. It makes you do things you would never do otherwise." His tired voice changed to soft whisper. "I actually killed a man in Germany." His father paused and took a few labored breaths. "Yeah. We came up over a ridge and surprised a German tank crew. They were all out of their tank with their shirts off, soaking up the sunshine."

"What happened?"

"Well, when they saw us, they all scrambled for their tank. I knew the tank commander would head for the TC hatch, so I trained my machine gun on that location, and when he showed up, I fired a short burst."

"Well, maybe you didn't kill him, Daddy."

His father stared at him coldly. "No, son, I saw the blood. He never made it inside the TC hatch. The driver started revving the engine, but the tank didn't move. I suspect the reason they were there all alone was that their transmission was shot. Anyway, when they turned their turret toward us, I ordered a platoon fire command. All my tanks fired. There was nothing left but flames. They all died."

Clark and his father said nothing for a while. It was if they were observing a moment of silence for those German soldiers who died so long ago. Clark could sense that his father had gotten some kind of closure and peace by telling him about it.

He began again. "You know, son, a lot of killin' that goes on in a war is impersonal: bombs and artillery shells… machine guns and rifles fired indiscriminately in the direction of the enemy. I did a lot of that myself. But that day was different. I actually saw a man die at my hand. I've thought about him a lot over the years—how my life turned out and how his ended. He didn't get to go home and start a family like I did."

185

"But he was the enemy, Daddy," Clark offered, even though he knew his limited military experience didn't qualify him to console his father on this point.

His father's dark, tired eyes stared at him. "He was a man, Bobby. He was fightin' 'cause his country told him to. Just like me." Despite the ravages of chemotherapy, he spoke with authority borne of wisdom.

"I guess that's right, Daddy."

"Yeah, it was just one of those tough situations the Army puts you in, son. I didn't have a whole lot of choice."

After a few silent minutes, his father cleared his throat. With a raspy voice he asked, "Son, would you please hand me a glass of water?" He took a couple of sips. "This case you're trying..."

"I'm not *trying* it, Daddy. I'm just working on it."

"Well, it sounds to me like you're in pretty deep if you're going to the autopsy."

"Yes, sir."

"Well, you need to keep your head about you, son. It's real easy to let your emotions get out of control with something like that." He stopped. Clark could tell he was getting tired. "You need to keep your head about you," he said again. He paused, seeming to ponder what he would say next. "You remember that poem I bought you when you were a little boy?"

"Yes, sir, the Rudyard Kipling poem. It's still hanging on the wall in my bedroom."

"Well, read it again, son. Read it carefully, and think about what he's sayin', 'cause he's right. What he's sayin' in that poem is what I tried to teach you."

"Yes, sir."

"And, be careful of the choices you make, son, 'cause they chart the course of your life and pretty much determine where you wind up." His father stared into space for a few moments. "And, one more thing," his father whispered, "before you decide somethin' is true, think long and hard about it." He wiped his mouth with a tissue and struggled to speak. "I hadn't been to law school, but I know that sometimes things aren't what they seem. The good guys don't always wear white hats, and the bad guys don't always wear black hats. Sometimes, evil smiles at you. And sometimes, good and evil aren't far apart. Sometimes, they're in the same person." He stopped and struggled with a few raspy breaths. "Remember, in your business you gotta be right. When you're prosecutin' a man, you're representin' the United States of America against one of her citizens. Make sure you know you're right." He lay back on the pillow and closed his eyes. He looked peaceful. Apparently, he had said all that he wanted to say, or he was too tired to say more.

Clark got up, tucked the blanket around his father, and quietly walked back to his bedroom. Staring at the framed poem hanging on the wall, Clark slowly whispered the words out loud:

If you can keep your head when all about you

Are losing theirs and blaming it on you,

Daddy quoted that line almost *verbatim*. Maybe he read the poem a few times himself over the years.

If you can trust yourself when all men doubt you,

But make allowance for their doubting too;

If you can wait and not be tired by waiting,

Or being lied about, don't deal in lies,

Or being hated, don't give way to hating,

And yet don't look too good, nor talk too wise:

I've been trying to do that all my life. I guess I'm just not very good at it. It's hard for me to trust myself, even when others don't doubt me. I get anxious; my hands get dripping wet. But then, I was the one who took on that motion *in limine* when nobody thought it was going to work. And yet it did. So maybe I do trust myself, even if it doesn't always feel that way.

If you can dream—and not make dreams your master;

If you can think—and not make thoughts your aim;

If you can meet with Triumph and Disaster

And treat those two impostors just the same;

If you can bear to hear the truth you've spoken

Twisted by knaves to make a trap for fools,

Or watch the things you gave your life to, broken,

And stoop and build 'em up with worn-out tools;

Daddy must have relied on that passage. Lord knows he's had his share of setbacks over the years. But he never complained. He just got back at it. Yeah, he didn't need to tell me to read this poem. All I have to do is think about how he's led his life.

If you can make one heap of all your winnings

And risk it on one turn of pitch-and-toss,

And lose, and start again at your beginnings

And never breathe a word about your loss;

If you can force your heart and nerve and sinew

To serve your turn long after they are gone,

And so hold on when there is nothing in you

Except the Will which says to them: "Hold on!"

Maybe I did learn something from having this poem all these years. If anything, I am determined. I guess I do whine from time to time about my setbacks, but I do stick with a task. That's what got me through West Point.

If you can talk with crowds and keep your virtue,

Or walk with Kings—nor lose the common touch,

If neither foes nor loving friends can hurt you,

If all men count with you, but none too much;

Daddy sure understood that line. Whether he was talking to the Mayor of Pemberton or a hardscrabble black farmer, he treated them with equal respect. The mayor didn't get any more consideration than the farmer. Daddy was right about that. We're all equal in God's eyes, and so it should be with each of us.

If you can fill the unforgiving minute

With sixty seconds' worth of distance run,

Yours is the Earth and everything that's in it,

And—which is more—you'll be a Man, my son!

That "unforgiving minute." It's plagued me my entire life. What is it Janelle said about me? 'He doesn't know how to have fun.' Maybe she's right. Maybe I've worried too much about that unforgiving minute.

His father slept most of the rest of the day. Occasionally, he would stir, and Clark's mother would run to his room to do whatever needed to be done. That night Darlene and Frank came over for dinner, and his mother fixed one of her great meals: fried chicken, mashed potatoes, green beans, and corn. The only thing missing was his father at the head of the table. Before they were finished, Clark's mother jumped up and said, "I'm gonna fix Daddy a plate. He always did like my fried chicken." She went into the kitchen and emerged in a few minutes with a plate full of food on a tray.

As she walked away, Clark turned to his sister. "That's a good sign, don't you think, Darlene? He's eating."

She shook her head. "He won't be able to eat any of that, Clark. But that dudn't stop her from tryin'. Let's clean the kitchen before she gets back."

They cleared the table and started doing the dishes and cleaning the kitchen, as they'd done so many times when they were kids. Frank went into the living room to watch a ball game on TV.

"You know Daddy's condition is really bad, don't you, Bobby?"

"Yeah. I hadn't expected to see him like this. He looks awful."

"Well, I don't want you to worry about Momma. If…" She stopped for a moment and sighed. "When Daddy passes, Frank and I will make sure she's all right. I know you've got a lot on your mind, being a lawyer and all."

Clark knew his sister was sincere. She was still looking out for her little brother, just as she had done when we were kids. He looked at her standing by the sink and smiled as he remembered the time she beat up a bully on the bus who'd been picking on him. That was back in her tomboy days. She had always looked after him, just as their father had looked after all of them. His eyes got glassy as he reflected on how lucky he was to have the family he had.

"Thanks, Darlene. That means a lot," he said, his voice a little shaky.

"I mean it. Don't you worry about her."

After they finished the dishes and cleaned up the kitchen, they sat down with Frank in the living room in front of the TV. Their mother joined them a few minutes later and made a big fuss about their doing the dishes and cleaning the kitchen, which was a far cry from when they were kids and she wouldn't let them leave the room until all the dishes were washed and dried and everything was cleaned and put away. They sort of watched the ball game, but none of them were really paying attention. They were all thinking about the man in the other room.

Still tired from his trip home, Clark headed to bed before the game was over. As he walked down the hall, he could hear his father snoring.

CHAPTER SEVENTEEN

"BOBBY, WAKE UP. Bobby, wake up."

It was his mother, hovering over him as she had done in years past when he was late for school. He could tell it was morning because sunlight was streaming through a crack in the curtains.

"Get up, Bobby."

It took a few moments for him to get oriented and to realize he was back in Pemberton and his mother was talking to him. As soon as he did, he knew something was wrong. She looked terrible.

"I'm afraid your daddy passed in the night."

Clark jumped up, pulled on his jeans, and raced to his father's bedroom, hoping she was wrong. His mother followed and opened the drapes, filling the room with light. His father looked pale and fragile. Clark touched his face with the back of his hand. It was cold.

"He's gone, Momma. I'll call Fletcher." "Fletcher" was Fletcher Thompson, a family friend who owned the funeral home in town. Clark's call came as no surprise. He told Clark he'd send a car over right away. After what seemed like only a few minutes, both the car and Fletcher arrived. Fletcher had a lot of experience with such situations and seemed to know exactly what to say and do. He moved calmly but with a purpose, and before long Clark's father had been taken away; his mother had signed all the paperwork for the casket; and funeral arrangements had been made.

The rest of the day, Clark struggled to pay attention to what was going on around him. Darlene and Frank came over, as did a parade of ladies from the town, bringing hams and all kinds of casseroles and vegetables. One would have thought they were feeding an army, rather than four sad, tired souls.

Clark remembered how, as a teenager, he had railed against the people who lived in his little town. He complained to his parents that the people in Pemberton were provincial and bigoted and that he wanted to leave as soon as he could. At the time, he didn't understand that by saying those things he was insulting his parents as well. They'd grown up in Pemberton, and the people Clark was criticizing included their friends, most of whom they'd known all of their lives. But he was now witnessing a very different side of those folks. One of their own—his mother—needed their help, and they were there for her. They fed his family, answered the phone, greeted visitors, and ran errands. Some of them even did things that didn't need to be done, like trimming the bushes and vacuuming the rugs. They were sincerely trying to help their neighbor and to show her how much she was loved. This was the way they'd been taught to do that.

His father's funeral was two days later. As if to fit everyone's somber mood, the weather turned unusually cold, and it rained. The clouds were low and gray, creating a fitting backdrop for those who gathered, all of whom were dressed in black or dark gray, except for Clark, who wore his uniform. Dressing in such somber fashion was one of those old-fashioned customs that people in small Southern towns still followed to show respect for one of their own who had gone on to meet his Maker.

The service was at the First United Methodist Church. Afterwards, the mourners gathered by the family burial plot on the church grounds. Although Clark couldn't remember exactly what

Reverand Stubbs had said during the service, he did remember that he hadn't been impressed. The preacher had known his father for years, and yet he didn't say anything that he hadn't said at a hundred other funerals. Clark's father deserved better than that. He most certainly was not an ordinary man.

After the burial, the family went home, where a crowd had already gathered. His mother's friends were scurrying everywhere, cleaning, laying out food, and generally trying to be helpful. His mother didn't say anything. She went straight to their bedroom, laid down on their bed wearing the clothes she'd had on at the funeral, and cried. Clark and Darlene checked on her a few times. After a while, she went to sleep. Her doctor had come by before the funeral and given her some pills to help her sleep. She must have taken them.

When the crowd drifted away, Clark telephoned Janelle and explained all that had happened. Although it was expensive to call Panama, he had to admit he hadn't thought about calling her until then, and he knew that wasn't right. But her reaction was strange: she didn't sound particularly sympathetic and just asked when he would be back. He told her he was going to try to leave the next day and would call her from the Air Force base as soon as he was sure he had gotten on a flight.

Next, he called Major Darst and, luckily, got him. His boss was very sympathetic and not at all the cold and stoic person that Clark had observed before he got the word to return home. He told Clark to take all the time he needed, not to worry about the Lydia Mendoza trial or anything else in Panama, and that he would update Colonel Allen and Captain Jackson. Clark assured him he would return as soon as he could get a flight.

Finally, Clark called Bob Jenkins, the Red Cross representative in Charleston, and told him what had happened. After giving his condolences, Mr. Jenkins said that he'd take care of things with his buddies at the base and could have Clark on a plane back to Panama the next day.

Clark wrote his mother a check to cover the phone calls to Panama. When she put up a big fuss and refused to take it, he gave it to Darlene and told her to deposit it in his mother's account. He knew she could sign their mother's name as well as his mother could.

Having finalized the arrangements for his return to Panama, Clark joined his mother and Darlene and Frank in the living room. That night they did something they'd never done before: they opened a bottle of wine and talked—no TV, no stereo, just conversation. Clark had never known his mother to drink at all, but he knew Darlene did. She'd brought several bottles of a pinot noir that she knew their mother liked. They had one glass after another and ate the wonderful food the people of Pemberton had brought. And reminisced.

It seemed to help his mother. They talked about old times, family vacations, and picnics. At one point, Darlene began to smile. They all knew she had something to say. "Do you remember the time we went to see Momma's family up in North Georgia?"

"We went up there a lot. What are you talking about, Darlene?"

"Well, you were little—you couldn't have been more than seven—and it was before the Interstate was built. We had to go on those old, two-lane roads that wound around and around the mountains. You got sick as a dog!"

"It's just like you to remember something like that."

"No. This is funny. You puked all over the quilt in the back seat. Daddy had to pull over and take it down to a creek and wash it off. It stunk to high heavens." She laughed and shook her head.

"That's a delightful story, Darlene. But I remember some, too." Clark looked at his mother, who was smiling at their repartee. "I remember when you were playing touch football with us in the front yard, and you fell into a pile of fire ants. They ate you up. You had welts all over your legs and your butt."

"Well, that's why I gave up football." She smiled.

"You used to play touch football?" Frank was suddenly interested.

"It was a phase."

"She dudn't play football now," Frank explained. "She dudn't even want me to watch it on TV." He looked at his wife and smiled to make sure she knew he was teasing. "What she does now is shop."

"I do not."

"Really? How come you're always goin' to Savannah?"

"'Cause you're always playin' golf." Like her mother, Darlene was adept at moving a conversation in a positive direction.

"I think y'all do a good job of givin' each other space," their mother said.

"Space? What are you talkin' about, Momma?" Darlene asked.

"In some marriages the man and woman smother each other. Either one of them is asking the other to do things for them all the time, or they want to know what the other one is doin' all the time. That dudn't work. People need space. Even when they love each other." She looked down and then looked back at them with glassy eyes. "Your daddy knew that. He knew when I needed to go to Savannah to shop. And Frank, that comment is for your benefit." She forced a smile. "No, children. You need to give each other space or you get smothered. Your daddy gave me space, and I didn't complain when he went huntin' or fishin', especially when he took you along, Bobby."

"Well, Frank gives me space, I suppose. And Lord knows I give him space, with his golf almost every week."

"It's not every week."

"Yes it is."

"Well, at least I don't play on Sunday, like Darryl and them. I go to church with you."

"And that's why I love you, Sweetie."

Clark watched his sister and listened to his mother. Those two women knew how to have a marriage. Why was his so fouled up? There was no give and take with Janelle. She was always in her own world, doing what she wanted to do.

"What's on your mind, Sugar?" his mother asked. "You've barely said two words."

"Nothin', Momma. I'm just thinkin' about what I need to do when I get back."

"Bein' a lawyer is tough, isn't it, Sweetheart?"

"Sometimes, Momma, but I manage. I just wish I knew what I needed to do to have the kind of marriage that you and Darlene have." Too much wine had loosened his tongue and made him forget, for a moment, that his mother's marriage was over.

She didn't feel the sting. "Well, Sweetheart, it's like we were sayin'. You need to give each other space."

"That's just it, Momma. All I've got is space. She's not interested in anything I'm doing. And she's not doing anything for me to be interested in, other than reading *People* magazine, if you can call that something." He knew he should shut up. He was talking about himself and his problems when he should have been comforting his mother. "Momma, you know what? I'll work it out. I'll figure it out. Let's talk some more about Daddy."

Darlene took a drink of wine and leaned forward. "I got another story to tell. Momma was talkin' about huntin'. Well, I remember when you shot your first deer. You couldn't have been more than twelve years old. And it was big."

"There's a picture in my room. But I wasn't really a good hunter. Daddy just put me on a good stand. The deer came right under the stand. I couldn't miss."

"That's not what I'm talkin' about. I'm talkin' about when y'all got home."

"Oh, I remember that," his mother smiled.

"Well, y'all have got one on me because I don't know what you're talkin' about."

"Daddy made you clean the deer in the backyard. You did it, but when you came inside, you were as white as a sheet." Darlene chuckled, and his mother and Frank joined in.

"Okay, so the little boy didn't want to cut up the deer. So what?"

"We're just teasing you, Sweetheart," his mother said. "That was a good deer. We ate on that venison for a long time."

Clark stood up. "This has been fun, y'all, but I've got to pack. I gotta leave tomorrow."

"So soon?" his mother asked.

"Now, Momma," said Darlene, "you know Bobby's got a lot of responsibilities back in Panama. Don't be fussin' at him."

"I know. I just hate to see him go. This was too short. And the circumstances, well…"

"I'll be back as soon as I can, Momma. I promise." Clark said goodnight and kissed his mother and sister, shook hands with Frank, and then, unexpectedly, gave him a hug. He walked down the hall, pausing outside his father's room, hoping to hear him snoring.

He went back into his bedroom and packed, making sure to leave out his uniform for the next day. Before he latched his suitcase, he took the Kipling poem off the wall and carefully tucked it in.

CHAPTER EIGHTEEN

CLARK WAS SO tired that he slept during most of the flight back to Panama. It wasn't until the plane touched down at Howard Air Force Base that he realized he hadn't given much thought to his job or the Lydia Mendoza case since he left Panama. As soon as he did, his anxiety returned, along with sweaty palms and a knot in his stomach.

What was the status of the investigation? Was it finished? Had Suzanne taken his place while he was away? He'd be lucky to have a minor role in the case. But then he quickly caught himself. He remembered what his father had said. Act like a professional. Show up to work tomorrow and do the work assigned to you. A soldier's job is to "saw the wood in front of him."

Although he had telephoned Janelle from Charleston, so she'd know when to expect him, she wasn't at the airport when he arrived. He retrieved his luggage and sat down in the waiting area with a copy of *U.S. News and World Report* that he'd purchased in Charleston. He merely looked at the pages, though. He was too distracted to actually read them. When Janelle finally did arrive, she gave no reason for being late. Nor did she give him a hug or even a smile. She simply said, flatly, "Glad to see you made it back."

They said nothing as they walked to the car. Clark loaded his suitcase in the trunk and got into the driver's seat. As he drove off the installation, Janelle's eyes were fixed on the road ahead. After a few minutes, Clark asked, "Is Ellie all right?"

"She's fine. I just have a lot on my mind." And then, silence again for several minutes. Finally, "Why didn't you call me until after your daddy's funeral?" Her emphasis on the word "after" made it clear that she was annoyed that he hadn't kept her apprised of what was going on.

"Well, for starters, it was a goddamn ordeal to get home. And then, there was a lot to do once I got there, and phone calls cost a bunch. I did the best I could."

"Why do you always start cussin' whenever I'm tryin' to have a conversation with you?"

She was particularly annoying when she staked a claim on the moral high ground. He was the one who had just lost his father. She should have been comforting him. But Clark didn't have the energy to argue with her or even respond. His emotional bank account was way overdrawn. So he just stopped talking at all, and they finished the trip home in silence.

His baby girl was happy to see him. He picked her up and got a big hug and kiss. "Daddy, I miss you soooo much. Will you read me story?"

"I sure will, Sweetheart. I missed you, too." Ellie hugged his neck again.

Nita, on the other hand, acted strangely and greeted him with a forced smile. Had Janelle and Nita gotten into some sort of an argument while he was away? He was too tired to try to find out. Instead, he headed to his bedroom to unpack.

As usual, Nita served up a great meal, almost as good as his mother's. Unfortunately, the mood didn't fit the meal: they ate in virtual silence—the conversation extending only to "please pass the salt." When he finished, he excused himself and retired to the bathroom for a hot shower. As promised, he read his daughter a bedtime story and then went to bed.

The next morning, he awoke early and quietly got ready for work while everyone was still asleep. As he headed toward the back door, he stopped by Ellie's room. She looked angelic in the early morning light that peeked through a gap in the curtains. Reluctantly, he left for work. No one was in the outer office when he got there. He made a pot of coffee and settled in to read his mail and other correspondence that had accumulated during his absence.

Around 7:30, he heard someone coming in. Suzanne soon appeared and offered her condolences. Apparently, the news of his loss had spread. After some perfunctory comments, her countenance changed to that of someone bursting to share gossip.

"You won't believe what happened while you were gone."

He just stared at her, knowing she needed no prompting.

"Major Darst went back to the States."

"What? What are you talking about? I just talked to him day before yesterday."

"I mean he's gone, and no one knows when he's coming back. It's all very mysterious."

Clark's stomach tightened, and his mind raced. Was the investigation of Major Darst closing in? Would the CID soon learn that he'd been in Major Darst's truck and should have known that it was his vehicle that almost ran them off the road that fateful night?

"And that's not all," Suzanne continued. "They have a suspect in the Lydia Mendoza case. Some guy named Gomez. The CID interrogated him while you were gone, and he asked for counsel. Trip Stephens is representing him."

"Really?" Clark assumed his best poker face and hoped she couldn't tell that he already knew. She rattled on until he told her that he had an important call to make. Surprisingly, she didn't question him about the call. She just said okay and left.

Clark needed to find out what was going on with Major Darst. He dialed a familiar number. "Jaime, this is Captain Clark."

"Hey, sir. Sorry to hear abou' you' dad."

"Yeah, thanks, Jaime. Listen, I need to come over and speak with you right away. Is now okay?"

"Sure, sir. Come on over."

As he drove to the CID Office, Clark contemplated what he would say to Jaime. How would he explain his failure to tell him about the truck that night? He decided to say that he was unsure of whether it was Major Darst's truck—which was true—and that he had been preoccupied with matters related to his dad's condition, which, of course, was not exactly true. Somehow he had to explain his delay in disclosing what could turn out to be critical information. He arrived at the back door of the CID Office and pressed the buzzer; Jaime was waiting and immediately let him in. They walked down the hall to the windowless room where they had first assembled to hear about the death of Lydia Mendoza. Clark's hands started to sweat, and the knot in his stomach tightened so much he felt nauseated.

Before he could say anything, though, Jaime began. "Does Colonel Allen know you' here?"

The question caught Clark by surprise. "I, uh, don't think so." But as soon as he said that, he wondered whether Suzanne the blabbermouth might have overheard his telephone call with Jaime. If so, there was no telling whom she might have told. Had he completely blown his chance to try the Lydia Mendoza case by coming to the CID Office? If Jaime was worried about whether Allen knew he was there, then he should be worried, too. But if the CID arrested Major Darst, and it later came out that he failed to tell Jaime that he thought it might have been Darst's truck behind them that night, then his career could be over. He had to come clean now.

"Well, you know wha' I tol' you abou' Agen' Robinson thinkin' tha' Major Dars' was screwin' Specialis' Weeks?"

Clark just nodded.

"Well, it turn ou' tha' i's no' Major Dars' a'ter all." He paused for exaggerated dramatic effect. "I's Colonel Allen."

"You're shittin' me. Colonel Allen was screwing Specialist Weeks?"

"Tha's righ'. Well, i' *look* like he was screwin' her. We go' a positive ID on the surveillance camera when he wen' to her apar'men' an' when he leave. More dan once. I don' thin' dey were watchin' TV."

"What about those pictures you showed me of Major Darst?"

"Tha' fuckin' guy—the inves'igator on tha' case tha' tol' me abou' Major Dars' didn' give me the whole story. Major Dars' did go to Week' apar'men', bu' the guy wha' stayed wid her wa' Colonel Allen, not Major Dars'. We don' know wha' Major Dars' was doin' over dere. He didn' stay lon' or go tha' much anyway."

"So, Allen is the guy, not Darst? Do you think Allen is involved with the drug guys in Panama?"

"No. It look' like Allen jus' screwing her. Agen' Robinson is piss' beyon' belief. General Kraus tol' him to forge' abou' the fraternization an' adultery charges agains' Colonel Allen an' bus' Weeks for drugs. As soon as we go' enough evidence, we gonna bus' her. But ge' this: her trial gonna be a' For' Leonard Wood."

"Wait a minute. You're going too fast for me, Jaime." Clark paused to process the news. "So, you're saying that Major Darst is no longer the target of an investigation, but Weeks is and you're going to arrest her?" Before Clark offered anything about Major Darst's truck, he wanted to be sure he clearly understood the situation.

"No' ye', bu' we close. We close to linkin' Weeks wid the Pan-amanian drug guys."

"Why Fort Leonard Wood?"

"Think abou' i', Captain Clark. She can' be tried here. No' when she been screwin' the Staff Judge Advocate. General Kraus won' admit i', bu' he know tha' Noriega don' wan' no drug trial down here involving Panamanians and soldiers. Noriega ge' pai' by dose drug guys, and so, fo' him, the less sai' abou' dem, the better."

"So, you're going to bust Weeks and then just let her walk?

"No. I don' thin' so. Dey will pro'ly le' Weeks plea to a lesser offense an' ge' a deal for no prison time. Dey may even admin'stratively discharge her fro' the Army. Bu', she definitely gonna be discharge fro' the Army."

"Why in the hell would Colonel Allen screw around with an enlisted soldier?"

"Ha' you seen hi' wife, Captain Clark? She so fat when she haul ass it take' two trips." Jaime chuckled at his own joke but then looked at Clark and realized that his attempt at humor hadn't worked.

"What kind of trouble do you think Allen is in?"

"Tha's wha' Agen' Robinson so pissed abou'. General Kraus say tha' if the only thin' is fraternization wid Weeks, den forge' abou' i', an' ge' Weeks outta here."

"But won't she try to bring up her relationship with Allen at her trial?"

"No' if she ge' a pre-trial agreemen'. An' if she don' ge' an agreemen', den the affair wid Allen don' have nothin' to do wid her dealings wid the Panamanian drug guys anyway." Jaime stopped and stared at Clark with a grave but inquisitive look—as if trying to determine whether Clark had understood him. "I don' thin' General Kraus wan' to deal wid tha' kinda mess, Captain

Clark. He jus' wan' Weeks outta here. Colonel Allen gettin' ready for reassignment anyway."

"What about Major Darst?"

"We go' nothin' on him now. I thin' he like' Weeks an' all, bu' I don' thin' he' involve' wid her or the drug guys."

"So, why did he go back to the States?"

"Major Dars' wen' back to the States? I didn' know tha'."

"Yeah, but I don't know why."

"Good thin' he no longer a suspect on anythin'." Jaime shifted in his seat and looked closely at Clark. "Now, wha' di' you wanna talk abou'?"

"I... I, uh, just wanted to get an update on the Lydia Mendoza case."

"Well, like I tol' you before, Captain Clark, you nee' to try dis case, especially if Major Dars' wen' to the States."

Remembering Suzanne's comment about Major Darst's departure being "mysterious," and thinking that maybe there was another shoe to drop, Clark decided to say no more about him.

Jaime continued, "You know tha' Agen' Robinson tol' General Kraus he though' you coul' try the case?"

"Seriously? Why would he do that?"

"Lo's o' reasons. Is an importan' case." Jaime stopped and gave Clark a big smile. "An', I tol' Agen' Robinson you coul' do i'."

"Why did you do that?" Clark wasn't sure he wanted General Kraus to know who he was.

"I wan' to nail dis guy, Captain Clark, an' you can do i'. Beside', General Kraus ask' Agent Robinson abou' the case. So he tol' the General wha' I tol' him." Jaime stopped again and looked at Clark. "You know General Kraus is pro'ly barely speakin' to Colonel Allen now. The general wan' him gone, too. So, I guess General Kraus wan' to talk to Agen' Robinson, 'cause he go' experience, an' the General trust hi' judgmen'. If Major Dars' is gone, den you are the bes' one fo' the job."

They sat in silence for a while. Jaime went to get some coffee and returned with two cups.

"Capitain Clark, I thin' you need to go to the office an' tell Colonel Allen tha' you wanna try the Gomez case."

Jaime was already referring to the case by the name of his prime suspect. Essentially, this was the same pitch that he'd made before, and yet this time, he said it with the kind of knowing smile that led Clark to believe there was more going on than he was revealing.

"Before you tell Colonel Allen tha' you wanna try the Gomez case, lemme tell you wha' we go'. Jus' a minute."

Jaime left the room again and returned with a thick redwell folder bulging with documents. He carefully explained all that he had done in the investigation and described what was in the folder. Clark flipped through some of the documents while Jaime was talking. The thing that caught his eye was the report of the medical examiner. At the top of the report, in a block entitled "Cause of Death," it stated:

> *It is my opinion that Lydia Mendoza, a 13-month old Hispanic female, died as the result of multiple blunt force injuries.*

"See, Capitain Clark, dis case is simple. Raul Gomez was alone wid Lydia for almos' six hour' jus' before she wen' to Gorgas. An', she die' jus' a few hours later. Who else coul' have done i'?"

"There are no other suspects?"

"Who coul' i' be, Capitain Clark? Carmen lef' the baby wid her brother-in-law aroun' 1800 hours and didn' ge' back until a'ter midnigh' when Lydia was asleep. The nex' day, Lydia wouldn' wake up, and so, Carmen and Raul too' her to Gorgas. We talk' to Raul the day you lef' to go home. He cry like a baby."

"I heard he asked for a lawyer."

"Yeah, but no' 'til a'ter he give us a statement." Jaime smiled as if he were giving Clark a birthday present.

"He gave you a statement?"

"Yeah, an' it a goo' one, too."

"He confessed?"

"No. Bu' he say tha' Carmen lef' Lydia wid him aroun' 1800 hours, an' he was alone wid her until Carmen go' back a'ter 2400 hours. He admi' tha' he was alone wid the baby fo' aroun' six hours."

"Can I see the statement?"

"Yeah, bu' don' tell nobody. I's really sensitive. In fac', we' no' suppose' to le' anythin' ou' until the whole repor' is finish' an' Agen' Robinson ha' review' i'."

"Sure. I understand. But you know the word is out. Suzanne told me this morning that Gomez was a suspect." Jaime nodded. "Have you ever been involved with a case like this before, Jaime?"

"Yeah. I ha' one a' For' Riley, an' some o' the o'her guys here in Panama ha' shaken baby cases in o'her places. I don' thin' nobody down here ever ha' one in Panama. Bu' I can hook you up wid the prosecutor from For' Riley. He can tell you wha' you gonna nee' to do. He' a goo' lawyer like you."

"That would be great, Jaime. See if you can set up a call with him tomorrow." Clark stared at Jaime, and he smiled back. "You know what, Jaime? Maybe I will go back and talk to Colonel Allen."

Jaime's smile widened. He'd won the debate.

On his drive back to the JAG Office, Clark briefly considered swinging by his quarters to see Ellie. But after meeting with Jaime, he had too much on his mind. Could he try this case? And if he could, how could he persuade Colonel Allen to let him be lead counsel, instead of bringing someone down from the States? He drove straight back to work.

Rather than return to his office and risk getting caught up in a conversation with Suzanne, Clark went directly to the SJA's office. He rarely came to see the SJA, so he got some surprised looks when he walked in.

"Is the SJA in?" he asked his secretary, a pleasant, but plump, middle-aged Panamanian woman who would never have had such a job in a Panamanian office downtown—she wasn't young and attractive enough.

"Yeah. Lemme see i' he' busy." She tapped on the SJA's door and stepped in. Clark couldn't hear the conversation, but when when she came out, she said, "He sai' to come in."

Clark walked into Colonel Allen's office and, like Trip Stephens, sat down and crossed his legs.

"What brings you down here, Clark?"

"I want to try the Lydia Mendoza case, sir."

"You do?" Allen dropped his pen on the desk, leaned back in his chair, and smiled.

"Yes, sir, I do."

"Well, homicide cases are tough, Clark, and they're high profile."

"Yes, sir, I know. But since Major Darst went back to the States, it leaves just Suzanne and me, and I think I can do a better job." He paused for a moment. "I've just come from the CID Office." Clark let that last comment hang for a moment and studied Allen's face. Seeing no glimpse of a reaction, and despite Jaime's admonition, he continued, "Agent Hernandez showed me the investigative file and briefed me extensively about the case. And, you'll recall that Major Darst had me attend the autopsy of Lydia Mendoza before I went back to the States."

"Slow down, counselor. Yes, I remember that you went to the autopsy. By the way, Clark, I was very sorry to hear about your father."

"Thank you, sir." Clark paused a moment to acknowledge his condolence. "I don't know if you also know that I was with

Jaime Hernandez when he interviewed the victim's mother, Isabel Mendoza."

"Yes, I'm aware of that as well, but you know Trip is representing the principal suspect."

"Yes, sir. Specialist Gomez."

"And Trip was trying cases before you arrived in Panama."

"Yes, sir, and in our first meeting in the courtroom, I beat him with a motion *in limine* that only I believed would be successful."

Colonel Allen looked at him with a slightly condescending smile. "Yes, you did a good job on that case, Clark, and it got a lot of attention. But I think we need to bring an experienced trial counsel down from the States."

That's not what Clark wanted to hear. If he was going to get the case, he knew he was going to have to fight for it. "With all due respect, sir, I have had extensive conversations with the CID investigators about all of their cases." And then, the trump card: "Agent Hernandez told me that Agent Robinson personally recommended me to the CG for this case."

That stopped Allen cold. He looked up from his desk and gazed intently at Clark. His face was pallid, except for the dark circles under his eyes, and his stare was piercing. Clark had pushed hard. He was sure that Allen was now asking himself why Agent Robinson was discussing the case with the General without his knowledge. And, he must at least suspect—given his currently strained relationship with the General—that his exploits with Specialist Weeks might be under investigation. Clark stared back in silence.

"Do you think you can do it?" Allen finally asked.

"Yes, sir. Agent Hernandez has been involved in a shaken-baby case before and said he would link me up with the prosecutor in that case to get a briefing on lessons learned."

Allen studied him for a long time, took a long draw on his cigarette, and then crushed it out. Clark said nothing. "Okay,

Clark. You've convinced me. But don't fuck it up! Homicide cases attract a lot of attention. Don't fuck this one up."

"Yes, sir." Clark had never heard the SJA use the "F" word before. In a sea of foul-mouthed soldiers, Colonel Allen was someone who rarely used profanity. Either Clark had gotten under his skin, or he was worried about his own fate. Or maybe he was worried that he had just assigned a high profile case to an inexperienced trial counsel. Whatever it was, Clark didn't care. He had gotten the case. Clark thanked Colonel Allen and left. Satisfied.

As soon as he got back to his desk, he called Jaime. "I did it."

"Did wha', sir?"

"I got Colonel Allen to assign the Mendoza murder case to me." Clark stopped short of confessing to Jaime that he had told Allen about seeing the investigative file and that Agent Robinson had recommended him to the General. He rationalized his betrayal of Jaime's confidence by concluding that Allen wouldn't tell anyone. Therefore, no harm, no foul.

Jaime was pleased with the news. "Outstandin', sir! Le's ge' Elmer and go celebrate."

"Okay, but this time let's stick to Mother's." Clark heard a chuckle on the other end of the line.

"Okay, sir. See you there at 1700 hours."

Clark's hand wasn't even off the telephone receiver before Suzanne was in the chair in front of his desk, red-faced.

"So, Boy Wonder, how in the hell did you get the Mendoza case?" She pursed her thick lips the way she always did when she was angry or stressed.

"I asked for it, Suzanne." He paused and carefully and consciously attempted to control his emotions. Although he wanted to tell her that he'd gotten the case because she was a terrible trial counsel, he restrained himself. "Suzanne, this case is too big for one person. You will definitely be co-counsel. And, I'll definitely need your help."

"But you'll be lead counsel."

"Who gives a crap, Suzanne. We'll both be sitting at the counsel table. In fact, you can do the opening statement."

She looked at him harshly for a few moments and then relaxed. "So, I would start the trial?"

"Why not?"

She smiled. His tactic had worked. And he hadn't taken much of a risk. The opening statement could be written in advance. He could review what she planned to say and make her rehearse it before the trial. And, it would be smart to open the case with a woman. Although Suzanne wasn't married and didn't have any kids, she looked like a mom. With the right script, she would set the tone perfectly.

"Didn't you say you knew someone in the States who had information about shaken-baby cases?" Clark asked.

"Yes. He sent me a bunch of good material. I'll make you a copy."

Suzanne was onboard. She immediately started talking about the research she had done, the people she knew who could help them, what she would say in the opening statement. The last topic almost caused a problem. "I think I'll start with a poem by John Donne," she said.

"What?"

"You know... the English poet. He was a cleric in the Church of England." Clark's face was expressionless as he struggled to control his reaction to her statement. "He wrote some moving poetry that I think will set just the right mood."

"No, Suzanne. The opening statement isn't a eulogy. It's our best opportunity to establish the theme of our entire case. And I doubt that any of the members will understand what you're doing by reciting a poem. Just think of your opening as a summary of the trial process and a preview of coming attractions."

"That's it?"

"Yup. And remember, KISS: keep it simple, stupid."

She pursed her lips and shrugged her shoulders. "All right," she said, dragging out the words to show her exasperation at Clark's opposition to what she thought would have been the perfect dramatic touch. Then, almost wearily, she said, "I'll put something together and let you look at it."

"Good. And if you could get someone to make me a copy of those materials you were talking about, I'll start reading them tonight."

"Sure."

"Oh, I almost forgot. Jaime knows a JAG who tried a similar case at Fort Riley. He's trying to arrange a call with him. And I want you on that call as well."

She perked up again and started taking notes. "When is the call?"

"I asked him to set it up tomorrow, if possible. Listen, Suzanne, we can make a name for ourselves with this case. By the way, the CID does think that Gomez is the guy."

"Yeah. It looks that way."

"Well, let's nail him, Suzanne." He looked at her, waiting for a reaction. "I really need your help," he said softly.

"I'm with you, Clark."

"Great. Jaime wants me to meet with him later today. So, the sooner you can get those copies to me, the better. I might be leaving a little early."

"Will do."

As Suzanne left his office, she seemed to be genuinely excited about the Mendoza case, although Clark unexpectedly felt a tinge of guilt. It dawned on him that he'd manipulated three people in less than two hours. But, he decided he needed to. It would have been a disaster if she had attempted to try the case as lead counsel. She would have gotten wrapped around the axle on something and have made a mess of it. Clark knew she would be a great ally. She had already read every child abuse case ever reported in the Military Justice Reporter, which meant he didn't have to. And she could research the hell out of any issue. He resolved that if he had to manipulate her or anyone else to win this case, then so be it.

CHAPTER NINETEEN

CLARK WAS FORTY-FIVE minutes late getting to Mother's Inn. As he walked in, he heard cheers and cat-calls coming from Elmer's corner.

"The judge is in the house. All hail the judge."

Elmer and Jaime had gotten there early. They sounded like they were well on their way. Through the blue haze of cigarette smoke, Clark found his comrades surrounded by a pack of grinning, semi-drunk lieutenants, beers and cigarettes in hand.

"Sit down, Judge. Grace us with your presence," said Elmer, making a sweeping gesture to invite Clark to join the group.

"You guys are too much," Clark replied.

"No... no. Congratulations, Counselor," Elmer continued. "We're happy that we now have a prosecutor who's gonna kick some butt."

"Easy, guys. I just got the case." Clark could tell they were both pretty drunk.

"Well, I thin' you gonna ge' the son o' a bi'ch wha' killed tha' lil' girl."

"Thanks, Jaime. But like I told you: I need your help. By the way, have you gotten in touch with that guy from Fort Riley?"

"Wha' guy?"

"The JAG that tried the shaken baby case."

"Oh, tha' guy."

"Yeah, that guy. You were gonna set up a conference call with him.

"I ge' i' done tomorrow. Tonigh', we nee' to celebra'."

Clark smiled. He couldn't be upset with his two loyal supporters. "Thanks, guys, but I think you're making too much of this."

Elmer turned to the lieutenants. "Would you guys excuse us for a minute? We've got some things we need to discuss with Captain Clark." Ever respectful of their favorite captain, the lieutenants picked up their beers and cigarettes and moved a couple of tables over, leaving the three of them alone in Elmer's corner.

Elmer turned back to Clark. "Listen to me, Clark." His face was uncharacteristically serious. No grin. Perhaps too much alcohol had caused a dark side of Elmer's personality to surface. "Have you heard the name José Rodriguez since you came to Panama?"

"I don't know what you mean, Elmer." Clark smiled, hoping Elmer was setting up some sort of a joke. "There are a lot of Josés and Rodriguezes down here."

"No. I'm talking about one Sergeant First Class José Rodriguez, a fat-ass piece of shit, assigned to my company when I was a line unit commander."

This was clearly no joke. Elmer's pale blue eyes were staring hard at Clark.

"No, Elmer. I haven't heard of him."

"Well, Rodriguez lived in the enlisted housing area here on Fort Clayton with his wife and four kids. But he wasn't like other married soldiers: he liked little boys." Elmer's voice was full of exasperation and venom. "In fact, Rodriguez liked one little boy in particular—Luis Martinez, whose dad was also in my company. Luis was six years old and lived in the same housing complex as Rodriguez. And in fact, Luis played on the playground with Rodriguez's kids. So, no one thought anything about

Rodriguez hanging around the playground all the time. One Sunday afternoon, he coaxed Luis off the playground and took him on 'an adventure,' as he told Luis, way back in the jungle that's next to the playground. But it was Rodriguez's adventure, not Luis's. Rodriguez butt-fucked that poor little boy. He stuffed Luis's Star Wars T-shirt in his mouth, and he beat him, and he butt-fucked him."

Clark stared at Elmer in silence.

"He didn't kill him, mind you, but he left him for dead." Elmer stopped talking and stared at Clark for a long time. "One of your marvelous predecessors prosecuted the case against Rodriguez, and he blew it. Fat boy walked out of the courtroom with a big fat smile on his face."

"So, Rodriguez came back to your company? What did you do?"

"No… No. Rodriguez didn't make it back." Elmer took a long draw on his cigarette, sat back in his chair, and exhaled. "Luis's father—an outstanding staff sergeant, I might add—stuck a knife in big ole' fat Rodriguez and damn-near killed him."

"Damn," said Clark. "What happened to Martinez?"

"Oh, that's where your wonderful justice system gets even better. They took Martinez to Fort Benning because there was too much publicity here." The disgust in Elmer's voice was obvious. "They knew no court-martial here would convict him. The prosecutor at Fort Benning got him convicted and sentenced to twelve years at Leavenworth. Yeah, you heard me right. Martinez got twelve fucking years in Leavenworth for stabbing that big fat fuck, and Rodriguez got medically discharged on full retired pay." Elmer took another long draw on his cigarette and then crushed it out in the plastic ashtray on the table. "And that, motherfucker, is why we need a prosecutor who will do his fucking job."

Jaime had said nothing during Elmer's monologue. He just sat and listened. When Elmer finally finished, he sat back in his chair and stared off into space. No one said anything for a long time.

Finally, Clark spoke. "I get where you're coming from, Elmer."

Elmer looked at him and gave him half a smile. "I'm sorry, man. I didn't mean to unload on you. As you can tell, that case still really pisses me off. Rodriguez should be dead, and Martinez should still be serving our country." Elmer took a long drink of beer. "And Rodriguez isn't the only case like that, Clark. Over the last two and a half years, there've been a bunch of bad guys who got off because the prosecutors were dumb shits. You gotta put this motherfucker away."

"Elmer, you know I'm going to do my best, but I'm up against Trip, and he's tried a lot more cases than I have."

"Bullshit, Clark. He's one of the guys we're talking about. He's a dumbass. And, you've already beat him once."

"Yeah, but I think I got lucky with that motion." Clark paused for a reaction and then sought to bolster his point. "It's the same as with anything else, Elmer: there's no substitute for experience."

"Listen to me, Clark. Trip is a dumbass. You'll run circles around him because you'll be prepared, and he won't. I've seen him in action. He'll try to pull things out of his ass."

Elmer took another long swig from his beer and smiled. Clark hoped it was a sign he was switching gears. "Have you ever noticed how Trip rarely talks to anyone under the rank of lieutenant colonel? The guy doesn't know any captains other than me. The only reason he talks to me is that my company clerk processes all of his administrative bullshit. Trip takes himself W...A...Y... too seriously." Elmer so loudly stretched out the word "way" that heads turned in his direction. But that didn't slow him down. The beer he'd already drunk was kicking in, and he didn't give a damn. "And, he is a consummate ass-kisser, which also means he expects anyone of lower rank—like the waitresses in here—to kiss *his* ass." Clark grinned at Elmer, relieved that the conversation had taken on a lighter tone. "Trip is lookin' for an easy way to the top, and he'll kiss anybody's ass if he thinks it will help him get there." Elmer leaned back in his chair as if to indicate that his rant was over. He lit another cigarette.

"Well, I hope you're right about Trip's ability in the courtroom, Elmer." Clark looked at Elmer, then at Jaime, and then back at Elmer. "I hope I didn't get myself in over my head." He stopped and took a drink of the beer the waitress had just put in front of him. "I heard Major Darst went back to the States." Elmer nodded. "So, now that he's gone, I don't have anybody in Panama with any trial experience who can help me get ready for this trial. You don't know what the deal is with him, do you?"

Elmer studied Clark for a few moments before responding. "Yeah. I don't know what the deal is with Major Darst. Colonel Allen himself called me and said Darst had a family emergency and had to get home right away. I figured it was something like the situation with your dad, but I don't know the details." Elmer discovered his beer bottle was empty and motioned for the waitress to bring him another. "He's about to run out of leave, though. He'll either be back soon, or he won't be coming back."

"What do you mean?" Clark asked.

"If his family situation doesn't get resolved by the time his leave runs out, the Army might give him a compassionate reassignment to an installation close to his home, or they might give him a compassionate discharge."

"So, he might never come back?" Clark asked, the pitch of his voice rising like an adolescent's.

"It's possible. But don't worry about it, Clark. Jaime's going to fix you up with that JAG from Fort Riley, and you've got Watkins."

"Suzanne? Come on, Elmer. You've got to be kidding me. I

mean, she'll help, but she doesn't know how to try cases. I need somebody with experience that I can talk to."

"Hey, I'll admit Watkins ain't much to look at," Elmer was grinning hard again, "but I heard she's pretty smart."

"Well, yeah. She is smart, and she's a good researcher. In fact, she's already read every reported court-martial case involving child abuse."

"Well, there you go. You're gonna be just fine. Anyway, Jaime says it's an open and shut case."

Jaime looked down to avoid making eye contact with Clark. He knew he wasn't supposed to be discussing cases with Elmer.

"I'm not sure there is such a thing as an open and shut case," Clark replied. "There's always something to worry about."

"Well, not tonight, my friend." Elmer flashed his trademark grin. "Like Jaime said, tonight we celebrate."

Elmer ordered another round of beer, so he had a spare, and then regaled Clark and Jaime with a vivid account of every good-looking woman in the brigade headquarters—the new ones, the ones who had left, the ones who were married, the ones who looked like they might put out. And, in Elmer's mind, all women would put out: it was simply a matter of time and persistence. The real question was how quickly they would put out. Clark lost track of time, and before he knew it, it was 8:00 p.m., and he remembered he hadn't called Jannelle.

"Hey guys, I need to get going. Things aren't going too good at home, and I forgot to call my wife and tell her I was gonna be late. She'll probably be pissed."

"Get going. It looks like your choker collar is gettin' tight," Elmer teased.

"Yeah. I hear ya." Clark tossed a ten dollar bill on the table and got up to leave.

"Look fellas," said Elmer, loud enough for the lieutenants ten feet away to hear him over the noise of the bar. "We got ourselves

a lawyer who actually buys other people drinks. It's fuckin'
amazin'. Must be all that etiquette he learned at West Point."
Turning to Clark, Elmer continued, in a mocking voice, "But
you know, Clark, the reason we love you is 'cause you got that
muther-fuckin' Ranger Tab." Elmer gave special emphasis to the
appositive that he'd assigned to Clark, and the lieutenants howled
and barked. Elmer was clearly playing to his crowd.

"Thanks, Elmer. That warms my heart," Clark said sarcasti-
cally. He turned to leave.

"You know we love you, right, Clark?" Elmer yelled as Clark
walked away. His mock sincerity cracked up his inebriated audience even more. Their howling changed to hysterical laughter by
the time Clark got to the door.

During the drive home, Clark anticipated his conversation
with Janelle. *The moment I walk through the door, she'll know
that I haven't been at work. She'll smell Mother's Inn, and she'll
start in on me. I'm tired of her crap. I've been through a lot lately,
and Jaime and Elmer were trying to help me. She'll just have to
like it or lump it.*

As he pulled into his driveway, he noticed that his quarters
were dark. The only light was coming through the back door,
which led into the kitchen. Nita was sitting at the breakfast bar.
She looked up at him with tear-stained cheeks. His first thought
was that she and Janelle had gotten into an argument again.

"What's going on, Nita?" She jumped up and turned to
face him.

"Oh, Señor Clark. I' so sorry," she began to sob.

"What's wrong?"

"Señora Clark and the baby have lef"."

"Left? What do you mean?"

"I mean dey lef', Señor Clark. Dey wen' to the airpor' and
took a plane back to the States."

"What? When did they leave?"

"Yes. She ma', Señor Clark."

"I don't understand. She's mad at you?"

"No, Señor Clark, a' you. She lef' you dis letter."

Nita handed him a sealed envelope with "Bobby" written on the front in his wife's handwriting. He dropped his briefcase and stared at the envelope. His stomach tightened, and his hands began to sweat. As he started to open the envelope, Nita put her hand on his arm.

"Before you rea' i' Señor Clark, I nee' to tell you somethin'. I can' stay here no more. I can' stay here when Señora Clark no' here."

"I don't understand, Nita." He sat down heavily on the other stool at breakfast bar. They were now at eye level.

"Señor Clark, you a married man. I can' stay here if Señora Clark no' here. I' gonna go stay wid my sister tonigh'. Dere's a bus a' 9:00 o'clock, an' I nee' to take it. I' sorry, Señor Clark. You a nice man, and you been goo' to me, bu' I can' stay here."

"Well, can you come during the day, and just not sleep here?"

"No, Señor Clark, I nee' a place to stay. I can' stay with my sister more dan one... two days. Goo' luck, Señor Clark."

His head was spinning. He didn't know what to feel. His world had turned completely upside down in a manner of moments.

Nita picked up her little suitcase and started for the door.

"Wait a minute, Nita."

She stopped and turned around. Tears were streaming down her face.

"You've been good to us, too," he said. He handed her $112, which was all the cash he had in his wallet.

"You don' owe me no money, Señor Clark."

"Take it, Nita. You might need it until you find another job."

She took the money and smiled as she tucked the bills into her purse. She gave him a hug and walked out the door. He watched her as she made her way down the street to the bus stop—small and vulnerable beneath the street lights. She disappeared into the darkness, and he knew he would probably never see her again. He stared out the back door for a long time. It was as if all the energy had drained out of him. He would miss her. She was one of the sweetest, most genuine people he'd ever known.

He knew he'd already had plenty to drink, but he didn't care. He got a beer out of the refrigerator and sat down at the dining room table. As he tore open the envelope, his hands began to shake. He couldn't take the letter out of the envelope. This can't be the end, he thought; it just can't be. When would he see Ellie again? No. He wasn't going to think about that. His insides seemed to be twisting into a tight, hot knot, and his hands wouldn't stop shaking. He quickly drank the rest of the beer and went to the kitchen to get another. When he returned to the dining room, he tried to settle down, but he couldn't. He moved to the living room, sat on the sofa, and tried to regain his composure. Finally, he read the letter.

Dear Bobby,

This is the hardest thing I ever had to write. I'm not sure how we got here or why. All I know is that I'm not happy and I've got to go home. I feel like you don't love me or respect me anymore. Ever since you went to law school all you think about is your career. You don't think about your family or our precious child. Children are a gift from God, Bobby. Marriage is a sacred bond. They must be cherished. Do you cherish her? Do you cherish me? I'm going home to try to figure this out. I don't know if I want to be married to you anymore. You are not the man I thought you were. You think only about yourself and what you want. I can't live like that and I don't want our daughter to live like that. When I get

*things figured out, I will write you a letter. I hope you will pray
about this. I think you need to.*

Your loving wife,

Janelle

He stared at the letter and read it again and again. Then
he started to talk to himself: As usual, everything is my fault.
According to her, our marriage is bad because I'm a bad husband.
And I'm a bad husband because I work all the time. I've given
her more than she could have ever dreamed of in that crummy
little town we grew up in. And yet, in her mind everything is
my fault. I'm sure it never occurred to her that it was terribly
wrong for her to take my daughter away from me without a single
word of warning. She obviously doesn't give a shit about me or
my feelings. On top of everything else, she's so disgustingly self-
righteous—telling me I need to pray. She makes me sick.

Clark got up from the couch and wandered from room to
room, trying to calm down. His anger at his wife turned to sad-
ness when he walked into Ellie's room. He recalled how happy
and excited she was to see him when he got back from the States.
He turned on the light and looked around. Not much had
changed, except that her favorite doll was missing. She must have
taken it with her. The silence and emptiness was too much to
bear. He dropped to his knees and began to cry. He hadn't cried
at his father's funeral, but that night—on his knees in his daughter's room, contemplating how difficult it would be to maintain a
relationship with her if his wife left him—he sobbed uncontrollably. After a few minutes, he slumped onto the carpet and curled
up into a fetal position. At some point, he fell asleep.

He awoke the next morning, still in uniform and still on
the floor. He got up and took a shower and shaved. He found a

clean uniform and finished getting ready. The house was strangely quiet—no giggling little girl dancing around, no Panamanian maid in the kitchen singing along with the radio, no wife in her bathrobe sitting at the table reading a magazine. His idea of preparing breakfast was to pour milk over dry cereal, but when he checked the cabinet, the box of Cheerios was empty. So, he skipped breakfast and left.

On the drive to his office, he tried to avoid thinking about Janelle and her letter and, instead, focused on the challenge of getting ready to try the "Gomez" case—he decided to adopt the name Jaime had given it. He also decided to focus hard on the case for the next few days and not call his wife until after she'd been away from him for a while and had had some time to think.

He entered the building and headed straight for his office, deep in thought, which was soon interrupted by the sound of Suzanne's voice.

"You look terrible. What's wrong with you?"

"I had a rough night."

"What's going on?"

"Nothing. Just a rough night."

"Too much drinking with Elmer and the boys, huh?"

"No, Suzanne. If you're finished with 'Twenty Questions,' I'd like to get to work."

Unfazed by his incivility, she continued, "That reminds me. Agent Hernandez called about the conference call with the guy from Fort Riley."

"Really? What time?"

"This afternoon sometime. He said he hasn't nailed it down yet."

"Well, you need to go with me, Suzanne. Let's see when he wants to do it."

Clark walked into his office and telephoned Jaime.

"Jaime, Captain Clark here. I heard you got a conference call set up."

"Yes, sir. Major Green sai' he coul' talk to you a' 1500 hours today, local time."

"I thought you said he was a captain."

"He go' promoted. An' he no' a' For' Riley no more. He' in the Pentagon."

"Okay, Jaime. If it's okay with you, Captain Watkins and I will come over to your office around 1430 hours."

Clark had decided it would be better—and more secure—to have the call at the CID Office. He spent the rest of the morning preparing. He didn't want to sound stupid, so he reviewed his notes and read Suzanne's case summaries. When they arrived at the CID Office later that afternoon, Jaime escorted them to the conference room, which had a speaker phone in the center of the table.

"Than' you for comin'," Jaime said, gesturing to both of them.

"No, thank you, Jaime. We really appreciate you setting this up. Can you tell us a little bit about Major Green?"

"Like a tol' you, he' a hot shit. Oh, sorry, Capitain Watkins."

"Don't worry about it, Agent Hernandez. Please continue."

"Well, they' no' too much to tell. Capitain Green did a goo' job a' For' Riley. He wen' to the Advance' Course, go' promoted, an' was assigned to the JAG personnel office in the Pentagon."

For a few minutes Clark and Suzanne talked with Jaime about the case and what to expect from Major Green. Shortly before the time scheduled for the call, Agent Robinson walked in.

"Are you ready, Captain Clark?"

"Not exactly, Agent Robinson. That's why we're here: to learn as much as we can."

Robinson began speaking as if he was working his way down a list. "Well, you know, General Kraus is especially interested in this case; he thinks it's a morale issue; all the wives are talking about it; he wants to nail this guy."

"I hear you, Agent Robinson. So do we."

Clark tried to sound like a team player but was annoyed that Robinson was turning the screws. Had Robinson bothered to advise General Kraus that he should refrain from making any comments about the case, since they could cause a court to throw it out on the grounds of unlawful command influence? Surely, Robinson knew that. The General should have known that, too. Only a couple of years before, the Court of Military Appeals had overturned scores of convictions from Fort Bragg because the general on that post was quoted in a newspaper article saying he would never grant clemency to a convicted "drug peddler." Nevertheless, Clark decided to forego a discussion of command influence and, instead, focus on preparing to try the case. After all, Colonel Allen was the one who was supposed to advise General Kraus on issues like that.

The time for the conference call arrived, and Clark was pleased that Agent Robinson decided to leave just as Jaime telephoned Major Green.

"Major Green?"

"Yes, this is Major Green."

"Dis is Agen' Hernandez, sir. How you doin'?"

"Fine, Jaime. So, you want to talk about shaken baby cases?"

"Yes, sir. Bu' firs', I wan' to introduce Captain Clark and Captain Watkins."

"Good afternoon, sir. This is Captain Clark."

"And, Captain Watkins, sir. Good afternoon."

"Well, glad to meet each of you on the phone. Jaime's told me a little bit about your case, and it does sound like the one that he and I worked on at Fort Riley."

"That's good to hear, sir. We've tried some cases but nothing like this one," Clark offered.

Major Green quickly got down to business. "The most important piece of evidence is the report of the autopsy. If Jaime hasn't interviewed the medical examiner, then he should do so immediately. You want to be sure he's not going to change his story from what he stated in his findings."

"Why would he do that, sir?" As soon as Clark asked the question, he realized it was a stupid one. He knew that witnesses change their testimony all the time under cross-examination.

"Well, defense counsel will try to make the examiner question his own findings. You need to be sure he's ready for a tough cross-examination."

"Yes, sir."

"The next thing you need to do is get the autopsy report up to the AFIP."

Suzanne and Clark both gave Jaime a puzzled look. Thankfully, the speaker phone had a mute button, which Jaime pressed. "He mean' the Arme' Forces Institu' of Pat'ology."

As soon as Jaime unmuted the phone, Clark said, "Yes, sir. We'll get on that right away."

"There are some good folks at AFIP. I used Major Horace Underwood on the case I had at Fort Riley. He's an Army doc, and he's taken a particular interest in shaken baby cases."

"I'll see if we can link up with him in particular, sir."

"Watch out for Commander Peterson. He's a jerk. And, unfortunately, he's Underwood's boss. And, he's board-certified in forensic pathology. Major Underwood isn't."

"So, a Navy officer is the head guy?"

"Yeah, for that section. All of the armed services use the same lab. You should also know that Peterson went to night law school after he became a doctor. He likes to match wits with prosecutors. And, he's a contrarian. Personally, I think he's unprofessional, although in my case his conduct wasn't bad enough for us to do anything about it."

After a lengthy pause, Clark asked, "Anything else I should know, sir?"

"Well, yeah."

The way Major Green answered his question made Clark again feel stupid for asking it. Soon it became clear that the pause was because Major Green had been talking to someone else in his office, not because he had finished providing advice.

"After you establish that the child's death was caused by her being shaken, you have to establish that the accused was the one who did the shaking."

"I don't think that will be difficult, sir," Clark interjected. "The suspect was the only person who had access to Lydia Mendoza for several hours before she became sick and was taken to the hospital."

"Well, that sounds good. It sounds like he's the sole suspect, then. Is there anyone else who could have done it?"

"No, sir, I don't think so. Don't you agree, Jaime?"

"Tha's righ'. We don' have no o'her suspec'."

"What about the mother?" Major Green asked.

"She's actually the suspect's sister-in-law," Clark replied. "She left the baby with her brother-in-law while she went out on a date."

"Well then get ready for the defense counsel to portray her as a slut."

"Sir?"

"Yeah. If he has no case otherwise, he'll try to say the mother was a slut who didn't take care of her child and that's why the baby died. He might even try to suggest that she had something to do with it."

"I'm not sure how that makes sense, sir."

"Well, Captain Clark, it probably doesn't, but you'll see it again and again as you try cases. When the defense counsel has nothing, he'll throw a bunch of shit on the wall to see if anything sticks. It doesn't have to make sense."

"Got it, sir."

Clark looked at Suzanne, who rolled her eyes and pursed her thick lips, suggesting that she thought Clark's questions were dumb. So, he turned the tables on her. "Captain Watkins, I've been asking all the questions. Do you have any for Major Green?"

"Uh… no. Not at this time," she stammered, her face flushing bright red.

"Listen, guys, I've got to get to a meeting. Jaime has my number. If you want to talk again, just get Jaime to set up another call." Without waiting for their response, he hung up.

Jaime pushed the button on the speaker phone to end the call and turned to the two captains. "I didn' wan' to say anyt'in', but I already sen' the repor' to Major Underwood. He lookin' at i', an' we gonna talk nex' week."

"Thanks, Jaime. That's great. By the way, is Major Green always that abrupt?"

"I don' know. Maybe he think' he' a big deal 'cause he' in the Pentagon."

"Well, I'm glad you've already sent the file to Underwood. If you talk to him next week, I'd like to be on the call with you, just to listen, if that's okay."

"Sure, Capitain Clark, bu' let' do i' a' your office. Agen' Robinson might no' like i' i' you there when I talki' to Underwood the firs' time. You know, he want' us to finish the investigation and our repor' and den give i' to you."

"I would like to be on that call, as well," Suzanne chimed in.

"I'm sorry, Suzanne. Of course, you need to be on it, too," said Clark. "My head is spinning with all there is to think about." Clark turned back to Jaime. "And there's no problem with doing it at our office, Jaime. We understand about the report. We definitely don't want to get you in any trouble with Robinson. We just want to get up to speed as fast as possible."

"No pro'lem, sir."

Wanting to leave before Agent Robinson showed up again, Clark said, "Thanks for setting this up, Jaime. Let us know about the call with Major Underwood."

On the drive back to the JAG Office, Suzanne didn't say anything, which was unusual for her. Surprisingly, she didn't even mention the possibility that, based on what Agent Robinson had said, General Kraus had probably lost his objectivity and shouldn't be the one to convene the court-martial or review the results. They could think of nothing other than the tasks that lay ahead of them—tasks that they had to accomplish without the help of their experienced boss.

As they walked into the reception area of their office, they encountered Trip, reading a copy of *Golf Digest*. He looked up when he heard them come in.

"Counselors. Just who I wanted to talk to."

"What's up, Trip?" Clark asked.

"Well, I'd like to talk to you about the Gomez case."

"The Gomez case?"

"Yeah, the alleged homicide case you're working on."

"Trip, the CID investigation hasn't been completed yet. Nobody has preferred charges against Gomez or anybody else."

"Yeah, I know. But I've heard that General Kraus has taken a special interest in this case. You might want to work something out before it's too late."

"Too late?"

"Yes, Clark, 'too late.' Ya'll don't have a case and you know it."

"We know nothing of the kind, Trip. As I said, the CID hasn't even finished its investigation yet."

"Yeah, Trip. We were just over there..." Suzanne stopped abruptly when she saw Clark glaring at her.

"Well, I won't be willing to deal later," Trip drawled. "I'll just go for a complete acquittal."

Trying to sound confident, Clark replied, as calmly as he could, "Do whatever you think you need to do for your client, Trip. But we won't be in a position to talk until the CID investigation is finished and we've reviewed their report."

"Suit yourselves, but Colonel Allen might see it differently," Trip snickered as he walked out the door.

After Trip left, Suzanne's insecurity resurfaced. "Maybe we should talk to him, Clark."

"Shut up, Suzanne."

CHAPTER TWENTY

AFTER THE UNPLEASANT encounter with Trip, Clark retreated to his office, closed the door, and carefully studied his notes and the documents related to the Gomez case, including the ones he'd just taken during the conference call with Major Green. He carefully re-read Suzanne's summaries of infant homicide cases and looked for similarities with the Gomez case. He wasn't in a hurry to head home. He knew his quarters would be empty, and he wasn't ready to face that.

By the time he left the office, it was dark, and there was no moon. There must have been a thick layer of clouds above, because he couldn't see any stars, which were normally abundant in Panama's night sky. As he left the area where the offices and quarters were located, the darkness closed in. It became thick—almost tangible. The trees on either side of the road arched over it, forming a tunnel of vegetation. The only lights he could see were his headlights, pointing down that dark tunnel. Then it started to rain, which was also unusual: normally, it rained in the afternoon. It began as a drizzle, but soon became a torrential downpour. He hadn't previously driven home when it was this dark or wet, so he'd never noticed the long stretches of road where there was nothing—no street lights, no quarters, no buildings—only an eerie darkness and the black jungle on either side. The only sounds were the rain pounding on his car and the slap... slap of the windshield wipers.

As he drove through the black tunnel, the reality of what he was facing became manifest. After only one case, he was now lead counsel on a murder prosecution. His co-counsel was scared of her own shadow. His mentor was thousands of miles away. His boss had a damaged reputation and no experience with criminal law. His investigator was a womanizer with a propensity to drink too much and talk too much. His opponent was the well-educated scion of a family of lawyers, who had probably been listening to discussions of legal issues since he was a child. And to top it all off, his wife had left him and taken his daughter with her.

Clark knew he didn't have a plan for dealing with all of that, and his stomach began to feel like it was twisting into its all-too-familiar knot. He tried to boost his spirits by reminding himself that he'd faced challenges before. It didn't work. His mind kept returning to a single thought: despite all these difficulties, achieving justice for Lydia Mendoza was in his hands.

When he pulled into his driveway, he was struck by how dark and empty his quarters looked. Not a single light was on. The rain continued to beat on his car as he stared at the black windows for what must have been several minutes. It was if he'd somehow stumbled into an Alfred Hitchcock movie. A flash of lightning startled him out of his daze. He hustled to the back door and got drenched in the process. Standing in his dark kitchen, shivering, he fumbled for the light switch. He'd forgotten to turn the thermostat up when he left for work, so the air conditioner had been running full blast all day. That, combined with his wet clothes, made him forget he was in the tropics.

He hurried toward his bedroom, peeling off his uniform and turning on lights as he went. On the way, he turned on the stereo to break the gloomy silence. Expecting some rock ballad, he was surprised to hear Ellie's voice, reciting her ABCs. He then remembered that he had taped her a few days before he'd left to go back to the States. Her little voice was so sweet and proud as she stumbled through the alphabet. He fell into a chair and began to weep.

He sat, sobbing, for a long time after the tape ended. The only sounds he heard were the rain beating on the roof and his heart pounding in his chest. And then, it was if all of his energy was gone. Half-dressed in wet clothes, he was too tired to get up, too tired to move. "Maybe she's right," he said out loud. "Maybe it is my fault. Maybe I've been too focused on my career and not enough on my family."

After staring at nothing for almost an hour, he finally found the energy to get up. He went back to the kitchen and poured a tall glass of Jack Daniels and then—almost as an afterthought— added a splash of Coke. He needed to sleep, and he thought that would do the trick. The drink went down in three gulps. He walked back into the dining room, sat down at the table, and gazed out at the storm. Lightening flashed, and he saw the iguana—the one that had terrorized his wife—standing on the picnic table under the covered portion of the terrace like a prince surveying his realm. Clark had decided to nickname him "John" after Ellie's imaginary friend.

"I guess you want to be out of the storm, too, don't you? What do you think, Johnny Boy? Should I have listened to her better?" The tall quick drink he'd just consumed on an empty stomach had gone straight to his head. He heaved and regurgitated some foul-tasting stomach fluid but didn't vomit. "You scared her by just showing up, didn't you? What do you think, Johnny? Did Bobby do a shitty job of listening?" Clark's voice was angry, not reflective. He sounded disgusted. Then his mood changed and his eyes welled with tears again. "Maybe if I'd listened to her, John, I wouldn't have wound up here, alone, staring at you."

The next morning, Clark walked into the JAG office with

bloodshot eyes. Although the Jack and Coke had gotten him to sleep, it had also given him a throbbing headache and a queasy stomach.

"Damn, Clark. You look like shit. What's going on?" Suzanne, in her inimitable way, got right to the point.

"Would you please join me in my office?"

"Your office? Uh… sure, Clark." Her confusion was understandable, since they were never so formal about such things. She followed him back to his office, past the civilian secretary and the enlisted clerks. He sat down behind his desk and motioned for her to shut the door. She did and then sat in the chair across from his desk, staring at him, wondering what was going on.

"My wife left me." He waited for her reaction.

"What?" she asked, wide-eyed. "When did this happen? Why did it happen?"

"I don't know why, Suzanne. It happened two days ago. I came home, and she was gone. She took Ellie and went back to the States. She just left a note saying she wasn't happy." He paused and wiped his hands down the sides of his face, ending with his palms touching as if he was about to pray. "I would appreciate it if you would keep this to yourself until I've had time to sort it out."

"Sure. No problem. I am really sorry, Clark." Suzanne actually sounded genuinely concerned.

"Well, we've got a trial to get ready for, don't we?" he asked, signaling an end to the discussion of his marital mess.

"Yeah, we got the CID report this morning."

"It's finished?"

"Yeah. And it's thick."

Suddenly, the reality of the case hit home—and hard. Now, it was "game on."

"Would you get someone to make me a copy?"

"They brought us two. Here's yours. I've already started making notes in mine."

"Great. Let me look through it, and then, let's compare notes around 1100 hours."

"Will do."

Suzanne retreated to her office, and Clark headed for the coffee pot. The coffee smelled burnt and tasted bitter, but it had become his habit. He instructed the clerks to hold his calls and headed back to his office to study the CID report.

The first thing in the folder was the autopsy report. On the first page, he again saw the plaintive words of the examiner's conclusion: "...Lydia Mendoza... 13-month old Hispanic female, died... multiple blunt force injuries." As his eyes fixed on the page, some words became bold and larger: Lydia Mendoza... 13-month old... died... died... DIED. He pressed his fingertips against his temples. They throbbed, and his head hurt. Last night's Jack Daniels wasn't the only cause. It was the pressure. His father. His wife. His job. His feeling that he wasn't up to the task. The task. His responsibility to a little girl and her mother.

He went to the latrine and splashed cold water on his face. It felt good. He cupped his hands and gulped down several handfuls.

But the pressure remained.

He went back to his office and continued his review of the CID report. It included a number of photographs taken at the autopsy, which were in an envelope attached to the inside of one of the file folders. He opened the envelope and looked at the first one. Lydia looked like Ellie, lying naked on that cold, hard table. The memories of that scene came flooding back, and it made him sick. The other photographs were even more graphic. He shoved them back in the envelope and decided to forego reading the rest of the autopsy report until after he'd examined the other documents.

There was a sworn statement from the emergency room nurse who processed Lydia's admission into the hospital. She said that Specialist Raul Gomez had told her that he had been babysitting his niece for his sister-in-law the night before. Although the nurse indicated that the sister-in-law was also present in the emergency room, she didn't record her name in the statement, which was odd, considering that Carmen Mendoza was Lydia's mother. Perhaps Carmen didn't say much at the time, because of her difficulty with English, or maybe she was intimidated by being in a U.S. Army hospital. The nurse further indicated that Specialist Gomez told her that Lydia had been bitten by a spider a few days before and had been acting strangely since then. That information was news. Clark's jaw clenched. How could Jaime fail to mention that? That bit of information could wipe out the prosecution's case. Clark quickly flipped to the statement of Dr. Gonzalez, the neurosurgeon who had operated on Lydia. No mention of a spider bite.

Next, he looked at the portion of the file related to Specialist Gomez. The first thing he noticed was that Gomez was in Colonel Bednar's battalion. He was surprised that Bednar hadn't called him about the case already, especially since he often called about much less significant matters. There was also a photograph of Specialist Gomez in his uniform. He was a big guy, with an intense stare and no hint of a smile. Clark suspected he was trying to look tough and intimidating for the picture. If he presented that demeanor in the courtroom, it would be good for the prosecution.

Next, Clark carefully read Gomez's sworn statement, which he had only glanced at previously in Jaime's office. Prior to taking the statement, Jaime had read Gomez his rights, so he knew he was a suspect. His statement confirmed what Carmen Mendoza had told Clark and Jaime when Jaime interviewed her in her parents' apartment: Specialist Gomez's wife and children had gone to visit some relatives, which left Gomez alone with Lydia for around six hours, while Carmen was out with Specialist Wallace, Lydia's father. But Gomez's statement also mentioned the spider bite, which he claimed was the cause of everything that led to bringing Lydia to the hospital. Gomez said that Carmen came into his room early in the morning screaming hysterically that something was wrong with Lydia. They slapped Lydia on the bottom and splashed cold water on her face, but she wouldn't wake up. When blood started to spill from her mouth, they bundled her up and raced to Gorgas Hospital. Clark tried to recall whether Carmen had mentioned a spider bite when they interviewed her. She had cried so much, and her accent was so thick, that he wasn't sure.

The report of the interview with Specialist Gomez indicated that he cried as he told his story of what happened. That was very different from what the emergency room nurse's statement recounted about Gomez's demeanor when he brought Lydia in for treatment. By the time Gomez gave his statement to the CID, he knew he was a suspect; he knew he needed to put on a good show.

Clark finished looking at all of the documents, except the autopsy report. It sat there on his desk in a separate file folder, neatly labelled. He went to the outer office and got another cup of coffee. It was worse than the first—pungent and bitter with an almost smoky aroma. No matter, he needed it. He went back to his office, picked up the autopsy folder, removed the photographs from the envelope, and spread them out on his desk. They were gruesome. And, they really didn't tell him anything he didn't already know. He looked at them briefly and then gathered them up and shoved them back in the envelope.

The autopsy report was nothing more than a written description of the procedure he had attended. It made no mention of the context of Lydia's death or of any consultation with Dr. Gonzalez. It didn't mention anything about a spider bite or about blood coming out of Lydia's mouth. Toward the end of the report, though, he discovered a bombshell. The medical examiner wrote that the evidence of multiple blunt-force injuries suggested that Lydia had been murdered, and her bruises suggested that she had been sexually assaulted.

Why hadn't Jaime said anything about that? Did he think he didn't need to? For Jaime, the case was "open and shut." For him, finding the perpetrator was simply a process of elimination. Specialist Gomez was the only person present with Lydia during a six-hour period shortly before her death, so he was the sole suspect. End of inquiry. In Jaime's mind, no one else could have done it, and the medical examiner had called it a murder. Case closed.

Nevertheless, Clark was troubled that neither the autopsy report, nor Dr. Gonzalez's statement, had said anything about a spider bite or blood coming from Lydia's mouth. Nor did the report elaborate on the evidence of sexual assault.

Clark recalled how Major Green, the prosecutor who had previously worked with Jaime, had advised them to focus on the autopsy report and the testimony of the medical examiner and to have the report reviewed at the Armed Forces Institute of Pathology. He also warned that the defense might try to use seemingly irrelevant evidence to confuse the members of the court-martial panel. It appeared that the Gomez case, like Major Green's shaken-baby case, would be won or lost on forensic pathology. And given all the questions Clark had after only a single pass through the report, he knew he was going to need the help of a really good forensic pathologist. He needed to talk to Jaime.

"Jaime, this is Captain Clark."

"Yes, sir. Wha's up?"

"I've been looking at the report you sent over…"

"We go' Gomez by the balls, don' you thin'?"

"Well, he's certainly the prime suspect, but I do have some questions."

"Capitain Clark, a lo' o' people reviewed dis repor'…"

"Jaime, I'm not quarreling with you. I just want to go over some things. Why don't I come over right now? Does that work for you?"

"You know it, sir. Dis case i' my top priority."

"I'll see you in a few minutes."

"Suzanne!" Clark yelled loud enough for her to hear but regretted it as soon as he did. He was afraid she'd think he was treating her like a clerk.

"Yeah. What's up?" She stuck her head in his door, apparently unfazed by the way she'd been summoned.

"I want to go over some stuff with Jaime. Can we push our meeting to 1400 hours? Does that work for you?"

"Sure. Do you want me to come along?" She stopped. "On second thought, never mind. I haven't finished reviewing the CID report. I didn't want to look at the autopsy photos." She stared at him dolefully and shook her head. Her cheeks flushed, as they often did. "I glanced at them, Clark, but I couldn't bring myself to study them."

"I know what you mean," Clark replied. "I just looked at them myself. They're awful."

"Major Darst was right," she said, "I had no business being at that autopsy. I can barely stand to look at the photos. I can only imagine what it was like actually being there."

"Yeah. It was a lot worse in person. You could not only see it, you could hear it and smell it."

She gazed at him for a few moments as if she were visualizing him at the autopsy. "Well anyway, I need to spend some more time with the report… including the photos."

"That's okay," Clark said. "Somebody ought to be here any-way. One of the commanders might call. We shouldn't both be gone in the middle of the day. I'll compare notes with you when I get back." As he started to leave, she grabbed his arm.

"I was mad at Major Darst that day for not letting me go. But he was right. You were the right person for that job."

"I'm not so sure about that, Suzanne... Look, I need to get going."

She gave him a half smile and went back to her office.

Jaime was waiting at the back door when Clark arrived at the CID Office. He let him in, and they headed to the conference room. To Clark's surprise, Agent Robinson was sitting at the head of the table.

"Good morning, Captain Clark. I hear you have some questions about our report."

"Uh, yes, sir, I do." Why was he calling him "sir"? He outranked him. Clark regained his footing and continued. "It seems to me that this case is going to turn on forensic-pathology evidence, and all we have so far is the report of the medical examiner."

"Well, I'm sure you realize, Captain Clark, that the medical examiner's report—and more importantly his testimony at trial—are examples of forensic-pathology evidence."

Clark couldn't tell whether Robinson was being condescending or defending the report, or whether he simply thought Clark was green. He tried to stay cool. "You're absolutely right, Agent Robinson. But I'd like to know more about the spider bite and the evidence of sexual assault."

"Spider bite? What evidence of sexual assault?"

It was clear that Robinson—regardless of whether he was a "hot shit," as Jaime had described him—didn't know what was in the report.

"Jaime?" Robinson asked in a way that demanded an explanation. Jaime looked at Robinson and then at Clark. Clark was afraid he might have just put his friend in a bad spot with his boss.

Jaime stammered an explanation. "Gomez mention' a spider bi', Boss, bu' none o' the doctors sai' anythin' abou' i'. An' the examiner sai' wha' he foun' abou' the sexual assault i' hi' repor'."

"Which wasn't much," Clark interjected. "But I do think it would be a good idea for Jaime and me to interview the examiner and Dr. Gonzalez again. The CID report is certainly complete, but I need to understand what these two key witnesses are going to say. And I need Jaime's help to do that."

"Who's Gonzalez?" asked Agent Robinson.

Had Robinson read anything in the report?

Clark answered, "He's the neurosurgeon who operated on Lydia Mendoza." At this point Clark wouldn't have been surprised if Agent Robinson had asked him who Lydia Mendoza was. Turning to Jaime, Clark tried to say something to show Robinson that Jaime's investigation had been thorough. "You know, Jaime, when we talked to Major Green, he mentioned the Armed Forces Institute of Pathology."

"Wait a minute." Agent Robinson was asserting himself again because he knew he had looked foolish. "Who's Major Green?"

"He' the JAG tha' trie' the shaken-baby case a' For' Riley."

"Oh, okay," said Robinson. "Did he give you some good guidance?"

"Yes. He sai' we shoul' talk to Major Underwoo' at AFIP."

"Yes. I'm familiar with him. He's a good man. Can you arrange to get him involved, Jaime?"

"I sen' him the repor', an' I been callin' him, bu' he been ou' o' the office. I'll try again."

"Okay, fine." Agent Robinson stood up and strode to the door. "Let me know if you need my help with anything further."

After Robinson was out of earshot, Clark turned to Jaime. "I hope I didn't get you into any trouble."

"No, you didn'. Tha' guy don' read nothin,' and den he wan' to ac' like he know everythin'. He hadn' handle' a case in years."

"I thought you liked him. I thought he was a stud."

"He i' a stud, but he' also an asshole. I' jus' sick o' dis damn case."

"What's going on, Jaime?"

"Nothin'." Jaime dropped his head and blew his nose into his handkerchief.

Despite his quick denial, Clark knew something wasn't right. "Really?" Clark asked.

"No. Dere is somethin' wrong." Jaime stopped and gazed at Clark with a pained expression. His eyes were red and watery, and his nose was running. He blew his nose again and then looked up at Clark. "My wife lef' me yes'erday."

"Damn, Jaime. What happened?"

"She foun' ou' I was screwin' aroun', an' she took the kids to Puerto Rico."

"I thought she was Panamanian?"

"No, I'm half Panamanian. She' a damn Puerto Rican. She wen' back an' move' in wid her parents."

"Oh man. I'm sorry to hear that." Clark waited for Jaime to look at him. "I need to tell you something. My wife left me, too."

"No shi'? When?"

"A few days ago, right after I got back from the States. She took my kid and went to Torrijos and flew back home. Left me a note."

"Damn."

"So, we're in the same boat, my friend. Please keep that information to yourself, would you?"

"Sure."

"Let's concentrate on this case and say to hell with these damn bitches," Clark said, attempting to rally their spirits.

"Yeah." Although Jaime responded in the affirmative, it was less than enthusiastic.

"Let's try to call Underwood," Clark suggested.

"Okay. Le' me ge' hi' number. We can use the speaker phone in here."

Jaime left the room and returned with a yellow legal pad. He dialed Major Underwood's number. It took a while to get through the clerks, but Jaime finally reached him.

"Major Underwood?"

"Yes. Who's this?"

"Sir, dis is Agen' Jaime Hernandez. You know. We worke' on the shaken-baby case a' For' Riley."

"Oh yes. How's it going?"

"I's goin' goo', sir. I wan' to talk wid you abou' tha' case I sent you las' week. I's the one fro' Panama."

"Oh, yes. I've seen it."

"I go' you on the speaker phone, 'cause I go' Capitain Clark, the prosecutor, wid me."

"Okay. Hi, Captain Clark. Jaime, I haven't had a chance to review your report yet. We're incredibly short-handed here, and things aren't managed very well. So, can you tell me what you've got?"

Jaime did a thorough job of summarizing the case. He recounted what was in the autopsy report and the statements from the nurse, Specialist Gomez, and Dr. Gonzales. He even mentioned the spider bite and the bruises that suggested a sexual assault.

"Sounds like a shaken-baby case to me, although I'd like to know more about the spider bite. The bruises were probably caused by the perpetrator man-handling the child. Why don't you give me a couple of days to review the file, and I'll call you back?"

"Sir, this is Captain Clark. If you could get right on it, we would appreciate it. I suspect that our general is going to want to convene an Article 32 hearing to review the evidence."

"Well, my review shouldn't hold that up."

"Yes, sir. But, uh, I must confess that I'm pretty new at this. I would like to have everything lined up as soon as possible."

"Okay. I understand. You'll have my report soon." He paused. "This kind of crime is especially loathsome."

"Yes, sir."

They ended the call and turned their attention to lining up interviews with the medical examiner and Dr. Gonzalez.

"Jaime, I've been meaning to ask you about Carmen Mendoza."

"Wha' abou' her?"

"When we interviewed her in her apartment, did she say anything about a spider bite or blood coming from Lydia's mouth?"

"No' tha' I recall."

"Well, you know Gomez mentioned it to the nurse when he was getting Lydia admitted, and he mentioned it again in the statement you took from him."

"Yeah. Bu' I thin' tha' bullshi'. Captain Clark, you gonna fin' tha' the evidence doesn' always line up like on *Columbo* on TV. You know, tha' guy wid the trenchcoa'."

Clark pressed on, ignoring Jaime's attempt to lighten the mood. "Well, the defense will make a big deal about the spider bite and anything else they can use to confuse the members of the court-martial."

"Yeah. Well, tha' where you do your lawyer stuff, Captain Clark. You ca' handle Captain Stephens."

"I hope so, Jaime. Anyway, I need to get back to the office. Let me know when you line up the interviews. If we need to go downtown, that's fine with me. I would just like to be there. It'll still be your interview, of course. I'll come up with some questions we need to ask them, and we can compare notes beforehand."

Clark found his way out the back door and headed to Fort Clayton. As he passed the entrance to his housing area, he reminisced about the times he took a detour to his quarters to have lunch with Ellie. He knew he couldn't let his thoughts go there now, though. He'd be worthless for the rest of the day, and he had a lot to do.

When he got back, he hurried toward his office. As he passed Suzanne's, he could see she was head-down, scrutinizing something. He decided to wait to see if she came to him. She did. No sooner had he gotten organized than she was seated across from him with a strained look on her face. "We've got a problem."

"What?" Clark was hoping this was real analysis and not more of Suzanne's paranoid drama.

"Did you notice the references to the spider bite?"

"Only in the nurse's statement and in Gomez's."

"Right. But nobody followed up on that. So I called over to Gorgas and talked to an ER doctor about spider bites."

"You didn't tell him it was in connection with this case, did you?"

"Of course not, Clark. Do you think I'm stupid? I just said that my kid had been bitten by a spider."

Clark smiled. "What'd he say?"

"What makes you think it was a 'he'? In fact, Clark, it was a female doc."

"Great, Suzanne, spare me the feminist bullshit and tell me what she said."

She pressed her thick lips together and shook her head. "Okay. She said that the spiders in Panama are really bad. There are two that can cause serious harm: a brown recluse and a black widow. And get this: a bite from a black widow can cause neurologic symptoms, especially in small children. The brown recluse causes necrosis…"

"Slow down. What's 'necrosis'?"

"Dead skin. So, it probably wasn't that, but it could have been a black widow."

"Before you go running down that road, Suzanne, remember that we want to convict this guy, not gin up a defense for him." She leaned back in the chair, crossed her arms, and glared at him but said nothing. "Jaime says that spider-bite business is bullshit. The only evidence of it comes from Gomez: he told the nurse there was a spider bite, and he repeated that story to the CID. There's no physical evidence of a bite. None of the doctors saw it. And as you know from looking at the autopsy pictures, none of them show anything that looks like a spider bite."

"Oh, funny me, Mr. Professional. I thought our goal was to seek justice. There were a lot of marks on that child; one of them could have been a spider bite." She glared at him, got up abruptly, almost toppling her chair, and left.

Later that day, Clark heard Suzanne packing up her things, although she left without saying anything to him. He wasn't anxious to be alone in his empty quarters, so he decided to call Jaime and meet up with him and Elmer. As he was reaching for his phone, it rang. The voice on the other end was officious. "Captain Robert E. Clark?"

"Yes. This is he."

"Stand by for General Kraus."

Clark's stomach tightened. But then he wondered: Could this be Elmer, playing a practical joke? He decided he couldn't take any chances.

"Captain Clark?"

"Yes, sir. This is he."

"This is General Kraus."

"Yes, sir."

"I've been speaking with Agent Robinson from the CID, and I understand you met with him today."

Jaime was right: Robinson was an asshole. "Yes, sir. We met to discuss the Mendoza homicide."

"That's what I want to talk to you about, Captain Clark. Agent Robinson tells me you have some reservations about the investigation."

Wonderful. Where was this going? Clark began to feel sick.

"Not exactly, sir. There were just some aspects that I felt warranted further investigation."

"Well, Agent Robinson thinks very highly of you, and I think very highly of him. Anyway, I want you to know, Captain Clark, that we selected you for this case because it's an important case, and Agent Robinson and I have confidence in your ability to do a good job."

"Thank you, sir," Clark replied. He quickly considered the General's wording. Had he just said that *he* selected Clark, not Colonel Allen?

"Well, you can thank me by doing a good job," General Kraus continued. "I want you to leave no stone unturned. If you need a witness, you can have him. If you need the AFIP to review the case, then do it. I want you to have everything you need to get a conviction. I want Gomez brought to justice."

Clark decided that it was not a good time to tell the General that he had lost his objectivity as the convening authority for a general court-martial.

"Yes, sir. Will do."

"Well, that's all I have at this time. Keep up the good work. Now, go home and see the wife and kids."

"Yes, sir."

Clark hung up the phone and sank into his chair, trying to process what had just happened. The Commanding General in Panama had just instructed him to get someone convicted before he'd even assigned an Article 32 officer to investigate the case and make a recommendation about whether there should even be a trial. Agent Robinson was probably sitting in the General's office when he made the call. The General was clearly taking his legal advice from a CID agent, not the Staff Judge Advocate. But that was Colonel Allen's problem, not Clark's. At this point, Clark's job was to ensure that the investigation yielded the evidence he needed to get a conviction.

Clark picked up the phone and dialed a familiar number. "Jaime, this is Captain Clark. You wanna call Elmer and meet at Mother's? I need a drink."

CHAPTER TWENTY-ONE

THE BARTENDER GREETED Clark as he walked into Mother's Inn. "They' in the corner, Capitain Clark. You wan' a Balboa or a Jack and Coke dis time?"

"Thanks, Carlos. A Balboa, please. How's Rita?"

"She' fine, Capitain Clark. T'anks fo' askin'."

Walking to Elmer's corner, Clark considered his relationship with Mother's Inn. Before he came to Panama, he'd been in a bar only about a half-dozen times. Why was coming to this bar now so routine? Probably because the only rule at Mother's was that you had to leave your worries outside, and Clark certainly had plenty of those.

The usual coterie of lieutenants was absent from Elmer's corner, and Jaime and Elmer were not engaged in conversation. Though sitting side-by-side, they were staring off into space in different directions. Elmer was in dire need of a shave—indicating that he hadn't been at work—and was wearing civilian clothes that were uncharacteristically grungy. He looked downright gloomy. Jaime was wearing his standard attire (a light blue guayabera and khaki pants) and looked equally glum.

"What's goin' on, fellas?" Clark asked. The two men looked up but said nothing. "Did someone die, and I didn't hear about it?"

"Hi' wife lef' him, too," Jaime explained.

"We're a great fuckin' bunch, aren't we?" Elmer blurted out to no one in particular.

"What are you talking about?" Clark asked.

Elmer stared at him. "We suck. All of our wives have left us."

So much for Jaime keeping Clark's secret. But he didn't really care; it was Elmer after all.

"What happened with you, Elmer?"

"Kinda like you guys. I came home yesterday, and she and the girls were gone."

"Did she leave you a note?" Clark asked. "Mine left me a note, saying she wasn't happy; all our troubles were my fault, so she was going back home to Georgia."

"Well, she didn't leave me a note like that," Elmer began. He stared at Clark for a while and then smiled sheepishly. "She just left a lab report on the dining room table, which said she had gonorrhea. On it, she had written: 'You might want to get checked.'"

"Damn," Clark said without thinking, "You think she was feeling guilty?"

"No, dumb ass, she was telling me that I'd given it to her. She never screwed around."

"Oh, yeah. Right. Sorry, man."

"Yeah. Well, I had to get a fuckin' shot in my ass today, and it hurt like hell." Elmer then tried to regain his stride by making light of his situation. "Remember, boys, in the future think positive; test negative." His grin was back, but it lacked its usual swagger.

"Are you going to try to work things out with her?" Clark asked, but immediately realized it was a stupid question. After all, he hadn't tried to reconcile with Janelle. He hadn't even called her. So why was he asking Elmer that?

"No," said Elmer. "I'm not going to try to work it out with her. I've been thinking about it, and I've concluded that I'm just

not the marrying kind. I guess I'm kinda married to the Army."
His last comment was delivered with a smirk.

Devotion to the Army wasn't Elmer's problem, but Clark
didn't think Elmer needed to hear that from him at that point.
Trying to lighten the mood, Clark said, "Let's change the subject,
guys. This is Mother's Inn, for crying out loud. I think we're brea-
kin' some kinda rule, talkin' about this depressing crap."

"I go' some news," Jaime offered.

"Yeah. What's that?" asked Clark.

"You know you guys bin askin' abou' Specialis' Weeks?" Clark
and Elmer nodded. "Well," his voice now hushed, "we gettin'
ready to arres' her."

"Arrest her?" Elmer asked. And then, shaking his head,
"That's one good lookin' piece of ass that'll be off the market."

"Damn, Elmer. Haven't you gotten in enough trouble already?"

"Fuck it," he replied, with no hint of a smile.

Jaime continued, "Yeah. We go' several controlle' buys fro'
her. She' bringin' the cocaine on pos' fo' the drug guys downtown. She sol' some cocaine to one o' our undercover agen'. I' was
tough findin' one she didn' know."

Elmer took a long draw on his cigarette, squinted his eyes,
and wrinkled his face as if he'd just tasted something sour. "So
why does Robinson have such a hard-on about investigating her?"

Obviously, Jaime had not told Elmer about Agent Robinson
wanting to hook up with Weeks.

"Robinson ha' a 'har' on,' all right." Jaime chuckled through
a big smile. "He ha' the hots fo' Weeks, bu' she wouldn' give him
the time o' day."

"No shit," said Elmer. "That old fart is damn near old enough
to be her father."

Clark looked at Jaime. "So, it's like you thought? Robinson is
jealous of Weeks."

"Yeah," said Jaime. He sat back in his chair, took a drink of his Balboa, and leaned forward again. In a lowered voice he continued, "Tha's why Robinson was so pisse' a' Major Dars'. He though' Dars' was screwin' Weeks."

"Whoa!" said Elmer, leaning forward in his chair. "Darst was screwing Weeks?"

"But he wasn't," Clark said, in a way that indicated he was asking for reassurance.

"No. I' wasn' Major Dars'; i' was Colonel Allen."

"Allen?" Elmer raised his eyebrows and scrunched his forehead in disbelief. "Allen was screwing Weeks? What could she possibly see in that short little shit. That he's a colonel?"

Clark was surprised by Elmer's reaction. Perhaps he wasn't clued in on everything that was going on at Fort Clayton. Or, maybe Weeks rebuffed a pass from the always-on-the-prowl Captain Jackson, as well as Agent Robinson.

"Yeah," Jaime continued, "she was havin' an affair wid Colonel Allen, bu' i's over. In fac', yes'erday Agen' Robinson tol' Colonel Allen to en' it, or the General was goin' to brin' him up on charges."

That explained why Allen got spooked when Clark told him that he'd reviewed all the CID cases. Allen must have suspected that his romantic tryst with Weeks was the subject of one of them. Clark smiled. He was beginning to learn how to stitch pieces of evidence together.

"Why did the General give Colonel Allen an out?" Clark asked.

"Generals don't like messy situations," Elmer interjected. "They don't mind busting some enlisted soldier, but they're slow to go after an officer, especially if the officer happens to be the chief legal advisor of the command. And especially for something as stupid as fraternization with an enlisted soldier. You don't have anything else on Allen, do you, Jaime?"

"No. Jus' foolin' aroun' wid Weeks."

"So," Clark asked, "Colonel Allen gets to walk, and Weeks is going to be arrested?"

"Think about it, Clark." Elmer leaned over the table in his direction and said in a lowered voice, "Allen might be guilty of screwing an enlisted person. Don't get me wrong: I agree that that's stupid. But Weeks was caught bringing cocaine on post. That shit's poison. And, she's the damn legal clerk for the defense counsel." Elmer paused and sat back in his chair. A new grin appeared on his face. "Trip Stephens is going to shit a brick."

"No shi'," said Jaime.

"When is she going to be arrested?" Clark asked.

"Pro'ly next week."

"I hope that doesn't screw things up with Trip." Clark took a drink of beer and contemplated how Trip would react to her arrest. "You know, he might ask for a continuance or something if his legal clerk gets arrested." Jaime and Elmer each shrugged their shoulders, as if to say, "So what?" Clark changed the subject. "What about Major Darst? Is he coming back?"

"Nobody knows anything about what's going on with him," said Elmer. "All I know is that it looks like he's going to be compassionately reassigned to Fort Sill. Something about takin' care of his mom in Amarillo."

"His mom?" Clark asked. "Is she sick or something?"

"I don't know. As I said, all I know is that they're going to reassign him to Fort Sill."

"When?" asked Clark.

"Don't know," Elmer replied.

Clark's thoughts began to spiral down. Who was going to help him with this case? Suzanne? She had no more experience than he did. He hoped he didn't regret getting the case. He could call Major Green again. But what would that do to his reputation? He could just hear the gossip at the JAG School: Clark lobbies to get a murder case that he can't handle. And then, of course, there was General Kraus. He made it damn clear that Clark had better win.

Elmer and Jaime started chattering about all sorts of subjects: baseball, fishing, women who are hot, women who are not, women who are a pain in the ass, how screwed up the Army is, *etc.* Clark only heard bits and pieces of the conversation.

"I wonder if she's the one who gave it to me?"

"'I' so, Elmer, you go' a pro'lem. She' married to a mas'er sergean'"

"No shit."

Clark again reflected on his first encounter with Major Darst and Specialist Weeks in the NCO Club. He recalled how chummy they seemed for a major and his enlisted clerk. Could the CID be mistaken? Was it possible that Colonel Allen *and* Major Darst had been having affairs with Weeks? And if Major Darst had been involved with Weeks, had he also been involved with the drug guys in Panama? Maybe it was Darst's truck that had tried to run them off the road that night. Maybe that was why Darst left Panama—out of sight, out of mind.

"Clark, are you deaf?" Elmer caught him, lost in thought.

"What, what did you say?" he stammered.

"Do you want to see how good that line is that I told you about?"

"What are you talking about?"

"Jaime, here, wants me to use my best line on the new waitress. Are you game?"

"I guess so."

Elmer motioned for the waitress to come over. Clark had not seen her before, although no one frequented Mother's as much as Elmer. The waitress was Panamanian—young and cute, although a little pudgy. She looked like she was no more than eighteen or nineteen years old.

"Señorita," Elmer began, the trademark grin having returned, "You have the opportunity to participate in a rare event. You have before you two 'Elmers.'" Elmer then gestured to himself and Clark. "We're out of glue, but we'll stick to you... either one of us... or both of us." Elmer looked at her expectantly, and then he and Jaime started laughing so hard they drew attention to themselves. It was clear the poor girl had no idea what Elmer was talking about. She gave a half smile tinged with trepidation and turned to walk away.

"No. No, Señorita. I'm serious," Elmer continued. She turned around and came back to the table, looking as if she thought an explanation was forthcoming. But Elmer persisted with his silly joke. "Seriously, Señorita, you can stick to either one of us." He started giggling as he spoke, which grew into a full-fledged belly laugh by the time he finished talking.

"*No entiendo*," she said softly and then smiled at Jaime, with a longing look, obviously hoping that a fellow Spanish speaker would explain what was going on. It was no use. He and Elmer were having too much fun at her expense. Jaime just kept laughing and motioned for her to go away.

"Rest assured, Elmer, I will never use that line."

"Fine with me. I'll save it for myself," Elmer sputtered through inebriated giggles.

After their laughter subsided somewhat, Clark said, "Guys, I need to hit the road."

"Come on, Counselor. You just barely got here. Have some fun." Elmer liked having a friendly audience for his antics, especially after a few beers had wound him up.

"No. I really have a lot on my mind. The General called me just before I came over here, telling me to do whatever I had to do to put Gomez away."

"No shit," said Elmer.

"Tha's goo', Captain Clark. Tha' mean you ge' wha'ever you wan'."

"Yeah, but I don't even know what I need. Darst is gone, the

SJA is no help, and I don't want to call that major in the Pentagon again. He'll think I'm an idiot."

"Quit sweating it, Clark," said Elmer, in a way that suggested he thought he understood the situation perfectly. "This case is a no-brainer. Just concentrate on what you're going to argue when it comes to punishment."

"It's not that easy, Elmer. There's stuff in the CID's report that's not been totally explained."

"You talkin' abou' the spider bi' again?" asked Jaime, breaching the confidentiality of his report yet again.

"Yeah, Jaime. It might be bullshit to you and Agent Robinson, but I don't want to give Trip something he can use. You heard what Major Green said about throwing shit on the wall and seeing if anything sticks. Well, that spider-bite issue is some serious shit." Clark paused and stared at both of them. "And, there's a lot of other stuff to worry about."

"Okay, Counselor. Go for it. That's why we love you," Elmer said. "We know you're gonna be prepared, and you're gonna kick Trip Stephens in the balls."

Clark smiled at his two friends. The old Elmer appeared to be back and had done a good job of cheering up Jaime. As he left, Clark could hear his buddies laughing, probably at another one of Elmer's stupid antics or a joke made at someone else's expense.

Driving home, Clark couldn't stop thinking about the Gomez case and the call from General Kraus. All eyes were on the case and him. As he turned into the entrance of his housing area, he passed a young officer in the front yard of his quarters, playing ball with his kids as the sun went down and evening began to emerge. His thoughts turned from the Gomez case to his own situation and, most of all, to his daughter. He decided he needed to try to call Janelle as soon as he got home. It was getting late, and he wanted to be able to talk to Ellie before she went to bed.

Clark walked in the back door and immediately headed for

his address book to look up his father-in-law's phone number. He didn't care that phoning from his quarters would cost him almost three times as much as using a calling card at the Post Exchange. When he picked up the phone to dial, however, he heard two men talking. Thinking it was Roy, the helicopter pilot who lived across the street, Clark decided to eavesdrop for a few moments to see if he could determine how long the call might last. Very quickly, though, he realized it wasn't Roy. He recognized one of the voices as Trip's when he heard Trip ask, "Well, what do you think I gotta do, Daddy?" He sounded anxious.

"Sometimes, the evidence against yo' client looks really bad, even though he's innocent," the other voice drawled, with a Southern accent that had a noticeable bourbon patina. Clark had heard that kind of voice around Pemberton. It usually belonged to some older gentleman who was either a lawyer or the beneficiary of inherited wealth, or both. Some of those men were polite and wise, while others were pontificating blowhards. If this was Trip's father, then Clark was eavesdropping on a sitting federal judge.

The second voice continued, "At other times, Son, there's virtually no admissible evidence against yo' client, even though you know fo' a fact he's guilty. What matters is what the jury thinks."

Clark couldn't believe what he was hearing. He knew it was wrong to listen in on a private conversation, especially if he heard something that might disqualify him from trying the Gomez case. He knew he should hang up.

But he didn't.

"They're called the members of the court-martial, Daddy, not members of a jury. And it's not like civilian juries full of sympathetic old ladies. These are hard-core infantrymen."

"Don't get smart with me, Son. I've had tough juries. When I started practicing law after the war, women didn't serve on juries. You talk about infantrymen. I had some tough old Mississippi farmers who had fought in World War II." He stopped, and Clark thought he heard ice clinking in a glass. "I know what you're thinking, Son, but a jury is a jury. You've got to sway them with emotion."

"Daddy, I think my client just might have killed that little girl. And today I heard that the smart-ass prosecutor has already been talking to a forensic pathologist."

How in the hell did Trip know that Clark had spoken with Major Underwood at AFIP? Would Suzanne have told him? Surely not. But then, she did seem to be overly impressed with Trip. Would Colonel Allen have told him? He was awfully chummy with Trip. Or maybe Allen told Weeks about it during one of their romantic rendezvous. But that couldn't be right. The timing was all wrong.

"Son, yo' job is not to decide guilt or innocence," the older man continued. "Yo' job is to protect yo' client and make the prosecutor do his job. The prosecutor must prove yo' client's guilt beyond a reasonable doubt. An' if he dudn't, then yo' client is not guilty, and he should go free. That's the way our system works."

"I wanna win this case, Daddy."

"It's not about winnin', Son. It's about doin' yo' job. Yo' client deserves that."

"What about that little girl, Daddy? What does she deserve?"

"If you're gonna be a lawyer, Son, then you've got to start thinkin' like one. Concentrate on swaying that jury." He paused for a moment, and Clark heard ice clinking again. Then the older man asked, in a voice that sounded like he'd just taken a sip, "What angle are you thinkin' about?"

"Angle?"

"Yes, Son, 'angle.' There's always an angle to every case. Where was the mother when this child was being abused?"

"She was on a date with the father of the child, tryin' to work things out about the baby. She wanted him to marry her."

"So, she's a whore."

"No, Daddy, she's a sweet young Panamanian girl who made a mistake."

"No, Son, she's a whore, who let a soldier get her pregnant. She's got loose morals, and this is the consequence. A baby was born without a proper family. No daddy around. This kinda thing happens in Mississippi all the time. These black girls especially, but the white trash, too. They don't even get out of their teens before they have a couple of kids. The social pathologies that result from that kinda behavior are horrible."

"What are you sayin', Daddy."

"I'm sayin' that the jury needs to understand that the baby died because her mother didn' take care of her. She's a slut who had a child out of wedlock, and then failed to take proper care of her." The older man paused for a moment and then continued. "And why did she leave her little girl alone with a man?"

"He's her brother-in-law, Daddy."

"You're not understandin' me, Son. You must paint a picture with yo' defense. You must show that this woman is a tramp."

"How does that show my client didn't kill that little girl?"

"Because the jury wants to be mad at someone for this horrible crime. The soldiers on that jury don't want to be mad at a fellow soldier. He's one of them. Make them mad at this woman. Even if yo' client gets convicted, his sentence will be less."

"She's not a whore, Daddy. She's just a kid. Besides, the whole argument sounds contrived."

"Don't get smart with me, boy. This is the way trials are conducted. If you don't have good evidence, then you must sway the passions of the jury. This man—yo' client—volunteered to serve his country. He's a married man. He wasn't makin' babies out of wedlock. The mother is the guilty party. How was he supposed to know how to take care of that little girl?"

Clark felt ashamed to be listening in on a private conversation. But he was transfixed.

"I understand what you're sayin', Daddy. But do you really think that's what I should do?"

"It sounds like it's all you got, Son."

Why didn't Trip mention the spider bite? Surely Gomez would have told him about that. Maybe Jaime was right. Maybe that story about the spider was BS, which Gomez came up with to explain what had happened to little Lydia. If Gomez didn't mention the spider bite to Trip, or Trip didn't believe it, then it probably wasn't true.

Trip and his father started talking about family matters, and Clark quietly put the receiver back on the phone. He couldn't believe what he'd just done but quickly rationalized his behavior on the grounds that he'd learned about a leak somewhere. Otherwise, how would Trip have known that he'd spoken to Major Underwood? It didn't occur to Clark that Major Underwood might have told his boss, Commander Peterson, who was known to be a frequent witness for the defense, and Trip in turn spoke with Peterson.

By the time Clark hung up, it was too late to call his wife and daughter, so he resolved to call them the next day. He was too agitated by what he'd just heard and felt the need to settle down. He went to the kitchen and poured some Jack Daniels in a tall glass of ice. With drink in hand, he retrieved a cigar from his makeshift humidor—a wooden cigar box with a humidifier in it—and went outside to think.

It was a beautiful night. A warm breeze was blowing, and the sky looked like a blanket of black velvet onto which God had sprinkled a million sparkling diamonds. He had never seen anything like it. It was magnificent.

Lying on his chaise lounge, staring at the stars, he finished his cigar and got a second drink. From time to time he thought he heard John moving around in his tree, though he never caught sight of him.

Clark didn't know what to do about General Kraus's apparent

lack of neutrality. Standard procedure called for the Staff Judge Advocate to address the issue with the commander. But Clark couldn't rely on Colonel Allen to deal with the issue—he'd compromised himself. Clark was also worried that someone in his organization was betraying confidences, but he couldn't talk to Allen about that either, since he or his former paramour might be the source of the leak.

Even though Clark's body was tired and he'd consumed one and a half strong drinks on top of the beer he'd drunk at Mother's, he couldn't relax. He looked up at the sky and tried to clear his head. His thoughts returned to Pemberton and his father. It was hard to believe he was gone. He'd been such an important part of Clark's life.

Memories of something that had happened when he was a child began to stir—something about replacing a fence on the back of their property. It happened when Clark was around thirteen years old. His father had gotten a copy of their plat from the courthouse and was using it to determine where to place the new fence, which they were installing about fifteen yards inside where the old one had been. Larry—one of his father's lifelong friends and the lawyer who later handled his estate—happened to be driving by and stopped to talk. He pointed to the old fence and asked why they weren't locating the new one there. When Clark's father explained that the old fence had actually been on his neighbor's property, Larry told him that he didn't need to worry about that. He said a legal principle called adverse possession states that a person can acquire title to someone else's real property without paying for it simply by holding the property for a specified time in a manner that conflicts with the true owner's rights. The old fence had been there long enough to meet the requirements of adverse possession under Georgia law. Larry said that a court would probably rule that his father legally owned the property inside of the old fence. But that didn't matter to Clark's father. He said he had known the neighbor all of his life, and he wasn't about to take something from him, especially by using "some legal loophole."

Looking up at the tree, Clark yelled, "My dad was a hell of a man, John. You hear me? They don't make 'em like that anymore!" By now, Clark was feeling the full effect of the Jack Daniels. The iguana had been watching him, and Clark's outburst caused him to scurry up the tree. "So you've been listening to me, huh, Johnny Boy?"

Clark downed the remainder of his second drink in one gulp. "I was proud of my dad that day, John." Clark continued to look up at the tree. "I'm sure you don't understand this shit, but we could've used that extra property. But that didn't matter to my dad. To him, it was a matter of integrity. And he never compromised that."

Clark lay back on the chaise lounge and was asleep within moments. Sometime during the night, he awoke, stumbled inside, and fell into bed.

CHAPTER TWENTY-TWO

A FEW DAYS later Raul Gomez's company commander preferred charges against him, the first step in the court-martial process. The next step would be the appointment of an Article 32 Officer to investigate the charges. Under the Uniform Code of Military Justice, serious crimes, like murder, are tried by a general court-martial, the highest-level trial court in the military. But before a general court-martial can be convened, an Article 32 Officer must conduct an investigation of the charges and make recommendations to the convening authority concerning whether the evidence warrants a trial. The convening authority is the commanding officer who is empowered to "convene" a general court-martial. In this case, it was General Kraus.

An Article 32 Investigation is somewhat like a civilian grand jury proceeding, except the accused at an Article 32 hearing has many more rights than a defendant at a grand jury hearing. For example, the accused's attorney may call witnesses and cross-examine them under oath at an Article 32. Defense counsel can't do that at a grand jury.

*

"Did you hear who General Kraus appointed as the Article 32 Officer for the Gomez case?" Suzanne was standing in the door of

Clark's office, clearly enjoying being the one "in the know" again. "Lieutenant Colonel Jacobs. That hard-ass from the Atlantic side of the Isthmus."

Clark looked up from his desk and thought out loud, "Maybe the General feels the case has gotten too much attention on this side."

"Really, Clark? You really think he cares about that? He appointed Jacobs because he knows Jacobs will recommend a general court-martial, regardless of the evidence." She stared at him, waiting for his acknowledgment that she was right. Getting none, she changed the subject. "What witnesses are you going to call?"

"Just Jaime."

"Really? Do you think that's enough?"

"Yeah. I don't want to show Trip our entire case. Besides, if you're right, the Article 32 Officer is going to recommend that Gomez be tried for murder anyway." Clark didn't notice that Suzanne smiled at her little victory. "I'm sure Trip will cross-examine Jaime, but Jaime can handle it. He's testified in a lot of trials."

"Who do you think Trip will call?" she asked.

"Probably some of our witnesses, like Dr. Gonzales. I'm sure he'll want to nail down their testimony."

"You think so?" Suzanne looked at him like she didn't understand what he meant.

"Yeah. If a witness testifies at the Article 32 under oath, then he won't be able to change his story at trial without losing credibility."

"Oh, I see," she said, nodding her head. "And if Trip questions them at the Article 32, then he'll have a better idea of what he'll encounter at trial and can figure out how to deal with it in advance."

"Right." Suzanne wasn't very good in the courtroom, but she was a quick study. "Remember, Suzanne, the Article 32 hearing is

Trip's only opportunity to question witnesses under oath before trial." He flipped through some files on his desk for a few moments and then stopped. "You know what?" he asked, without making eye contact. "I'll be surprised if he doesn't call every last witness listed in the CID file."

The Article 32 hearing took place a few days later, and Clark was indeed surprised. Not only did Trip fail to call any witnesses, he didn't even cross-examine Jaime, the one witness Clark called. Clark couldn't believe it. Trip's one chance to cross-examine witnesses under oath before the trial, and he took a pass? Surely, his father had not advised him to do that, unless he didn't understand what a defense counsel could do at an Article 32. And, Trip made no effort to bring up the spider bite—not even with Jaime. That one was really puzzling. Did Trip think Gomez was lying about it? Or was he planning to spring it on Clark at trial? Or maybe Elmer was right about Trip being lazy.

As Suzanne predicted, the Article 32 Officer recommended that Gomez be tried for murder, and to no one's surprise, General Kraus convened a general court-martial. The next big question was: Who would the JAG Corps send to Panama to preside over this case?

*

On a Wednesday evening, two weeks or so after his wife and daughter had gone back to the States, Clark was working late in his office when the phone rang.

"Captain Clark speaking. This line is unsecure."

"Aren't you ever goin' to call me, Bobby?" Janelle asked.

Surprised by her call, he stammered, "I, uh, tried to call you the other night, but I got sidetracked. You could've called me, you know. You're the one who left without so much as saying goodbye. And, I've been incredibly busy preparing for the Gomez trial."

"You're always 'incredibly busy,' Bobby. That's the problem. All you care about is your work. There's nothin' left for me and Ellie."

"That's not true, and you know it," he shot back.

"No, I don't know it. You've been that way your whole life. I thought maybe things would change when we got to your first JAG assignment, and you weren't goin' out in the field all the time, but they got worse. You never had time for me and Ellie— only work."

"Can you put her on the phone?"

"No. She's asleep."

"So I don't get to talk to my daughter, is that it?"

"You could if you ever bothered to call."

"For your information, I've tried to call you during the little bit of free time that I've had."

"You mean when you aren't at Mother's Inn with your buddies?"

"What do you think you know about that? You don't know anything." Clark tried to speak with as calm a voice as he could muster. "For your information, Janelle, I'm trying to learn a new job. I've only been out of law school for a little over a year, and I'm already responsible for a murder trial against an experienced lawyer, whose father—who happens to be a federal judge— is coaching him on how to defend it. And, oh, by the way, my father just died. So, forgive me if I'm just a little bit stressed." He strained to keep his composure. "And thanks, by the way, for adding to that stress by leaving me."

"I'm not going to apologize for leavin'."

"Well, you should…"

"I've got a right to be happy, Bobby."

That comment really ticked him off. He no longer tried to sound calm. "Well, Janelle, I've been bustin' my ass for a lot of years trying to build a future for us, tyring to make you happy, and believe me, it's not been easy. But nothing ever satisfies you. And another thing," he yelled, his anger now boiling over, "when my dad died, you didn't even give a shit. You were just pissed off that you didn't get to go back to Pemberton."

Deep down, Clark knew that she'd been unhappy for a long time. He also knew that he was over-reacting, but he didn't understand why. The stress he'd been under had completely eroded his ability to deal with anger and frustration. Unfortunately, his wife didn't understand that either.

"I'm not goin' to listen to you yell and cuss at me. I called to talk to you, but I can see that you aren't interested in havin' an adult conversation." She hung up.

Before his hand was off the telephone receiver, he was startled by Suzanne. "What's going on, Clark?"

"What are you doing here?" he snapped, still angry from the conversation with his wife.

"I work here, remember? You said you wanted to go over my opening statement tomorrow, so I'm working on it. What was that call all about?"

"My wife. She has a way of pressing my buttons."

"Is there anything I can do?"

"Yeah," he said, almost shouting at her, "Stop asking about my personal life and help me prepare this damn case!"

"Well, when you calm down, let me know," she shot back, turned on her heel, and left.

Clark knew he had been out of line but decided to let some time pass before he talked to her. Later that evening, he walked into Suzanne's office waving a tissue as if it were a white flag of truce.

"Can we talk?" he asked timidly.

"Yes, if you can do so respectfully," she said, without looking up from her work.

"I'm sorry, Suzanne."

"Are you, Clark?" She looked up, eyes blazing. "I've been trying to help you, and yet you treat me like a clerk. And now you've decided you can talk to me that way, too. Well, I'm not gonna put up with it. I'm your colleague, and you need to treat me that way." Her face was stern and her jaw clenched, but her cheeks were flushed. Clark could see that she was serious and furious at the same time.

"You're absolutely right, Suzanne. I've been a jerk, and I apologize. I was a jerk to my wife on the phone, and I was a jerk to you. I don't know what's wrong with me. There's just too many things piling up. I lost my dad; I'm feeling the pressure of this trial; and in the middle of everything, my wife leaves me. And then she has the gall to call me and say that everything is my fault—my fault for working hard to give her and our daughter a life that I can assure you she never dreamed of."

"Maybe that's the problem, Clark." Suzanne's voice was soft and comforting. The anger was gone.

"What? What are you talking about?"

"She never dreamed of it, because you and she have dramatically different visions of what you want out of life."

"I don't understand what you mean."

"Look, anyone who knows you knows that you're ambitious and you're willing to work your ass off to get ahead. I was only around Janelle a few times, but she seems to me to be a simple country girl. She wants to grow old in that little town you guys grew up in. She wants to sit in her rocker on the porch and snap beans, or whatever it is old Southern women do."

Clark took a deep breath, sighed, and stared at the lights outside Suzanne's window. "Yeah, I guess I screwed things up."

"It's not a question of screwing things up, Clark. You are who you are, and she is who she is. Maybe the problem is that you two just don't go together."

"But everyone back home always said we were a cute couple."

"Gimme a break. You got married because of that line of bullshit?"

Clark didn't have a good answer and decided not to even try to offer one. After an uncomfortable period of silently staring at each other, Suzanne abruptly changed the subject: "Listen, I got some news about the Gomez trial."

"What?"

"I found out that the military judge they've appointed is a guy named Colonel Walter O'Brien."

"You're shittin' me."

"You know him?"

"Yeah, he was teaching at the JAG School when I was in the Basic Course. I was actually in his Bible study group."

"Bible study?" The look of disbelief on Suzanne's face suggested Clark wasn't living up to the image she had of guys who went to Bible study.

"You're surprised by the fact that I was in a Bible study group?"

"Well, you just don't seem like the Bible-study type, Clark."

"What's that supposed to mean?"

"Nothing. Tell me about Colonel O'Brien."

He began slowly, the sting of her previous comment still fresh. "Well, let's see. He's a straight arrow, as you might imagine. I'm sure he won't be wanting to go to the bars downtown when he gets here. He knows military criminal law backwards and forwards. He's a by-the-book kind of guy, which I think will be good for us. And, I think I have a pretty good reputation with him."

"All that sounds good, but we still have a problem."

"That spider-bite bullshit?" he asked, without attempting to hide his irritation.

"No, no not that." She paused to gather her thoughts. "Major Underwood phoned earlier. He wants us to call him back. It seems his boss, Commander Peterson, is giving him a bunch of crap."

"About what?"

270

"He disagrees with Underwood's conclusion that this is a shaken-baby case."

"Great. Just like the case at Fort Riley," Clark sighed.

Suzanne's expression was pained. "I know Major Green told us that Underwood was good, but I've got a bad feeling. This is the second time that we know of where he went against his boss." Clark sensed that Suzanne's anxiety was kicking in again, which annoyed him. But he knew it was because she was trying to do a good job. He had to admit she was a loyal colleague, and he felt guilty for suspecting that she had given confidential information to Trip.

"Remember, Suzanne, the guy at Fort Sill got convicted. Underwood's side won."

"Yeah, but maybe Peterson is looking for a rematch." Suzanne had an unmatched ability to see the glass as half empty. She could make a baby's baptism depressing.

"Did he say when we should call?" he asked.

"Anytime. He gave me his home number."

"Well, let's do it now. Would you mind calling him? When he gets on the line, I'll go to my office and pick up."

Suzanne dialed the number. "Major Underwood, please. This is Captain Watkins from Fort Clayton... Yes." Suzanne then looked at Clark and put her hand over the mouthpiece of the receiver. "It's his wife. She said he's expecting us... she's going to get him." Clark hurried to his office, picked up the phone, and pressed the button for the extension. Suzanne was speaking. "Hello, sir, this is Captain Watkins, and I believe I now have Captain Clark on the line as well."

"Hello, counselors."

Clark kicked things off. "Sir, we were calling to see if you have had a chance to review the Lydia Mendoza file."

"I have, and I agree with the medical examiner at Gorgas Hospital that this is a classic shaken-baby case."

"Good," Clark said.

"Well, not so good," Underwood replied. "My boss, who's a Navy officer, disagrees with me." The way Underwood said the word "Navy" indicated that the long-standing interservice rivalry between the Army and Navy was continuing in full force at the Armed Forced Institute of Pathology. "He's been contacted by the defense counsel, a Captain Stephens, and he plans to testify for the defense."

"About what? I thought you just said this was a classic shaken-baby case." Clark's response must have lacked sufficient military decorum for Major Underwood.

"Well, Captain Clark." Underwood emphasized Clark's rank, as if to underscore the distance between Clark's and his. "He disagrees with me. His name, by the way, is Howard Peterson, and he's a Navy Commander, which is like a lieutenant colonel in the Army."

"Yes, sir," Clark replied, respectfully trying to reassure the major that he understood that both he and Commander Peterson outranked him. "We're familiar with the Navy's rank structure. So, what does Commander Peterson base his conclusion on?"

"He questions every shaken-baby case we get," Underwood explained, with obvious disgust. "He thinks that other forensic pathologists, including me, are too quick to call a death a homicide and too quick to call an infant death a shaken-baby case. He said there are too many unanswered questions in this case."

"Like what, sir?" Suzanne asked.

"Captain Stephens sent him some sworn statements that said something about a spider bite. But there wasn't any mention of a spider bite in the autopsy report, and I didn't see any evidence of a bite in the photographs."

"Could the child's death have been caused by a spider bite?" Suzanne asked.

"Excuse me just a minute, guys." Major Underwood put his

hand over the mouthpiece, but Clark and Suzanne could still hear him. "Honey, would you please make the kids be quiet? I can barely hear these people. They're in Panama."

Underwood took his hand off the receiver and returned to talking to them. "Sorry about that guys. We're trying to get the kids to bed. Do either of you have kids?"

That question pricked an unhealed wound. "Yes, sir, I have a three-year-old daughter," Clark replied.

"Uh, not yet, sir, but I hope to someday," replied Suzanne. Clark heard a wistfulness in Suzanne's voice that he'd never heard before. He couldn't see her face, because she was in her office, but it sounded like she'd just revealed a side of herself that he didn't know existed.

"Well, they can be a challenge," said Underwood. Now, where were we? Oh, yeah, the spider bite. If she had received a fatal spider bite, the symptoms would have been much more pronounced, and Dr. Gonzalez would have noted them. Although I've never seen a spider bite that was fatal, I have seen a lot of cases like this one. This is a shaken-baby case, guys, plain and simple."

"That's the way we're preparing it, sir," Clark said. "I just hope we don't have any problems with Commander Peterson."

"Well, you should know that Peterson doesn't have any kids. He's not even married. So he's got no real-world experience in this area. I, on the other hand, have five kids, and I've seen it all. Believe me. This is a shaken-baby case."

"Will it make you uncomfortable to take a position in opposition to your boss?" Suzanne asked.

"No way. I do it all the time. I have professional standards that I adhere to, and besides, I want to see this murderer go to jail." He paused for a moment and then added, "If someone did this to one of my little girls, I wouldn't wait for a trial. I'd kill him."

The line was silent for an uncomfortably long time. That kind of passion could backfire at trial. And yet, Major Green had said that Underwood was a compelling witness.

"Are you still there?" asked Underwood.

"Uh, yes, sir," said Clark. "Could you... could you tell me what Commander Peterson is like?"

"Well, he's kinda weird. He keeps to himself a lot. Very bookish. In fact, he went to law school at night. Did you guys know that? And did I mention that he's never been married?"

"I thought you said he was a pathologist," Suzanne interjected.

"He is. He's a medical doctor, and he's board-certified in forensic pathology. But he's also a lawyer. Well, I guess he is. He went to night law school and passed the bar."

"Oh... that's interesting," Suzanne mused.

"And you guys better get ready. He likes to spar with counsel. He thinks he can outwit them."

Clark probed further. "'But you won the argument at Fort Riley, didn't you?"

"Oh, yeah. And it pissed him off. It always pisses him off when my side wins. In fact, I've won more times than he has."

"Do you see any merit to what he's questioning about this case?" Suzanne asked.

"No. If the spider bite had been significant, then the medical examiner would have mentioned it in his report. His conclusion is clear, and I believe the evidence supports it."

Clark decided they needed to wrap up this call, especially since they were intruding on Major Underwood's family time. Also, they needed to do some more homework. "Okay, sir, well, we might need to have another conversation with you, and I suspect that we'll need to call you as a witness."

"Fine with me. I've never been to Panama."

They hung up, and Clark walked back to Suzanne's office. She was sitting at her desk with a puzzled look on her face.

"What do you think?"

"I don't know, Clark. He seems a little weird."

"What do you mean?"

"Did you hear him say all that stuff about killing someone who hurt his child? And why did he make such a big deal about Peterson not being married? It was all just kind of weird."

"Well, in fairness, Suzanne, when he talked about killing someone he was referring to someone shaking his daughter to death. A lot of dads would feel that way. As for the bit about not being married: I don't know. Maybe he was hinting that Peterson is homosexual."

"So? What difference should that make?"

"He'll be testifying in front of a bunch of infantrymen, Suzanne. They're not like the people you went to law school with."

"Don't patronize me, Clark."

"I'm not. Anyway, who knows?" said Clark, shrugging his shoulders and shaking his head. "It doesn't matter. Well... it shouldn't matter. And it doesn't mean Underwood will be a bad witness for us."

"Maybe. But it's not just that he seemed weird. His answers were pretty superficial, too. And he seems so adamant for someone who's relying on what's in the medical examiner's report." She paused for a few moments, collecting her thoughts. "I don't know, Clark. He just seems so weird. Do you think he might be some kind of zealot? All those comments about 'my side' when he was referring to testifying for the prosecution. Do you think he's objective?"

"I don't know. But he's all we've got at this point. And all he's got to go on is the medical examiner's report."

"Yeah. I guess you're right. I just thought there would be more depth to his analysis."

Suzanne now sounded like she was focused on winning, and Clark wanted to encourage that sentiment. He also realized that she had raised some legitimate concerns about Underwood. "You know, Suzanne, maybe we should talk to Major Green again. Would you mind doing that?" She perked up. "See if you can find out how this interplay between Underwood and Peterson played out in his trial at Fort Riley. And find out how deep he got into the technical stuff with Underwood on the stand. I think a lot of that stuff will be over the head of the members of the court-martial. Don't you agree?" She nodded. "And, I guess we should ask Major Green about his cross-examination of Peterson."

"I'm on it, Clark." She seemed pleased that Clark had delegated to her the development of the person who might turn out to be their most important witness.

"We also need to start thinking about how we're going to structure the case," he said. "We'll need Jaime and Carmen Mendoza, of course, and Dr. Gonzalez." He put his elbows on her desk and leaned forward rubbing his forehead. Then he leaned back in the chair. "Jaime said Dr. Gonzalez should be a great witness. He says he's very distinguished-looking—has a thick mane of silver hair and mustache." Clark turned to look out the window and started chewing his thumbnail. "I can't remember the name of the medical examiner or what he looked like."

"Dr. Arias."

"Right. Arias. What's wrong with me, Suzanne? Why can't I remember this stuff?"

"Calm down, Clark. You've got a lot on your mind. Just take a deep breath, relax, and go to your office and start making a list. That's what I do. I make lists. That way, I don't miss anything. And, it calms me down."

"Good idea." He went back to his desk and pulled out a yellow legal pad. The first thing he recalled was that he'd talked with Jaime about re-interviewing Dr. Gonzalez and the medical examiner but hadn't done that yet. He wrote that down as Item #1. What else had he let slip? That anxious, gut-tightening feeling began to creep over him. He struggled to organize his thoughts but made no progress. Suzanne said good night around 9:30, leaving him alone in the office.

It was so quiet he could hear the flourescent lights hum. But it wasn't like the peaceful quiet in the morning before everyone arrived. It was a tense quiet, as if something was lurking in the darkness outside his window and down the hall. He glanced at the clock on his desk. It was almost 11:30. How had so much time passed? He decided to quit for the night.

On the drive home, thoughts of his wife and the trial and all that he needed to be doing kept swirling in his head. As soon as he entered his quarters, he went through his night-time routine as fast as possible and went to bed, hoping sleep would relieve that nagging, anxious feeling. It was no use. He couldn't turn off his mind. He got up and headed for the kitchen but decided against a late-night drink and instead went outside. He laid down on the chaise lounge and looked up at the vast array of stars. He looked to see if John was watching from the tree but saw no sign of him. And then, without thinking, he looked up in the sky and prayed out loud, "God, help me deal with all that I have to do. Please guide me and direct me. Give me peace, so that I may rest and be ready for the challenges that lie ahead." It was almost 2:30 a.m. He got up, went inside, and went to bed.

Finally, sleep came.

CHAPTER TWENTY-THREE

CLARK TELEPHONED JAIME as soon as he got to work the next day. He was anxious to schedule the interviews with the two doctors.

"Jaime, Captain Clark here."

"Yes, sir. Wha's up?"

"You remember we talked about interviewing Dr. Gonzalez and the medical examiner again?"

"Yes, sir. You know I go' statements fro' each o' dem in the file."

"Oh, yeah, I read them. The statements are good, but I also want to ensure that the docs are ready to be cross-examined. Last night, I found out from Major Underwood that Captain Stephens is going to bring up the spider bite."

"How di' he know tha'?"

"Because Stephens sent Commander Peterson the nurse's statement and some other documents that mention the spider bite. Besides, what else has he got?"

"So, Commander Peterson gonna testify fo' the defense again. He nothin' but a fuckin' *maricon*."

Although Clark hadn't been in Panama long, he knew that "maricon" was Panamanian slang for faggot. And, he knew he didn't want to let Jaime start down that road.

"So what if he is, Jaime? He's going to be our opponent; I've got to be prepared to discredit his testimony when I cross-examine him. So, let's get those interviews set up."

Jaime didn't say anything for a few moments, and then, "Tha's wha' I like abou' you, Captain Clark, you workin' har' to nail dis son o' a bi'ch."

"Call me back when you get the interviews lined up, would you? Tell them it's urgent."

Around 2:00 p.m., Jaime phoned and said that he had arranged to conduct both interviews later that afternoon. Impressed that Jaime had responded so quickly, Clark gathered his notes and headed to the CID Office. Jaime came outside when Clark drove up and said he would drive because he had already been to the doctors' offices and knew where they were. That was fine with Clark. He hated driving in downtown Panama.

Dr. Gonzalez's office was in a modern office building in a nice part of town, so Clark was surprised when he walked in and saw the sparse and somewhat tattered *décor* of the waiting room. The floor was covered with light beige tiles, many of which were cracked; there were several mismatched rattan chairs, arranged in no particular order; and the covers on the flickering fluorescent ceiling lights were yellowed and cracked—basically, a pretty grim-looking place for the office of the man who was supposed to be the leading neurosurgeon in Panama.

Some of the patients in the waiting room were dressed in the latest fashions, while others wore threadbare work clothes. But they all bore the same solemn look—a testament to the serious medical issues that Dr. Gonzalez handled. Heads turned when Jaime and Clark walked in, and expressions changed from solemn to bewildered. Under the circumstances, that was understandable: a big, burly Hispanic guy wearing a guayabera and a Norteamericano in an Army uniform, walking into a doctor's office in downtown Panama. That *was* a bit unusual. The patients continued to stare until an attractive nurse, wearing a 1950s-style, immaculate white uniform and cap, came out to the waiting room and said something to Jaime in Spanish. He signaled Clark. "Le's go."

They walked down a narrow hallway into Dr. Gonzalez's private office, which, in contrast to the waiting room, was nicely furnished. The doctor was sitting in a high-backed leather chair behind a massive carved mahogany desk. Behind him were two matching bookcases, full of books and framed family photographs. Original artwork adorned the walls, which were covered with what appeared to be expensive flocked wallpaper. Jaime was right about Dr. Gonzalez's appearance: Hollywood could not have selected a better person to play the role of the distinguished surgeon.

As soon as they sat down, Dr. Gonzalez began. "Gentlemen, I do not mean to be rude, but I am very busy today. Agent Hernandez has told me about the urgency of this meeting, and so, I made room for it on my schedule. Please forgive me, though, if we get straight to the point and move this along."

"That is perfectly fine with me, Doctor Gonzalez," Clark began. "Thank you for seeing us on such short notice." Pulling a yellow legal pad from his briefcase, he continued, "I know that you have provided a sworn statement to Agent Hernandez, but I was wondering if you might also tell me what you remember about this case in your own words."

"Well…" He stroked his mustache with his thumb and index finger. "It was a terrible case. That beautiful little girl… just terrible. By the time I got to her, there was little that I could do. She had severe brain edema."

"Excuse me for interrupting, Doctor Gonzalez, but we'll need to explain words like 'edema' to the members of the court-martial. And remember, when you testify, I'll ask you questions, but you should look at the members when you give your answers. And when we're finished, the defense counsel will cross-examine you."

"Yes, Capitain, I have testified before," he said with raised eyebrows and a shake of his head. He stared at Clark for a few moments and then continued, "Several years ago, I testified in a case at Fort Clayton involving a terrible car accident, in which someone was killed."

"I'm sorry, Doctor, I should have asked you about your prior experience with military courts-martial."

"No pro'lem, Capitain Clark. As I was saying, this little girl was in very bad shape by the time I saw her. A young Army doctor called me in, and he assisted me. I do not remember his name, but I can get it for you if it's important."

"I' do dat, Doctor," Jaime said.

"Thank you, Agent Hernandez." Turning back toward Clark, Dr. Gonzalez continued, "We tried to reduce the edema—the swelling—by giving her dexamethasone, which is a steroid. But it wasn't effective. So we went to surgery, and I removed a piece of her skull in an effort to provide more room for the brain. Unfortunately, her brain pressed out of the opening. I told the nurse to give the child ten more milligrams of dexamethasone. The capitain was worried about damage to her liver, but I tol' him that we could not worry about that. I tol' him the child would die if we could not stop the swelling. We watched the monitors for a long time. Maybe forty-five minutes or an hour. I cannot remember. We watched the signal on the heart monitor get weaker and weaker, as the little girl faded away from us. Nothing we did made any difference. We watched the monitors. And then..." Dr. Gonzalez took off his glasses and raked his fingers through his mane of silver hair. He pulled a handkerchief from his pocket and wiped his eyes. "I'm sorry, gentlemen. This was a very difficult case for me. There was nothing I could do. Her condition was too serious by the time I was brought in. I don' think the capitain could have done anything either. The little girl's condition was jus' too serious.

"The capitain had a very difficult time with it. It was the firs' time he had lost a patient. I tol' him that it is part of the job. In my field…," the doctor's voice faltered, "it happens all too often. I tol' him he must shield his psyche. As you can see by looking at me now, that is difficult to do." He forced a smile. "We cannot allow ourselves to become too emotionally involved, but sometimes that is difficult, too."

"I think I understand, Dr. Gonzalez. I got a taste of what you're talking about at the autopsy. As Jaime will tell you, I didn't do too well."

"You di' fine, Capitain Clark."

"Well, gentlemen, this was a terrible, terrible case."

Thinking forward to the trial, Clark hoped Dr. Gonzalez would come up with another adjective besides "terrible," although it wasn't the right time to make a suggestion.

"What do you think caused her brain to swell like that?"

"Well, I was told she had been shaken. Isn't that what you said, Agent Hernandez?"

Good grief. Clark couldn't believe that Jaime had made a suggestion like that during a fact-gathering interview. Clark shot a glance at Jaime, who nodded awkwardly in response to the doctor's question and then looked down.

"We must be careful, Doctor, to stick with what you saw," Clark said. "Otherwise, the defense counsel will object that your testimony is based on hearsay."

"Oh, I understand. Well, I could say that her brain edema could have been caused by shaking her. The brain of a child that young is not fully grown. When they are shaken, the brain rattles around inside the skull and can become bruised. The bruising often leads to edema. Therefore, what I observed with this child is consistent with cases where a baby was shaken."

"Could anything else have caused it?" Clark asked.

"Well, I suppose the baby could have fallen, but that usually leaves a big bump on their heads. This baby did not have a bump."

"Did you see any evidence of a spider bite?"

"Spider bite?"

"Yes. The accused is claiming that the baby was bitten by a spider a few days before you saw her."

"Well, no. I did not see a bite, but then, I was focused on addressing the baby's brain edema. I did not perform a complete examination. There was no time for that."

"Do you think a spider bite could have caused the edema?"

"I have never seen a spider bite cause edema of the brain. A bite from a black widow spider can cause neurologic symptoms, but nothing as severe as the brain edema this little girl had."

"Thank you, Doctor. Is there anything else I should know?"

"No, Capitain, I just hope you bring this man to justice." Dr. Gonzalez pushed a document across the desk in Clark's direction. "I think this might be useful to you. It is my *curriculum vitae*. It lists all of my credentials and will help you establish that I am an expert in the field of neurosurgery." He stared at Clark for what seemed like several minutes. "This was a terrible crime against a precious little girl, Capitain Clark. I hope you can bring this man to justice."

"We're going to try to, Doctor. Thank you for your time. When I learn the details of the date and time of trial, I'll be in touch. Oh, and by the way, if you are ever asked what I told you to say when you testify, would you please say that I told you to tell the truth, the whole truth, and nothing but the truth?"

"Certainly, Capitain Clark. That is what I will do. And, please give me as much notice of the trial as possible, so that I can arrange my schedule."

"Yes, sir. Thank you for your time." Clark stood up, and then Jaime stood up. They each shook hands with Dr. Gonzalez and then walked out to the hallway where the nurse who had shown them in was waiting. She escorted them out.

Back in the car, Jaime began. "I thin' tha' wen' very well."

"Well, I can't believe I didn't ask him about his credentials," Clark said.

"Tha's okay, Capitain Clark, I forge' to as' thin's like tha' sometimes. He was jus' tryin' to be helpful. I like the way you tol' him to tell the truth."

"Well, I meant it." Clark looked straight ahead and said nothing for a few moments. "I'm still pissed off at myself, though, for forgetting to ask him about his credentials. That was stupid. You know, Jaime, it's the little things that can cause you to lose a case." He turned and looked at Jaime with wide eyes. "I didn't even ask him how many shaken-baby cases he'd seen, for chrissake. I didn't ask him if there was other evidence indicating that Lydia had been shaken. Damn it! I was sloppy."

"Tell you wha', Capitain Clark," Jaime said in a calm voice, "when you ge' back to the office, si' down and write down everythin' you can thin' abou'. Den, pu' the lis' in a drawer and wai' 'til tomorrow. Den, take i' ou' again an' read i'. If you lef' somethin' off, you'll pro'ly thin' of i', an' den I can take the questions to Dr. Gonzalez an' ge' dem answered for you."

"Couldn't I just call him?"

"I don' thin' he woul' take the call, Capitain Clark. Doctors in Panama are a big deal. You have to come see dem."

"Really?" Jaime nodded. "Okay. Well, I'll do that. I'll get you the list of questions tomorrow. I should have done that before we came down here." Clark stared ahead for a few moments and then added, "Oh, and by the way, thanks."

"No pro'lem, Capitain Clark. You still wanna see the medical examiner, don' you?"

"Oh yeah."

As Jaime navigated his way down Panama City's potholed

streets, Clark was, again, glad that Jaime was driving. The streets were crowded with brightly colored chiva buses, some of which had elaborate murals painted on the sides. There were dented and rusty compact cars and people on scooters and bicycles. And no one seemed to give much regard to traffic rules. Most of the buses and cars spewed out smoke, indicating their valve seals were shot. The heat, the smoke, the swerving through traffic, and the tension created by the task at hand combined to make Clark nauseated, which caused his stomach to heave. When they got close to the medical examiner's office, which was near Gorgas hospital, the traffic eased, so Clark opened his window to get some fresh air.

Although Gorgas was an Army hospital, it was not fully staffed with Army doctors. Many of the doctors were Panamanian civilians, like Dr. Gonzalez, who worked part time and were called upon when their particular skills were needed. Because the medical examiner was one of the doctors who had been associated with Gorgas for a long time, his office was nearby. The neighborhood was not as affluent as the neighborhood where Dr. Gonzalez's office was located, but the office itself was nicer. Although it wasn't lavish, everything in it was clean and orderly. As they walked in the door, Clark saw a sign, which read: "Doctor José Ramone Arias." Why did he have so much trouble remembering that name?

Jaime approached the receptionist, an attractive woman who appeared to be in her mid-twenties. She was wearing a tasteful, but rather tight, dress, which showcased her ample bosom. Jaime spoke to her in Spanish and then came back to get Clark.

Jaime walked toward Clark with a big smile on his face. "Di' you see the rack on tha' one?"

"Hard to miss it, Jaime," said Clark, staring intently at nothing. He was too anxious about handling this interview properly to join Jaime in what seemed to be his favorite pastime. Soon, the young woman with the shapely figure escorted them into Dr.

Arias's private office, which was also nice, but starkly utilitarian, in contrast to Dr. Gonzalez's. Jaime did some preliminary explanation in Spanish, and then Dr. Arias turned to Clark. "What would you like to ask me, Capitain Clark?"

"First of all, Doctor, thank you for seeing us on such short notice."

"I am happy to do so, Capitain."

"I know you have prepared a detailed report of your autopsy of Lydia Mendoza, but I was wondering if you would please describe again what you saw."

"Certainly." Dr. Arias then proceeded to recite, almost verbatim, what he had written in the autopsy report.

This man was certainly proud of what he wrote. When he finished, Clark asked, "Is there anything else you would like to tell us about this case? Anything that we should know?"

"I don't understand, Capitain Clark. What else would there be? I tol' you that there was evidence of multiple blunt force injuries and of sexual assault."

"Did you see any evidence of a spider bite?"

"A spider bite?"

"Yes."

"No, Capitain Clark. This little girl had been—how do you say—'manhandled.' She was bruised on her legs, and there were bruises around her vaginal area."

"So that's why you concluded that she'd been sexually assaulted?"

"Those injuries are consistent with a sexual assault."

"It's hard to imagine, Dr. Arias, how such a small child could be sexually assaulted. Could you explain?"

"Certainly. And it is, indeed, disgusting, Capitain Clark. But I've seen it before. The little girl's hymen was intact, but the tissue around her vagina was bruised, suggesting that it had been manipulated in some way, perhaps by the assailant's finger."

That description gave Clark a mental image of what must have happened, and it made him sick. He stared at Dr. Arias in silence for a few moments.

"Is everything all right, Captain Clark?"

"Uh, yes. Everything is all right. You are correct, Dr. Arias. It is a disgusting thought. Could anything else have caused it?"

"Perhaps the little girl fell on something, but I do not think a fall would have produced the kind of bruises she had."

"In any event, those bruises were not related to the injuries that caused her death, were they?"

"Only in the sense that they were evidence that she had been manhandled and shaken."

"And you still believe that her injuries support the conclusion that she was shaken to death?"

"Yes. And sexually assaulted."

"Okay. Well, I think that's about it, Doctor. Jaime, did you have anything?"

"No."

"Well, Dr. Arias, I will try to find out as soon as possible what the schedule for trial is, and I'll let you know."

"Thank you, Captain Clark. I would appreciate receiving as much notice as possible."

"Of course. By the way Doctor, could I have a copy of your *curriculum vitae*? I'll need it to establish you as an expert witness."

"Certainly. I think this is all you will need, Captain." Arias picked up an envelope on his desk and handed it to Clark. It had a typed label on it that read:

Curriculum Vitae
of
Dr. José Ramone Arias, M.D.
for
Captain Robert E. Clark,
Judge Advocate, Fort Clayton

Clark and Jaime stood up, and each of them shook Dr. Arias's hand. Back in Jaime's car, they rode in silence for a while.

"I thin' you' ready, Captain Clark."

"Well, at least I remembered the damn c.v. But I'm still… Crap, Jaime!"

"Wha'?"

"It just dawned on me that I forgot to ask Dr. Arias about how many infant autopsies he'd performed and how many of them were shaken-baby cases. Within the span of less than two hours, I've made the same stupid mistake twice. What's wrong with me?"

"Don' be so har' on yourself, Captain Clark. Dis is no' easy"

Clark stared ahead for a couple of minutes. "What did you think about all that stuff about sexual assault?"

"I don' thin' dere is enough evidence to convic' Gomez of sexual assual'. I thin' I woul' jus' stick wid the murder charge. O'herwise, the members of the cour' martial will ge' confuse'."

"Yeah. I'm sure you're right. Would you mind taking some questions to Arias, too?"

"No pro'lem, Captain Clark. You write dem down, an' I ge' dem answered."

"Thanks, Jaime." For a few minutes Clark mentally recapped the two interviews and then said, "I've got to ask you a question, Jaime."

"Wha'?"

"I thought Dr. Gonzalez was this big deal neurosurgeon, and yet his office looked like crap, while Dr. Arias—who is a nice guy and all, but not as important as Dr. Gonzalez—had a relatively nice office. I don't get it."

"Well, Dr. Gonzalez is rich, bu' he don' want to look rich. Dr. Arias is doin' okay, bu' he no' rich, an' so, he tryin' to look

288

like a big deal, especially for the Americans. Tha's why he go' tha' job a' Gorgas."

"I don't follow you."

"Capitain Clark, in dis country, i' you rich, somebody gonna wan' somethin' from you. So, Dr. Gonzalez don' wanna attract no attention."

"Oh, I see." Clark nodded. How could he ever describe this hot, crazy place to the folks back home?

CHAPTER TWENTY-FOUR

CLARK'S MEETINGS WITH Dr. Gonzalez and Dr. Arias did little to boost his spirits. In the past, he'd always been able to gain confidence by thoroughly preparing for whatever tasks lay ahead of him. But that tactic wasn't working this time. As the trial date grew near, his anxiety increased. Despite devoting an enormous amount of effort to preparing for trial, he didn't feel confident. He got in the habit of checking the telephone in his quarters several times each evening to see if he might catch Trip and his father talking on the party line. Each time he tried, he resolved never to do it again. But his resolve always succumbed to his anxiety. In the end, it didn't matter. He never heard them again. He did, however, learn that Angela and Roy—his neighbors across the street—were expecting another baby and that Angela liked to talk on the phone—a lot. And, from that first call with Trip and his father, he'd learned that Trip would probably try to paint Carmen as an unfit mother—a woman who went out partying, instead of taking care of her baby. Major Green had warned him to be ready for that defense strategy. Clark knew he needed to be ready to respond.

He and Suzanne pored over every document in the CID report, and Clark read every case in the Military Justice Reporter that dealt with child abuse, even though he had previously read

Suzanne's summaries of those cases. All of his hard work failed to decrease his anxiety, but it did have a profound effect on him. The more he prepared the case and studied the autopsy report and other evidence, the more he saw Raul Gomez as a monster. He had a mental image of Gomez shaking the life out of little Lydia Mendoza. He thought about describing Gomez as a "monster"— a monster that weighed ten times what Lydia Mendoza weighed when he violently shook her to death.

The tension was constant. On the one hand, he felt he could never prepare enough to know—deep down—that he was ready. On the other, he wanted to do everything within his power to put Raul Gomez behind bars for a long time. Feeling particularly uneasy one afternoon, he decided to bounce some ideas off Suzanne. He went to her office and dropped into a chair across from her, the way she often did in his office. She was writing something that she apparently wanted to finish before engaging in conversation. While he waited, he glanced around her office. Like Suzanne, everything in it was neat and orderly—plain, but neat and orderly. No family pictures or anything else to personalize it. The only thing hanging on the wall was her diploma from the University of Dayton School of Law. Not a top-tier law school, he thought, but maybe that's all she could afford. Finally, she looked up.

"What brings you here, Counselor?"

"I'd like to brainstorm with you a little bit."

"Okay." What had been the hint of a grin widened into a big smile. Clearly, she was pleased to be consulted on his trial strategy.

"I don't know whether Trip will put Gomez on the stand…"

"Judging from his past performance, he'll do whatever is the easiest."

"Maybe. But if he puts Gomez on, I need to be ready to cross-examine him."

"Well, I've been working on that, Clark. I think…"

"Yeah, but that's not why I came here."

"Okay. Then why did you come here?"

"I'm thinking he won't put Gomez on the stand and risk having him incriminate himself."

"That's probably right."

"So, I think our most important witness just might be Carmen Mendoza. What do you think?"

"Possibly."

"Think about it. Even though Major Underwood will be important, it is Carmen who can establish the timeline when Lydia was with Gomez. And more important, she can help us appeal to the emotions of the members of the court-martial and focus them on the fact that Lydia was a living, breathing little girl, whose life Gomez ended before it had a chance to begin."

"You sound like you're making your closing argument already," she teased. But when his expression immediately darkened, she realized she'd touched a raw nerve. "No… no, Clark, I think it's good. A little passion in a prosecutor is a good thing."

"Well, I've been thinking. As important as Carmen is, her testimony needs to be great. But you know she'll be nervous. She's just a kid, and on top of that, she'll be coming to a courtroom on Fort Clayton, not the Enlisted Club."

"And, she'll be testifying about the baby she lost just a few weeks ago," Suzanne offered.

"Good point. So, what do you think about having Jaime bring her to the courtroom one evening this week? We can show her what the courtroom looks like, where she'll be sitting, and all that. We could even let her sit on the witness stand. You know, let her get used to the surroundings. Don't you think that would help her to be less nervous at trial?"

"I think that's a great idea. What can I do to help?"

"Well, I'd like for you to be there. Jaime came on kind of

strong when we met her at her parents' apartment downtown. Besides, she's pretty, young, female…"

"So, you want a woman present. I get it." She pursed her thick lips as if she was getting ready to spit.

"Spare me the feminist, crap, Suzanne. You're my colleague. I want your help as a lawyer *and* as a woman."

She blew out a sigh and said, "Well… all right."

Clark returned to his office, called Jaime, and explained his plan. Jaime agreed to contact Carmen and arrange a time. Later that afternoon, Jaime called back and said he would bring Carmen to the office that evening at 1800 hours.

Promptly at the appointed time, Jaime and Carmen arrived, and the group gathered in the reception area. When Clark introduced Suzanne and Carmen to each other, Suzanne eyed the young woman from top to bottom—like the president of a high school science club might check out the head cheerleader. A study in contrasts. Suzanne: frumpy, overweight, unattractive, but well educated and smart. Carmen: fresh, beautiful, voluptuous, but poor and uneducated. He hoped Suzanne's icey stare wasn't a sign that she was about to lose perspective.

After the introductions were over, Clark left to check the defense counsel's offices, which were adjacent to the courtroom. He wanted to ensure they wouldn't be observed or overheard. The door from the courtroom to the defense counsel's outer office was unlocked, which wasn't unusual, so he went in to verify that everyone had gone home.

Surveying the room, he envisioned how things would change when Specialist Weeks was arrested. Despite all the activity surrounding the Gomez trial, everything was in order—no documents, files, or books lying around. He looked at her desk. The only thing on it was a photograph of what looked like Weeks as a little girl and a black man in Army fatigues, kneeling beside her. Probably her father.

She was such an enigma. Her uniform, her demeanor, even her desk—everything suggested she was a model soldier—and yet, she was involved in serious criminal activity. And, of course, she had been consorting with at least one married man, who happened to be his boss. And maybe Major Darst, too. Clark couldn't understand. She appeared to be so professional. But, he didn't have time to think about that. He made a mental note to remember to ask Jaime if her arrest could be delayed until after the Gomez trial was over. He didn't want to give Trip an excuse for delaying the trial.

When Clark returned to the courtroom, Jaime was explaining something to Carmen in Spanish, and Suzanne was quietly watching them. When Jaime finished, he looked at Clark as if to say "your turn." Clark began to speak to Carmen in English.

"Do you understand what will take place here?" Carmen stared at him blankly. "Do you understand that this is where the court-martial will take place?"

"Cour'-mar... *No entiendo.*"

"A court-martial. It's like a trial in court."

"*Entiendo.*"

"Let's stick to English, Ms. Mendoza. You will need to testify in English at the court-martial. You can do that, can't you?"

"Yes. I' goin' to testify?"

"Yes. You will be a witness in the court-martial. I will ask you questions, and you must answer them. Do you understand?"

"Yes. You wan' me to talk abou' Raul?"

"Sort of. I want you to answer my questions about what happened the night you left Lydia with Raul."

"You wan' me to tell you now?"

"No... no." Clark stopped and stared at her, which caused her to suddenly look frightened.

Suzanne finally said what everyone had been thinking, "We're going to need an interpreter."

"No!" Clark shot back. "There are a million ways the translation process can get fouled up, Suzanne. I want the members of the court-martial to hear her testimony from her, not some interpreter, who will probably be a man, by the way." He emphasized the word "man" for Suzanne's benefit.

Suzanne walked over to Carmen and held both of her hands. "Do you understand that Raul might go to jail? Carmen nodded her head. "Do you understand that we believe he is the one who killed Lydia?"

"Yes," Carmen replied, shaking her head. The tears that had been pooling in her eyes began to stream down her face.

"Do you think you can testify in English?" Suzanne continued. "Yes."

Despite Carmen's responses, Clark wasn't sure she understood the gravity of the situation. He asked Suzanne to have Carmen sit on the witness stand, then went to his office and retrieved the case files. When he returned, he took the autopsy photographs out of the folder and started toward the witness stand. Suzanne stepped in his way. "She understands, Clark. Now, you're just being insensitive. Stop it." Her voice was calm, but firm.

"All right." Clark closed the file folder and laid it on the counsel's table. Turning back to Carmen, who was still seated on the witness stand, he asked, "Carmen, do you understand that the evidence we have clearly shows that Raul shook Lydia to death? It's not our opinion. It is a fact."

She nodded yes. Jaime started speaking to her in Spanish again. Clark understood little of what he was saying because he was talking so fast, although judging from how animated he was, Clark suspected Jaime was furthering the argument that Carmen's brother-in-law was, without a doubt, guilty. Carmen's lips began to quiver, and within moments she began to cry so intensely that she gasped for breath. Suzanne snapped, "We're going to take a break." She took Carmen's hand and escorted her out the door toward the women's latrine.

After they left, Jaime said, "Dis is a really goo' idea, Captain Clark. She gonna do a lo' better jo' on the stan' at trial, now tha' she seen the cour'room."

"I hope so. That's the idea, anyway. I hope she hasn't used up all those tears. We're going to need them at trial." Jaime raised his eyebrows and nodded yes. "Do you think she's worried about testifying against her brother-in-law?" Clark asked.

"No' anymore," said Jaime. "You an' Captain Wa'kins tol' her, an' I tol' her tha' the son-o'-bitch kille' her daughter. Her baby come firs'. I don' thin' she tha' close to her bro'her-in-law anyway."

Suzanne and Carmen walked back in. Carmen had washed her face and seemed to have composed herself. Suzanne asked her to sit on the witness stand again and explained where the judge and the members of the court-martial would be during the trial, as well as where Gomez and Trip would be.

Clark studied Carmen. She was wearing a pair of frayed shorts, a faded blouse, and sandals. "Jaime would you explain to Carmen what she needs to wear at the trial?" Clark wanted to be certain she looked the part of the grieving mother, both on the stand and in the gallery.

"Sure, Capitan, Clark. Wha' you wan' me to tell her?"

Clark searched for the words to describe what he wanted. "Tell her to dress like she's going to church. That should present the right image and underscore the seriousness of the proceeding." Jaime said a few words to Carmen in Spanish, and she nodded her head.

Clark was still concerned about the need for an interpreter, especially in anticipation of Trip's cross-examination. He stared at Carmen and slowly explained, "If anyone asks you a question that you don't understand, you should look at the judge, who will be sitting here." He walked over to the bench and put his hand on top of it. "And say that you don't understand." What Clark was thinking, but didn't say, was that if Trip bears down on you too hard, my dear, the sympathies of the members of the court-martial will be with you, especially if you cry. At least, he hoped it would work that way.

Clark then finished with what, by now, was his standard interview closing. "Always tell the truth, Carmen, and if anyone asks you what I told you to say, tell them that Captain Clark told me to tell the truth no matter what. Will you do that?"

"*Si, Señor.* I mean, yes. Yes. The whole tru', no matter wha'."

Clark smiled and nodded his head. He turned to Jaime and asked him to take Carmen back to her parents' apartment. Shortly after they left, Suzanne said she was going to get some dinner and asked Clark if he wanted to join her. He declined. She gathered her things and left him alone in the darkened courtroom.

He sat at the counsel's table for a long time, thinking about what was going to happen there. This trial would probably be the most important one of his JAG career, and yet it was only his second. He couldn't think of anything else he could do to prepare. He rubbed his fingers on his temples and forehead. He felt just like he did before he took the Scholastic Aptitude Test. If he hadn't done well on that test, there would have been no West Point, no law school, no life outside of Pemberton. He took a deep breath and blew it out, as if that might clear his head.

He kept recalling what the criminal law professors at the JAG School used to say: "a squad of facts can defeat an army of law." In other words, focus on the evidence. That rule had not applied to his first trial, which he won with a motion *in limine*— a purely "legal" maneuver. This trial would be different. The evidence would determine the outcome. And it wouldn't be enough to simply state the facts. He would have to present the evidence and make his arguments in such a way that the members of the court-martial would have to conclude that Raul Gomez killed Lydia Mendoza. He had to be part motivational speaker, part showman, and part lawyer. And he had no idea how to pull that off. His fledgling confidence sunk again.

On the way home he stopped by the post office to check his mailbox and found a letter from his mother. When he got home, he poured some Maker's Mark over ice—Elmer had suggested he might like it more than Jack Daniels—and steeled himself to read the words he was dreading. He turned on the porch light, walked out to the terrace, and sat down at the picnic table. "Well, she certainly got straight to the point in her opening line, John," he said, looking up in the tree, expecting to see his green nemesis staring back. "She says the word around Pemberton is that Janelle and Ellie are not going back to Panama." He looked down at the letter and read a few more lines. The paper fluttered as his hands began to tremble ever so slightly. "She wants to know what's going on." His voice cracked, so he took another sip of bourbon to sooth his throat. "She wants to know why I haven't said anything about it to her." He put the letter down and took a long drink. "I'm not going to drag my mom into this mess with Janelle." His voice was disgusted and angry. "You know what that's like, don't you, Johnny Boy? You got her fired up by just showing up in the backyard." He looked down at the letter again. "My mom has enough to worry about. She doesn't need to be worrying about me. I'd better answer her tonight."

He stood up, a little wobbly. The bourbon was kicking in. He went inside, set his drink and the letter on the dining room table, and headed to his desk. His mother had given him some writing paper for his birthday; he figured this was an appropriate time to use it. He topped off his drink and sat down to compose the letter. He knew Janelle and Ellie were not coming back. His stomach tightened, and his throat felt hot and constricted. He took another long drink.

After all that his mother had been through, he couldn't let her get drawn into his mess. It was his job to fix things. Leaning back in his chair, he stared at the ceiling and hoped for inspiration. He had to be very careful. She was still grieving and emotionally fragile. After collecting his thoughts, he bent over the table and wrote her a short letter, telling her that he and Janelle had had some disagreements, but after he got this trial behind him, he would resolve things with her. That was the truth of course. He wanted to focus on the trial, get it finished, and then deal with his damaged relationship with Janelle. He hoped this letter, though short, would put his mother's mind at ease. He thought about writing Janelle, too, but he was too tired. He resolved to write her the next day.

CHAPTER TWENTY-FIVE

JUDGE O'BRIEN WAS not happy. The Gomez trial was supposed to have begun at 8:00 a.m., but it didn't get started until almost 11:00. Fortunately for Clark, he had nothing to do with the delay, which was at Trip's request. Clark suspected that Trip might have been trying to convince his client to plead guilty. Whatever the reason, the late start meant they didn't get much accomplished the first day. The judge took Gomez's plea of not guilty. Then, Trip and Clark went through the process of questioning and selecting the members of the court-martial, known as *voir dire*, and the judge ruled on their objections to some of the proposed members. By noon, they had a court-martial panel comprised of two Infantry captains and five sergeants—two senior NCOs and three buck sergeants. One of the senior NCOs and two of the buck sergeants appeared to be Hispanic. While Judge O'Brien was instructing them prior to recessing for lunch, Clark studied their faces. They were stern, serious, and intently focused on the proceedings. A good sign for the prosecution.

When the court reconvened after lunch, the trial got underway in earnest. Suzanne made the opening statement for the government. No poem included. She outlined for the members of the court-martial what was going to happen during the trial and what the evidence would show—in effect, giving them a preview, just as Clark had suggested. Clark and Suzanne had rehearsed her performance several times, including twice in the courtroom. As a result, her delivery was outstanding. Her best passages came dangerously close to arguing what the members should conclude from the evidence, though she didn't cross that line. In opening statements attorneys are prohibited from arguing what inferences should be drawn from the evidence. They must stick to "what the evidence will show."

The best part of her opening statement was when she gave a preview of the evidence: "Gentlemen, Carmen Mendoza, Lydia's mother, will tell you that she left her child with the accused, who happens to be married to Carmen's sister. Ms. Mendoza will tell you that Lydia was alone with the accused for over six hours on the evening of December 18, 1982, that the next morning Lydia was lethargic, and that she was unable to wake her. Ms. Mendoza will tell you that the accused took her and her baby to Gorgas Hospital. But it was too late. Although Lydia was operated on by Dr. Roberto Gonzalez, one of the leading neurosurgeons in Panama, he was unable to save her. Dr. Gonzalez will tell you that Lydia's brain swelled inside her skull and that the swelling—called edema—is what killed her. Dr. Gonzalez will also tell you that the injuries he observed on Lydia were consistent with her having been shaken violently. Dr. José Arias, the medical examiner who performed the autopsy on Lydia, will also tell you that Lydia's injuries were consistent with a violent shaking. And finally, you will hear from Major Horace Underwood, a medical doctor assigned to the Armed Forces Institute of Pathology. Major Underwood examined all of the evidence in the case, including samples taken during the autopsy. He will provide his expert medical opinion concerning what happened to little Lydia. He, too, will tell you that her injuries indicate that she was violently shaken to death. As you listen to that evidence, gentlemen, ask yourselves who had the opportunity to commit this crime against this precious child? Who had the ability to violently shake that little girl to death? Those are important questions for you to consider as you see and hear the evidence."

After Suzanne finished and sat down, Trip made a short opening statement for the defense. "Gentlemen, it is a tragedy that Lydia Mendoza has died. There's no getting around that. But it would compound that tragedy if you convict Raul Gomez of killing her, because the evidence will show he didn't. The evidence will show that Lydia died from a spider bite—a spider bite that need not have been fatal. Had Lydia's mother taken her to the doctor sooner, she might be alive today. Instead, gentlemen, Lydia's mother—Carmen Mendoza—was more interested in going to night clubs than she was in taking care of her sick baby. She left her child with her brother-in-law, Raul Gomez, while she went out on the town. And although Specialist Gomez is a good soldier and a good father, he was ill-equipped to deal with Lydia's condition. He lacked the sensitivity of a good mother. But unfortunately, so did Carmen Mendoza. While she was drinking and partying with the man who got her pregnant in the first place, her baby got sicker and sicker. The next morning—after Carmen had been out all night—it was Specialist Gomez who insisted on taking Lydia to the hospital. But unfortunately, it *was* too late. It's horrible that this little baby died, gentlemen. But the evidence will show that her death was not at the hand of Specialist Gomez. After you see and hear that evidence, you will know what your duty is. You will know that you must return a finding of not guilty. Thank you."

Even though Trip crossed the line and started arguing his case, Clark didn't object. He felt it was best to say nothing. He didn't think Trip had done any real damage and wanted to avoid giving the impression he was worried about anything Trip had said. As Trip was wrapping up his opening, Clark again studied the faces of the members of the court-martial but saw nothing to indicate they had been moved.

Trip's opening statement was baffling. Maligning Carmen made no sense. That approach would backfire if the members of the panel felt sorry for this young mother. And it had little connection with Trip's principal argument that Gomez shouldn't be held responsible for failing to detect that Lydia was sick from a spider bite. But even with that argument, Trip would have a tough time of it. Raul Gomez fathered, and was raising, three children, the eldest of whom was seven years old. The members of the court-martial would surely conclude that Gomez should have been able to detect that Lydia was very sick. And how could Trip explain the bruises and other evidence indicating that Lydia had been mistreated?

Clark recalled that when he eavesdropped on the conversation between Trip and his father, he heard Judge Stephens tell Trip to make the victim's mother out to be a slut. Even though that advice was baseless, Trip seemed to be following it to the letter. Did it occur to him that his father didn't know the facts of this case—that he shot from the hip with his advice and was probably half-drunk when he did? Perhaps the Stephens legal dynasty was not such a formidable opponent after all.

As the trial proceeded in the courtroom, Carmen and Jaime waited out of sight in an unused office in the Legal Assistance Section. When it became apparent that Carmen would not be called to testify that day, Clark sent word to Jaime to take her home. Judge O'Brien instructed Clark to be ready to put on witnesses the next morning at 0800 hours. He then sent the members of the court-martial home with instructions not to talk about the case with anyone.

The next day the trial started on schedule. Suzanne led off by questioning Dr. Arias, whom she quickly qualified as an expert witness. He testified by giving an almost verbatim recital of his autopsy report—just as he had done when Clark and Jaime questioned him in his office. When Dr. Arias got to the part about sexual abuse, the members of the court-martial leaned forward, waiting for some salacious testimony that never came. The only evidence supporting the conclusion that Lydia had been sexually assaulted was the presence of bruises around her groin. Suzanne and Clark had decided it couldn't hurt to mention it, and it definitely caused the members of the court-martial to perk up. The main purpose of Dr. Arias's testimony was to present his conclusion that Lydia died from having been shaken violently.

Trip's cross-examination of Dr. Arias was weak. Surprisingly, he didn't ask a single question about the spider bite. Clark guessed that Trip was adhering to the old advice about cross-examination: don't ask a question unless you know what the answer will be. Trip could've easily learned Arias's answer to the spider-bite question if he had bothered to call him as a witness at the Article 32 hearing, which had taken place weeks before. His failure to do so was a big mistake.

Dr. Gonzalez was next. Suzanne also took his testimony, and it could not have gone better. First of all, his appearance was perfect—distinguished, confident, compassionate. He told the members of the court-martial how he attempted to save "this precious little girl," but was unable to do so. And, like Dr. Arias, he concluded that Lydia died from having been shaken violently.

Again, Trip's cross-examination was weak. Again, he didn't ask Dr. Gonzalez about the spider bite. And again, Clark was puzzled. It was odd—and very risky—for Trip to fail to ask these two doctors about the central thesis of his defense. Even if they had testified that they had seen no evidence of a spider bite, Trip could have impugned the quality of their work by later introducing clear evidence of the spider bite, assuming he had some.

Suzanne had done a good job with her opening statement and direct examinations of Dr. Arias and Dr. Gonzalez. Now, it was Clark's turn. He wanted to personally conduct the direct examination of Major Underwood, whose testimony would be complicated and yet extremely important. Clark hoped Undewood would bring a degree of scientific authority to the conclusions of the two medical doctors who had just testified.

Considering the composition of the court-martial panel, Underwood's appearance could not have been better. He looked like a model soldier as he strode to the witness stand—big and tall and in good physical condition. His blonde hair was cut short, and his uniform was impeccable. A Meritorious Service Medal and Airborne wings were on display above his left pocket. More important than his appearance was his performance as a witness. Clark asked him some preliminary questions to qualify him as an expert and then just backed off and let him go.

"How many cases involving these kinds of injuries have you been involved in, Major Underwood?"

"Seven."

"That's quite a few, isn't it?"

"Yes, but it's seven too many if you ask me. I've focused much of my research and work on shaken-baby cases because it's such a despicable crime—grown adults inflicting terminal injuries on defenseless children."

"Objection, Your Honor." Trip was on his feet.

"Sustained," said Judge O'Brien. "Major Underwood, please confine your testimony to the evidence and the expert opinions you have developed that are based on that evidence."

"I understand, Your Honor. I apologize."

Using a large chart depicting the anatomy of a child's brain, Major Underwood explained, in simple terms that the members of the court-martial could understand, all of the medical terminology involved in the case. The best part of his testimony was when he described how the injury occurred.

"Can you tell us, Major Underwood, how Lydia might

have suffered the fatal injuries that are documented in the autopsy report?"

"Yes."

"Objection, Your Honor. We're not interested in what 'might' have happened," said Trip. "We need to hear what did happen."

Clark had learned his lesson in his previous trial. He waited for the judge. And he wasn't disappointed.

"Overruled," said Judge O'Brien. "He's testifying as an expert, Captain Stephens. Obviously, he wasn't there when the child received the injuries in question. He's expressing an expert opinion based on a review of the evidence after the fact. If you want to cross-examine him on that, you'll have an opportunity to do so."

Clark couldn't have argued it better himself, and he hoped the members of the court-martial understood that the judge had just given Trip remedial instruction on a basic principle of trial practice.

"Continue, Major Underwood," said Judge O'Brien.

The major cleared his throat and took a drink of water. "The autopsy concludes that Lydia Mendoza died because she was shaken violently, and in my expert opinion, the evidence supports that conclusion."

"Can you elaborate on how that injury might occur?" Clark looked at Trip to see if he was going to object. Nothing.

"Yes. Like all children her age, Lydia's brain was smaller than the interior of her skull. Therefore, when she was shaken violently, her brain rattled around inside of her skull, became bruised, and began to swell. The evidence in the autopsy shows Lydia Mendoza's brain was bruised and swollen, and it also notes that there were bruises on her extremities, indicating that she had been grasped tightly while being shaken."

"Could she have received these same injuries by falling?"

"Possibly, although there would have been evidence of a bump on her head, and the autopsy revealed none."

"That's all I have, Your Honor. Your witness," Clark said, turning to Trip.

As he had done with the other witnesses, Trip asked only a few questions on cross-examination, establishing only that Major Underwood was not board-certified in forensic pathology. Clark was again surprised. Surely Commander Peterson had prepared Trip and told him how to discredit Major Underwood's testimony. But then, maybe Peterson wasn't that good. Maybe he wasn't going to be a formidable witness after all.

"Does the government have any more witnesses, Captain Clark?" Judge O'Brien was staring at Clark over his glasses, which appeared to be floating on the end of his nose.

"Just one, Your Honor. Carmen Mendoza."

"All right. Let's take a ten-minute break." Turning to his left, the judge continued, "Members of the court-martial may use the latrine but do not make any telephone calls or discuss the case with anyone, even amongst yourselves. Court will be in recess." He banged his gavel and stood up.

"All rise," said Clark, and everyone complied. After the judge left, the members of the court-martial began to file out of the courtroom, as did some of the spectators in the gallery. When Suzanne started to leave, Clark grabbed her arm. "Would you come to my office, please?" She nodded yes, but her face was anxious.

As soon as they entered his office, Clark shut the door and sat in the chair next to Suzanne. "Does Trip really think the my-expert-is-better-than-your-expert argument is going to persuade this panel?"

"Apparently," she said, raising her eyebrows and shrugging her shoulders.

Clark leaned toward her and continued, "His cross-examination has been pathetic. Don't you think?"

"Yeah. It's as if he didn't prepare anything. Maybe he's counting on Commander Peterson to carry the day."

"Maybe. What did you think of Major Underwood?"

"I thought he did a good job. I didn't see any of that weirdness we heard on the phone."

Suzanne could tell that Clark was feeling insecure. She smiled, pleased that he was reviewing the progress of the trial with her.

"Do you think the members will care much about that board-certified business?"

"You would know better than I, Clark. Don't infantrymen put a lot of stock in all those badges they get for the schools they attend?"

"Yeah, but this is different. I don't think they'll relate to the board certification of a medical doctor." Clark stopped and stared into space, as if he was calculating something. "If Trip is basing everything on Commander Peterson's testimony, then I think we're in good shape, unless Peterson is a spectacular witness."

"I think you're right."

Someone knocked on Clark's door. "It's time to reconvene, sir."

Clark looked at Suzanne with wide eyes and the hint of a smile. "Let's go."

They walked back into the courtroom together. The bailiff had also notified the members of the court-martial, as well as Trip and Gomez. Everyone was in place except Judge O'Brien. The door behind the bench opened, and Judge O'Brien stepped up onto the bench. Not waiting for the bailiff, Clark said, "All rise."

Judge O'Brien struck his gavel on the bench. "The court will come to order. Please be seated. Captain Clark, you may proceed."

"Your Honor, the government calls Carmen Mendoza," Clark announced in a strong, confident voice. But that confidence evaporated almost instantaneously, when Carmen walked into the courtroom. Her spike heels clicked across the linoleum floor as she ambled to the witness stand. She looked like a prostitute from downtown Panama and bore no resemblance to the sweet, young, grieving mother whom Clark had brought to the courtroom just a week before. Her skirt was short, tight, and bright red. Her make-up was overdone and slutty-looking: thick eyeliner, pale-blue eye shadow, false eyelashes, a heavy layer of blush, and fire-engine red lipstick. Her hair was pulled back and off her neck, held in place with some sort of gaudy barrette adorned with large, obviously fake, gemstones. But worst of all, the cleavage of her ample bosom was on full display. Trip had wanted to portray her as a slut, and Carmen had unwittingly obliged him by dressing the part.

Clark's anxiety increased as he began to question Carmen. She sounded and acted like a melodramatic actress in a television *novella*—what the Panamanians call a soap opera. He knew he needed to change course fast. Departing from what he and Suzanne had prepared, he went to the counsel table and retrieved an enlarged copy of one of the most gruesome autopsy photographs, which Suzanne had introduced into evidence when Dr. Arias testified. When he picked it up, Suzanne scowled at him. But it was not the time for sensitivity. Carmen needed to start crying. Clark walked to the witness stand and shoved the photograph into her hands.

"I'm handing the witness Government Exhibit Number 13. Ms. Mendoza, can you identify the person in this photograph?"

"Yes." As before, her eyes immediately filled with tears.

"Who is it?"

"I's Lydia. I's my daugh'er, Lydia Mendoza." Her glassy eyes gazed at Clark as if he'd betrayed her. Tears began streaming down her cheeks.

"Are you certain, Ms. Mendoza? Please look carefully."

Clark knew it was a callous tactic, but it worked. Carmen began to sob and gasp for breath, the way she did on the evening of their courtroom orientation. She bent forward and put her face in her hands. Clark glanced at Suzanne. She was squirming in her seat as if she wanted to get up and rescue Carmen by taking her to the latrine again. Clark considered asking the judge for a brief recess but decided to let the members of the court-martial observe the Carmen he had planned for them to see: a grieving young mother, overwhelmed and completely distraught. She might have looked like a prostitute when she walked in, but now she fit the part she was supposed to play.

Carmen's tears caused her eye make-up to run down her face. Clark handed her a box of tissues from the court-reporter's table, and after a few minutes, she composed herself. Clark was able to elicit—from the now grieving mother—all the facts that he needed concerning the night she left Lydia in Gomez's custody.

"That's all I have of this witness, Your Honor." And then, turning to Trip, "Your witness."

Unlike his weak cross-examinations of the previous witnesses, Trip came at Carmen like a predator on the attack. "Isn't it true that you had sexual relations with Robert Wallace?" (Specialist Wallace was Lydia's father.)

"Objection, Your Honor." Clark was on his feet. "That question has nothing to do with this case." He was almost shouting and, as a result, got a stern look from Judge O'Brien.

Trip turned to the judge and then cut his eyes toward Clark and said, with a faint smirk, "We are establishing the paternity of the victim, Your Honor."

Before Judge O'Brien could respond, Clark blurted out, "Well, then, it's irrelevant, Your Honor."

"Restrain yourself, Captain Clark. I'll rule on your objection. If I want to hear from you, I'll ask you." The judge turned back toward Trip. "Captain Stephens, it is uncontroverted that we have a victim and that this witness is her mother. The identity of the child's father is irrelevant at this point, unless you want to make an offer of proof of why it would be relevant, in which case I'll need to excuse the members."

"Uh, no, Your Honor. I withdraw the question." The smirk was gone.

"Why did you leave your daughter with Specialist Gomez on Saturday evening, December 18, 1982?" Trip asked.

Clark stood up. "Objection, Your Honor."

"Overruled." Carmen looked puzzled and scared. "Please answer his question, Ms. Mendoza," Judge O'Brien said in a calm, comforting voice.

"Wha' ques'ion?"

"Why did you leave your daughter with Specialist Gomez on Saturday evening, December 18, 1982?" Trip asked again.

"Her question was addressed to me, Captain Stephens, and I'll answer it." Turning back toward Carmen, the judge asked, "Do you understand, Ms. Mendoza, that sometimes the lawyers will object to questions? If you don't know what to do, just ask me. Do you understand?"

"Yes," she replied, nodding at the same time. Judge O'Brien's fatherly demeanor seemed to have comforted her.

Judge O'Brien continued, "Please tell Captain Stephens why you left Lydia with Specialist Gomez."

"I wan' to talk to Roberto."

"You are referring to Specialist Robert Wallace, Lydia's father?" Trip asked.

"Yes."

Trip approached the witness stand. "You wanted him to take you to the Enlisted Club, didn't you?"

"No. I wan' to talk to him." Carmen looked afraid.

"But he took you to the Enlisted Club, didn't he?"

"Yes, bu' I wan'…"

"You've been to the Enlisted Club many times, haven't you, Ms. Mendoza?"

"Objection, Your Honor."

Judge O'Brien leaned forward. "Captain Stephens, do you have some sort of theory that you want to offer as to why that question is relevant?"

"No, Your Honor."

"Then don't ask it or any other question that isn't relevant. Objection sustained." Judge O'Brien's face was flushed, and his brow creased. He was now intimidating, not fatherly, and obviously annoyed.

Trip appeared unfazed by the judge's admonition and continued his questioning. "What time did you get home from the Enlisted Club on December 18, Ms. Mendoza? Or was it December 19?"

Carmen stared at Trip and then looked at Clark and then at the judge. "Please answer that question, Ms. Mendoza," said Judge O'Brien.

"Roberto take me to my sister' house aroun' twelve o'cloc'."

"Did Specialist Wallace agree to marry you, Ms. Mendoza?" Trip sounded haughty and insensitive.

Carmen's eyes became glassy again, and she shook her head from side to side.

Trip continued in the same tone of voice. "Please answer orally, Ms. Mendoza. The court-reporter needs to hear your answer and take it down."

Trip thought he was being tough, but he was actually only persuading the members to feel sorry for her. Good, thought Clark.

"No," said Carmen, almost whispering. "He no' goin' to marry me."

Clark glanced at the members of the court-martial. They

looked like a bunch of concerned older brothers and cousins. Trip wasn't scoring any points.

Trip continued, "Did you feel it was safe and appropriate to leave your daughter with Specialist Gomez?"

Carmen looked at Judge O'Brien. "*No entien...* I no' un'erstan'."

"Rephrase the question, Captain Stephens."

Now, Trip looked perplexed. "You left your daughter with Specialist Gomez, correct?"

"Yes."

"And you felt she was safe with him?"

"Yes."

"Miss Mendoza, do you think it was prudent to leave Lydia with your brother-in-law when she was sick?"

"I no' understan'... pruden'?" As Clark had instructed, Carmen looked up at Judge O'Brien, wide-eyed and innocent. Clark couldn't believe it. She looked more pitiful than he could have possibly hoped for.

Judge O'Brien looked at Trip over his glasses, which were still hovering on the end of his nose. "Rephrase the question, Captain Stephens."

And so it went. Repeatedly, Trip asked Carmen questions using vocabulary and phrasing that were difficult for someone with limited English ability to understand. He liberally used words such as "prudent" and "behoove" and "bald assertion." And each time he did, Carmen followed Clark's instruction: she looked up at Judge O'Brien and said she didn't understand. And each time Carmen did that, Clark smiled inside. He knew the members' sympathy for her had just increased another notch. Their faces told the story.

At the end of his cross-examination, Trip finally asked Carmen about the spider bite. To Clark's surprise, she said she hadn't seen any spider bite. Undeterred, Trip pressed ahead but got

313

nowhere: Carmen said she didn't know whether a spider bite had anything to do with how sick Lydia got. Clark suppressed a smile. Trip needed convincing testimony on the spider bite, and it was unclear where he was going to get it.

As Clark watched Carmen on the witness stand, he could sense palpable tension between Gomez and her—something different from what he had expected. Several times during the cross-examination, her eyes darted in Clark's direction as if she was trying to signal something. So, as an afterthought—always a dangerous path for a trial counsel—he decided to ask Carmen additional questions on redirect examination about what happened after she returned to Gomez's quarters. That topic was fair game because Trip had brought it up during his cross-examination.

"I'd like to redirect, Your Honor."

"Proceed."

"Ms. Mendoza, you said that you got back to your sister's house around midnight on December 18. What, if anything, happened when you got there?" Carmen stared back at Clark. They had not discussed this topic during her preparation. Her expression was strained, almost frightened. Clark waited a few moments for an answer and, getting none, tried a different approach. "Did the accused say anything about how Lydia had been while you were away?"

"No." Her answer was strong, quick, and matter-of-fact.

Clark knew he was on to something. His stomach was doing cartwheels as he tried to decide what to do next. Why didn't he ask her about the details of what happened when he interviewed her? How stupid! Now, he had to go for it.

"Could you explain what you mean for the members of the court-martial?"

"Objection, Your Honor." Trip was extremely agitated. "It's unclear what counsel is asking the witness."

"Rephrase the question, Captain Clark."

"Did the accused say anything to you when you got to his quarters?"

"He was ma'." Carmen looked down at her lap.

"Mad about what?"

"I tol' him no," she said, now staring straight back at Clark.

"You told him no about what?"

"He wan' to sleep wid me, an' I tol' him no."

"When did he want to…"

"Objection, Your Honor." Trip's aggressive demeanor again brought a look of fear to Carmen's face, which Judge O'Brien noticed.

Before Clark could think of anything to say in response to Trip's objection, Judge O'Brien responded firmly: "Overruled." He turned to Carmen and in a calming voice said, "You may answer that question, Ms. Mendoza. Repeat the question, Captain Clark."

"When did the accused say he wanted to sleep with you?"

"When I go' to hi' house tha' nigh'…"

"Which night is that, Ms. Mendoza?"

"The nigh' Lydia stay wid him, an' I wen' ou' wid Roberto."

"You are referring to December 18, 1982?"

Trip was up again. "Objection, Your Honor. He's leading his own witness."

"Overruled. We all know the language issues we're dealing with here, Captain Stephens. Continue, Captain Clark."

"When you got to your sister's house on the evening of December 18, is that when the accused said he wanted to sleep with you?"

"Yes. He grab me an' star'ed pulling my clothes off. I say leave me alone. You married to my sis'er, and he sai' she no' like you. She fat."

"Objection, Your Honor, hearsay."

Clark waited for a sign from Judge O'Brien. "Your Honor,

Ms. Mendoza's testimony concerning what the accused said to her is not being offered for the truth of the matter stated in his words. Instead, it is offered as evidence of what she heard, in order to explain her actions." Judge O'Brien nodded and smiled. Clark had just demonstrated that he understood the lessons he'd been taught at the JAG School on the complicated subject of hearsay—taught by none other than Judge O'Brien.

"Objection overruled."

"Did the accused say anything else, Ms. Mendoza?"

"He pushed me down on the couch and sai' you fucked Wallace, why don' you fuck me."

Trip objected to Carmen's use of the "F" word, but Clark countered that she was merely repeating what she had heard. Although Judge O'Brien overruled Trip's objection, Clark was concerned that the casual way in which Carmen said "fuck" might have damaged her image as a grieving mother.

"What happened next?" Clark asked.

"I tol' him to leave me alone, and he wen' into the bedroom where Lydia was sleeping because all the shoutin' wake her up, an' she wa' cryin'."

"Did you follow him into the bedroom?"

"No. It all happene' so fas'. By the time I go' up fro' the couch an' fix' my clothes, he was back in the livin' room."

"And then what happened."

"He wen' to hi' bedroom and slammed the door. I wen' to see Lydia and go' her back to sleep."

"How did Lydia look when you went in the bedroom?" Carmen looked puzzled. "What was Lydia doing when you went into the bedroom?"

"She was jus' sittin' on the blanket cryin', and so I picke' her up and hel' her until she wen' back to sleep."

Clark took a deep breath. He decided to quit while he was ahead. "No further questions, Your Honor."

Trip stood up, started to speak, hesitated, and then said, "No questions, Your Honor."

"Then are we finished with this witness?" asked Judge O'Brien.

Simultaneously, Clark and Trip answered, "Yes, Your Honor."

"Ms. Mendoza, you are excused," said Judge O'Brien. "Court will be in recess until 0800 hours tomorrow. Members are admonished not to discuss this case with anyone." He struck the gavel on the bench, stood up, and retreated through the door behind the bench.

Clark sat down and glanced in the direction of the defense table. Trip was hard to read, but Gomez looked scared. His face was pale, and he was staring at the members of the court-martial who were filing out of the courtroom. Clark hoped the members saw Gomez's expression. At his own table Suzanne looked stunned, which Clark hoped the members had not noticed. As he stood up and turned to leave, he saw Elmer in the back of the gallery, grinning from ear to ear.

CHAPTER TWENTY-SIX

ON THE THIRD day of the Gomez trial, Clark awoke to glorious Panamanian sunshine streaming through his bedroom window. It was the end of the first good night's sleep that he'd had in quite a while. He rolled over and stared out the window, trying to wake up. The sky was the color of his mother's hydrangea bush, and there wasn't a cloud in it. A gentle breeze swayed the trees outside in a hypnotic rhythm. For the first time in what seemed like a long time he felt at peace. His thoughts weren't dominated by the problems with his wife and by the pressures of his job. But this detachment from reality was short-lived. Thoughts of the trial and what was left to be done soon began to creep in. The bed felt good, but he knew he couldn't stay. He got up and shuffled to the shower.

The warm water hit his face and jolted him back into his role as a prosecutor. He had a trial to finish. He began to review what had happened so far. The examination of the two doctors had gone well, and they were the only witnesses who had first-hand knowledge of how Lydia Mendoza died. Commander Peterson will have to draw his conclusions based on what Dr. Arias wrote in his autopsy report. And Trip didn't lay a glove on Arias during his cross-examination. So, the autopsy report will be the key, unless Trip has a surprise.

Clark dressed quickly and headed out the door without pausing for breakfast or even coffee. As he drove to the office, he continued to think about the progress of the trial. Despite a shaky start, Carmen had turned out to be a great witness. Even though she hadn't dressed the part, she ended up coming across as a sweet, young grieving mother once her tears began to flow. The members had seen her genuine grief, and Clark felt they had been moved. Trip's attempt to cross-examine Carmen had been clumsy and oafish. Best of all, though, was the gamble that Clark had taken on his redirect examination of Carmen. When she testified that Gomez had come on to her, she sealed his fate. That testimony gave Clark the evidence of motive that he needed: Carmen spurned Gomez's advances, which made him angry, and he took his anger out on Lydia. Clark doubted that Trip would put Gomez on the stand. So he thought it would all come down to Commander Peterson.

Clark arrived at the office with ten minutes to spare. Judge O'Brien emerged from his chambers precisely at 8:00 a.m., and Clark was ready. "All rise."

After arranging his papers, Judge O'Brien leveled his gaze at Clark. "Captain Clark, before we start this proceeding, and before the court reporter starts transcribing, I want to admonish you concerning the manner in which you conducted yourself yesterday. I know that you are a capable lawyer. And I have every reason to believe you are also a professional one. The courtroom histrionics that you've seen in movies and on television are unacceptable and will not be tolerated in my courtroom. Govern yourself accordingly." He paused and stared at Clark, as if to say, "I'm not kidding."

"And lest your smirk returns, Captain Stephens, let me say that your behavior yesterday was only marginally better. I know you come from a distinguished line of lawyers and jurists. They would be appalled at your courtroom conduct yesterday. I know

319

that you know better, and I expect you to live up to your family's reputation. Now, Mrs. Early," he said, turning to the court-reporter seated below him, "we'll begin. The court will come to order. Bailiff, please have the members of the court-martial take their seats." After they were ushered in from the deliberation room, Judge O'Brien turned to Clark. "Captain Clark, you may proceed."

Clark stood up and faced the judge. "The government rests, Your Honor." As soon as he said those words, his stomach reminded him of what they meant. It is not a phrase that is taken lightly. After telling the judge that "the government rests," it is virtually impossible to admit additional evidence. If he and Suzanne had failed to put on at least some evidence for each element of the offense charged, then the trial would be over, and the government would lose. That's what happens when defense counsel makes a "motion for a finding of not guilty." It's what caused Suzanne to lose her first trial against Major Darst. Every prosecutor experiences the same feeling at this juncture. Clark had carefully reviewed the evidence that he and Suzanne had admitted, and he knew they were in good shape. He looked at Suzanne. For once she looked confident.

In his typical perfunctory style, Trip moved for a finding of not guilty, but it was pointless. There was no doubt that Clark and Suzanne had introduced at least some evidence for every element of the offense. It seemed to be yet another example of Trip merely going through the motions of defending his client—based on some general principle or on his father's advice—rather than thinking for himself about what he was doing in this particular trial. Judge O'Brien took little time to deny the motion, which didn't seem to bother Trip.

The next step was for Trip to put on the defense's case. "The Defense calls Commander Howard J. Peterson," Trip said in a strong, sonorous voice. He must have thought his theatrical flair would compensate for his abysmal performance as a defense counsel. Or, he was completely clueless.

Commander Peterson walked into the courtroom wearing his Navy service dress white uniform, consisting of a white tunic with black shoulder boards, white trousers, and white shoes. Clark had to admit it was a sharp-looking uniform. But Peterson himself appeared to be exactly the kind of wimp that infantrymen detest—skinny and bespectacled, with a wispy beard that looked anything but manly. His beard, which the Navy allowed at the time, would have been *verboten* in the Army, and so it probably annoyed the infantrymen on the panel even more. Given the way he strutted to the witness stand, it appeared that Peterson thought his service whites made him look cool. Unfortunately for the commander, no uniform—in any military service—could overcome the impression that he was a complete nerd.

Pursuant to the procedures of the Manual for Courts-Martial, Clark swore in Commander Peterson as a witness, and then Trip began his direct examination. He asked Peterson questions to establish that he was an expert, taking great pains to point out that he was both a doctor and a lawyer and was board-certified in forensic pathology. As Peterson started listing his credentials— *magna cum laude* from Columbia University, graduate of the Johns Hopkins School of Medicine, pathology resident at Johns Hopkins, law degree from George Washington University—Clark had to admit that they—like his uniform—were impressive.

In addition to looking like a wimp, Peterson further undermined his credibility by consciously trying to sound like President Franklin D. Roosevelt—an erudite member of the Eastern establishment. Clark suppressed a grin as he imagined how that style would play with the members of the court-martial, who were either Southerners or Hispanics. And what's more, the accent sounded fake.

When Trip's questions started getting into the meat of the autopsy report, Clark focused carefully on how Peterson answered.

"As an expert in the field of forensic pathology, Commander Peterson, have you formed an opinion on the cause of death of Lydia Mendoza?"

"I have."

"And what is your opinion?"

"In my opinion, Lydia Mendoza died of a spider bite of unknown type."

"Thank you." Trip turned to Clark. "Your witness."

Clark already knew he didn't like Peterson. He was clearly arrogant and—worse than that—he was a Navy officer. Clark's blood was olive-drab green. In addition, Major Underwood's innuendo about the commander's sexuality appeared to be correct. Despite his beard, Peterson's demeanor was almost feminine. His legs were crossed, knee-over-knee, and he was taking a drink of water with his elbow and pinky finger extended in dramatic fashion. He set the glass down, looked at Clark with a smirk, and cocked his head to one side.

Clark could feel his body generating heat. Leveling his gaze, he took a deep breath and walked toward the witness stand. "Isn't it true, Commander Peterson, that you never examined Lydia Mendoza?"

"Captain Clark," Peterson sneered, "you obviously don't understand what we do at the Armed Forces Institute of Pathology."

"Well, you obviously don't understand how to answer a simple question."

"Captain Clark!" Judge O'Brien was red-faced. "Do we need to have a session in chambers?"

"No, Your Honor."

"That is your last warning."

Now on thin ice, Clark consciously restrained himself and repeated the question. "Commander Peterson, isn't it true that you never examined Lydia Mendoza?"

"That is correct, Captain Clark, because that it not what we do at the AFIP."

To prevent Peterson from starting to explain what he did at the AFIP, Clark quickly proceeded to his next question. "Isn't it true that Major Underwood disagrees with your conclusion concerning the cause of Lydia Mendoza's death?"

"Major Underwood is incorrect, and I should point out that he is not board-certified in forensic pathology."

"Did you have access to documents and materials that were not available to Major Underwood?"

"No, I did not. Major Underwood is in error. He drew conclusions that are not supported by the evidence."

"Would it surprise you to learn, Commander Peterson, that both the medical examiner and the doctor who treated Lydia Mendoza also concluded that she was shaken to death?"

"I read the file in this case, Captain Clark. So, that would not surprise me. The doctors down here have obviously not received the education and training that we have in the United States." Peterson's derisive expression and condescending tone suggested that he believed he was getting the best of Clark.

Clark, on the other hand, thought that the members of the court-martial were quickly getting their fill of this pompous jerk.

"Would it change your mind, Commander Peterson, to learn that Dr. Gonzalez, who treated Lydia Mendoza, made no mention of a spider bite during his testimony at this trial?"

"Perhaps I wasn't clear in my previous answer, Captain Clark. I read the report, and so I know what Dr. Gonzalez concluded." He took great pains to say the name "Gonzalez" with a Spanish accent, although it wasn't clear whether he was trying to pay homage to Dr. Gonzalez's heritage or to mock him. In either case, Peterson sounded stupid.

"I was referring to his testimony at trial, Commander

Peterson, not his sworn statement that was included in the CID report."

"Well, he didn't mention it in his sworn statement either, Captain Clark."

"So, it does not surprise you that he didn't mention it in his testimony at trial?"

"That is correct."

"Since neither the autopsy report nor Dr. Gonzalez's statement mentioned a spider bite, why do you conclude that a spider bite was the cause of death?" Clark knew it was risky to ask that question. Lawyers know it's generally considered a bad idea to ask a witness "why" on cross-examination because witnesses always have a reason. And Clark didn't know what answer Peterson would give, which violates another rule of cross-examination.

"The caretaker of the deceased little girl and her mother both confirmed that she had been bitten by a spider."

"The 'caretaker'?"

"Yes. Specialist Raul Gomez."

"You are referring to something the accused said, are you not?"

"Yes, Captain Clark, I am, and I'm also referring to what the victim's mother said before you coached her."

"What?" Clark raised his voice and took an aggressive step toward the witness stand.

"Captain Clark!"

"This witness is impugning my integrity, Your Honor."

"Then act professionally and object to it."

"I object, Your Honor."

"Objection sustained. Commander Peterson you will confine your testimony to answering the questions you are asked. You may give your expert opinion, but you must refrain from speculating on what a witness might or might not have been told."

"I was commenting on how her story changed, Your Honor."

"Well, you weren't asked anything about how the witness's testimony might have changed, Commander Peterson. Furthermore, you were speculating. Your credentials suggest that you are educated enough to know the difference between proper testimony and speculation. I am directing you to answer counsel's questions, and if you don't know the answer, say so. Nothing more, nothing less. Am I clear?"

"Yes, Your Honor."

Turning to the members of the court-martial, Judge O'Brien said, "You are to disregard the comments of Commander Peterson concerning the testimony of Ms. Carmen Mendoza. Continue, Captain Clark."

"Isn't it true, Commander Peterson, that in the past you and Major Underwood have disagreed on what the evidence in a case file establishes?"

"We frequently disagree. He's a zealot."

"Objection, Your Honor," said Clark.

"Sustained. Commander Peterson, I thought I made myself clear. Do you need further clarification about your role in this trial?"

"No, Your Honor."

Hoping that perhaps Judge O'Brien was beginning to become annoyed with Commander Peterson, Clark decided to press hard. "Isn't it true, Commander Peterson, that when you and Major Underwood testified in a similar case at Fort Riley, your side lost and his side won?"

Trip was instantaneously on his feet, objecting and waving his arms hysterically. "That's irrelevant, Your Honor. What happened at Fort Riley has nothing to do with this case. I move for a mistrial."

Judge O'Brien banged his gavel hard. "Counsel will approach the bench." He was seething. "Captain Clark, are you trying to have a mistrial?"

"No, Your Honor."

"Then, shape up. And Captain Stephens, constrain yourself and start acting like a professional." He paused for a moment and then said each word distinctly for emphasis, "I thought I made myself clear: no more theatrics from either of you. Is that now clear?"

In unison, Clark and Trip replied, "Yes, Your Honor."

Clark continued his cross-examination of Commander Peterson. "Let me ask a different question, Commander Peterson. Isn't it true that the only evidence you have of a spider bite is the statement of the accused, Specialist Gomez, which has not been admitted into the evidence of this trial?"

"I also have the nurse's statement."

"Well, no nurse has testified at this trial. And so, Commander Peterson, your opinion is, at best, based on facts that are not in evidence and, therefore, without merit."

"Objection, Your Honor." Trip was on his feet, clearly more restrained this time. "Counsel is arguing his case, not asking questions."

"Sustained," Judge O'Brien responded quickly. "Captain Clark, stick to cross-examination."

Clark continued, "Commander Peterson, you don't even know what kind of spider made this alleged bite, do you?"

"I do not, but I assume that there are venomous spiders here in Panama, such as the black widow and the brown recluse."

"Oh, that's true, Commander Peterson, but you have no evidence that the victim was bitten by a venomous spider, do you?"

"Only because you and the CID Agent have intimidated witnesses."

Clark charged the witness stand. "Excuse me? Who do you think you are?" The judge's gavel came down so hard he broke off its head.

"Court's in recess. Counsel in my chambers, now!" Judge O'Brien's face was beet red.

As he walked out of the courtroom, Clark glanced at Suzanne. Her confident look seemed to have been replaced by the same look he'd seen when she tried her first case. She followed them to Judge O'Brien's "chambers," which were nothing more than an empty office near the courtroom. It was bare, except for a gray metal desk and a few chairs.

"Captain Watkins, you may return to the courtroom," said Judge O'Brien. "Sit down, gentlemen." The two remaining captains complied, like two little boys hauled before the principal. The judge continued, "I have never seen such an unprofessional display in my courtroom or any courtroom. Have you two never tried a case? Captain Clark, you are perilously close to having me declare a mistrial. And Captain Stephens, I would think by now that you would know the proper way to make an objection. Moreover, did you even consider whether Commander Peterson's opinion was based on evidence that was in the record?"

"I thought I would get it in with subsequent witnesses, Your Honor."

"Well, that's not the way it works, Captain. Are you not aware of that? Do your homework when you prepare for trial. Your client is depending on you to get it right. And you, Captain Clark, how long have you been in the military? Did they teach you nothing about customs and courtesies of the service at West Point?"

"He said some reprehensible things, Your Honor," Clark mumbled.

"And you obliged him by acting like an idiot. Would you have behaved the same way if he'd been a lieutenant colonel in the Army, instead of a Navy commander?"

"I guess not, Your Honor."

"You 'guess not.' Is that all you have to say?"

Clark's emotions began to get the best of him. "This trial is very difficult for me," he stammered. "Ever since I saw that little girl on the table during the autopsy…" He struggled to keep his composure. "She looked like my daughter, Your Honor. What this man did… it's so wrong, so unfair." The judge stared at him in silence, which Clark couldn't bear for long. "When I saw her there, Judge, I…" Losing his composure again, he blurted out, "I didn't want to send him to jail, Judge, I wanted to send him to hell."

"Well, that is not your job, Captain." The judge punctuated his point with another icy stare. "Start acting like a professional." He paused to let that sink in and then said, "I thought you told me at the JAG School that you were a Christian."

"I don't know what you mean, Your Honor. I am a Christian. I'll confess I'm not always a very good one, but I try."

"Well, if you were a Christian, then you'd know that it is God's job to decide who goes to hell. Your job is to do your job. You should have faith that God works these things out the way they're supposed to be worked out." He paused and stared at Clark, appearing to be trying to assess whether Clark understood what he was saying. "Whatever your role is in life, Captain Clark, you should do your best, but you should trust God to deliver the results that He wants. To do otherwise is presumptuous."

Clark glanced at Trip, who was squirming by this point. Clark suspected that Trip had never heard such frank talk about God and faith in his Episcopalian congregation, although it had been common at the First United Methodist Church in Pemberton, Georgia.

Thankfully, his lecture seemed to calm the judge down, or maybe God did. "Gentlemen, we are going to go back out there; and Captain Clark, you are going to finish your cross-examination of Commander Peterson in a professional manner. No more outbursts or unprofessionalism from either of you. Am I clear?"

This time, Trip responded with, "Yes, Your Honor," but Clark said, without thinking, "Yes, sir," temporarily reverting to the courtesies he'd learned growing up and in the Army, instead of his training as a lawyer.

When Judge O'Brien and the two captains returned to the courtroom, every member of the court-martial panel was sitting on the edge of his seat, wide-eyed and staring back at them, waiting to see what was going to happen next.

"Court will come to order." Judge O'Brien rapped the head of the gavel, which he was now holding in his hand, on the bench. "Continue, Captain Clark."

Clark stood well back from the witness stand. "Commander Peterson, I remind you that you are still under oath."

"Clearly."

"Do you have any direct, first-hand evidence that Lydia Mendoza was bitten by a spider?"

"The CID Report said…"

Clark took two steps forward. "Excuse me, sir, but I asked about any direct, first-hand evidence that you have."

Peterson glanced at Judge O'Brien, who was leaning over the bench and glaring at him.

"Uh, no, Captain Clark," he said softly. "I don't have any direct evidence of a spider bite."

"No more questions, Your Honor."

After Trip waived the right to re-direct examination, Judge O'Brien let out an almost audible sigh. He'd had enough of them for one day. Surprisingly, because it was still relatively early in the day, he announced that the court was going to be in recess and gave the members his standard admonition about not speaking with anyone about the case. He directed them to be ready to proceed the next day at 0800 hours and then dismissed them. Turning back to face the attorneys, he pounded the head of his gavel on the bench and recessed the court.

As Clark gathered his files and papers, he reviewed what had just happened. Judge O'Brien had been hard on him, but Clark felt that he'd accomplished what he set out to do. He felt good about his performance.

When he got to his office, Suzanne was already there. She greeted him with a big smile. "You gave 'em hell, Boss."

"I don't know, Suzanne, Judge O'Brien got pretty mad at me."

"Who gives a damn? You're winning. You made Peterson look like a bleeding-heart liberal with an agenda. And isn't it perfect that he's a Navy officer?"

"Yeah, I don't think the members of the court-martial like him."

"Let's go to Mother's and have a drink. I'm buying."

"I can't, Suzanne. I'm beat. I've got to go home."

"Okay, but I want a rain check."

"You got it. See you tomorrow." Clark packed his briefcase and headed for his car. The sunshine and fresh air felt good, especially after having been cooped up inside all day. A warm breeze carried the scents of Panama—an odd mixture of fragrant flowers and burning grass. Despite the problems with Judge O'Brien, Clark felt relaxed and thought he had scored some points with the members of the court-martial. The trial was going well. He stopped to get gas and went inside the store to buy some cigars to reward himself for a successful day. In Panama, even gas stations sold premium cigars.

Clark's route home took him through one of the manicured neighborhoods where the Zonians lived. He happened to notice an old gardener on the side of the road. He was bent, like one of the gnarled live oak trees on the courthouse square in Pemberton, and had a pronounced hunched back, probably the result of years of hard, manual labor. His clothes were worn thin and ragged, and he was carrying a cardboard box on his back that contained rakes and other gardening tools.

Something came over Clark, when he saw the old man, shuffling along in the late afternoon sun. He imagined how hard he must have worked all day in the oppressive heat—a stark contrast from Clark's air-conditioned courtroom. And although the old man's day had been much more arduous than Clark's, he'd probably earned no more than ten or fifteen dollars. Clark decided he wanted to help him, so he pulled his car over to the curb and got out.

"*Buenas tardes, señor, tengo algo para usted,*" Clark said as he walked in the old man's direction. What Clark "had" for him was an opportunity to work for some of Clark's neighbors, who were Army officers, not ungrateful Zonians. The gardener smiled nervouslly at him but kept shuffling along. Clark suspected that his Army uniform had intimidated him. It wasn't unusual for such men to be hassled by the U.S. authorities in the Canal Zone. Unfortunately, Clark's limited ability to speak Spanish prevented him from explaining the opportunity he had in mind, so he simply pulled a five-dollar bill out of his wallet and offered it to the old man. At first, he looked confused, clearly not understanding what Clark was doing. But soon, a grin appeared on his weathered old face and then a toothless smile. "*Muchas gracias, señor, muchas gracias.*"

"*En el nombre de Jesucristo,*" Clark said, thinking he should give credit to the inspiration for his gesture. He shook the old man's hand, which was so calloused it felt like a leather glove, and then got back into his car. As he drove away, Clark could see the old man in the rearview mirror, alternately staring at the five-dollar bill and looking up, waving to Clark.

CHAPTER TWENTY-SEVEN

THE NEXT DAY Clark was at his desk by 6:00 a.m. He was anxious to finish the trial. The only thing left was his closing argument; that is, unless Trip put Gomez on the stand. That was a possibility, since Commander Peterson had not been the savior Trip had apparently hoped for. Around 7:00 a.m., Trip appeared.

"Clark, I need to talk to you about something." His face was gaunt, except for the gray, puffy bags beneath his eyes. There was no hint of his previous swagger.

"What's up?" Clark asked, looking up from the papers on his desk.

"Gomez had to be taken to Gorgas Hospital last night. He took a bunch of pills."

"He what?"

"Took a bunch of pain killers. Trying to commit suicide." Trip seemed to have stepped out of the role of advocate. He sounded more like a concerned friend.

"With aspirin. Or was it Tylenol?" Clark squinted as he stood up from behind his desk. "Come on, Trip, this is a stunt."

Trip fidgeted in the doorway and looked out the window. "Well, I'm just telling you what I know, Clark." It was clear Trip didn't want to argue.

"You know that Judge O'Brien will want to have a 39(a) session to sort this out and decide whether we can proceed."

"You mean out of the presence of the members?"

"Well, yeah, Trip. That's the way it's done."

"Yeah, I guess that's right," Trip mumbled.

Clark felt the need to orient him further. "It's just like the 39(a) we had in the Rodriguez case." Trip stared vacantly. "The motion *in limine*, Trip."

"Oh, yeah. Okay, I'll see what I can find out about his status."

Clark and Trip heard Judge O'Brien arrive at 7:30 a.m. and went to the office he was using as his chambers. Trip delivered the news about Gomez and the pills, and the judge was not happy. Although Judge O'Brien was not a "screamer," the chaos of the previous day had snuffed out his normally friendly demeanor. Just as Clark had predicted, the judge convened an Article 39(a) session at 8:00 a.m. to put the information about Gomez's alleged suicide attempt on the record. After hearing Trip's report on Gomez's status, Judge O'Brien directed Trip to get either Gomez or his doctor into court by 12:00 p.m. Then he had the bailiff bring in the members of the court-martial and advised them that there had been a "delay," although he didn't elaborate on the cause. He told them that they were free to go but must return by noon, and, as was his habit, warned them not to discuss the case. Judge O'Brien's demeanor had definitely changed, and the members noticed it. They looked at him like new recruits waiting for their drill sergeant to tell them what to do next.

The delay caused by Gomez worked to Clark's advantage. He was able to spend the time preparing, while Trip was busy trying to find out what was going on with his client.

Clark stuck his head in Suzanne's office. "What did you think of the 39(a) session? Do you think Gomez was really trying to kill himself?"

"I think it was a silly stunt from a guy who knows he's going to prison. I think we've done a pretty good job, partner."

"Me too. Your opening statement was outstanding." Suzanne smiled, clearly pleased with his compliment. "And, you laid out a convincing case with Arias and Gonzalez." Clark looked out her window for a few moments and then turned and asked, "What do you think about the rest of the case?"

Suzanne dropped her pen on the desk and leaned back in her chair. "So far, I think Peterson is their entire defense. And I don't think that any of Trip's cross-examination was effective." She stopped and glanced away, as if contemplating something. She narrowed her eyes and said, "He might have made a few points here and there, such as Underwood not being board certified in forensic pathology, but all-in-all I don't think he had much of an impact." She leaned forward and her eyes widened. "And, Underwood was great—a lot more articulate and passionate than Peterson. And he looked like a soldier. Peterson just looked out of place."

"What did you think of my cross of Peterson?"

"You kind of lost it, didn't you?"

Clark immediately became agitated and began to pace. "The guy's an asshole, Suzanne, he…"

"Yeah, but you let him get the best of your temper, and it got you crosswise with Judge O'Brien." She stopped and then punctuated that thought with, "I think he's pissed."

Clark spun around, put both hands on her desk and leaned in. "Well, screw him. My job is to nail this guy." He stood up and turned back toward the window.

"Okay, Clark, but be careful. You don't want the members to think you're as big a jerk as Peterson is."

Gazing out the window, he mumbled, "We have a great view from here, don't we?" He knew Suzanne was right about how he'd behaved, but she just didn't understand how difficult it was to cross-examine a witness like Peterson. He decided to change the subject. "What do you think about the lack of evidence of the spider bite?" He turned around to hear her answer.

"I thought you handled that pretty well, and I made some notes..."

Suzanne started thumbing through her papers on her desk, and Clark turned back to the window. Something seemed to keep drawing his mind away from the trial. There was a cruise ship coming through the Canal, glistening in the sunshine. From his vantage point it appeared to be gliding through the grass. Clark could see passengers on the deck, milling around and waving to the workers manning Miraflores Locks, which lowered the ship from the level of Lake Gatun to that of the Pacific Ocean. Where did all those people on the ship come from? And where were they going?

"Hey! Are you listening to me or am I wasting my time?" Suzanne seemed slightly irritated.

"Yeah. I'm listening." He turned around to make eye contact.

"Okay," she continued, "Peterson commented several times on things that were not in evidence: the nurse's notation about the spider bite and what Dr. Gonzalez said in his statement. Peterson has no direct knowledge of those matters. So, he shouldn't have been testifying to them."

"Dammit," said Clark, pounding his right fist into his left palm. "You're right. I should've objected."

"Don't beat yourself up. I wanted to say something to you during your cross of Peterson but was afraid the judge would say we were tag-teaming him. Anyway, you can still make the point. Just argue it to the jury in your closing... I mean to the members of the court-martial. Harp on the fact that Peterson never saw Lydia—that he formed his opinion based on what the accused told him." She paused as if she'd just had an epiphany. "You know, Trip has kind of put himself in a corner on that point."

"What do you mean?"

"Well, if he wants to mount a spider-bite defense, then he'll have to put Gomez on the stand."

"Of course!" Clark said, looking straight at her. "He's got nothing else, does he? I definitely need to be ready to cross-examine him. But I haven't even thought about it."

"And what about Carmen's news that Gomez made a pass at her? That was big. Do you think it's true?" Suzanne seemed intrigued by the salacious nature of that revelation.

"I don't know. But we've got to figure out how to address it if I have to cross-examine Gomez."

They talked more about how Clark should cross-examine Gomez if Trip put him on the stand and what the theme of Clark's closing argument should be. It was almost 11:00 a.m. by the time they finished. Because he hadn't eaten in over twenty-four hours, Clark decided to get some lunch at the NCO Club before the trial began again.

He exited the building and stepped into Panama's heat and humidity, which immediatley wilted his uniform and made him sweat. Although the NCO Club was only a short walk across a parking lot, he was dripping by the time he entered the front door. He found a waiter, told him he was in a hurry, and said he needed a hamburger and fries fast. By the time his food arrived, it was 11:30 a.m.—only thirty minutes before he needed to be back in court. He started gulping down his lunch and, in the process, dropped a french fry on the front of his shirt, causing a large and very noticeable ketchup blob. He jumped up and raced to the bathroom to clean it off. Unfortunately, his efforts were for naught, and he was left with a large, faded-red wet spot in the middle of his chest. When he looked at himself in the mirror, he lost it. He started kicking the trashcan as if it were Jimmy Walker's dog, which used to chase him when he delivered newspapers on his bicycle. The commotion attracted the attention of the club manager, who barged through the door in a huff. But when he found Clark, squatted down, picking up the paper and putting it back in the trashcan, he said, "I'll get that, Captain Clark." He took the container from him and picked up the remainder of the spilled trash.

"Sorry," Clark explained. "I managed to spill ketchup on this uniform, and I've got to be back in court in a few minutes."

"I know a trick," the manager said. "Come with me." He led Clark to the bar, where he cleaned the spot with club soda. "It'll dry fast, and nobody will notice." He looked at Clark with sincere eyes. "We're counting on you to nail that guy." Clark didn't reply. He just nodded and smiled.

As Clark hurried back to his office—again becoming wet with sweat—it dawned on him that virtually everyone on Fort Clayton was focused on this trial. Everyone was wondering whether he was going to "nail that guy."

When he got back, he learned that Trip had come by to report that Specialist Gomez would be present in the courtroom. He went to his office and spent the remaining few minutes in in front of a fan, drying his shirt and cooling off. Precisely at noon, Judge O'Brien walked in the courtroom, sat down behind the bench, and banged his gavel—a replacement for the one he'd broken earlier. "Court will come to order. This is an Article 39(a) session, out of the presence of the members of the court-martial." He stared at Clark. "Counsel, stand up and approach the bench." Clark complied, his eyes staring straight ahead. Judge O'Brien glared at him for an uncomfortably long time before he finally spoke. "Your behavior yesterday was deplorable." Clark suddenly realized that the court reporter was transcribing what the judge was saying, which meant that this tongue-lashing was going to be a part of the permanent record of this trial. It would be reviewed, and probably talked about, at the appellate division in Washington—not a good thing for a budding JAG career.

Trip was also standing in front of the bench, a few feet away. Judge O'Brien continued, "If I get so much as a hint that either of you are stepping out of the bounds of proper decorum, or are even thinking about stepping out of bounds, I'll do everything within my power to see that neither of you ever tries another case. Captain Stephens, is your client ready to proceed?"

"Yes, Your Honor."

"Bailiff, please bring in the members of the court-martial." Clark and Trip retreated to their seats. Suzanne sat at the counsel table, staring straight ahead, the epitome of apprehension.

As soon as the members were seated, Judge O'Brien banged his gavel again. "This court will come to order. Captain Stephens, call your next witness."

"Your Honor, the defense calls Specialist Raul Gomez."

Gomez looked ill as he slowly walked to the witness stand. He must have been feeling guilty to have taken an overdose of pain killers, even if he really wasn't trying to kill himself. Whatever his reasons, he looked like hell as he was sworn in and took his seat on the witness stand.

Trip first had Gomez testify as to all the events that led up to Lydia being taken to the hospital. He then pursued a long series of questions about the spider bite and how Lydia started acting lethargic afterward. Gomez looked both frightened and agitated as he testified. When he finished, Trip stared at Gomez and then at the members. He turned to walk toward his counsel table but stopped abruptly and turned around. With pathetic melodrama he asked one last question. "Specialist Gomez, did you love your niece?"

The answer was utterly predictable. "A'solutely."

"Your witness." Trip acted as if he'd just won an acquittal.

Clark stood up and—mindful of Judge O'Brien's warning—asked as politely as he knew how, "Isn't it true, Specialist Gomez, that you never saw a spider bite your niece, Lydia Mendoza?"

"Sir? I don' understan'."

In his peripheral vision, Clark could see Judge O'Brien hunched over the bench, watching him closely. Slowly, Clark repeated the question. "Isn't it true that you did *not* see a spider bite your niece?" He emphasized the word "not" for the benefit of Gomez and the members of the court-martial.

"I sorry, sir. I don' understan'."

Judge O'Brien chimed in, "Rephrase the question, counsel."

"Specialist Gomez, did you see a spider bite your niece?"

"No."

"So, why did you testify that she had been bitten by a spider?"

"She star'ed actin' funny."

"What do you mean 'acting funny'?"

"She star'ed actin' sleepy."

"Don't all babies get sleepy from time to time?"

"Yes, sir, bu' she look sick and sleepy a' the same time."

"Why didn't you take her to the hospital?"

"I di'."

"You and Carmen Mendoza took her to Gorgas Hospital on Sunday morning, December 19th, didn't you?"

"Yes, sir."

"Did you tell them that Lydia Mendoza was your daughter?"

"No, sir. I jus' sai' she wa' real sick."

"If she was 'real sick,' why didn't you take her the night before?"

"I jus' though' she was sleepy."

"Lydia Mendoza was alone with you until Carmen returned after midnight, wasn't she?"

"Yes, sir."

"Where were your wife and children?"

"Dey were a' her aun' in Colon."

"So, your wife and children were at her aunt's house in Colon and you were alone with Lydia?"

"Yes, sir."

"How many children do you have, Specialist Gomez?"

"T'ree."

"Did any of them ever have a serious spider bite?"

"No, sir."

"Did any of them ever have the flu?"

"Yes, sir."

"Did you take them to the doctor?"

"Yes, sir."

"So, why didn't you take your niece to the hospital that night?"

"I didn' know she was tha' sick. I wish I ha', Capitain Clark. I wish I ha'."

Gomez then began to cry, sobbing so much that Trip asked Judge O'Brien for a recess. But the judge—still in a testy mood—denied the request. As Clark waited for Gomez to compose himself, he noticed that Gomez was looking piteously at Carmen, who was now seated in the gallery. Gomez's expression seemed to be begging her for forgiveness and support. Clark glanced back at her. She looked as cold as a marble statue.

When Gomez finally composed himself, Clark began again. "Did you talk to Dr. Gonzalez when you were at Gorgas Hospital?"

"Yes, sir. He tol' Carmen an' me tha' Lydia was dead."

"Did he say that Lydia died from a spider bite?"

"No, sir."

"Did you talk to any other doctors at Gorgas Hospital?"

"Jus' the captain tha' was wid Dr. Gonzalez."

"What was his name?"

"I don' remember."

"Did that captain tell you that Lydia died from a spider bite?"

"No, sir."

"So, it's just your opinion that Lydia died from a spider bite, isn't it?"

"Objection, Your Honor," said Trip, now on his feet, but without the cockiness he'd shown before. "Counsel is arguing evidence, not eliciting it."

"Sustained," said Judge O'Brien, staring at Clark with a look of admonition. "Rephrase the question."

Clark fumbled a bit. Trip's objection had knocked him off guard. "Did any of the doctors you talked to about Lydia tell you that she died from a spider bite?"

"No, sir. Bu' Carmen thin' she die' fro' a spider bite, too."

"You are referring to your sister-in-law, Carmen Mendoza, who is Lydia's mother, right?"

"Yes, sir."

"You heard her testify that she never saw a spider bite, didn't you?"

"Yes, sir."

"But now you say that Ms. Mendoza thinks that Lydia died from a spider bite?"

"Yes, sir. She changin' her story."

"You made sexual advances toward your sister-in-law, Ms. Mendoza, didn't you, Specialist Gomez?"

"No, sir. I di' no'. Dat's a lie!" Although tears were welling up in his eyes again, he was puffed up and looked rather theatrical. Clark didn't think the panel members were buying it.

As Clark walked toward his counsel table, he looked at Suzanne and remembered one more question. He turned around to face Gomez. "One more question, Specialist Gomez. How much do you weigh?"

Trip was on his feet instantly. "Objection, Your Honor. His weight is irrelevant."

Trip had again responded in a perfunctory manner. Why did Trip care whether Gomez testified as to his weight? Did he think that the members of the court-martial would be more likely to convict him because he was overweight? Without thinking, Trip had teed up Clark's argument about Gomez weighing ten times what Lydia weighed.

"Your Honor, the accused is charged with shaking Lydia Mendoza to death. Dr. Arias testified that Lydia Mendoza weighed twenty-one pounds at the time of the autopsy. The size and strength of the accused are relevant with respect to the issue of his ability to shake the victim in the manner charged."

"Objection sustained."

Clark was surprised. The judge's ruling was incorrect, but it didn't matter. The members of the court-martial had heard Clark's explanation. He'd made his point.

"No further questions, Your Honor." Clark walked to his chair at the counsel table and sat down.

Now Trip was at his critical juncture in the trial. He had to decide whether to say those fateful words: "the Defense rests." After a long and awkward period of silence, Trip said, with great solemnity, "The Defense rests, Your Honor."

"Do you have any rebuttal witnesses, Captain Clark?"

"Yes, Your Honor. The government calls Carmen Mendoza." Suzanne looked startled. They hadn't discussed putting Carmen back on the stand.

"What are you doing?" she whispered.

"Trust me."

Trip was on his feet again. "Objection, Your Honor. She's been present in the courtroom, listening to all the testimony ever since she testified."

"Captain Clark?" the judge asked, awaiting an explanation.

"Your Honor, Carmen Mendoza is the victim's mother. She has a right to see the prosecution of the crime against her daughter. Furthermore, Specialist Gomez has introduced an issue when he testified that she had changed her story."

Trip spoke up, but with restraint. "May I be heard, Your Honor?"

Judge O'Brien sighed and leaned back in his chair. "Perhaps counsel should approach the bench." Then, having seen the whispered interchange between Clark and Suzanne, he added, "You, too, Captain Watkins." He directed them to move to the right side of the bench, opposite of where the members were sitting, and then asked, "Captain Stephens?"

"Your Honor, government counsel makes the point that Ms. Mendoza heard the testimony that she will now be asked about. That's prejudicial to the defense, Your Honor."

"That's the way it's supposed to work, Counselor," said Judge O'Brien, his professorial demeanor having returned, at least for the time being. "Everything the government presents is prejudicial to the defense. The question is whether it is *unfairly* prejudicial. Do you see a risk that the members will weigh her testimony based on non-legal factors in such a way that it will outweigh the probative value of her testimony?"

"No, Your Honor. I just think she should have been sequestered."

"What do government counsel have to say?"

Suzanne looked at Clark, and he nodded for her to proceed. She faced the judge and said, with confidence, "Your Honor, Ms. Mendoza was sequestered for most of the trial. She had no opportunity to hear the testimony of the other government witnesses or their cross-examination. The only testimony she heard was that of the accused. Now, however, she is being called as a rebuttal witness, to defend what she said on direct examination. Her testimony now will be limited to the issue of whether she's changed her story as the accused claims."

The judge looked at Trip. "Your Honor, she was able to see and hear the testimony of Specialist Gomez, which is what she'll be questioned about."

The judge turned back to Suzanne, who felt his gaze and fidgeted for a few seconds before saying, "Your Honor, we would be permitted to provide context to our questions of Ms. Mendoza, even if she had been sequestered. For example, we could tell her what Specialist Gomez said and ask her to respond."

Judge O'Brien turned back to Trip. "Captain Watkins makes a good point, Captain Stephens. I don't think it's unfairly prejudicial to allow the government to question Ms. Mendoza on this particular point. So, objection overruled. But let me caution government counsel to limit your questioning of Ms. Mendoza to rebuttal, nothing more."

As they sat down at their counsel table, Clark leaned over and whispered, "Great job, Suzanne. Do you want to question her?" Suzanne smiled but shook her head.

Trip slumped in his chair with a sullen look on his face, clearly sending the wrong signal to the members of the court-martial, who were seated directly across from him.

Clark stood up. "The government calls Carmen Mendoza." She walked up to the witness stand, appropriately attired this time, thanks to further guidance from Jaime. "Ms. Mendoza, you testified before, and I want to remind you that you are still under oath."

"I un'erstan'."

"I have only one question for you. Do you believe that your daughter died from a spider bite?"

Carmen hesitated, and Trip was immediately on his feet. "Objection, Your Honor, Ms. Mendoza is not an expert witness. She can't provide opinion testimony on medical issues."

"Sustained."

At that moment Clark realized that he should have objected to Gomez expressing a similar opinion, but he'd missed it. Now, he needed to regroup quickly. "Ms. Mendoza, I guess I am going to have to ask you some more questions." He smiled at her and then glanced at Judge O'Brien, who nodded his consent to proceed. Clark turned back to Carmen. "Let me ask another question. Did you see a spider bite Lydia?"

"No."

"Did anyone tell you that a spider had bitten Lydia?"

"Nobody bu' Raul."

"You're referring to the accused, Specialist Raul Gomez?"

"Yes, sir."

"Do you have any reason to believe that a spider bit Lydia?"

"No."

"Did you see any evidence of a spider bite?"

"I no' un'erstan'…"

"Did you see any marks on her skin that looked like a spider or other insect had bitten her?"

"No sir."

"No further questions, Your Honor."

"Captain Stephens?"

Trip paused for a long time. He turned his head to one side, twisted his neck, and tugged at his shirt collar as if it were too tight. Finally, he stood up and, in his normal voice, without theatrical flair, announced, "No questions, Your Honor."

Judge O'Brien turned to address the members of the court-martial to his left. "Gentlemen, we've heard a lot of testimony over the last few days. I want to recess the court at this point. Tomorrow, each counsel will present closing arguments. After that, you will retire to deliberate. I want to remind each of you that you must not discuss this case with anyone—that includes colleagues, superiors, spouses, friends… anybody. Is that clear?"

Each of the members nodded in agreement. The acrimonious way the trial had progressed had so hardened Judge O'Brien that General Patton wouldn't have dared to cross him at this point.

After the members of the court-martial had left, Judge O'Brien turned toward Clark. "Counsel, today went a lot better than yesterday. But let me make one thing perfectly clear," he then turned toward Trip, "you two had better act like professionals tomorrow—no ifs, no ands, no buts. Understood?"

"Yes, sir," Clark and Trip replied in unison.

Despite having been chastised several times, Clark felt good about the trial. If he and Suzanne failed to get a conviction, it was not for a lack of trying.

As they were walking out of the courtroom, Clark saw Jaime and Elmer, sitting in the last row, grinning like two spider monkeys. "Damn fine prosecution, Counselor," said Elmer. "Bring it home tomorrow." Elmer had a way of sounding eloquent in a redneck sort of way.

"You gave 'em hell, Captain Clark," said Jaime. "You were better dan Major Green. You gonna nail dis guy."

Fortunately, Suzanne had not slowed down, so she didn't hear the two spectators fail to comment on her performance. "Thanks, guys, but I had help." Clark nodded in the direction of Suzanne, who at that point was exiting the courtroom. "And, we still have to do closing arguments tomorrow." He sat down in the spectator row in front of them, turning around to face them and resting his arm on the back of the bench. "And, I have no idea what the members of the court-martial are thinking."

"You got 'em, sir," said Jaime. "I saw i' in dere faces. Dey was noddin' when you were talkin'. Jus' go in dere tomorrow an' nail his ass."

"Thanks for the vote of confidence, Jaime. I'm gonna do my best. But right now I need to make some notes and get ready for tomorrow."

"Tha's goo', Captain Clark. Keep workin' har'."

"Thanks guys." Clark stood up, gathered his files, and headed to his office. Even though things had gone well, he was anxious. Everyone in Panama had been following the trial. His reputation—and probably his future in the JAG Corps—was riding on how it ended. If he lost the case, the only thing anyone would remember was the tongue-lashing that Judge O'Brien put on the record.

Clark really did want to make some notes, but he was too restless to think clearly. He decided to go home early and relax. As he walked down the stairs, he bumped into Colonel Allen on the second floor.

"Captain Clark. Headed home?"

"Yes sir. I'm pretty worn out. I'm going to do some work at home later."

"Oh that's fine. You and Watkins have been burning the midnight oil."

"Yes sir."

"I've heard good reports about the trial."

"Thank you, sir. Closing arguments are tomorrow."

"Well, you've done a good job, Clark. I must say, I had my doubts, given Trip's family and his experience, but you've done a fine job."

"Thank you, sir." Clark smiled politely. "But now I think I need to get home and take a nap."

"You've earned it. Good luck tomorrow. Make me proud."

Although Clark had tried to be pleasant, Colonel Allen's remarks were annoying. As he drove home, he couldn't stop thinking about them. Did Allen actually think that a lawyer's ability was genetic? The outcome of a trial was supposed to be determined by the evidence that each side had to work with and how they used it in the courtroom. But then, why should Clark care about what Allen thought? He was the one sleeping with an enlisted woman who was a suspected drug dealer.

The sun was going down as Clark pulled into his driveway. He decided it was a perfect evening for a cocktail and a Romeo y Julietta on the terrace. As he walked outside with his Maker's Mark and cigar, it began to thunder and lightning the way it normally did in the early afternoon in Panama. The setting sun had colored the evening sky with rich array of red, orange, blue, and purple, and when the lightning flashed, it made for a spectacular sight. Clark settled into a chair beneath the metal roof of the porch and watched God's light show. The rain came in torrents and pounded the roof with an almost rhythmic beat. As the wind blew through the water that was streaming off the edge of the roof, it cooled the air and made everything smell fresh. The gully behind his quarters was soon full of rushing water, as well as all manner of debris. It was as if God was giving His creation a thorough cleaning. The rain stopped just as Clark was finishing his drink and cigar. Everything was peaceful and fresh, and there was a rich earthy smell in the air. He felt like Adam in the Garden.

CHAPTER TWENTY-EIGHT

WHEN CLARK AWOKE the next morning, the sky was black. He looked at his digital clock. The red numerals read 2:00. Although he'd slept only three hours, he was wide awake. He couldn't stop thinking about his closing argument, which still loomed in front of him. It was the part of the trial that everyone would remember—the part everyone would talk about, regardless of how the trial turned out. His boss, the other JAGs, other commanders and soldiers, even the manager of the NCO Club—all of them were waiting to see what happened—waiting to see if it was like Perry Mason or some movie they'd seen. If the trial went well, they would talk about how brilliant the closing argument was—just the right amount of passion, touched on just the right points of law, hammered home the key evidence. If the trial went badly, they would talk about how he'd screwed up—what he'd left out, what he should have said, how he should have said it.

He knew he needed more sleep. In a few hours he would have to "perform." And everyone would be watching. His anxiety made him sweat so much he soaked the sheets. Realizing it was pointless to try to go back to sleep, he got up, showered, and got ready for work. He put on his uniform trousers but left his shirt hanging on a hook on the bedroom door; he didn't want to wrinkle it while he was getting ready.

He paced from room to room, collecting his things, but his movements weren't efficient. First, he forgot some of his notes in the spare bedroom and had to look for them. Then he couldn't find his wallet, then his keys. Finding no clean T-shirt in the drawer, he had to look in the dryer. As he paced about, he noticed the click-click sound of his shoes on the terrazzo floor. When he stopped, it was quiet and still—as if no one lived there. That desolate silence reminded him of that other set of problems in need of his attention. But he had a trial to finish. Only then could he focus on that.

Looking around his dimly lit quarters, he decided to practice his closing argument there. For one thing, there was no risk of being overheard. At his office, Suzanne, or even Trip, might be lurking outside his door. He took the chairs from the dining room and lined them up in the living room as if they were the members of the court-martial panel. He draped his uniform shirt over the first chair. Not enough. He went to his daughter's room and gathered up a couple of her dolls and a stuffed animal. His "panel" would be comprised of Raggedy Ann, a stuffed Easter Bunny, a teddy bear, and his shirt. He stood in front of them and tried to imagine the seven men he would face in a few hours. It wasn't a convincing array, but it would have to do. Then he practiced. Over and over, he practiced. For almost two hours he practiced without stopping. But it wasn't working. His delivery was all wrong. It was too rehearsed, too stilted, too devoid of passion.

Picking up his daughter's teddy bear, he walked out to the terrace to clear his head. He heard rustling in the tree and looked up. There was his pal John, staring back at him in the moonlight. "Why do you always show up when I'm frustrated?" The iguana seemed to sneer back at him. "Fuck you, John!" Clark stormed back into the living room and threw the teddy bear into the chair. It landed sideways. "Sit the fuck up, asshole!" he yelled at Ellie's toy. Sweat formed under his arms and slid down his sides. That awful feeling began to form in his gut—as it always did before he began to cry about Ellie. But he couldn't allow himself to go there. He had to be ready to finish the case.

He walked back into his bedroom and undressed. Now, his movements were quick and purposeful. He showered and dressed again and then walked back into the living room. His shoes click clicked on the floor.

"Gentlemen, I want to thank you for the time and attention you've given to this trial…" The words began to flow. He carefully considered each gesture, each movement to and from the lectern, each turn of phrase. And he nailed it. He knew he did. He put on his uniform shirt, gathered his files and papers, and turned off the lights.

Clark got to the parking lot around 5:45 a.m. and was surprised to find Suzanne's car already there. When he got out of his car, he heard soldiers in the distance, singing "jody calls" as they ran in formation. He looked up at his building in the dim, pre-dawn light. The windows beneath the terra cotta awnings were all dark except for the emergency lights in the stairwell. Entering the ground floor, he started up the stairs to the Criminal Law Section but stopped when he noticed the heavy, metal gate, made of welded rebar, across the front door of the liquor store. It was secured with a thick chain and a large padlock. Strange that he'd never noticed it before. He turned and continued up the stairs.

The reception area of the Criminal Law Section was dark and empty, but he could see light coming from the hallway where Suzanne's office was located. Not wanting to startle her, he announced his arrival with, "Anybody home?" No answer. The door to her office was open, and she was at her desk, staring intently at a document. She looked up, her face so ashen she looked like a cancer patient. "We have a problem."

Clark took a deep breath. He had to make a conscious effort

not to sound irritated. "I thought you were feeling confident about where we were."

"That was before I reviewed my notes on those cases I researched."

"What's the problem?" he sighed, disheartened that Suzanne's persistent paranoia appeared to be taking control of her again.

"None of the doctors ever looked at Lydia Mendoza's medical records."

"What are you talking about, Suzanne?"

"Well, if she had some disease or illness, they wouldn't have known it."

"She didn't have any medical records, Suzanne. Remember, she's Panamanian. And, they examined her."

"Yes, but Dr. Gonzalez said he was focused only on the edema. I don't think he gave her a complete examination."

"Why are you looking for trouble?" Clark asked, squinting his eyes and slightly shaking his head from side to side. Suzanne's eyebrows dropped, and he saw her lips quiver slightly as they pursed and turned downward. "Look, Suzanne, I'm sorry. I don't mean to be short with you. I'm just ready to get this trial over with. I'm sure Dr. Gonzalez made a thorough examination of Lydia when he was treating her."

"But remember, Clark, he didn't even see the spider bite."

"There was no spider-bite, Suzanne. The only person who testified about it was Gomez. Even Peterson's testimony was based on what Gomez told him."

"Yes, but Dr. Gonzalez said he was focused on treating Lydia's symptoms. What if he missed something that would tell us why she died?"

"She died because Raul Gomez shook her to death, Suzanne. Why is this bothering you, anyway?"

"Well, some of the civilian cases I reviewed reversed the

convictions because the doctors ignored the medical histories of the victims—just like our doctors did."

"You know what? I'm not worried about that. First of all, this is a court-martial, not a civilian criminal trial. Second, nobody believes that spider-bite story. And third, Dr. Gonzalez and Major Underwood were the two most convincing witnesses. If they had thought anything in Lydia's medical history was important, they would've brought it up." Clark waited for a response but got none. "I've got to go get ready for my closing argument."

"I thought you had already prepared it."

"I did, but I need to go over it some more. You know, Suzanne, you kill confidence faster than a quarterback with slippery hands."

"Spare me the sports analogies, Clark. I'm just trying to do my job."

"You have been, Suzanne. Now, I've got to get ready to do mine."

Clark turned on his heel and went to his office, where he retrieved a yellow legal pad that he'd left on his desk. It contained the notes he had taken when he last discussed the case with Suzanne. He stepped back into her office, reading from the pad, "Yesterday, you told me to, quote, 'harp on the fact that Peterson never saw Lydia and was, therefore, forming an opinion based on what Raul had told him' end quote. What's different now?"

"I told you, Clark, I've been reviewing my notes…"

"Look, Suzanne, as far as I'm concerned, Peterson's testimony is all the defense has. You said so yourself. Despite his tears, Gomez was unconvincing, and none of Trip's cross-examination was effective. So, it seems to me that discrediting Peterson is the key. The members of the court-martial need to conclude that there is no reasonable explanation for the death of Lydia Mendoza other than what you said in your opening statement: 'Raul Gomez brutally shook Lydia Mendoza, causing her brain to swell, which ultimately led to her death.' You said that, remember? And that conclusion is what all the evidence points to. There is no credible evidence that a spider bite caused Lydia's death."

"You obviously don't need me, Counselor," she said, sitting up straight and tucking back her chin and shoulders. "Go for it." She raised her eyebrows and pursed her lips—clearly no longer on the verge of crying.

Before long it was 7:30 a.m., and the outer office was abuzz. Everyone knew this was the big day, and they wanted to get a good seat to watch. As Clark was gathering his materials to go to the courtroom, he looked up to see Trip, looking lost and—especially strange for Trip—almost humble. "Listen, Clark, however things turn out, I, uh, hope that we can still be friends."

"Uh, yeah... sure, Trip. We'll be friends, regardless."

Trip gave a half smile and then turned and walked away. What was Trip trying to do? It never had occurred to Clark that Trip thought of him as a friend. The only thing they had ever done together was that first trip to Mother's Inn. Clark concluded that Trip knew he was going to lose and was making a lame attempt to save face.

Shortly before 8:00 a.m., Clark and Suzanne walked into the courtroom; Judge O'Brien entered shortly after. The judge wasted no time with pleasantries and got straight to the point. He called the court to order and had the members of the panel come in and take their seats. Then he looked at Clark and Suzanne and said, "One of the government counsel may address the members of the court-martial."

Suzanne turned toward Clark, so that her back was to the panel. She looked intently into his eyes and whispered, "Go get 'em. You've got this."

He took a deep breath, stood up, and walked to the lectern with his notes. "Gentlemen, thank you for the time and attention you have devoted to this trial. Yours is an important and solemn duty. Although this trial has been long, I shall be brief because the evidence in this case is clear.

"By his own testimony, the accused told you that he was alone with Lydia Mendoza for six hours before her mother arrived and before she was taken to Gorgas Hospital. Thus, it is uncontroverted that the accused had the opportunity to commit this crime." Clark studied their faces to see if he was connecting. They could have been playing poker.

"He also had the means. You can see for yourself that the accused is a large man." Clark gestured in the direction of Gomez. "Decide for yourself how much you think he weighs." Clark glanced at Judge O'Brien out of the corner of his eye but saw no reaction. "Clearly, gentlemen, a man of this size would have no trouble shaking a little girl who weighed only twenty-one pounds."

Clark left the lectern and approached the members of the court-martial without his notes. "Dr. Roberto Gonzalez, the most prominent neurosurgeon in Panama, explained to you what can happen when a small child is shaken violently." He raised his arms so that his hands were in front of his face, as if he were holding a small child, then imitated a violent shaking. He stopped and put his arms down. As he looked into the eyes of one member and then another, he said, "A child's undeveloped brain rattles around inside of its skull and becomes bruised. That bruising leads to swelling and, ultimately, to death. The evidence you heard proves that that is exactly what happened to Lydia Mendoza. Dr. Gonzalez told you that he tried to relieve the pressure on Lydia's brain by taking out a piece of her skull, but it wasn't enough. Her brain continued to ooze out of the hole."

Clark walked back to the lectern to transition to his next point. "In addition to Dr. Gonzalez, you heard from Dr. José Arias, who performed a complete autopsy on Lydia Mendoza, carefully examining every part of her body. Like Dr. Gonzalez, he also concluded that Lydia died from being shaken. And remember, gentlemen, the only doctors who actually examined Lydia Mendoza were Dr. Gonzalez and Dr. Arias." Clark paused to let his last statement hang in the air and stared at the members to underscore its importance.

"Major Horace Underwood—from the Armed Forces Institute of Pathology—testified next. He is a medical doctor who specializes in forensic pathology, which, as he explained, is the sub-specialty of pathology that focuses on determining the cause of death by examining a corpse. Major Underwood carefully reviewed all the evidence that the Criminal Investigation Division collected in this case, including the autopsy report and tissue samples from the autopsy. He reached the same conclusion that Dr. Gonzalez and Dr. Arias reached: Lydia Mendoza was violently shaken to death. There is, therefore, no doubt that the accused had the means to commit this crime."

Clark glanced at his notes to signal a change of topic and then looked up at each face on the panel. "This leads us to the final question: Why would the accused do something so horrendous? What was his motive?" Clark stopped talking and made eye contact with the members of the court-martial. He wanted to emphasize what was coming next. "Carmen Mendoza gave you the answer to that question when she testified under oath." Clark gestured toward the witness stand, hoping the members would recall her testimony. He walked over to it and turned to face the members. "Miss Mendoza told you that Raul Gomez was angry— angry because his beautiful sister-in-law had rejected his sexual advances. She challenged his manhood when she told him that she didn't want to sleep with him. And on whom did the accused take out his anger?" Clark paused for a long time and then said, in a soft voice, "His thirteen-month old niece, who weighed only twenty-one pounds." He allowed that comment to sink in and then continued in his normal voice, "Recall that Carmen testified that the accused went into the room where Lydia was crying immediately after she rejected him. A big angry man, shaking a tiny little girl, led to a terrible result."

Clark slowly walked back to the lectern to check his notes and then continued. "You also heard from Commander Peterson. He testified that Lydia Mendoza died from a spider bite. But that was pure speculation: Commander Peterson never saw Lydia Mendoza. He only reviewed photographs and the reports prepared by the two doctors who did examine her. They testified that Lydia died from brain edema brought on by a violent shaking. And note, gentlemen," at this point Clark's voice became louder and more intense, "I use the word 'speculate' advisedly because there is no evidence that a spider bite killed Lydia Mendoza or that she was even bitten by a spider. Even the accused admitted he never saw a spider bite her. Both he and Commander Peterson are speculating. And speculation is not the same as reasonable doubt."

Again, Clark approached the members of the court-martial without his notes. In a softer voice—almost a whisper—he said, "The evidence in this case clearly demonstrates, beyond any reasonable doubt, that Lydia Mendoza died because Raul Gomez cruelly shook her, as if she were an inanimate object. That act of violence by a man ten times her size caused Lydia's brain to swell and killed her. Your duty, gentlemen, is to do justice." He looked at the faces of each of them. "The evidence in this case calls for justice. Lydia Mendoza calls for justice. Thank you."

The members of the court-martial almost nodded at him. After he sat down, Suzanne leaned over and whispered, "Good job, partner." Clark gave her a tiny nod and the hint of a smile and then whispered, "I hope so."

Trip gathered his papers, stood up, and strode confidently to the lectern. "Gentlemen of the jury," he began. Snickers rippled through the members, who at this point knew that they were referred to as "members of the court-martial," not "gentlemen of the jury."

"Excuse me," Trip continued. "I mean members of the court-martial. I guess the word 'jury' flows off my tongue when I think of these proceedings because juries are a sacred part of our judicial system, and you gentlemen are filling that important, sacred role."

Even Clark had to admit that was a good recovery.

"All that stands between Specialist Raul Gomez and a miscarriage of justice are the discussions you will have in that deliberation room." Trip pointed to the door behind the members. "Conduct those deliberations carefully, gentlemen. This man's future—and the future of his family—are in your hands.

"Lydia Gomez died from a spider bite. That is the conclusion of the only board-certified forensic pathologist who testified in this trial. None of the other doctors who testified have passed the rigorous examination that is necessary to become board-certified in forensic pathology.

"Carmen Mendoza, the victim's mother, now has a convenient memory lapse about the spider bite. Now, she assuages her guilt for not caring for her illegitimate child by accusing Specialist Gomez of making a pass at her. You saw him testify, gentlemen. You saw how emotional this soldier became when he spoke of his little niece. Do you really think that such a man is capable of harming a defenseless child? Trip gestured toward Gomez as if he'd rehearsed the movement, except it wasn't smooth. He looked like a kid who'd been forced to play a part in a school play. "He has three children of his own, whom he dearly loves. Why would a caring father do something so heinous as shaking a little girl to death?

"No, gentlemen, there is another reasonable explanation for Lydia Mendoza's death. She died from the bite of one of the most poisonous spiders in the world. And doctors Gonzalez and Arias didn't even bother to look for evidence of a spider bite. They had their scapegoat. There was no need.

"Do not convict this man based on the flimsy evidence you have heard." Trip's voice rose in a way that suggested he was trying—unsuccessfully—to sound like a great orator. He continued, "Captain Clark is right about one thing, gentlemen: your job is to do justice. And justice demands that you acquit Specialist Gomez."

Trip then turned and walked back to his seat. No "thank you" to the members of the court-martial. No "the end." He just stopped, turned around, and walked back to his seat.

"Any rebuttal, Captain Clark?"

Clark studied the faces of the members of the court-martial, trying to discern whether Trip's argument had swayed any of them. They all looked serious. He had no idea what they were thinking. But he did sense that Judge O'Brien had heard enough from him, and he didn't want to give the members of the court-martial the impression that Trip had said anything of consequence. He stood up and confidently replied, "No, Your Honor." As he sat down, he tried to gauge Suzanne's reaction. She was staring straight ahead, her jaw clenched and her face taught.

CHAPTER TWENTY-NINE

ALL THE EVIDENCE was in. Each side had argued its case. Now it was time for Judge O'Brien to give the members of the court-martial panel specific instructions, which he had discussed with the attorneys in an earlier session. Although lawyers often anguish over the fine points of a judge's instructions, Clark doubted they would mean very much in this case. He was right: the members' faces were blank, their eyes glazed over, as the judge read what Clark was sure they would refer to as "legalese" when they returned to the deliberation room.

The members knew what they needed to do. If they believed that Gomez shook Lydia, then he was guilty; if he didn't, then he wasn't. There wasn't much else to this case. The spider-bite story wasn't believable, and all the government witnesses had said that Lydia had been shaken to death. Gomez was the only person with opportunity, means, and motive to commit the crime.

As Judge O'Brien read the instructions to the members, Clark scanned the courtroom. Elmer and Jaime were again on the back row. They saw him looking at them and started grinning and giving him the "thumbs up." Clark frowned like a teacher reigning in a couple of rowdy schoolboys. They dropped their hands but kept on grinning. Suzanne saw them, too. "They're so juvenile," she whispered through clenched teeth.

Clark turned and looked at Trip, who was huddled with his client, apparently in deep conversation. That didn't look very good. The members were listening to the judge, and the man with the most to lose was not.

After the judge finished his instructions, the members retired to the deliberation room. Clark had heard in law school that if a jury comes back quickly, it's good for the prosecution. But, if a jury stays out for a long time, it usually means there is disagreement among its members, which is good for the defense. He wasn't sure whether that same conventional wisdom applied to court-martial panels. A lot of other factors might alter the process, he mused, chief of which was that although they were missing work, they weren't missing any pay. And, it was a lot cooler in the deliberation room than on the firing range or in the motor pool. In any event, it appeared that the members were going to be out for a while because they sent word that they wanted lunch brought in.

Clark wasn't too worried until later in the afternoon, when the president of the court-martial panel sent word that they wanted the judge's permission to go home and continue their deliberations the next day. That news brought a big smile to Trip's face. It was a good sign for him. Clark couldn't understand what was taking them so long. As expected, Judge O'Brien granted their request and told everyone to reassemble at 0800 hours the next day.

Clark went back to his office and flopped into his chair—tired, and yet anxious and fidgety at the same time. He tried to read the CID reports concerning new investigations, but it was no use. Although his eyes scanned the same sworn statement three times, he had no idea what it said. He needed to break the tension, and he knew exactly how to do it. Picking up his phone, he dialed a familiar number from memory. "Elmer, this is Clark. You want to meet me at Mother's? I've got to wrap up a couple of things here, but I could meet you there in about forty-five minutes."

"Of course, Counselor. Jaime's here, too. He just said that we should call you. We'll meet you there."

Clark felt guilty for not inviting Suzanne, especially since she'd offered to take him a couple of days before, but he just didn't want her to come along. He wasn't in the mood to deal with her pessimism. He was afraid she'd start worrying about something they'd missed—which, of course, they couldn't do anything about now—and he just didn't want to think about that. He needed to relax, and he knew that Elmer and Jaime were experts at that. He tried to slip past her office, but she saw him. "Hey, partner, want to get some supper tonight? I know a good place downtown…"

"No thanks, Suzanne. I'm beat. I think I need to go home and relax." He cringed inside when he told that lie but tried to convince himself that he was sparing Suzanne's feelings.

When he arrived at Mother's Inn, Elmer's motorcycle was parked in its usual spot. The boys were ahead of him. As he walked through the door, he heard someone yell, "Here he is." The lights started flashing on and off, and popcorn came showering down on him. Elmer walked up, put his arm around Clark's shoulder like a buddy, and shouted for everyone to be quiet. And then, he started. Sounding like a combination of a Southern politician doing a stump speech and a television evangelist begging for money, Elmer announced to those who had gathered around: "We've been waiting a long time to get a prosecutor with some balls. Well, gentlemen, we got one. And I just watched him kick some ass today!"

The crowd cheered, although Clark was pretty sure that the semi-drunk lieutenants in front of him had no idea what Elmer was talking about. His stomach tensed because he knew Elmer's victory speech was premature. Nothing is certain in a trial until the members of the court-martial come back with their verdict. Elmer quieted the rowdy group and turned toward Clark with an expectant look. Clark wasn't about to give a speech, so he smiled and said, simply, "I need a beer." A raucous cheer erupted, and Elmer led

Clark through the crowd to his corner. As they approached Elmer's table, Clark saw Jaime sitting there looking as if he'd just won the office pool on the Super Bowl.

A waitress arrived with a cold Balboa, as Clark raked popcorn out of his hair. He looked up at her and smiled, but she just shook her head like a mom, perplexed by the antics of little boys. He took a long swig. The beer tasted good and signaled to his stomach that it was, indeed, time to relax. More beers followed as the three of them recounted all that had happened during the trial.

"If the members see it the way you guys did, then I think we're in good shape," Clark said after he'd finished about half of his second cold one.

"Of course they will," Elmer replied, "I especially liked it when you yelled at that Navy commander. He was such a prick."

"Do you think the members thought I was unprofessional?" Clark stood up, untucked his shirt, and shook out several kernels of popcorn.

"Are you kidding me?" Elmer wrinkled his nose and squinted his eyes in mock disbelief. "They would've done the same thing to that wimpy little maggot."

"What about O'Brien calling me into his chambers?"

"They're probably laughing about you gettin' your ass chewed. They don't give a shit about stuff like that. Hell, I thought it was funny, too."

"Tha' shi' happen' all the time, Capitain Clark. I wouldn' worry abou'," Jaime added.

When Elmer and Jaime finished stroking Clark's ego, the three men started watching the antics of a group of lieutenants at the table next to them. They were building a beer-bottle pyramid, which grew to almost five feet before it came crashing down, creating a mess of broken glass that they proceeded to ignore. Their sideshow ended when the club manager came out from the back

room and yelled at the lieutenants, directing them to help the waitress sweep up the broken glass, which they promptly did.

Elmer and Jaime turned back to face Clark, which prompted
him to ask, "What did you guys think of Trip's performance?"

"I told you, Clark. I can't decide whether that guy is lazy or stupid or both," said Elmer. Jaime nodded in agreement. "He sounded
like he was pulling everything out of his ass. And it looked that
way, too. He didn't do anything on cross-examination except go
over what Watkins and you had just asked the witnesses. And his
closing argument was pathetic. The guy is completely superficial."

"What do you mean 'superficial'?" Clark asked, surprised by
Elmer's answer.

"Well, for one thing, he should have brought up the issue of
intent. You nailed him on opportunity, means, and motive, but
Trip could have said that even if Gomez might have shaken the
kid a little bit, there was no evidence that he intended to hurt her."
Again, Jaime nodded in agreement.

"That would have been a good defense, I suppose," said Clark,
"but I don't think Trip wanted to allow Gomez to admit that he'd
even held Lydia."

"Well, that was stupid," Elmer replied. "How could he babysit
her for six hours and not hold her? He should have said, 'Yeah, I
held her, but I sure as hell didn't intend to kill her.' That would
have been plausible, and he might have gotten off with a conviction of a lesser included offense like negligent homicide."

"Yeah. Capitain Stephens didn' even try to go fo' somethin'
like negligen' homicide. Tha' would ha' been my trial strategy."

"You know, you're right," Clark said. "Now I'm feeling stupid for not anticipating that. I should have thought about lesser
included offenses."

"Aw, bullshit, Clark," said Elmer. "You did fine, especially when
Carmen said that Raul tried to rape her. Did you know that?"

"No. She never mentioned it before."

"You're kidding, right?" Elmer stared at Clark, apparently trying to discern whether he was really that naïve.

"I guess I should have asked her about it."

"Well, no shit," Elmer replied. But when he noticed that his comment had caused an immediate change in the valiant warrior's expression, he shifted gears. "Well, so what? In the end it didn't matter. You sure as hell made good use of it." Clark managed a faint smile. "But next time you talk to a pretty woman, dumbass, ask her about the sex angle. There's always a sex angle, especially down here."

"I guess you're right." Clark took a long drink of his beer and then rallied a defense. "But you know, Elmer, she looked like a kid when I met her."

"Well, she sure as hell didn't look like a kid when I saw her." Elmer and Jaime started laughing like high-school sophomores.

"She's a kid, Elmer."

"Yeah. Yeah. I get it."

Turning to Jaime, Clark said, "Thank God you got her appearance squared away before she testified in rebuttal."

"Yeah. I shoul' have looke' a' her the firs' time. She di' look a little too hot tha' firs' time."

"Hey, guys, I gotta hit the head," Elmer said as he got up and headed for the latrine.

"I thin' you di' a goo' job, Capitain Clark. I' sorry I didn' check ou' Carmen before the trial. I didn' thin' she woul' dress like a *puta*."

"Don't worry about it, Jaime. I think we're in good shape. I should have given you better guidance, anyway. But, you know what? We made our point. I think the members got it. It was clear that she's a grieving young mother."

"Yeah. An' I don' thin' dey believe tha' spider bite bullshi'."

Jaime and Clark watched as Elmer "worked the room" for a few minutes like a politician running for office. When he returned, he had a pensive expression on his face, as if he'd been pondering something. "You know, Trip's biggest problem is that he failed to connect with the members of the court-martial."

"How so?" Clark asked.

"You do it naturally, Clark, because you're one of us. You got that muther-fuckin' Ranger Tab, don't you?"

"You think the Tab makes that much difference?"

"Not the Tab, stupid. The fact that you're a soldier. You understand soldiers. Most of the members of that court-martial have never been in a country club, except maybe to caddie or wash dishes. If they heard somebody ask for a G&T, they'd think they were talkin' about some kind of medical procedure." Clark and Jaime gave that lame joke more laughter than it deserved. "Trip is a typical country club guy; you're a fuckin' soldier. Have you ever even been in a country club, Clark?"

"I caddied at one in Savannah one summer."

"See. What did I tell you? Did you notice how they talk?"

"I'm not sure what you're getting at."

"The guys that go to country clubs go on and on about their new sports cars and their vacations to Europe… their golf trips and their custom clubs… their hunting trips to Argentina and their expensive shotguns." Elmer paused to take a drink of beer. "And, sometimes, after they get a little drunk and don't think any of the help are listening, they talk about all the women they're screwing."

Elmer had a far-off look on his face, as if he were looking at something that Clark and Jaime couldn't see.

"I didn't hear that much, Elmer. Where's your information come from? Did you caddie, too?"

"Nope. My dad's a lawyer. We belonged to the Bellerive Country Club in St. Louis when I was a kid."

"Really?"

"Yeah, ain't it funny? More incongruity from Captain Elmer T. Jackson. First, you find out I went to Oral Roberts University.

Then you find out that my wife is a bar fly from the Fort Benning Officers' Club who got knocked up by somebody other than
me. And now you find out that my dad's a lawyer and I grew up
goin' to a country club. Shockin', ain't it?" Elmer took another long
drink of beer.

"Not really."

"And, I was also valedictorian of my high school class."

"Really?"

"No, dumbass, I'm fuckin' with you. I was smoking too much
dope back then."

Clark looked at Elmer in wide-eyed disbelief.

"Don't worry, Clark. I reformed when I joined the Army. But
admit it. You thought I was some redneck hillbilly, didn't you?"

"I don't know. I thought you were like me, I guess."

"I am like you. That's what I like about you. You're the real
deal. You know: what you see is what you get. But Trip is like
every other asshole I saw at that country club. I figured out a long
time ago that I didn't want any part of that bullshit. They're just
a bunch of pretentious pricks trying to out-brag each other. And
most of them have never done shit. You ever hear that Army com-
mercial about how we do more before breakfast than most people
do all day?"

"Yeah. I like it," Clark said. Jaime nodded.

"Well, those country club dudes ain't even out of bed before
0900 hours. A lot of 'em are livin' off their daddy's money. If they
have jobs, they got them because daddy or granddaddy was some
big shot. My father was a big deal because his father was a judge."

"I thought it was that way only in the South."

"It's that way all over, Clark." Elmer shook his head. "I decided
a long time ago that I'm gonna make my own damn way. That's
why I joined the Army." He took the last draw on his cigarette and
crushed it out as he exhaled.

For several minutes the three men sat quietly drinking beer, until a new waitress came over to gather their empties. All three of them eyed her with interest. She was gorgeous—probably in her mid-twenties, with a stunning figure that she didn't mind showing off. Cleavage yielded more tips, after all. She smiled and loaded her tray with their empty bottles. As she walked away, they continued to stare—her hips swaying in a seductive way that seems to come naturally to Latin women.

Clark broke the silence. "Have either of you guys talked to your wives lately?"

Almost in unison, they said no.

"I don't intend to go crawling back to her," Elmer said. "I don't need her."

"Me neither," Jaime mumbled. "She can go to hell."

Clark said nothing, and neither of his friends asked about his wife. He figured they didn't want to risk appearing sensitive, as if they cared about something as touchy-feely as his relationship with his wife. Despite all their macho talk, though, it was clear that all three men were hurting. As the evening wore on and their bar tab grew, they began to get philosophical.

At one point, Clark looked at Elmer and slurred, "Did you really graduate from Oral Roberts U?"

Continuing to stare into his beer, as if the bubbles were tealeaves, Elmer said, "No, Clark. I told you that."

"I forgot what you said. So you didn't graduate?"

"No! They were as full of shit as the men at the fuckin' country club—just a different kind o' shit. I went there lookin' for somethin' but didn't find it, so I quit."

Sensing he needed to change the conversation, Clark blurted out, "I did something kinda good a couple days ago."

Jaime and Elmer looked at him as if to say, "Okay, what?"

"I was driving through the front part of Curundu... you know, where all the Zonians live. And I noticed this old guy, all bent over, carrying a box with rakes and other yard tools in it."

"Yeah, I've seen that old dude shuffling along, too," said Elmer.

"Well, I stopped and gave him five bucks and told him that I did it in the name of Jesus Christ."

"Well, you just blew it, Counselor," said Elmer.

Clark looked puzzled.

"I may be an Oral Roberts drop out, but I remember the parable of the widow's mite."

"What's that got to do with this?"

"Don't get me wrong, Clark. It was a nice thing to do. That old guy works his butt off to earn five bucks. But if you talk about your gift, you ruin it. It means you did it because you wanted to brag about it."

"No, that's not it at all."

"Maybe. But I think you should keep that kind of stuff to yourself. Get the benefit Christ wanted you to get from making a gift. Don't go lookin' for praise."

"I wasn't…"

"I'm sorry, Clark." Elmer looked at him with his honest blue eyes. "I'm being an asshole. I know you weren't lookin' for praise. You're not that kinda guy. I just think that things like that are better when they're free of bullshit. If you do something good, don't say anything about it. It makes it better." He threw his arm around Clark's shoulder.

Elmer was, without a doubt, the most unusual, enigmatic person Clark had ever met. He seemed to have a deep understanding about things, and yet his lifestyle was crazy. One minute he was chasing married women and the next he was quoting Jesus, with the kind of confidence that only comes from a true understanding of the Bible. Maybe he was one of those people Daddy was talking about there at the end—one who was both good and bad at the same time.

CHAPTER THIRTY

CLARK STABBED HIS key at the lock twice—and missed both times—leaving two deep scratches on the side of his Nova. Looking down at them in the shadowy light, he mumbled, "How the hell am I going to explain that to her when she comes back?" The third time the key hit the mark, and he unlocked his car. He knew he'd had way too much to drink and probably shouldn't drive home. But, he figured his reputation among the MPs on Fort Clayton had grown and doubted that any of them would bust him for DUI.

The night was moonless, and the stars were obscured by clouds, because the only light he saw came from his headlights. They guided him through the thick, black jungle that surrounded the road, forming a tunnel of vegetation. It wasn't the first time he'd driven home on such a night, but it was no less haunting. Given his semi-drunk condition, he had the good sense to drive at a cautious pace.

The steering wheel jerked in his hands. "What the hell was that?" he said out loud. "I must have hit something." He pulled over to the side of the road and grabbed his flashlight from the glove compartment. After checking for oncoming traffic, he turned on his flashers and got out to investigate. He hadn't walked far before he saw his victim: an iguana, much bigger than John. It was writhing in the middle of the road. He picked up a large rock from beside the road and smashed it on the iguana's head. The writhing stopped. He picked up the rock, tossed it away, and got back in his car.

When he got to his quarters, he shuffled from the back door to his bedroom and fell onto the bed—still in his uniform, sweaty and exhausted. But he couldn't get to sleep. Despite Elmer's optimistic predictions, he was scared. Why had the members of the court-martial stayed out so long? Obviously, courts-martial were different from civilian criminal trials. He tried to convince himself that the length of the deliberations didn't mean that Gomez was going to be acquitted. It was hopeless, though. He couldn't stop worrying and was so nervous he soaked his uniform and sheets with sweat. At some point during the wee hours, he finally fell asleep.

Morning came, and he awoke exhausted, having slept no more than a couple of hours. His head felt like it was splitting apart, which reminded him that Elmer and Mother's Inn and celebrations were not a good combination. When he looked at the bedside clock, the numerals read 6:50, which was way too late to be waking up. Thankfully, he had one more clean uniform, since he'd trashed the one he'd slept in. He quickly shaved and got ready to face one of the momentous days of his life.

When he arrived at the JAG Office, the parking lot was full, which was unusual. Inside, a crowd had gathered in the hallway outside the courtroom. There were soldiers, including some officers, and a few civilians, some of whom appeared to be Panamanian. In a strange way, it made Clark feel good that so many people were concerned about a little girl named Lydia Mendoza. They were here because they wanted to see the fate of her killer. They wanted to see if she got justice.

As he made his way down the hall, Suzanne blocked his path. "Listen, Clark, I wanted to say…"

He held up his hand. "If you're going to lecture to me, Suzanne, don't. I can't deal with that right now."

"No… no. I just wanted to say that yesterday I got all paranoid because you didn't address the matter of reviewing Lydia's medical records, and I want to apologize. You played the hand you were dealt, and you did a great job." The words tumbled out of her mouth as if she'd rehearsed them.

"Oh. Thanks. But I'm still not sure what you mean." He squinted his eyes—and held his breath so she couldn't smell it.

"I mean you can't change what people did. They either did or didn't review the records. You can't control that. You argued the case well."

"Oh. Okay. Thanks. I need to get some coffee." He walked over to the pot, poured a cup, and took a big drink, hoping to cover up his booze breath. Heading to his office, he motioned for Suzanne to follow him. He went to the window, so as not to be too close to her, and motioned for her to shut the door. He sat down on the sill, stared at her for a few moments, and then asked, "Why do you think the members have been out so long?"

"Come on, Clark. You know why. They aren't sweating their asses off outside somewhere. This is cushy duty, so they're stringing it out."

"I hope you're right."

"Look, I need to return a call before we get started." She turned and left.

He looked at the clock on the wall. It was 7:50 a.m. He closed the door and sat down in his chair to gather his thoughts. At this point, the course of the trial was set. If he won he would try to appear magnanimous to Trip, and if he lost, he would act as if he was above it all. But the only way he could lose would be for the members to make an incredibly stupid decision, and he had no reason to think they would. By the time he walked into the courtroom, his personal pep talk had given him more confidence than at any point during the trial.

Judge O'Brien called the court to order. "Do the members of the court-martial need more time for deliberations?"

Captain Hargrove, the president of the court-martial, stood up and announced in a firm voice, "No, Your Honor. We have reached a verdict."

"Are your findings reflected on the findings worksheet?"

"Yes, Your Honor."

Judge O'Brien told the bailiff to retrieve the findings worksheet. He examined it and gave it back to the bailiff, who immediately handed it back to Captain Hargrove.

"Captain Stephens," said the judge, "will you and the accused please rise?" Then he turned toward the court-martial panel and said, "Captain Hargrove, please announce the findings to the court."

Clark felt like he was going to throw up. Being hung over was no condition in which to wait for a verdict.

Captain Hargrove read from the worksheet, "Specialist Raul Gomez, this court-martial finds you guilty of the charge and its specification, in violation of Article 118 of the Uniform Code of Military Justice."

Clark wanted to jump up and cheer. Lydia Mendoza had received justice. He looked at Suzanne, who was smiling but fidgeting. She looked at him and mouthed the words, "We did it." Clark nodded slightly. He turned and looked at Gomez, who was crying much harder than before. Trip had his arm around Gomez's shoulder and was saying something to him. Gomez kept looking toward the gallery, and when he did, Clark could see that his face was wet with tears. Each time, he shook his head no.

Turning to see who Gomez was looking at, Clark noticed a Hispanic woman sitting on the front row of the gallery, who appeared to be looking at Gomez. She was approximately the same age as Carmen, and she was also crying uncontrollably. Clark assumed she was Gomez's wife and Carmen's sister. She was, in fact, a little chubby and not nearly as attractive as Carmen. Hearing sobbing from the other side of the gallery, Clark turned to see Carmen, who was bent over with her face on her knees. An older woman had an arm around her, consoling her. Jaime was there, too.

The courtroom got too rowdy for Judge O'Brien; he pounded his gavel so hard he broke it again. "Order in this court!" The room fell silent, as the head of the gavel tumbled to the floor in front of the bench. All eyes turned to the judge. When he spoke again, he sounded more like a priest, comforting his parishioners, than a tough judge presiding over a contentious trial. "I realize this is an emotional time in this proceeding, but I must have order in this court. These are serious matters that must be addressed with dignity. If you are unable to restrain yourself and maintain the decorum of this court, then you must leave immediately." Neither of the weeping sisters left.

The judge then explained to the members of the court-martial how the sentencing phase of the trial would proceed. Both the government and the defense would be permitted to present appropriate matters to aid the members in determining the kind and amount of punishment to be imposed. When he finished, the judge excused the members and then instructed Clark and Trip on what he expected of them during the next phase of the trial.

After a short break, the members of the court-martial were brought back in, and Judge O'Brien reconvened the proceeding. From Gomez's charge sheet Clark read the data concerning his age, pay, and length of service. Because Gomez had been a pretty good soldier prior to this crime, there wasn't much adverse evidence to present about his duty performance. Trip, in turn, introduced evidence of Gomez's awards and certificates of merit. He also introduced and read to the members an affidavit from

Gomez's previous company commander, which basically confirmed that Gomez had been a good soldier. Clark thought Trip read the affidavit with far more emotion and drama than its author would have exhibited, had he testified in person.

After all of the evidence was submitted, each side argued for an appropriate sentence. Clark went first.

"Gentlemen, I want you to reflect on what you've heard during the course of this trial. I want you to focus on the fact that Specialist Gomez ended Lydia Mendoza's life before it had a chance to even begin. Think about that for a moment." Clark paused and looked at their faces. "That little girl will never learn to ride a bike... or swim... or dance... She'll never go to prom or have a boyfriend or be kissed in the moonlight. She'll never grow up, get married, or have children. Her life is over." He stared at them and let those comments sink in. "And who remains?" Clark pointed to Carmen, who was sitting in the front row of the gallery behind the rail, still sobbing softly. "Lydia's mother, Carmen Mendoza, who loved her little girl dearly and, for the rest of her life, will have a hole in her heart where a precious little girl should be. None of us can know how great her hurt is. None of us can know how hard it is to hear the silence that was once filled with the giggles and laughter of her little girl." At that point Clark decided he'd said as much as he needed to. Not wanting to begin to bore the members, he thanked them and sat down.

Trip stood up and walked to within two feet of the members of the court-martial. "Gentlemen, I'm at a loss for what to say..."

Was Trip going to say they made a mistake?

"This father of three young children would never intentionally hurt a child, especially his niece..."

Elmer was right. Trip should have argued intent. It was too late for that now, though. The members had just concluded that Gomez had the intent to hurt Lydia when he shook her to death. Judge O'Brien had instructed them that they could infer that

Gomez "intended the natural and probable results of an act he purposely does." In other words, if a person did something intentionally that was likely to result in death, then the members of the court-martial could assume he intended to inflict death. And that's exactly what they did.

Trip continued, "As I said, gentlemen, Specialist Raul Gomez has a wife and three young children. Don't deprive this family, especially those children, of his presence in their lives."

Another lame argument. Why would the members of the court-martial want to return a baby killer to a home where three little children lived? After Trip finished, Judge O'Brien asked Clark if he wanted to make a rebuttal argument. He declined. The members had heard enough, and he had already said what he needed to say. The judge gave the members some instructions about what the maximum punishment could be, as well as other matters concerning sentencing, and they retired to deliberate.

Clark didn't want to talk to anyone until it was all over. Fortunately, Suzanne said she had to return some phone calls, so she went straight to her office and closed the door. After about thirty long minutes, the bailiff knocked on Clark's door. "They're ready, sir."

When they reassembled, Judge O'Brien directed the bailiff to retrieve from Captain Hargrove the sentencing worksheet that Clark and Trip had prepared for the members to use in deciding on the sentence. After the judge reviewed it, he handed it to the bailiff and directed him to return it to Captain Hargrove. "Would defense counsel and the accused please rise?" Trip and Gomez stood up and faced the members of the court-martial. The judge continued, "Captain Hargrove, please announce the sentence."

The young captain looked somber as he stood up. His voice was deep and resonate. "Specialist Raul Gomez, it is my duty as president of this court-martial to announce that the court-martial, with all members concurring, sentences you to be reduced to the grade of E-1; to forfeit all pay and allowances; to be confined for twenty-five years..." There was a loud gasp, immediately followed by wailing so loud it was impossible to hear the remainder of Gomez's sentence, although it sounded like Captain Hargrove said dishonorable discharge. The woman who Clark had assumed was Raul's wife was the loudest. Judge O'Brien pounded his hand on the bench, although it was pointless. Clark just sat in his chair and tried hard not to smile.

Gomez had his head down on the counsel table, bawling. A big military policeman came and put his hand on Gomez's shoulder. As he was led away, Gomez continued to cry and look longingly at his wife. After some final administrative matters, Judge O'Brien adjourned the court. Clark glanced at Suzanne, who had a completely blank look on her face. She turned toward him, gave him just the hint of a smile, and stood up. They walked out of the courtroom together, not even noticing Elmer and Jaime in the back row. Clark went back to his office and collapsed into his chair. He decided it would be smart to call Colonel Bednar to let him know that they had gotten the conviction and Gomez was going away for twenty-five years.

"Sir, this is Captain Clark."

"Hot damn, Counselor! I've already heard the news. Damn good job! That sonofabitch needed to go down—killing a little baby, for chrissake."

"Yes, sir. We were pleased with the result."

"You should be proud, Captain Clark. I'm gonna make sure the SJA and the Commanding General know how pleased I am."

"Thank you, sir." Clark hung up the phone.

"Who was that, Clark?" Suzanne was standing in the doorway, the same strange look still on her face.

"I called Colonel Bednar to tell him about the result, but he already knew."

"Oh yeah, he had one of his sergeants up here watching

the entire trial. I'm sure he reported the result as soon as it was announced." The momentum of her disdain for Bednar was carrying her forward. "Did you good ol' boys talk about anything else?"

"No, Suzanne. Are you ever going to drop it?"

"Probably not. He annoys me. He's such a pig."

"He's a lieutenant colonel, Suzanne."

"Oh yeah, that's like a Navy commander, right?"

"*Touché.*"

"Actually, before Elmer and Jaime and your other buddies steal you away to celebrate, I want to buy you a drink and tell you how proud I am of you."

"Well... thanks, Suzanne. Sure. Let's go to Mother's Inn. Everybody will be there. But let me call Colonel Allen first."

When Clark finally got him on the line, the SJA was not happy. "I suppose you're calling to tell me about the result of the trial, but I've already heard it from Colonel Bednar. I must say I was a bit embarrassed that he found out about the result before I did."

At this point, Clark decided it wouldn't be prudent to tell Colonel Allen what he was thinking: that Bednar had had a representative present throughout the trial and that's why he knew the result so quickly, even though Bednar was all the way across post while the SJA's office was only one floor below the courtroom. So, Clark just apologized and said they had been busy wrapping up some administrative matters.

"Well, call me first, next time. I don't like getting surprised. What if it had been General Kraus on the phone? I would have looked like a fool if I didn't know the result and Bednar did. I want to be the first person you notify, not Bednar." Clark didn't respond. After an awkward pause, Allen continued, "But don't let me rain on your parade, Clark. You did a fine job against a worthy opponent."

"Thank you, sir. Suzanne played a key role as well."

"Indeed she did. Tell her I said so. I need to go. Congratulations."

Clark hung up the phone. "*Worthy opponent*"? Why was Colonel Allen always going out of his way to say complimentary things about Trip? Had he forgotten that Clark had now beaten him twice? Why did Allen think Trip was such a "worthy opponent"? He was terrible in the courtroom. But then, Colonel Allen knew next to nothing about being a trial counsel. He was probably just impressed with Trip's family and their money.

Clark turned to see Suzanne standing in his doorway. "The boss says to tell you 'congratulations,'" he said glumly.

"Sure, Clark. C'mon. Let's go have a beer."

CHAPTER THIRTY-ONE

AS THEY WERE walking into Mother's Inn, Suzanne grabbed Clark's arm and confessed, "You know I've never been in here before."

Clark smiled. After she gets inside, she'll wonder why anyone would want to come to such a dump.

They walked into the cool semi-darkness and found the place almost empty, except for a couple of guys in a corner, eating. Not finding Elmer in his usual spot, Clark suggested they grab a table away from "Elmer's corner" and order some beer.

Before she sat down, Suzanne carefully inspected the chair and used a paper napkin to wipe the seat. Apparently, she'd already noticed that the place was pretty grubby. No sooner had they sat down than Suzanne looked at Clark with smiling eyes and said, "You did a great job, Clark. You've made quite a name for yourself."

"Thanks, Suzanne. You did a great job, too. We make a good team." A waitress deposited two Balboas in front of them, and Clark took a long drink. "You know, the SJA sure was pissed." He put down his beer and looked at Suzanne to gauge her reaction. Seeing none, he continued, "He seemed more concerned that I hadn't called him right away than he did about the outcome of the trial."

"Aw, don't worry about that, Clark. He'll get over it." After a few sips on her beer, she mused, "I'm thinking Allen might just make you Chief of Military Justice."

"Really? I don't think so. That's a major's slot, and it'll be a long time before I get promoted."

"Well, in case you haven't noticed, Boy Wonder, we no longer have any majors, other than the Deputy SJA, and he's got a job. Darst isn't coming back."

"Maybe they'll get another major from the States," Clark suggested, trying to sound modest.

"Not for a while. Besides, after this trial, you are definitely the fair-haired boy. I'm sure the CG has heard all about it."

"Yeah, Jaime probably told Agent Robinson, and I wouldn't be surprised if Robinson went over to the General's office and briefed him in person. What's the deal between him and the General, anyway?"

"I heard they go back to Vietnam. They were in the same unit or something." Suzanne seemed to know the personal details on everyone. "Maybe Robinson knows something about the CG that the CG doesn't want anyone else to know—like My Lai or something."

"Are you kidding? Our general? He is the straightest of straight arrows."

"Maybe," she replied, raising her eyebrows and pursing her lips.

Clark said nothing further but wondered if Suzanne might be right. How many people in Panama had he encountered who turned out to be very different from what they first appeared? Racists. Philanderers. Cheaters. Criminals. Deceit grew in Panama like mold.

They'd been there for about an hour, when junior officers started shuffling in for happy hour. All of a sudden, Elmer burst through the front door with an entourage of lieutenants in tow.

He took off his sunglasses and announced to all who could hear, "I saw the conquering hero's car outside, and so, I know he's in here." As his eyes adjusted to the darkness, his gaze turned to Clark. "There he is. Out-fucking-standing, Counselor! Twenty-five years? We haven't seen a sentence like that since I've been in Panama. Well done. Well done." Turning to the bartender, he shouted, "Javier, this man's drinks are on me tonight."

After Elmer's speech, the lieutenants with him and most of the other customers in the bar came up to congratulate Clark. Although he tried to point out that Suzanne was part of the team, it was hopeless—all the attention was on him.

Then, Elmer held court. The crowd grew as he gave a blow-by-blow account of the trial. He described Clark's performance as "outstanding" and said that he'd "kicked ass." And as he did, he would gesture grandiloquently toward Clark. Watching him go on and on, Clark marvelled at Elmer's gift for storytelling and thought that perhaps he got that talent—or at least learned it—from his lawyer-father.

It wasn't long before Suzanne had heard enough and told Clark she needed to go. He wasn't surprised: Elmer had said nothing about her contribution, and his praise of Clark's performance was a bit much. It also occurred to Clark that—despite her compliments on the way he'd handled the case—Suzanne was still a friend of Trip's, and Elmer's description of the trial showed Trip no mercy. He had called him "a pitiful excuse for a lawyer" and said that Clark had "wiped the floor with him."

As Suzanne was walking out the door, Clark finally interjected, loud enough for her to hear, "Elmer, we need to change the subject. We've got real warriors here. They need to learn their craft, so they can keep the bad guys at bay. Let's talk about that."

Not missing a beat, Elmer continued to address his audience. "Did I also mention that our prosecutor has a muther-fuckin'

Ranger Tab? Plan, recon, control, and security, gentlemen. Remember that, fellow Rangers? PRC-S."

Pronounced prick-s, Elmer was referring to an acronym based on an Army radio called the "PRC-77," for Portable Radio Communication, which had been in the Army's inventory since before Vietnam. Soldiers called it a prick 77. So, in Ranger School they used that acronym to remind patrol leaders of what they should do when they were in charge of an operation. They just added an "S."

Elmer was on a roll—fueled by the beer he'd consumed during his monologue. "Yes, gentlemen. This Ranger-lawyer used those same principles to win this trial. Remember that: PRC-S. It will serve you well, just as it served Captain Clark when he vanquished the enemy."

"Okay, Elmer," said Clark. "I've got to insist on another topic. Let's talk about women." That comment brought laughter, whoops, and catcalls from the group, most of whom knew that Elmer's two favorite topics were: the Infantry (and, in particular, the Rangers) and women, although the priority between those two topics varied from time to time.

"Counselor, you're right. We've talked about this enough. Let's you and me retire to our spot and allow these gentlemen to go do what they came here to do: drink beer and tell each other lies." Elmer's last line brought some chuckles from the group, which began to disperse as Elmer led Clark to his corner. Before long, Jaime came strolling in with a big smile on his face.

"Agen' Robinson sai' the CG is really please' abou' the Gomez trial. He congratulate' Agen' Robinson on a goo' investigation, an' you know wha' he sai'? He sai' 'thanks,' bu' we also ha' a goo' prosecutor fo' a change.' An' Agen' Robinson sai' the CG sai' 'I thought so.' Tha's pretty goo' don' you thin'? The CG know' who you are an' how goo' you di' tryin' dis case."

"Hell, Jaime, he should've heard Elmer tell about it." Jaime looked puzzled. "Never mind, man. Thanks for the report."

After Jaime had settled in and drunk most of his first beer, Elmer said, "Gentlemen, this evening we are going to celebrate properly, and I don't want to hear any bullshit, Clark. Jaime, you're driving. I'll pay this tab." As Elmer picked up the check, he said, "Damn, Clark! We drank some beer. I've never had a bill this big." He turned and smiled. "And it was worth every fuckin' penny." With that, Elmer almost jumped to his feet, signaling that whatever he was planning for the rest of the evening was underway.

They all went to the parking lot and piled into Jaime's car—Jaime and Elmer got in the front and Clark in the back. Clark was glad to have a big, Spanish-speaking CID agent as chauffeur to drive downtown because he knew he'd had way too much to drink, and so had Elmer. Not surprisingly, Elmer's inebriated condition did little to deter him from taking a leadership role in whatever adventure he was taking them on.

After they left the post, Jaime reached under the seat and pulled out a bottle. "Dis is some goo' shi'. And dis i' the time to drink i'." He spun off the cap with the thumb and index finger of his right hand, while his left hand held the steering wheel. He took a long swig and handed it to Elmer.

Looking down, Elmer read the label. "Santa Teresa 1796. That's that Venezuelan rum, isn't it?" Jaime nodded. "Damn, Jaime. That's some expensive shit."

"Well, dis i' the time to drink it, don' you thin'?"

"Hell, yeah," said Elmer. "HOOAH!" He took a long swig and handed the bottle to Clark.

After inspecting the label to see what all the fuss was about, Clark took a drink, too. It was good, but he held onto the bottle until Elmer asked for it back. He wasn't too keen on Jaime swigging rum as he wound through the narrow dark streets. He and Elmer were pretty tipsy. No, they were drunk. At least Clark had on a Class B uniform, which was a little more presentable downtown than Elmer's boots and olive-drab fatigues. Jaime looked okay because he hadn't drunk as much and, as usual, had on a guayabera and khaki pants.

Clark had no idea where they were going. It seemed as if Jaime had been driving for almost half an hour. He began to feel woozy in the back seat as the car made hard turns in one direction and then another.

As they pulled into a gravel parking lot, Clark sensed that he'd been there before, although the darkness and the copious amount of beer and rum he'd already consumed made it difficult to remember when. He got out of the car and noticed an eight-foot, concrete-block wall surrounding the parking lot and a building. Then it came back to him: this was Club Iguana, the whorehouse that Elmer and Jaime had brought him to after he'd won his first case. His conscience was telling him to say "no, take me home." But he was drunk, and Elmer and Jaime were so excited that he couldn't bring himself to be the spoiler, so he rationalized going inside. There wasn't any harm in merely entering the place, he thought. After all, the girls were not going to be walking around naked or anything. But then, they weren't going to be dancing either.

The interior of the club was just as Clark remembered it: cool and dark, with soft music playing in the background, and eight or ten candlelit tables. A few well-dressed men were sitting at each table, along with several equally well-dressed, attractive young women. Jaime said something to the hostess in Spanish, and she led them to another room. There was a bar on one end and a number of couches. Like the other room, this one was well decorated. Men were lounging on the couches, surrounded by gorgeous young women. The hostess ushered them to an empty, L-shaped couch in the corner and asked Jaime something in Spanish that sounded like a request for a drink order.

Almost as soon as Clark sat down, a young waitress appeared

and bent over to offer him a drink. Her soft, round breasts seemed to be spilling out of her dress. For a fleeting moment, he was reminded of Nita. But that thought didn't last, because suddenly there were women everywhere. Clark had one on each side of him. The one on his right had her arm around him. She was petite and looked like a high-school girl, dressed up for prom. Her long black hair hung down on her bare shoulders, and her heavy makeup looked out of place on her young face. The other woman was older—but no more that twenty-five—with light skin and a shapely figure like Nita's. She looked like a Hollywood starlet from the 1950s, complete with a tight red cocktail dress and a cigarette clasped between the first two fingers of her left hand. She rested her right hand on Clark's inner thigh and started to squeeze gently.

Clark was uncomfortable. He knew he was in the wrong place, but it was clear he was the only one who felt that way. Jaime and Elmer were enjoying themselves, and their female companions were laughing and giggling at everything. Although it had been quite some time since Janelle had left him, Clark kept reminding himself that he was still a married man. As the evening wore on, though, he and his buddies drank more—a lot more. What was once a crowd of girls became three: one paired with each of them. Despite the low lights, Clark could see Jaime and Elmer kissing and fondling the girls they were with.

The younger girl had moved on, leaving Clark with the older, shapely one, who spoke to him in English. "You no' like me?" she asked—her big brown eyes, wide and inviting. He smiled, dumbstruck. She continued, "You no' thin' I' pretty?"

He couldn't let that question go unanswered, especially since she spoke English and had been so nice to him. "Oh, no, I think you're beautiful." She smiled and dropped her chin. "It's just that I'm married." He held up his left hand to show her his wedding band.

She stood up and gestured around the room. "No pro'lem, señor. All dese men married."

"Really?" asked Clark, attempting to sound like he was unfamiliar with such places.

"Yes. Men work har' and nee' to relax. Sometime', they wife don' help dem relax."

"You're right about that," he sighed.

"Woul' you like massage?"

"Yeah, but there are a lot of people around." Clark looked up at her. His eyes narrowed and his head tilted to one side, signaling his confusion.

She curled her right index finger and said, "Come wid me." She took his hand and led him down a hallway, which was dimly illuminated with small, glowing blue lights. They entered a room that had mirrors on the walls and a massage table in the center. It was as dark as the hallway. Sexy soft music hung in the air, complementing the dreamy state that was overtaking him. She handed him a towel and told him to "get comfor'ble" and then left the room. Clark stripped down, put the towel around him, and laid down on the table, face down. He was exhausted and rationalized that a massage was all right under the circumstances.

After a few minutes, he heard her come back into the room. In the dim light he could see that she had exchanged her cocktail dress for tight, white shorts and a tight, white T-shirt, both of which glowed in the blue light. She rubbed oil onto her hands and then started kneading his shoulders, his back, his buttocks. It had been a long time since he'd felt a woman's touch, and he'd never felt anything quite like this—her soft, sure hands against his skin. It was if she were pressing out all the stress that had built up over the past several weeks. He forgot about his wife leaving him. The trial that had been dominating his thoughts for months was over. Before long, she was leaning over him, and he could feel her groin press against his shoulders and then against his arms, as she moved around the table. The fragrance of her perfume was almost as intoxicating as what he'd been drinking. It smelled elegant—like Paris, not K-Mart.

She told him to turn over, and he promptly complied. Smiling, she pulled off her T-shirt, exposing her round, young breasts. He was transfixed. Although the light was dim, he could clearly see that her body was perfect: luscious breasts, pale and luminous in the soft blue light; a slim waist; and round Latina hips.

She continued to massage his arms and legs. Lying on his back, with his palms facing upward, Clark looked up at her. Her raven hair hung down and framed her face. He could see her naked breasts, gently swaying as she worked and occasionally brushing against his skin. She bent over and her left breast brushed against his open palm. Her nipple was erect, and he could feel it gently riding across the bumps of his fingers. When she stood up again, he reached up and gently caressed her breast with his right hand. She stopped and smiled. Her teeth were very white—a fitting accent to her perfect face. Her cheekbones were high and sculptured; her eyes, narrowed ever so slightly, focused intensely on him; her nose, slender and perfectly symmetrical. Her lips were full and moist, and her mouth was feminine and erotic like Marilyn's. After she'd massaged his legs and arms for a few minutes, she reached under the towel and started caressing his erection.

He was rock hard. She removed the towel and continued to glide her soft hands over his shaft, and then... her lips. She created a sensation unlike anything he'd ever experienced. He didn't want to think about how she'd learned that skill or the fact that he was still married. Then her shorts were off, and she was on top of him. She was moist and tight—very different from his wife, the only other woman he'd ever been with. She began to undulate her pelvis in a sensual, fluid motion. He looked at her mound, as she moved back and forth. Like her breasts, it was pale, unkissed by the sun. Her abdomen was flat and tight, and yet, at the same time, she was soft and feminine. Her breasts hung above him, as she leaned over him, with her hands resting on the table on either side of him. Clark looked up at her—her captivating smile and her beautiful face, framed by luxurious black hair. He'd never seen a woman so breathtaking. Soon, he climaxed, and her smile widened: she realized she'd done her job. She got off him and stood beside the table. In the dim blue light she looked like a Renaissance painting—a work of art.

She removed the condom—which he hadn't even noticed her putting on—leaned over, hugged him, and kissed his cheek. She wrapped a towel around her and turned to leave.

"Don't I owe you something?" he asked, still lying on the table.

She flashed her gorgeous smile. "No, señor, your friends pay for you." She was out the door and gone.

He didn't want her to leave. He was sad that it was over but felt wonderful. He'd never had anyone treat him the way this beautiful young woman had. She was so sweet, and yet so erotic at the same time. He must have lain there for ten minutes—relaxed, refreshed, blissful. Finally, he got dressed and found his way back to the room with the couches. Jaime and Elmer were waiting for him. Their girls were gone, and they each looked like the proverbial cat that swallowed the canary.

"So, how goes it, Counselor?" asked Elmer, his shit-eatin' grin plastered across his face.

"It was great, guys, but I need to get back to my car at Mother's," he said, staring at the floor. "And, uh, by the way guys, thanks." He looked up and smiled sheepishly.

CHAPTER THIRTY-TWO

THE PARKING LOT was empty. Evidently, they were the last to leave. It was late, and the night was still. The normally noisy street on the other side of the concrete-block wall was quiet. Their feet crunched the gravel as they walked to Jaime's car. Clark heard a lone truck drive by on the other side of the wall. It needed a new muffler and some valve seals. He could smell the burnt oil. Somewhere nearby there was a chorus of frogs croaking at each other. They probably were in one of the many drainage canals the city had built to prevent flooding during the Rainy Season. The noise of the city must have masked their symphony when Clark and his buddies arrived a few hours earlier. The sound of the frogs reminded him of summer evenings along the Ogeechee River back home.

Jaime cautiously pulled his car out of the parking lot and headed back to Mother's Inn, so Clark could retrieve his Nova and Elmer could get his Harley. As they wound through the dark streets of the city, Clark sat quietly in the back seat while Jaime and Elmer laughed and chattered away in the front. The reality of what had just happened started to sink in. Even though he was angry with his wife for leaving him, and uncertain of the future of their marriage, he knew what he had just done was wrong.

Clark opened his window to let the cool night air blow on

his face. He needed to sober up. As they approached a bridge over one of the drainage canals, Jaime slowed down to avoid hitting a pothole too hard. He and Elmer stopped talking as he maneuvered the car around it, and in the stillness Clark heard the frogs again—even louder than before. They must have been near the bridge. Their sounds made him smile and think again about all those unhurried summer evenings back in Pemberton. His thoughts drifted and then settled on a childhood memory: a Sunday school lesson, in which his teacher had told the class how to boil a frog. A roomful of wide-eyed ten-year old boys listened as she explained that you don't just drop the frog into boiling water, because as soon as his feet touch the hot water, he'll jump out. Instead, you put the frog in a pot of water at room temperature and slowly heat it up. The frog doesn't perceive the danger, falls asleep, and then succumbs to the rising temperature. She told the boys that if sin slaps you in the face, it's obvious and you can avoid it. The real challenge is when sin slips up on you slowly— like the frog, you might succumb before you know it.

Clark felt like a boiled frog. He had drunk too much and worried too much about what his friends thought of him. He knew he should have told them he couldn't stay at that place, just as he had the first time. In the back seat of Jaime's car that night, he remembered that ten-year old boy he once was and quietly asked God to forgive him.

When they got to Mother's Inn it was late—or, more accurately, early the next day. There were no cars in the parking lot and no rowdy junior officers hanging around. The white, concrete-block building looked almost serene in the moonlight. Clark needed to get some sleep; he still had all the administrative matters related to the Gomez trial to deal with. He said a quick goodnight to Jaime and Elmer and slumped into the driver's seat of his car.

As he drove home alone, his thoughts kept returning to

what he'd done. In his mind's eye, he could see the girl—beauti-ful, sweet, sensual. There was no question that he had enjoyed being with her. But when those memories began to arouse him, he became disgusted. Are you an animal or a man? he asked himself. Have you forgotten that what you did was wrong? Put that encounter—and any thoughts of her—out of your mind, or you'll wind up going back. Think about your family, stupid. Think about Ellie. Stop thinking about yourself.

He walked in the back door and went straight to bed, not even stopping to brush his teeth. But as was the case the night before, sleep didn't come easily, despite the hour. He tossed and turned for a long time before finally nodding off into restless sleep. In his dreams he was an adult, but his elder sister was a baby. Darlene was in a high chair, and he was feeding her baby food while smoking a cigar. He could see his father and grandfa-ther, standing behind a rail fence and looking down at the scene. They were talking, but he couldn't make out exactly what they were saying. His father kept shaking his head, and Clark thought he heard him say something about losing his way.

Clark jolted awake, disturbed and not wanting to go back to sleep. He got out of bed and went to the kitchen. As he gulped down a glass of water, he looked out the window. Was John out there, somehow polluting his dreams? He went outside and looked up in the tree. No sign of him or his mocking sneer. He went back inside, but before getting in bed, he knelt down and prayed. He closed his eyes and begged for forgiveness again. When he finished, he was still troubled. Had his father looked down from heaven and seen him with that girl? Slowly, he got up, walked to the window, and looked up into the night sky. All the booze he'd consumed had made him maudlin. "I love you, Daddy," he whispered. "I hope you're not ashamed of me. You told me God forgives. Well, I'm counting on that. I'm so sorry." He got back into bed and promptly went to sleep.

At 6:00 a.m. the alarm went off, and Clark bolted out of bed. Getting up so fast made the room start spinning. He felt terrible and raced to the bathroom where he deposited the remaining contents of his stomach into the toilet. It was then that he noticed it. His crotch was itching like crazy. Could he have contracted something from the girl? He remembered the note that Elmer's wife had left him—the one where she told him to get checked. He took a quick shower, thoroughly scrubbing his groin and rinsing it with the hottest water he could stand. He shaved, put on a clean uniform, and headed for the door.

The JAG office had calmed down considerably since the previous day. The parking lot was back to normal, and there was no crowd in the hallways and reception areas. Suzanne was already at her desk; Clark just smiled and nodded as he walked by. He didn't even stop to get a cup of coffee: his stomach wasn't ready for that. He'd no sooner sat down than he sensed someone in his doorway.

"You had quite a day yesterday," Suzanne smiled.

"You can say that again."

"Well, just for the record, you look like shit."

"No kidding. Never party with Elmer."

She pursed her lips. "Don't worry. That will never happen." Changing her tone, she announced, "I have something important to tell you." Clark looked up. "Judge O'Brien is still here and wants to see you."

"Great. Did he say what about?"

"No, but I suspect it's about your charming demeanor during the trial. He's in the same office he's been using." She smirked and walked away.

Clark couldn't tell whether Suzanne was pleased that he might still be in trouble with Judge O'Brien or whether she was just being a smart aleck. He stopped by the latrine to see if he could improve upon his appearance. She was right: he did look like shit. And that itch. That maddening itch. After making a few minor adjustments and buffing his shoes with some toilet paper, he made his way to the office where Judge O'Brien was working. He took a deep breath and knocked.

"Come in."

"Sir, Captain Watkins said you wanted to see me."

"Yes, Clark, sit down. I want to talk to you about the trial."

His stomach started to knot, which was especially bad given its delicate condition, and he readied himself for the tongue-lashing that he knew was coming. As soon as he sat down, the itch started again. He squirmed in the seat, wishing he could scratch. Leveling his gaze at the judge, he tried not to think about his discomfort and what might have caused it. The judge stared back at him with a strange expression. He wasn't smiling, nor did he look angry. Instead, he seemed to be studying Clark. Could Judge O'Brien sense how guilty and ashamed he was feeling? Not because of the way the trial had gone. Because of the events of the prior evening and that infernal itch. Finally, the judge broke the uncomfortable silence.

"What do you think of your performance at trial?"

"The result was good," Clark mumbled.

"I'm sure you feel that way, but what I'm concerned about is your behavior in the courtroom. When I met you at the JAG School, I thought you'd make a fine trial counsel. You always looked like a soldier, and you had a clear understanding of how we JAGs can help make the Army better." He stopped, took off his glasses, and shook his head slightly from side to side, saying, "But you seemed to have lost your way."

"Sir?" Clark's thoughts flashed back to his dream. Wasn't that what his father had said? Something about losing his way?

"Do you remember the class on professional responsibility?"

"I'm sorry, sir. What did you say?"

"Are you all right, Clark?"

"Yes, sir. I'm just not feeling too well this morning."

"I asked if you remembered the class on professional responsibility at the JAG School."

"Yes, sir. Of course, you taught it."

"Well, go back and review the materials. A trial counsel's job is to seek justice, Clark. You need to remember that. You looked and sounded like a vigilante in there," he said, pointing in the direction of the courtroom. Judge O'Brien stared again for an uncomfortably long time. "I must say that I'm disappointed in you."

"I'm sorry to hear that, sir." Clark squirmed in his chair, wanting to scratch.

"Well, I hope you will take to heart what I've said. You could be one of the best prosecutors in the Army, but you've got to get off your high horse. Don't go into a trial thinking you're going to right all wrongs and vanquish the enemy. Seek justice and do so professionally." He paused and a half-smile appeared. "Remember, Clark, you do your job and let our Lord do His."

"Yes, sir."

"Now, get back to work and behave like the professional that I know you are."

"Yes, sir."

As Clark walked back to his office, he was a little annoyed by Judge O'Brien. The judge hadn't tried a case in years. He had probably forgotten how damn difficult it was. It was easy for him to sit there and talk about being professional. His butt wasn't on the line. He didn't feel the commanding general breathing down his neck.

Suzanne met him in the hallway. "So, how'd it go?" she asked.

"It went okay. He told me I didn't act like a professional."

"So, what'd you say?"

"Are you kidding? I just said 'yes, sir.'"

"Yeah, I guess that's the right approach. It's hard to argue with the truth."

"What do you mean by that?"

"Come on, Clark, you weren't exactly Perry Mason in there."

"Perry Mason was a defense attorney, Suzanne."

"You know what I mean."

"No," Clark replied, making no attempt to hide his irritation with her, "I don't know what you mean. Trying a case is a tough job, especially when it involves a child victim."

"I know that, Clark. I was co-counsel on this one, remember? I'm the one who briefed you on every reported court-martial case concerning child abuse because I read every one of them. I'm the one who..."

"You're right, Suzanne. I'm sorry." But he wasn't convincing. His words were perfunctory and insincere, and she knew it.

Suzanne gave him a hard look, but then softened. "I just think you ought to take Judge O'Brien's advice to heart, Clark. I think he's a good guy, and he seems to be genuinely concerned about you."

"Well, you're entitled to your opinion." Clark pressed past her, went into his office, and closed the door.

The rest of the morning was taken up with administrative matters related to getting the record of trial prepared and answering telephone calls from folks all over Panama who wanted to congratulate him on his victory. At lunchtime, Clark made a trip to the post infirmary to get checked. It was crowded, and he had to wait more than two hours to be seen, but it was worth it. The doctor said that he had a bad case of tinea cruris (jock itch), nothing more. He told him that he shouldn't have washed the area with soap—it further irritates the already irritated, sensitive skin—and he should only wear his jock strap once before washing it. Doing laundry was one of many domestic chores Clark had let slip.

It was late when he got back to the office. Suzanne had already left, and the clerks were locking up and getting ready to head home. Clark decided to stay and write his wife a letter. If he went home, he'd just get distracted. The trial was over. And he'd resolved to put thoughts of the girl behind him—thank God he hadn't contracted anything. Now, it was time to focus on putting his family back together.

Dearest Janelle,

I'm writing to tell you how much I miss you and our precious little Ellie. After you left, Nita left, too. So, I've been fending for myself. Our quarters are very lonely with just me here.

The Gomez trial is finally over, and I hope that my life will get back to normal now. I know that I was withdrawn from you while I was preparing for this trial and didn't act like a good husband. I am one of those people who must focus very hard in order to accomplish difficult and complex tasks. It doesn't come easy to me, and I know that I probably wasn't very pleasant to be around. I apologize.

Now that my first murder trial is history (I won, by the way. Gomez is going to prison for 25 years.), I hope you will return to Panama and allow me to make it up to you. My family means everything to me. Please don't destroy it. I need you in my life. I will lose my way without you.

I know that when you called a while back I was not very polite. I apologize for that, too. I will try to call you on Saturday afternoon. I hope you get this letter before then. It will mean a lot just to hear your voice—and Ellie's. I miss you both so much. I need you back here with me.

Love,

Bobby

CHAPTER THIRTY-THREE

CLARK LEFT THE office, drove straight to the Fort Clayton Post Office, and dropped the letter in the mail. He wanted it to go out as early as possible the next day. Driving home, he realized he hadn't eaten anything all day, so he decided to go to The Happy Buddha, the Chinese restaurant that he, Janelle, and Ellie had visited shortly after arriving in Panama. As he pulled into the parking lot, he debated about whether to go inside wearing his uniform and concluded it would be all right. At least the patrons and staff would know he wasn't a Zonian. No one seemed to take any notice of the uniformed Norteamericano when he walked in. The hostess seated him at a small table in the back, and he quickly began reading the menu. Then he heard a familiar voice.

"You don' loo' no worse fo' wear, Capitain Clark." Clark looked up to see Jaime Hernandez smiling down at him.

"Hell, Jaime, you should've seen me this morning. How are you doing?"

"Oh, you know. Tryin' to kee' the ol' lady happy." He gestured to another table where a Hispanic woman was looking in their direction and smiling.

"That's your wife?"

"Yeah. She came bac' jus' a li'le while ago. I thin' we gonna make i'."

"Congratulations, Jaime. I'm glad to hear that."

"You know, Capitain Clark, I tol' her abou' you, an' she wan' you to join us. We no' start' eatin' yet."

"I couldn't do that, Jaime. It's your first night back together."

"No, Capitain Clark. She heard me talk abou' you. She want' to meet you."

Clark stood up and walked over to their table. Jaime introduced him to his wife, whose name was Camila. Although—as Jaime had complained earlier— she was a little heavy, she had a pretty face and a warm, engaging smile.

"Pleased to meet you, ma'am," said Clark, extending his hand. Camila shook it with her soft plump fingers but didn't get up. "I hope I didn't cause Jaime to have to work too hard."

"No, Capitain Clark. He like' workin' wid you. He sai' you are a goo' prosecutor. You go' tha' horrible man twen'y-fi' years, righ'?"

"Yes, but I had a lot of help—not only from Jaime but also from my co-counsel, Captain Watkins. She handled the opening statement and almost all of the direct examinations."

"A woman?" Camila scrunched her nose and forehead as she arched her right eyebrow. She looked at Jaime and then back at Clark.

"Yes," Clark explained. "She did most of the research, too."

"Jaime, you didn' tell me tha' one of the prosecutors was a woman."

Jaime shrugged his shoulders and shook his head. "She work wid Capitain Clark, *mi amor*. He wa' runnin' the show."

Sensing where the conversation was headed, Clark quickly explained, "Oh, that's right, Camila. I was lead counsel, and so, I was the one interacting with Jaime. He did a great job, by the way. A lot of this stuff is new to me, and he was very patient. He helped me a lot." Camila smiled and looked at her husband. "Oh, and so did Captain Watkins," Clark added, as an afterthought.

"And, uh, she did a lot of work, too. In fact, Camila, Captain Watkins is all about work. All she does is work."

Camila smiled again and said, "Well, I hope Jaime will stay home more now. His chil'ren miss him. Do you ha' any chil'ren, Capitain Clark?"

"Uh, yes. Yes, I do. I have a little girl, but she's back in the States right now with her mother."

The waiter arrived with their dinner. He was the same young man who'd been insulted by the Zonian woman during Clark's first visit to The Happy Buddha. He seemed more confident to be waiting on a Spanish-speaking woman and looked expectantly at Camila. She looked up at him and said, "*El cerdo agridulce es para mí.*" She took the plate and motioned for him to put the other plate on the other side of the table. "I wou' like to mee' you' wife an' daugh'er when dey come back," said Camila. She smiled and waited for Clark to respond.

"Oh, yes, that's right. We'll have to get together, for sure."

"*Perdóneme*, Capitain Clark, bu' I nee' to go to the *baño*. I jus' flew in a li'le while ago, an' i' wa' a rough fligh'." Camila got up and looked at Jaime. "*Cuidame la comida, por favor.*" Jaime nodded, and she walked away.

Jaime smiled as he watched her leave. Then he sat down and motioned for Clark to sit in Camila's seat. Making sure no one could overhear them, he whispered, "I nee' to tell you somethin'. We arrest' Weeks at her apar'ment a li'le while ago."

"Really? How'd it go?"

"I thin' she kinda knew it wa' comin'. Mos' o' the stuff in her apar'ment was packed in boxes. Like she wa' movin' ou'.

"No kidding."

"Yeah. An' she called Capitain Stephens. He came o'er to the CID Office. He tol' her no' to say nothin', bu' she no' gonna say nothin' anyway."

"Where is she now?"

"We pu' her in pretrial confinemen', 'cause she from Panama, an' so, she' a fligh' risk."

"I guess the magistrate will be reviewing that tomorrow."

"Yeah, but don' worry abou'. We shippin' her off to Fort Leonar' Woo' tomorrow, anyway. General Kraus wan' her outta Panama."

"Good."

Camila reappeared, and both men stood up.

Clark seated Camila in her chair but didn't sit down himself. "Camila, I appreciate your sharing this time with me, but since you just got home, I think you and Jaime should enjoy this evening with just the two of you. I'll take you up on that offer of getting together when my wife and daughter get back. Maybe you can teach her how to make *arroz con dulce*."

"Oh, okay. Yes, we will do tha', Capitain Clark."

"And thank you for sharing Jaime with me," Clark added. "I couldn't have done the trial without him." Camila smiled and then turned and looked admiringly at her husband.

As he walked back to his table, Clark reflected on Jaime's knack for dropping things in his lap. He knew he needed to tell Colonel Allen about Weeks's arrest and was glad to hear that he wasn't going to have to deal with her court-martial. That would be a nasty case. Her defense counsel would probably try to drag in the SJA and, possibly, Major Darst. As Clark considered how that trial might proceed, he started to wonder whether Weeks's arrest might also lead to the arrest of Major Darst. He still wasn't convinced that Darst had left Panama for a "family emergency."

Clark finished his dinner quickly. On the drive home he became restless as he reflected on his own family situation. He was glad that Jaime had gotten his wife back, but he was also a little envious. He walked through his back door and tripped over the trash can and then kicked it, spreading trash across the kitchen floor. "Stupid fucking trash can," he said, as he ignored the mess he'd created and walked into the dining room. Physically and emotionally he was worn out, but there was no way he could rest. His emotions were too unsettled.

He opened the middle drawer of the buffet and took out the tablecloth—the one Janelle had claimed was a Christmas gift for his mother—and spread it out on the table. He ran his hands over the intricate embroidery. It was beautiful, although clearly something Janelle had purchased for herself. She knew his mother would have said it was "too fancy." He imagined Janelle venturing into downtown Panama City to shop. She would have looked at every single tablecloth before making a decision. Then, she would have told the proprietor—in English, of course—that it "cost" too much. (She never pronounced the final "s.") And then she would have stared and waited for him to concede to a price reduction, usually ten to fifteen percent.

Walking into the kitchen, he slipped on some of the garbage he'd strewn, but he caught himself on the counter. He poured a tall drink—Maker's Mark on the rocks—and got a Honduran cigar from his makeshift humidor. He stepped onto the terrace and checked the tree. No sign of John, though Clark suspected he was watching from a concealed vantage point. The night sky was clear and black, with a stunning array of stars. He lit his cigar and sipped his drink. After he'd downed about half of it, he lay down on the lounge chair and looked up at the stars. Finally, he began to relax. As he enjoyed the earthy aroma of his cigar and watched the smoke swirl in the gentle breeze, memories of the night before crept into his thoughts. But he caught himself and sat up. Stop thinking about her, he thought. That's not who you are. That itching could have been something serious. It could have meant the end of everything. Concentrate on getting your family back, stupid.

He lay back and focused again on the stars, although his eyelids began to get heavy. As he was taking the last draw on his cigar, he looked up, and there he was—looking at him, mocking him. "Leave me alone, John." Clark got up from the lounge chair and pointed a defiant finger at him. "Get the fuck out of here, you piece of shit! Go back to hell where you belong." He yelled so loud the iguana scampered up the tree into the darkness. A light inside the quarters behind him came on and then an outside light. Quickly gathering his glass and matches, Clark went inside and turned off his outside light. He peeked out the window to see if his neighbor had come outside. Fortunately, he hadn't, and his lights soon went out.

He opened the cabinet next to the sink and retrieved a bottle of aspirin from the top shelf—put there to be out of Ellie's reach. He shook out four tablets, which he downed while drinking an entire glass of water without stopping. Then he drank another—advice from Elmer on how to avoid a hangover. He paced around his quarters for a half hour, occasionally running his hand across the embroidered tablecloth. As if he were planning a military operation, Clark thought through each step of how he'd get Janelle and Ellie back to Panama. He would take leave. He'd earned it, after all. And Elmer could help him get a flight back to the States again. He'd go to Pemberton and persuade her, face-to-face, to come back to Panama. That would do it. He'd always been able to persuade her. Yes, that would work.

Having satisfied himself that he'd developed a good plan, he went to bed. Unlike the previous evening, he slept as if he'd been tucked in by his mother.

He arrived at work early the next morning and went straight to Colonel Allen's office to report what Jaime had told him about Specialist Weeks being arrested. He didn't want to be criticized again for failing to keep his boss informed. The lights were off in the outer office, although he could see light shining beneath the SJA's door. He knocked.

"Come in."

"Sir, I wanted to give you some news about Specialist Weeks."

"You mean about her being arrested last night. Trip's already told me."

"Okay, sir."

Clark wasn't surprised. Of course, Trip would immediately report the arrest to his chief sponsor and cheerleader.

"How did you find out, Clark?"

"I saw Jaime Hernandez and his wife at The Happy Buddha last night." Clark could see that Allen was puzzled. "Jaime is the CID agent who worked on the Gomez case. He told me about Weeks."

The SJA stopped stroking his chin and started rubbing the back of his neck with his right hand, as if he was trying to loosen a tight muscle. Staring off into space he asked, "Why didn't the CID call me? Wouldn't you think they would have contacted me before arresting one of my legal clerks?"

"It seems like it, sir. But I'm sure they had their reasons. Maybe they thought that because she technically works for the Trial Defense Service…"

"That doesn't make any sense, Clark. They should've coordinated with me. Why would they cut me out of the loop?"

Colonel Allen knew the answer to that question. The CID hadn't contacted him, because they didn't trust him. Allen was probably worried that his affair with Weeks was about to be revealed, which would not only jeopardize his marriage, it might also mean that he was about to be prosecuted under the UCMJ for fraternizing with a subordinate or maybe even adultery.

"I'm going to have to get a new Chief of Military Justice," Allen sputtered. "I need someone to stay on top of these things."

"Do you have anyone in mind, sir?"

"No," Allen replied, looking down at his desk and continuing to rub his neck. "I guess I'll need to requisition someone from the States."

"So, it's definite that Major Darst is not coming back?"

"No, he's not coming back. He's got some serious family issues to deal with back in Texas. The Army is reassigning him to Fort Sill."

"Do you think Major Darst might have been involved with Specialist Weeks?"

Allen looked at Clark as if he'd kicked him in the groin. "Why would you say such a thing?"

"Well, they worked closely together and seemed pretty chummy when I first met them."

"No, there was nothing going on there," Allen said with a pained expression. "Trip told me that Weeks is suspected of being connected with some sort of drug business in Panama City. Major Darst would never be connected with anything like that."

"Will we be handling the case?" Clark asked, even though he knew the answer.

"Well, I don't know. I don't see why not."

Allen was definitely not in the loop, and he was running scared. He lit a cigarette and took two long draws.

"The wife says these things are going to kill me. Got started in 'Nam, and now I can't stop." He took another long draw and then crushed it out. "Why don't you call this Agent Hernandez fellow and see what you can find out about Weeks?"

"Yes, sir." Clark interpreted the last question as his cue to leave, so he stood up. "I'll see what I can find out and get back to you ASAP, sir."

Climbing the stairs to the Criminal Law Section, Clark reconsidered all that he'd just heard. Allen was probably being sincere when he insisted that Major Darst wasn't involved with Weeks. He should know, after all, since he was carrying on with her himself. Still, Clark was unsure about Darst. He had changed so much before he left. There was no longer any sign of Jake, the fishing buddy he'd had so much fun with. And his departure was so sudden—as if he wanted to get out of Panama one step ahead of the CID.

Clark went to his office and telephoned Jaime. A clerk answered the phone and said that Agent Hernandez had not come in yet, but she expected him any minute.

"When he gets in, tell him that Captain Clark is coming over."

Jaime must have seen Clark pull into the CID Office parking lot. He was waiting at the back door. "Goo' mornin', sir. Goo' to see you las' nigh'."

"Yeah. Good to see you, too, Jaime. I enjoyed meeting Camila." The two men walked down the hall to the now familiar conference room.

"Yeah. She wa' happy to finally mee' you, too. Wha' bring' you here dis mornin'? Week' i' already on her way to For' Leonar' Woo'."

"Good. The SJA wants me to find out everything about Weeks's arrest."

"Wha' you nee' to know?"

"Was she charged here in Panama? Is our office going to be involved in her case at all? That sort of thing."

"Well, he ough' to be gla' he no' on the plane wid Specialis' Weeks," Jaime chuckled.

"Right. I still don't understand why he's not in hot water."

"I thin' General Kraus jus' wanna get her outta here an' don' wan' a lo' o' fuss." Jaime paused a few seconds and then continued, "An' Agen' Robinson advise' him tha' dis i' the bes' way. I thin' Robinson want' Week' gone, too."

"Spurned suitor, huh," said Clark with a grin. Jaime cocked his head to one side, either not understanding him or failing to see the humor in that comment. "Never mind. So, if I hear you right, the JAG Office in Panama is not going to be involved at all?"

"Tha's right. General Kraus prefer' charges agains' her, bu' the cour'-martial gonna be convene' by the general a' For' Leonard Wood. The prosecutor a' For' Leonard Wood even drafted the charges fo' General Kraus to sign."

"So, I guess we're totally out of it." Jaime nodded. Clark repositioned himself in his chair—signaling a change of subject—and leaned toward Jaime. "Off the record, Jaime, do you think Colonel Allen is going to get pulled in?"

"I don' thin' so. They pro'ly gonna offer Weeks an a'ministrative dischar', an' I thin' she gonna take i' an' come home to Panama. I don' thin' they gonna have a trial. I' dey have a trial, i' woul' be ba', 'cause we go' a lo' o' pictures of Colonel Allen comin' an' goin' from her place. Look a' dese."

Jaime pulled a stack of 8 X 10 photographs out of the file. The guy in the picture certainly looked like Allen, but the images were pretty grainy.

"An' we even go' a bunch o' videos tha' are real clear. You can see dem huggin' each other on her porch."

"Allen had better pray they don't have a trial." Clark stood up. "Thanks for the update, Jaime. I need to get back and let Colonel Allen know that the Weeks case is going to be handled entirely at Fort Leonard Wood."

As the two men walked to the back door, Jaime said, "Don' say nothin' abou' the res' o' wha' I tol' you, 'bout Colonel Allen an' all dat."

"Oh, for sure. I understand." Clark pushed open the back door and stepped into the sunshine. Then, turning around, he said, "Tell Camila that I look forward to getting together soon—as soon as my wife and daughter get back to Panama."

CHAPTER THIRTY-FOUR

WHEN CLARK GOT back to his office, he immediately phoned Jaime. "Hey, I forgot to ask you. Do you know *when* Weeks is going to be tried?"

"No, sir. I's up to the guys a' For' Leonar' Wood."

"Okay, thanks. Talk to you later."

Suzanne overheard Clark and was in his office as soon as he put down the receiver. "What's going on? Did I hear you say something about Specialist Weeks?"

"Yeah. She's been arrested by the CID."

"What?" Suzanne's eyes widened, and her jaw dropped. "Arrested for what?"

"Apparently she's mixed up with some drug guys downtown."

"Soldiers?"

"No. Panamanians. But she was bringing the drugs on post and distributing them to selected dealers in the units."

"Wow!" Suzanne said the word slowly, expelling a sigh in the process. "And to think she was operating right here under our noses."

"Yeah. She read all the CID reports, knew exactly how they operated, who the undercover agents were—basically, everything she needed to avoid detection."

"Incredible." Suzanne tilted her head to one side, still in a daze. She turned back toward Clark and narrowed her eyes. "I always thought there was something odd about her. You know, she and Major Darst had a strange relationship. Are we going to prosecute her?"

"No, we're not." Suzanne scrunched her nose and pursed her lips—an expression waiting for an explanation. "Look. It's complicated, Suzanne. She's going to be tried at Fort Leonard Wood."

"Fort Leonard Wood? That's in the middle of nowhere."

"Yeah, I know, but I don't have time to speculate on why they're doing it. Right now, I've got to go brief the SJA."

"So, you're the Chief of Justice, now?"

"No, Suzanne, I'm just the guy they briefed about the case." Attempting to shift her focus, he continued, "But the SJA did say this morning that he's going to appoint someone soon."

"Really?" She lit up, her annoyance having been displaced by curiosity.

"Yeah, I suspect it'll be Trip."

"No," she replied, stretching out the word and shaking her head, "he just got through appointing him as the Senior Defense Counsel. In fact, they need an additional defense counsel." She looked at him with a smirk and said, "Besides, Boy Wonder, you just beat Trip in a murder case. Just ask Elmer—he'll tell you all about it."

Clark grinned, assuming she was teasing. "Maybe he'll bring someone down from the States."

"You know he's not going to do that, Clark. Go brief the SJA."

As he turned to leave, Clark couldn't tell whether Suzanne was happy or annoyed that he might become her boss.

The SJA was looking intently at some documents on his desk when Clark was ushered into his office. "Sir, I wanted to let you know that Specialist Weeks has been sent to Fort Leonard Wood for trial."

"What?" He looked up. "Leonard Wood? She's not going to be tried here in Panama?"

"No, sir."

"Where'd you hear that?"

"The CID. Remember? This morning you told me to talk to Jaime Hernandez."

"Oh, yeah. Well, I guess that makes sense, don't you think?" A nervous smile came across Allen's face. "She is half Panamanian, after all. Probably don't want to have a courtroom full of relatives."

"It makes perfect sense, sir. And, you know she was very close to a lot of people here."

At first Allen looked puzzled, then relieved, at the news that Weeks's trial would not be in Panama. And he did an excellent job of feigning ignorance of the reason for the change, which he no doubt understood. After fidgeting for a few moments, he lit a cigarette. "Have you played any golf down here, Clark? We need to play together sometime." Allen studied him for a few moments. "Oh, don't get me wrong: I'm still a hacker, but it's fun and not very expensive."

"Uh, no, sir. The only time I've ever been on a golf course was to caddy at a country club when I was in high school."

"Well, you should try it. Take a lesson or two. I think you'd enjoy it."

Since Allen seemed to be in a good mood, Clark thought the time was right to bring up the topic of Major Darst's replacement.

"Sir, have you thought anymore about the Chief of Justice slot?"

"I haven't made up my mind," he said, slightly shaking his head from side to side and jutting out his chin. "Trip has the most experience, of course."

"That experience didn't seem to help him in the two cases he tried against me."

"Oh... well... Clark, that motion you filed was a good piece of lawyering. But the Gomez case... well, Trip had a tough case to try, didn't he?" Allen took a long draw on his cigarette. "I mean, you and the CID had the goods on old Gomez, didn't you?"

Clark couldn't believe what he was hearing. Did Colonel Allen actually think he just strolled into the courtroom and won the Gomez trial without breaking a sweat? Maybe if he had come to the courtroom and watched at least part of the trial he'd understand how difficult it was. But Clark knew that now was not the time to appear annoyed.

"Uh, not exactly, sir. It was a little more complicated than that." He took a deep breath. "Sir, I'd like to be considered for the job."

"You?"

The disbelief in Allen's voice stung a bit. This wasn't going to be easy. "Yes, sir. I think I'm the best person for the job. Trip was only recently assigned to the Trial Defense Service, and no one else, other than Captain Watkins, has any experience with criminal law, and I have date of rank on her."

Allen leaned forward on his desk and rubbed his nose. "Don't get me wrong, Clark, you've done a good job since you've been here, but you've only tried two cases."

"And I got good results in both of them, sir." Clark paused for a moment but got no response. He decided to go for it. "Besides, sir, I'm sure the prosecutor at Fort Leonard Wood will want to coordinate with the Chief of Military Justice on the Weeks matter. Jaime gave me a full briefing on that investigation this morning." Clark emphasized the word "full" to make his point, although he was bluffing about the rest of it. He knew that if the prosecutor coordinated with anyone in Panama it would be someone at the CID Office, not the JAG Office.

"So, you got a, uh, full briefing, huh?" Allen spluttered. He stood up, turned around, and looked out the window behind his desk.

"Yes, sir. They even have surveillance videos and photographs."

Allen turned and looked at Clark. His droopy eyelids had narrowed his dark eyes to slits, which he focused on Clark. "They've got surveillance videos and photographs?" Allen sat down at his desk but almost immediately got up and paced to his other window, still puffing away.

Undaunted, Clark moved in for the kill. "Yes, sir, lots of photographs. Most were taken outside her apartment to record the comings and goings of various individuals." The SJA spun around and stared at Clark with his slit eyes.

"Did you recognize anybody? I mean... I assume that... that the person was one of her drug guys. Right? Could you tell if he was, uh, a Panamanian?

"Not exactly, sir. I only saw a couple of the photographs, and they were pretty grainy. Jaime said the videotapes were much better, but for some reason he wasn't able to show me those."

Allen walked back to the window behind his desk and looked out, his back to Clark. "Well, you know, Clark, that probably does make sense," he said slowly. "If the folks at Fort Leonard Wood call, they'll want to coordinate with the Chief of Military Justice, and you've already been briefed and all. Besides," Allen turned back toward Clark with a look of forced nonchalance. "Trip did go down to the CID Office and represented himself as Weeks's lawyer." Allen raised his eyebrows and shook his head from side to side, "So, *he* can't coordinate with them, can he?"

"No, sir."

"And, we would look silly to the folks at Leonard Wood if we had Weeks's lawyer as our Chief of Military Justice, wouldn't we?"

"I couldn't agree more, sir."

"Now Clark, you know that criminal law is not really my area."

"Well, sir, I know that you've spent most of your JAG career dealing with administrative law matters, if that's what you mean."

"Bullshit, Clark." Allen was trying to be chummy. "You know I don't know shit about criminal law." Clark smiled and shook his head to say no. Allen continued, "Well, I want you to promise me that you'll have my back and keep me out of trouble with this criminal law stuff."

Clark knew what Allen was getting at. But he also knew that he could legitimately say "yes"—meaning that he would ensure that all criminal law matters were handled properly.

"Absolutely, sir."

Clark sat silently for a few moments until Allen continued, "Good. Then, uh, I'll get the paperwork drawn up. I know the General will support it. I heard that Bednar was so pleased with the Gomez trial that he went to the General in person and told him you did an outstanding job. You made us look good, Clark, and I'm counting on you to continue to do that. You're my Chief of Justice, now."

"Thank you, sir," Clark replied, trying to sound nonchalant. Having accomplished what he set out to do, he stood up and headed for the door.

"By the way, Clark, are you going to the dining-in tonight?"

"Yes, sir, I planned to."

"Good, because I can't make it. Family emergency. Be sure you let the General know that I wish I could be there, but I can't. You'll be our representative."

"Yes, sir. I hope it's nothing serious."

"Huh? Uh, no, I just need to take care of some things with my wife. I promised to take her out tonight. Frankly, I forgot about the dining-in."

That comment surprised Clark. Dinings-in were big events in the Army, especially in the Infantry. Clark would have never missed one, unless he had a really good reason. His face must have revealed what he was thinking because Allen quickly attempted to explain. "Well, you know, Clark, you gotta keep 'em happy. Wives, that is. How's your wife getting along?"

Allen obviously didn't know what was going on between Clark and Janelle, and Clark wasn't about to tell him. "Uh, she's back in the States right now, sir."

"Well, give her my regards, and let me know how the dining-in goes." Allen began looking at some papers on his desk, signaling that their meeting was over.

Clark took the stairs two at a time, as he headed back to his office, suppressing a smile the entire way. He kept saying to himself, over and over, "I can't believe it. I'm the Chief of Military Justice." For a moment, Clark considered going to Trip's office to deliver the news but decided against it. No way did he want to anger Colonel Allen—he might change his mind. Besides, if he told anyone, he should tell Suzanne.

Clark sat down at his desk, surprised that Suzanne hadn't come rushing in as usual to demand a report. He walked by her office a few times on his way to the coffee pot and each time saw her at her desk with her head down, intently reading something. Lunchtime finally came, and he decided he couldn't wait any longer to tell her.

"Suzanne, do you want to go to the NCO Club and grab some lunch?"

"Sure. Am I getting invited to lunch by my new boss?" She smiled. No hint of sarcasm this time.

"Sorta."

"What do you mean sorta? I knew he was going to name you Chief of Justice. Congratulations."

"You were right. He didn't want to move Trip since he's just appointed him to the Senior Defense Counsel slot, and they're not going to send a replacement for Major Darst for a while.

And, I do have date of rank on you. So, appointing you wouldn't work either. It was sort of a process of elimination."

"Well, the new boss has to buy lunch." She grabbed her cap and started for the door.

"You got it," Clark replied as he followed her, pleased that she seemed to be taking the news well. "Hey, are you going to the dining-in tonight?"

"I never have before. I heard it's just a bunch of good ol' boys trying to act like they're from some British regiment."

"No, that's the old Army. Now, it's more collegial. You know, just a chance to dine with some fellow officers you don't get to see that often. Come on. It'll be fun. Your buddy Colonel Bednar will be there. He might even buy you a drink."

"Please. Spare me." Suzanne shook her head several times but then looked at Clark and shrugged her shoulders. "Okay, I'll go. But I've got to see if my dress whites still fit. I had them made when I got down here, and I've lost weight since then."

"Good. I'll meet you there then."

"Hey, I know you think that I'm not happy about this, Clark, but I am."

"Thanks, Suzanne. That means a lot coming from a colleague. I think we make a good team."

CHAPTER THIRTY-FIVE

WHEN HE GOT home later that day, Clark went straight to his bedroom to check on his dress white uniform. He panicked when he opened the closet and couldn't find it right away. As he sorted through several things that were still in plastic bags from the laundry, he came across a red cocktail dress that Janelle had worn to the Christmas Party at Fort Hood when he was still a lieutenant. He pulled up the plastic and ran his hand along the brocade. His mind went back to that party. The dress had cost him a week's pay, but it had been worth it. He'd never forget the expressions on the faces of his fellow lieutenants when he walked into that party with Janelle. Bringing the dress close to his face, he inhaled to see if it still smelled like her. It didn't. She had probably taken it to the laundry right after the party. That was only five years ago. It was hard to believe. So much had happened since then. He pulled the plastic back over the dress and put it in the closet. After sorting through a few more garments in the closet, he was relieved when he finally found his dress whites. He carefully laid them on the bed.

He retrieved a small leather box from the top drawer of the dresser. It had been given to him by his high-school English teacher—a former Marine named Joseph Bray. Mr. Bray had told Clark to store his insignia in it while he was at West Point.

He opened the box and dumped the contents onto the bed. As he sorted out what he needed, he reminisced about what a great mentor Mr. Bray had been—stern, demanding, and uncompromising when it came to right and wrong.

All of Clark's medals and insignia had been in the leather box since he arrived in Panama, and he was shocked to see how tarnished they were. That had never happened before. What was it about Panama that caused everything to deteriorate? The U.S. insignia, in particular, were almost black. Fortunately, he'd never worn the JAG Branch insignia. They were new and still had lacquer on them from the manufacturer, which had to be removed. His captain's bars were badly tarnished, too. He scooped everything up and went to the kitchen.

The cleaning supplies were stored under the sink, and he hoped a can of Brasso was among them. He found the blue-and-white striped can, shook it vigorously, and then took off the red cap and went to work. Although Brasso was normally effective, his insignia were so badly tarnished that it took extra effort to get them back to their normal condition. And experience had taught him that even if the brass appeared to be clean, he had to make sure that he buffed off every bit of the residue. Otherwise, it would make black smudges on his white uniform when he pinned it on.

As he was polishing the brass, Clark thought more about Mr. Bray and what he had told him when he gave him the box. He said to learn everything that West Point had to teach about being a leader because most people who accomplish anything in life—regardless of their fields of endeavor—are leaders. He told Clark that he'd decided to become a teacher when a college professor explained that the word "educate" comes from a Latin word that means to lead forth. And Mr. Bray had taken that explanation to heart: for him, Chaucer and Shakespeare were merely tools for motivating a bunch of South Georgia country kids to think more

417

deeply about themselves and the world around them. He was a special man.

Cleaning everything had taken Clark longer than he'd expected. He hurried back to the bedroom and quickly, but carefully, pinned on each piece, as well as his medals, his Airborne wings, and his Ranger Tab. If he was going to represent the JAG Office, he needed to look sharp.

After he showered and shaved again, he put on the shirt and trousers of his uniform but left the jacket on a hanger, so it wouldn't get wrinkled on the drive over.

The scene at the Officers' Club looked like the set of a Hollywood movie from the 1940s: officers were standing around in crisp white uniforms, cocktails in one hand, cigarettes or cigars in the other. Clark spotted Elmer across the room and made his way over. Elmer had a Balboa in each hand and, as usual, was surrounded by an entourage of lieutenants. Clark chuckled as he approached Elmer who appeared to be regaling them with a story of his exploits during Ranger School.

"Hey, Elmer. I've got some big news."

"What might that be, Counselor?"

"Well, it's sort of confidential."

"That's no problem. We were finished, weren't we, gentlemen?" Elmer grinned and looked around his group. "Besides, you need some more beer anyway." The lieutenants headed to the bar. It wasn't the first time Clark had broken up one of Elmer's sessions, but he didn't seem to mind. He turned back to Clark and said, "I'm guessing confidential can only mean one thing. Your wife came back."

Clark's smile disappeared. "Uh, no. Not yet." He cleared his throat. "It's about work. Allen says he's going to appoint me to be the new Chief of Military Justice."

Elmer's eyes widened, and he responded—in typical Elmer

fashion—with the volume he used at company formation. "Out-fucking-standing!"

Heads turned their way, and officers began asking him what he was talking about. Apparently already forgetting that the news was confidential, Elmer explained to all who were interested that the brigade finally had a Chief of Military Justice with some balls and, of course, a "muther-fuckin' Ranger Tab."

"Guys, it's not exactly official yet," Clark attempted to explain, but it was no use. Elmer was fired up and on a roll, fueled in part by the large quantity of beer he'd already consumed. But then, Clark really didn't try to slow him down. He was enjoying the attention too much. Elmer proceeded to deliver a mini-version of the speech he'd given at Mother's Inn after the Gomez trial. Clark just stood next to him and tried to look modest.

To signal the end of the cocktail hour, the presiding officer of the dining-in—known as the "President of the Mess"—came out and loudly announced, "Please be seated." At that point, everyone got rid of their smokes and headed to the formal dining room.

Clark located Suzanne, standing by herself on the other side of the room. Her right hand was clutching her left elbow, and her expression was vacant—like a lost child at the mall. Her baggy uniform merely completed the picture. When she saw him walking toward her, an awkward smile quickly emerged.

"Looks like all that running did you a lot of good, Suzanne."

"Huh?"

"Your uniform. It certainly isn't tight."

"Oh, yeah." She laughed nervously.

"My trousers are a little snug." Clark raised his eyebrows and patted his stomach. "Too much good food and not enough exercise." She shrugged and shook her head no. "Is Trip here?" he asked.

"No. I asked him about it, and he said he came last year and hated it. Everybody got drunk. And, now that he's in the Trial Defense Service, he saw no point in coming again."

"Well, I know he was invited. Major Darst always made it a point to attend when he was Senior Defense Counsel. He said it was fun, but he also wanted to show the commanders that he was a regular guy." Clark looked at Suzanne to see if she was going to say anything else about Trip—pro or con. She didn't, so he continued. "And as for drunkenness, you know General Kraus isn't going to put up with that."

"We'll see," she said, shrugging her shoulders.

They found a table with some other staff officers and sat back to watch the evening unfold.

The traditions associated with a dining-in are elaborate. Of course, there is always a head table. At this dining-in, the head table was on a raised platform. There was an array of flags behind it: American, Panamanian, Army, and one for the 193rd Infantry Brigade, which also had streamers on it to commemorate each of the battles the brigade had fought. A large, full-color representation of the unit patch hung on the wall behind General Kraus, who was seated in the middle of the head table. Unlike the round tables positioned around the room, the head table was in the shape of a rectangle. Colonel Bednar was seated on the General's right, with the other battalion commanders and members of the general staff on either side. The effect was that of a formation, presiding over the room. Clark noticed an empty seat at the end of the table and wondered if it was for Colonel Allen.

After the room settled down, the President of the Mess, whose table was directly in front of the head table, called for the presentation of the meat. A waiter in a short white jacket and black trousers appeared, rolling a cart bearing a roasted prime rib carving station. The waiter sliced off a piece, put it on a plate, and presented it to the President of the Mess, who sampled it with great flourish and then announced that it was "tasty and fit for human consumption." After some more folderol, dinner was served and everyone settled in and began eating and chatting. Clark glanced at Suzanne, who was the only woman at their table. She wasn't saying anything, and the officers seated beside her weren't talking to her either. She looked like a lost little girl again.

When they finished eating, the President of the Mess directed the chief steward to prepare the Brigade Punch. The waiter who had presented the meat reappeared, only this time he was pushing a serving cart carrying a massive silver bowl. With great ceremony and fanfare, the President of the Mess directed the waiter to pour wine, spirits, and other liquids into the bowl, while he explained how each ingredient had some passing connection with the history of the brigade. The only one that seemed to make any sense was pineapple juice, which represented the period when the brigade was stationed in Hawaii. After the waiter had poured everything into the bowl and mixed it with a large silver spoon, the dining staff rolled the cart around the room and charged each person's glass.

There were formal toasts to the United States of America, the President of the United States, the Army, and fallen comrades. After those toasts were over, the President of the Mess directed a young lieutenant—referred to as "Mr. Vice"—to light the smoking lamp. That was the signal for the cigars to come out. And they did. Officers got up and started milling around—exchanging cigars and giving each other "lights." Clark got up and moved to the seat next to Suzanne.

"Are you enjoying this?"

"Are you kidding?"

"I guess these guys aren't used to having a woman at the table."

"You noticed that, too, huh?" She folded her arms, leaned back in her chair, and let out a deep sigh. The room began take on a blue haze, as officers strutted around puffing on cigars. Clark looked at Suzanne, whose face had taken on a greenish hue. She leaned over toward him. "I've got to leave," she groaned. "This is making me sick."

"Stay a little while longer. Pretty soon, they'll start making toasts. It'll be fun. You'll see."

A few minutes later, officers started clinking their glasses and asking the President of the Mess for permission to speak. Although some toasts were serious, most were silly or funny. One sycophant toasted the General's cocker spaniel, Leonidas—calling him a "mighty warrior." A few officers made toasts in the form of limericks, in response to General Kraus's previously published guidance for the dining-in. It had directed participants to maintain proper decorum—which wasn't the way dining-ins normally went—and to refrain from coarse language and jokes—also a departure from tradition. The guidance even went so far as to recommend the use of "sophisticated humor, like limericks." Junior officers, in particular, thought that recommendation was laughable and had poked fun of it all week during happy hour at Mother's Inn by reciting every lewd limerick imaginable.

Across the room from Clark and Suzanne, Elmer rose and clinked his glass. After being recognized by the President of the Mess, Elmer announced, "I would like to propose an unusual toast." The room got quiet. Elmer's reputation as a wild man always preceded him, so everyone wanted to hear what he was about to say.

Elmer dramatically surveyed the room, and then, using his best "command voice," normally reserved for company formations, he began. "There once was a man from Nantucket..." He paused, and a big, devilish grin emerged on his face—even his eyes were smiling. You could have heard a pin hit the terrazzo floor. Every eye was on him, wondering whether he really was going to continue with that bawdy and shopworn rhyme. "Naw. I can't go there." The whole room erupted in laughter—even

General Kraus. After things quieted down, Elmer clinked his glass again.

"Yes, Captain Jackson, you have more?" asked the President of the Mess, barely able to keep his composure.

"Yes, sir, I do. Tonight, we've heard many toasts to the men in the field and to those who have gone before us. Indeed, they deserve our admiration and respect. But, ladies and gentlemen, it takes a lot to make a unit like the 193rd Infantry Brigade successful. Napoleon said famously that 'an Army runs on its stomach.' Well, I submit to you that what makes an army effective is discipline." He stopped to punctuate that comment. "Discipline comes from good leadership, which we have in the 193rd." Elmer nodded in the direction of the head table. "But the discipline of our brigade is also a function of the quality of its JAG officers. And, we have two fine representatives here tonight: Captains Clark and Watkins." Elmer turned and gestured in their direction.

All eyes in the room were on Clark and Suzanne, which immediately caused red blotches to form on the pale skin of Suzanne's neck and face. Where was Elmer going with this toast? Clark hoped it wasn't a repeat performance of Elmer's comments from earlier in the evening.

"I learned this evening that Captain Clark..." Elmer reverted to his command voice again. "who recently obtained a twenty-five-year sentence for a child murderer..." Whistles and loud applause erupted and drowned out what Elmer was saying, causing him to stop and smile at Clark, who squirmed in his seat. The audience quieted, and Elmer continued. "As I was saying, I learned this evening that Captain Clark has been named the new Chief of Military Justice of our brigade." Elmer then increased his tempo and volume, sounding like a football coach in the locker room at half time. "Woe be unto the bad guys, gentlemen. They're going down!" More applause and shouts of "HOOAH." After the crowd settled down, Elmer motioned toward Clark. "Officers of the 193rd Infantry Brigade, I give you Captain Robert E. Clark." Elmer raised his glass in Clark's direction, and the room erupted again.

Now, it was Clark whose cheeks were flushed. He knew that Elmer was trying to be nice, but this was too much. He stood up and gave a nod of acknowledgment to the applause, glancing quickly in the direction of the head table. The General smiled and nodded his head, which Clark hoped meant that he wasn't bothered by Elmer's toast, considering he hadn't approved Clark's appointment.

Clark sat down, and another officer rose and clinked his glass to make a toast. Clark didn't hear what he said: he was still reeling from the reaction to Elmer's toast. He leaned over and whispered into Suzanne's ear. "Can you believe it? All those Infantrymen applauded for a toast to a JAG officer?"

"They're drunk, Clark," she said sardonically. "They also applauded for the General's dog. Has your appointment been officially announced? And by the way, that brigade punch is awful." She looked at him and cocked her head. "This is supposed to be fun?"

"Maybe they're tired of seeing bad guys 'get away with it,' Suzanne. Maybe..."

"How much are you paying Elmer anyway? He's a hell of a PR man."

"Very funny, Suzanne. He mentioned you, too."

"Oh yeah, the Great Captain Clark and his sidekick Captain Watkins vanquished the enemy." She was not smiling.

"Are you pissed?"

"No. I just think this whole thing is stupid. Is it okay to leave now?"

"No. You're supposed to wait for the General to leave first."

"Well, if anyone asks, just say that I went to the ladies room." She gathered her things and slipped out a side door.

That's just what his wife used to do. Whenever she'd had enough of a situation, the bathroom was her ultimate refuge—her get-out-of-jail-free pass.

Clark couldn't blame Suzanne, though. He should have known she wouldn't like all the silliness that goes on at a dining-in. And it was just as well that she wasn't around to hear the stream of officers who came by their table to congratulate him on the Gomez trial and his appointment as the new Chief of Military Justice. She'd heard enough about that already.

Clark kept his eye on the head table because he wanted to tell General Kraus about Colonel Allen's "family emergency" and to apologize for Elmer's premature announcement. When he saw the General get up to talk to the President of the Mess, Clark decided it was time to approach him. He excused himself from his table and quickly made his way through the crowd. General Kraus was surrounded by a group of captains, each trying to impress the brigade commander. When Clark approached, the crowd parted, most likely because of his recently acquired celebrity.

"Sir, Captain Clark."

"Well, it seems you're the man of the hour, Captain Clark."

"Not by choice, sir," Clark replied, tucking back his chin slightly and shaking his head. The general gave a slight shrug, and Clark relaxed a bit. "Sir, I wanted to inform you of two things." He paused and waited for the General to nod, signaling his permission to proceed. "First, Colonel Allen was unable to attend tonight because of a family emergency, and he sends his regrets."

"I trust it's not too serious."

"I don't think so, sir. One of those wife things." General Kraus nodded his head and smiled. "The second thing, sir, is that Captain Jackson's toast was premature." The General's expression changed, and Clark couldn't read it. Was he upset? Clark quickly tried to salvage the situation. "I mentioned to Captain Jackson that the SJA had indicated that he was considering appointing me to that position, but of course he would have to obtain your approval and coordinate with your staff on that and…"

"That's fine, Captain Clark. If Colonel Allen wants you as his Chief of Military Justice, then it's fine with me. I'm very happy with the result you achieved in the Gomez trial. In fact I agree with Captain Jackson: we are quite ready to see the bad guys go to jail." After nodding in a way that signaled the end of the conversation, the General turned to his aide, who led him through the crowd and out of the dining room.

Clark found Elmer, who was again surrounded by a coterie of lieutenants. As he walked up to the group, Clark grinned and held up his hands as if to say "no more." Elmer got the message and continued his story about a river crossing during Ranger School when he was selected to swim across with the rope that was used to create a one-rope bridge. Clark's mind was elsewhere, although he did hear Elmer say that the water was so cold his balls retreated into his body, causing his sack to shrivel.

Later that evening, as Clark drove home from the dining-in, the applause was still echoing in his ears. He was concerned that the SJA might hear about Elmer's toast, and he knew he had to find a way to get Elmer to tone it down. Other than that, his life was *almost* perfect. If he could just get his wife and daughter back, it would be perfect indeed.

CHAPTER THIRTY-SIX

CLARK SLEPT LATE the next morning. By the time he got up, got dressed, and ate breakfast, it was almost noon. He went to the Post Exchange, paid for a call to Georgia, and telephoned Janelle at her father's house. No answer.

He walked around the PX, looked at watches in the jewelry department, and wound up in the toy section. A Cabbage Patch doll, just like Ellie's, caught his eye. He recalled how much she loved that doll, calling it her "Babbage Patch doll." Part of him wanted to smile at that memory, but the stark reality that she was over a thousand miles away prevented it. He tried to think of other pleasant memories. He recalled the other words Ellie used to mispronounce, the funniest of which was "fire truck," which came out sounding a lot like a word he hoped her sweet little mouth would never say. And then, he realized he couldn't remember exactly what her voice sounded like. He took the doll off the shelf and stared at it through the cellophane on the front of the box. What did she sound like? He couldn't remember. Impulsively, he strode to the front of the store and bought the doll. She might need it when she returned. She might forget hers in Pemberton.

He went back to the phones and waited in line for another twenty minutes. He called his father-in-law's house a second time. Again, no answer. Back to the end of the line with his purchase, he waited for another twenty-five minutes to call again. Still no answer. Holding the doll tightly under his arm, he looked at his watch. It was now 3:40 p.m.—4:40 p.m. in Pemberton. Maybe they went to a movie. He looked at his watch again. The minute hand had barely moved. When he finally made it to the front of the line, it was 5:15 p.m. in Pemberton. Janelle's father didn't have an answering machine—said he didn't care about talking to anyone that much. So, the phone just rang and rang. A young soldier behind him in line snorted and sighed as Clark let the phone ring ten, eleven… fifteen times before he finally hung up. He could feel his stomach twisting again. He needed a drink of water. Why didn't she answer the phone? She should have received his letter, telling her that he would be calling. He decided to wait until Sunday and then try again. To avoid wasting another afternoon standing in line, he purchased a calling card for $60—a lot of money on his captain's pay. But at least he could use it to call from his home telephone.

After the Exchange, he wasn't in the mood to do anything. He hung around his quarters the rest of the day and watched an episode of *General Hospital* on TV. What did people see in that crap? He turned it off, got a beer from the refrigerator, and flipped through some magazines, one of which was a copy of People magazine. Victoria Principal—one of the stars of a TV show called *Dallas*—was on the cover. She was gorgeous, but the article on her, as well as the rest of the magazine, was stupid. Why would anyone waste time with such dribble?

He found a steak in the bottom of his freezer and decided to try his hand at grilling. In view of his inexperience as a cook, the result was surprisingly good—nothing like Nita's cooking but not bad. He topped off his feast with a cigar and a drink on the terrace. He looked for John but saw no sign of him. Maybe his tirade a few nights ago scared him away for good.

Sunday morning started with a glorious sunrise, and Clark

decided not to rush the day. He sat out on the terrace, enjoyed some coffee and the newspaper, and tried to think of something other than calling Janelle. He knew that Janelle, Ellie, and Janelle's father would go to church and then to lunch somewhere after that. There was no point in calling her before about 2:00 p.m. (Georgia time), which was 1:00 p.m. in Panama. After anxiously waiting for the minutes to pass, he called her but got no answer.

After four calls and no answer, he began to get panicky again. He'd used up a lot of minutes on his calling card but hadn't reached her. He went to Ellie's room and retrieved the doll he'd purchased the day before. He placed it on the dining room table for good luck and then tried to call again. Nothing.

What was going on? Why wasn't she answering the phone? That was not like her. Her daddy's Sunday schedule was excruciatingly predictable. He went to church, ate lunch somewhere in town—probably the Swanson Inn—and then went home and watched NASCAR races on TV. They should have been back to his house by early afternoon. Clark chewed on his lower lip and stared at the phone, then the doll, then the phone, as if the doll had some magical power. He went to the kitchen and poured two shots of Maker's Mark in a glass with no ice. Although it was not yet 2:30, he tossed it back—no sipping this time. He stared at the doll again, and then it came to him. He'd call his mother, even though that would probably use up all the time he had left on his calling card. But his mother would know what was going on.

"Hey, Momma, it's Bobby."

"Oh, Sweetheart, what a pleasant surprise."

His mother's Southern drawl was like a sip of iced tea on a hot day. "How are things going, Momma?"

"I'm doin' fine, Baby. Your sister is takin' real good care of me. But we didn' plant a garden this year. Just couldn't bring myself to do it without your daddy... first time in thirty-six years."

"Well, maybe next year, Momma." Clark needed to change the subject fast. "It's good to hear that Darlene is helpin' you."

"And Frank, too." Clark could almost hear her smile. "He's even skipped golf on a few Saturdays to help me. He cuts the grass and keeps the yard lookin' good."

Clark swallowed hard. His brother-in-law was doing things for his mother that he should've been doing. "Has everything been settled with Daddy's estate?"

"It has. Larry's been wonderful, and your sister helped me with all the paperwork."

Larry, his mother's lawyer, had grown up with Clark's father. They had been good friends since childhood and had even enlisted in the Army together. Clark knew his mother was in capable, caring hands.

"Are you all right, Sweetheart? You sound troubled."

"Yes ma'am, I'm all right."

"Well, you'll be happy to know that Janelle and Ellie look great." His mom could read him like the cover of a book. "I saw them at the Swanson Inn after church today. She said they were gonna go see her uncle this afternoon. She was pretty talkative, but her daddy didn' say two words."

"Well, you know, Momma, he's always been kinda strange. That's just him."

"She said she'd bring Ellie by tomorrow for a visit."

"That's nice," he said, though his voice belied the comment.

"What's gonna happen with you two, Sweetheart?" she asked wistfully.

"I don't know, Momma." His voice faltered, and he cleared his throat. "I've been so busy with this trial and everything that I haven't talked to her. I wrote to her, but that's about it." He paused, trying to decide what to say next. "I tried callin' her yesterday and today, but she didn't answer. So, I'm glad to know that you saw 'em and that they looked good." For a moment

Clark considered telling his mother how worried he was about the future of his marriage and, more important, his relationship with Ellie. But he decided his mother had enough problems of her own, so he changed subject. "I won my trial, by the way."

"That's great, Baby." She paused. "Now, which one was that?"

"The murder trial, Momma."

"Oh, yes, that's right. Well, that's good, Sweetheart. He killed a little girl, didn' he?"

"Yes, ma'am. You know, Momma, I'd better get goin'. This call's gonna cost a bunch."

"All right, Sweetheart. Well, it's so good to hear your voice. Call me again sometime. And write me a letter now and then."

"Yes, ma'am. I love you, Momma."

"I love you, too, Baby."

Regrettably, Clark concluded that the prospect of a call from him wasn't important to Janelle. He knew she hated her uncle. When she was in high school, he tried to put his hand up under her skirt during Easter Dinner. She never told her daddy, because her uncle was his only relative, but from then on she hated him and thought he was a pig. And yet, she decided to visit him on Sunday afternoon rather than wait for a call from Panama. Surely, she had received his letter, letting her know he was going to call. Was she avoiding him? He twisted his wedding band around his finger. It had been there for almost ten years. He took a deep breath and let it out. If she was plotting on how to keep Ellie from him, all she had to do was stay in Pemberton while he was deployed to God-knows-where.

His chest tightened. His stomach began to churn. He looked around his quarters for something to get his mind off his situation. On the buffet was a copy of *The Last Lion*, a biography of Winston Churchill. Janelle had given it to him for Christmas, although he'd only started to read it. Deciding that was just the distraction he needed, he spent the remainder of the afternoon and early evening on the terrace, engrossed in the book. As a tribute to the British Bulldog, he switched from bourbon to scotch whiskey and smoked two Cuban cigars. The book described Churchill's early life and rise to prominence during World War II. But what captivated Clark was its vivid description of Churchill's dogged determination. It inspired him to apply that same kind of determination to repairing his fractured family.

On Monday morning, Clark decided he should brief the SJA about the dining-in as soon as he got to work. He knew his boss would be wondering whether his absence was noticed and, if so, whether the General seemed to be bothered by it. Clark arrived before any of the office staff and found Colonel Allen at his desk.

"Sir, I thought I'd let you know what happened Friday night."

"Friday night? Oh, yeah, the dining-in. Sure, Clark, come in and sit down. I'm just trying to catch up on some paperwork." Allen took off his reading glasses and started rubbing his chin. "So, it, uh, it went well, I take it?"

"Yes, sir."

"Did the General say anything about me not being there?"

"No, sir. I explained that you had a family emergency."

Should he mention Elmer's premature, congratulatory toast concerning Clark's selection as the next Chief of Military Justice? It appeared that Allen hadn't heard about the toast, even though he lived next door to Colonel Bednar, who, among other things, was a blabbermouth. Clark decided to avoid mentioning it.

"General Kraus didn't seem to be annoyed by my absence, did he?"

"No, sir."

Allen sighed and sat back in his chair. "Well, that's good, isn't it?" Clark nodded. "Well... I, uh, better get back to this administrative BS. Got to get you appointed to that Chief of Justice slot." Allen smiled, jutted out his chin, and nodded his head, indicating that it was time for Clark to leave.

Clark plodded up the stairs to his office. Should he have told Colonel Allen about Elmer's toast? He sat down in his chair to process what had just happened. Suzanne showed up a few minutes later and, after depositing her briefcase and purse in her office, came to see Clark.

"Did anyone notice that I left early?"

"From the dining-in? No, I don't think so. You didn't miss much."

"No more toasts to the mighty Captain Clark?"

"No, Suzanne, spare me the sarcasm."

"I'm just teasing you, Clark. And I'm glad you encouraged me to go to the dining-in. I wanted to see what it was all about. Now I know I don't ever need to go again." She rolled her eyes and cocked her head to one side. "I really don't have anything in common with those people. And all that smoke made me sick."

"Yeah. It did get pretty bad." His voice was flat, and Suzanne's sixth sense told her that something was wrong.

"What's up, Clark?"

"Nothing. What do you mean?"

"I mean you sound like something is troubling you. And you certainly don't look like the toast of the brigade."

"It's my wife, Suzanne." His eyes began to get watery.

"She's divorcing you?"

"No," he said quickly—his expression, more hurt than shocked.

"I'm sorry, Clark. I didn't mean anything by that comment. It's just that I figured it must be something really bad."

"I can't get in touch with her."

"What? What are you talking about?"

"I mean I tried to call her all weekend and couldn't reach her, even though I wrote her a letter last week telling her I was going to be calling her on the weekend."

"Well, maybe your letter didn't get there in time. You know how terrible the mail service is down here."

"I doubt it. My mom saw her and my daughter after church, and she told my mom that she was going to her uncle's house."

"So, you see—a logical explanation."

"No. She can't stand her uncle. He's a creep. He made a pass at her when she was in high school."

"Yuck. You Southerners. You've got some strange ideas."

"No, Suzanne. He's a redneck creep, and she can't stand him for good reason." Clark stared at his colleague so intently she could see the bright red rims around his eyes. "She knew I was going to call her, and yet, she chose him over me."

"You can't be sure of that, Clark," she said, her voice more soothing than normal. "Isn't she staying with her father? Fathers have a way—especially with their daughters—of making their children feel guilty."

"My dad never did that."

"I said daughters. Are you listening? He probably wanted to go see his brother and talk about monster trucks or moonshine or something."

"They're not that redneck, Suzanne."

"Well, I'd say it's pretty redneck to make a pass at your niece." Clark hung his head down and didn't look at her. She knew he was hurting. "Forget the redneck stuff, Clark. I'm just saying that there might be an explanation." He didn't raise his head. "So, don't get yourself all upset. You've just had a big victory, remember?" Although Suzanne wasn't a mother, she certainly knew how to sound like one.

"Yeah. I guess so." Clark replied, sounding like a little boy who needed reassurance.

"It's going to work out, Clark. Why don't you ask Allen for some leave and go home?"

"I should. I thought about that the other night." Clark

stopped talking because his lower lip started to quiver. He took a deep breath and looked at Suzanne. "But she didn't even wait for a telephone call that she knew was coming."

"Who is this guy I'm talking to?" Suzanne asked, now sounding surprisingly like his English teacher, Mr. Bray. "Is this the guy who filed a motion *in limine* that nobody—including me—thought he could win? And then he won it. Is this the guy who took on an experienced defense counsel in a murder case and wiped the floor with him?" She stopped and smiled at Clark. "Yeah. I was listening to Elmer, and he was right. You go after things and get them done, Clark. Now, do the same thing with your marriage."

Clark felt guilty for ever thinking ill of Suzanne. She was the real deal. She might not fit the mold of the typical Army officer, but she was a good person and a good friend. He smiled at her and said, simply, "Thanks."

"Okay. I've got work to do. You work out this leave stuff with Colonel Allen and your buddy Elmer. I'll take care of things here while you're gone."

Suzanne went back to her office, and Clark could hear her scurrying around doing something. He stared out the window at the Canal and thought about the cruise ships that he'd seen glide through, loaded with people enjoying themselves and each other.

CHAPTER THIRTY-SEVEN

"WE NEED TO talk," Suzanne announced later that day, as she walked into Clark's office holding a handful of pink telephone message forms.

"What's all that?"

"All your messages from Elmer, congratulating you again and again and again." She delivered the line like a vaudeville comedian and was disappointed when Clark just frowned at her attempt at humor. She sighed and pursed her lips. "It's all the stuff that came in while we were preoccupied with the Gomez trial. None of it's too serious, but we need to get back to them."

"Yeah. I guess life does go on, doesn't it? Would you mind looking through them and dividing up the work? I need to be sure that the record of trial and the rest of the Gomez stuff gets wrapped up. Just tell me which of them I need to answer."

Pleased with her delegated responsibility—especially since she would be determining Clark's workload—Suzanne smiled and went back to her office. For the rest of the week, they busied themselves with catching up. A lot of the work involved advising commanders on nonjudicial punishments—known as Article 15s—and administrative discharges, most of which resulted from soldiers failing random drug screenings.

At 4:45 p.m. on Friday afternoon, with only a few minutes left until the start of the weekend, the record of trial arrived from Judge O'Brien's office. The judge had reviewed and authenticated it. Now, Clark had to prepare the post-trial review for General Kraus. He winced as he flipped through the pages of the transcript and recalled what had happened in the courtroom, especially when he got to the part where Judge O'Brien chastised him on the record. The guys in the appellate division would have fun with that when Trip filed an appeal. But he got Gomez convicted; that should be all that matters. Although the subject of the trial was distressing, Clark was proud of the work that he and Suzanne had done. He sat the record on his desk, thinking he would dig into it in depth on Monday. It was time for the weekend.

As he was leaving his office, he received an unexpected call from Major Underwood.

"What brings you to call, sir? Did you forget something down here?"

"No, Captain Clark, there is something I need to discuss with you."

Underwood's voice sounded strange—almost rehearsed. "Has the SJA prepared his post-trial review and advice for the Gomez trial, yet?"

"No, sir. We just received the authenticated record of trial today from Judge O'Brien's office. I've only glanced at it. But it reminded me of how critical your testimony was in achieving a conviction. Thanks again for all your hard work. Is there a problem? Is Commander Peterson upset?"

"He's always upset about something; I really don't care about that." Underwood paused and then quickly sputtered, "I'm going to need to submit a report to the SJA for him to consider as part of his review of the record of trial."

"What kind of report?" Clark's tone was blunt, and he omitted the obligatory "sir" at the end.

"I've come to the conclusion that the opinion I expressed at trial was incorrect."

"What? Why?" Clark's voice was shaky. He sat upright and stiff in his chair, as if he were a plebe at West Point again. He waited for Major Underwood to continue, but there was only a foreboding, heavy silence on the other end of the phone. Clark stood up and then sat back down. His chest felt tight, and his hands began dripping with sweat. He began looking for an unfinished glass of water that was somewhere in his office. He'd had it only a few minutes ago. His office suddenly felt small and tight—crammed with too much furniture, too many pictures. He took a deep breath and tried to compose himself. What on earth was this man talking about? Was he about to undo what they had worked so hard to achieve?

Clark couldn't take it anymore; he broke the silence. "Sir, I don't understand."

"I stopped by Gorgas Hospital after the trial and learned that neither Dr. Gonzalez nor Dr. Arias reviewed Lydia Mendoza's medical history with her mother. That surprised me, so I reviewed the microscopic brain and spinal cord sections obtained during the autopsy."

"I'm not following you, sir."

"To put it bluntly, Captain Clark, I've concluded that Lydia Mendoza died of meningitis."

"Meningitis?"

"Yes. I wasn't sure until I returned to the AFIP and was able to confirm what I suspected. Meningitis is an inflammation of the membranes covering the brain. I now think that she experienced large-scale inflammation of her subarachnoid space, which was caused by her immune system responding to the entrance of bacteria into her central nervous system. I don't need to tell you that Panama is not exactly a clean place. I must say that I missed it when I first reviewed this file because we normally see this kind of infection in much younger children."

"I'm afraid I still don't understand, Doctor. So, you don't believe she died from being shaken?"

"No, I don't. I think the meningitis killed her. Her brain responded to some kind of bacterial infection by releasing large amounts of cytokines, which recruit other immune cells and stimulate other tissues to fight the bacteria. That reaction caused her blood–brain barrier to become permeable, which led to her cerebral edema. In other words, her brain swelled due to fluid leakage from her blood vessels. Large numbers of white blood cells were in her cerebrospinal fluid. I believe that also caused inflammation of the meninges, which led to more edema due to fluid between her brain cells. The walls of the blood vessels in her brain were also inflamed, which caused a decreased blood flow, which in turn led to additional edema. The other notable fact I overlooked is that when she was admitted to the hospital her blood pressure was low, which means that it was harder for blood to enter her brain, and so, her brain cells were deprived of oxygen."

"Sir, I thought the alternative diagnosis, or, rather... I thought Commander Peterson said that she died from a spider bite."

"He didn't know what he was talking about." Underwood's response was quick and adamant. "In case you didn't notice, he's a well-educated pompous ass. He likes to be a contrarian and spar with counsel, but he's not a thorough forensic pathologist."

"Well, I can't argue with that, sir. But I'm confused about this meningitis theory. I thought..."

"It's not a theory, Captain Clark. The evidence is clear."

"Sorry, sir. I didn't mean to sound argumentative. This is just a lot of medical information to take in."

"I understand. But the important thing is that I've got to correct the record. I'm no longer happy with my testimony. This man might have been wrongly convicted."

"What about Doctor Gonzalez and Doctor Arias? They both agreed with your opinion that Lydia had been shaken to death."

"I can't control what they did or didn't do. I'm only concerned about my testimony. It was incorrect, and I need to correct the record. In my opinion, though, they were sloppy and took the easy path. It's clear from Doctor Arias's report that he didn't investigate the possibility of meningitis." Major Underwood paused for a moment. "The bottom line, Captain Clark, is that none of the doctors who reviewed this case—not me, not Commander Peterson, and certainly not Doctors Gonzalez or Arias—did his job properly."

"So, nobody drew a correct conclusion?"

"Right. But remember, these things aren't easy. Forensic pathology is an art as well as a science. Judgment is important." Underwood paused again. "I've talked to our JAG here, and he pointed me to paragraph 85 of the Manual for Courts-Martial, which says that the SJA's review may include matters outside the record of trial that might have a bearing on the action of the convening authority."

"I'm not sure what you're trying to accomplish, sir."

"I told you Captain Clark: I'm trying to correct the record. I don't want to wake up at night, five years from now, because I participated in wrongfully sending a father of three small children to jail for twenty-five years. They'll be lucky if they ever see him. And when they do, what will they think of him? That he's a murderer? I don't want any part of that."

Clark was annoyed by the melodrama but more concerned that his great achievement was coming unraveled.

"At this point, sir, we have a conviction. All that remains is for the convening authority to approve it."

"That's just it, Captain Clark. The Manual for Courts-Martial says that the convening authority has the power to disapprove all or a part of the findings. It seems to me that the correction of my testimony is an important factor for him to consider."

"I'm not completely familiar with that section, sir, but I don't think the convening authority can simply do whatever he wants."

"You're the JAG, not me, but what was explained to me is that the convening authority can consider something that might make him conclude that Gomez was not guilty or that he deserves to be retried. He doesn't have the power to change a not guilty verdict to guilty—only the other way around."

"Could you give me some time to consider this, sir?"

"I'll be happy to wait and discuss my report with you before I send it to the SJA, but I want to be clear: if I conclude that I need to send him a report—which is where I am right now—then I'm going to send it. It's not my job to do the convening authority's job, or the SJA's job, or your job, for that matter. But it is my job to set the record straight concerning my expert opinion and my testimony."

"I understand, sir. Can we talk again on Monday at this same time?"

"Sure. I'll call you again."

Clark hung up the phone and leaned back in his chair. It felt as if someone had placed an anvil on his chest. A dark, sinking feeling began to form deep in his gut. This was a disaster. Major Underwood had been so confident at trial. Now, he was pulling the rug out from under the prosecution. Clark worried that if the SJA included Underwood's report in his post-trial review, General Kraus would set aside the conviction. He didn't know whether the Manual would allow Gomez to be retried or not. Taking the Manual off the shelf, he began to turn the pages furiously. Even if Gomez could be retried, the General probably wouldn't refer charges again. Worst of all, Clark would soon look like an idiot. No matter that he had presented the evidence, argued the case, and gotten a conviction, it would look like he fouled up the case—just like his predecessors. He needed help.

"Suzanne, could you come here a minute, please?"

CHAPTER THIRTY-EIGHT

"WHAT'S UP?" SUZANNE asked as she came into Clark's office. "Are you wanting to buy me a drink now?"

"No." Clark's expression communicated the seriousness of the situation. "Shut the door, would you?"

"Everyone's already left. It's just us." Clark stared at her hard. Her smile disappeared, and her jaw clenched. "Now what?"

"Underwood wants to submit something to the SJA saying that the opinion he provided at trial was incorrect."

"What?" She stretched out the word, to further express her disbelief.

"Yeah. He thinks Lydia died from meningitis. He reeled off all sorts of medical mumbo jumbo about why he's now concluding that meningitis is what caused her death."

"Why is he saying this now?" She emphasized the last word, which captured Clark's feelings exactly.

"He says that nobody reviewed Lydia's medical records or considered her medical history."

"I knew that was going to be a problem." Suzanne pursed her lips and shook her head slightly.

"Are you playing Monday morning quarterback, too?"

"No, Clark, I told you about those cases where they didn't look at the medical records. But I also told you that there was nothing you could do about that at trial. The facts are what they are."

"Well, now the guy who we thought was our star witness is going to wind up screwing us. Do you realize how stupid I'm going to look?"

She glared at him like one of his Sunday school teachers back in Pemberton. "Well, first of all, stop worrying about yourself and start thinking about what a professional would do."

"You're right," he sighed. "But what do I do now?" Although he was angry, Clark tried to restrain himself and not take it out on Suzanne. He knew she was right, and he knew he needed her help.

Suzanne began thinking out loud. "We both learned this in law school, right? To convict Gomez, we had to introduce evidence that proved each element of the offense beyond a reasonable doubt." Clark nodded in agreement. "We did that," she continued, "but now Underwood wants to take back his testimony." She stopped to organize her thoughts. "Now, General Kraus might consider the change in Underwood's testimony to be significant and set aside the conviction altogether." She raised her eyebrows and pursed her lips. "But that doesn't mean Gomez is innocent: it just means the General concluded that doubt has been cast on at least one element of the offense. So, he's not guilty. In that case, he couldn't be retried. Alternatively, the General might conclude that the evidence in the record is still sufficient to convict Gomez, but to ensure everyone feels the process was fair, he could order a rehearing."

"Do you think he'd do that?"

Lost in thought, Suzanne ignored his question and continued, "Or, he could say that Underwood's change in testimony shouldn't change the result, since Gonzalez and Arias both said Lydia died from being shaken, and we proved that Gomez had the opportunity, means, and motive. In that case, he'd affirm the conviction."

"Where does all that leave us? What do we do now?" Clark slumped back in his chair. "I should've seen this coming," he moaned. "I should've listened to you and quizzed those guys during trial prep about whether they checked the medical records."

"Look, Clark, just chalk it up to experience." She waited for him to respond and then with a tentative smile added, "And remember: experience is something you don't get until just *after* you need it."

"No shit. Ain't that the truth?"

"I'm not sure I have this all straight in my head," she said. "Let's step back a minute. Let's both review the Manual for Courts-Martial, think about this situation, and then regroup and compare notes."

"That makes a lot of sense, Suzanne. Thanks for thinking clearly about this crap."

"Well, I've got to go now." Clark looked up, surprised to see her almost radiant. "I have a date, believe it or not. But I'll be in here tomorrow, bright and early."

Clark's jaw slacked a bit but he said nothing, and neither did she. She just smiled and left. Wonderful. She was happy. She was downright perky. Because she was going on a date. Their case was falling apart, and she was going on a date. Great. Just when he needed her. Clark picked up his Manual and slammed it on the desk. After pacing back and forth for several minutes, he sat down and took a deep breath. He thought about how Suzanne had looked when she left. How could he be mad at her? This was her first date in over two years. And she had been a damn good team player. If there was a way to avoid disaster, Suzanne would figure it out.

The provision of the Manual that Major Underwood was referring to was part of what the military called the post-trial review of the convening authority. It's a unique aspect of the military justice system that gives the convening authority broad powers to act on a case. It starts with the staff judge advocate's review of the record of trial and recommendation concerning what action the convening authority should take. After the convening authority reviews the record of trial and the SJA's recommendation, he may suspend all or part of the sentence, disapprove a finding or conviction, or decrease the sentence, but he may not increase the sentence or change a finding of not guilty to guilty. In certain cases, he may order a rehearing. That's why Major Underwood wanted to make his report to the SJA. He wanted to influence the SJA's recommendation and, in turn, the General's.

The weekend stunk. Normally, weekends in Panama were filled with fishing, water skiing, night-clubbing, relaxing by the pool. For Clark, this one consisted of one anxious moment after the other, slowly plodding towards Monday. He knew he should go to the office; he knew Suzanne would be there, working away. But he just couldn't.

Around noon on Saturday, he decided to go to a restaurant. He was hungry because he hadn't eaten since Friday lunch, but he wasn't interested in cooking for himself. Although The Happy Buddha was usually his first choice, he didn't want to risk running into one of the officers from post. So, he sucked it up and drove into downtown Panama to Casa Pacifica, a seafood restaurant that Jaime had told him about. Ironically, it was near Club Iguana. He made it to the restaurant and sat at a table in the back. He ordered some ceviche and began watching a Panamanian *novella* on a black-and-white TV perched high on a shelf. Of course, it was in Spanish, but it kept his mind off of what he didn't want to think about.

"Wha' the hell are you doing here, Capitan Clark?"

Clark looked up to see Lieutenant Martinez, one of the usual members of Elmer's band of merry men. "Oh, I thought I'd sample some authentic Panamanian cooking."

"Well, dat's no' cooked. You know dat, righ'," he looked at Clark with a teasing smile.

"Oh, yeah, of course. It's ceviche."

"Hey, sir. Coul' I come an' tal' to you abou' law school sometime? Do you thin' I coul' ge' in tha' program you went to? I's called FLEP, righ'?"

"Yeah, that's right," Clark answered curtly. He wanted this kid to go away.

"The way you kicked tha' guy's ass. Tha' was ou'stan'ing! Tha' wha' I wan' to do. I'd like to be a prosecutor, like you." He smiled as if to say did-you-like-that-compliment.

"Yeah, well, FLEP is a pretty involved and competitive process. I'd be happy to talk to you about it sometime, but I've got to be going. Gotta meet someone."

Clark stood up and in one motion took his last swig of a Balboa and picked up his keys off the table. He glanced back at the lieutenant, who seemed stunned by his quick departure. Clark had come downtown to avoid encounters like that. Just his damn luck. All the officers at the dining-in thought he was a big deal because of the Gomez verdict, and now it was going down the drain.

He couldn't bring himself to go to the office, so he headed back to his quarters, stopping on the way to fill up his Nova at the post gas station, which was just inside the back gate. He didn't notice the midnight blue BMW that was parked on the other side of the pumps; that is, until he heard that familiar Southern drawl. "Afternoon, Robert. Are you still celebratin'?"

"Oh, hey, Trip. No, uh, you know, just getting ready for next week."

"What's happenin' next week?"

Clark's gut tightened. "Oh, nothing. Just the usual."

"I haven't had a chance to congratulate you on your recent appointment. Under the circumstances, you'll understand if I don't wish you good luck." Trip smiled at his own joke, but Clark just nodded and put the nozzle back on the pump.

"Oh, yeah. Well, thanks, Trip. I, uh… I've got to get going. I've got some stuff to do at the house." Trip nodded and headed inside to pay.

As soon as Trip was inside, Clark hopped in his car and drove away, hoping to avoid any further interaction with him.

When he got back to his quarters, he couldn't relax as he had planned. He didn't even want to sit on the terrace or smoke a cigar. He was a wreck—pacing around all afternoon like a caged jaguar. He didn't feel like eating dinner and didn't sleep very well either. He could not stop thinking about the repercussions of Major Underwood's report to the SJA. All the praise that had been heaped upon him would be recalled. From General Kenneth W. Kraus down to Captain Elmer T. Jackson, Clark would be viewed as just another JAG weenie who couldn't get the job done. All the "muther-fuckin' Ranger Tab" crap would be history. They'd probably check his personnel records to see if he'd actually earned one. Any way Clark looked at the situation, it was a disaster. He couldn't think clearly about it at all.

Monday morning finally came. Clark was anxious to find out if Suzanne had come up with something brilliant over the weekend. He arrived at the office early but found no one there. He followed his usual routine, made a pot of coffee, settled into his office, and started reviewing correspondence. He couldn't bear to look at the Manual for Courts-Martial anymore. Suzanne arrived around 7:30 a.m. He heard her walk into her office, drop her things in her chair, and head toward his office.

"We need to talk," she said grimly.

"Did you come up with anything?" he asked, wide-eyed and leaning forward in his chair.

"Well, I was up here all weekend doing research, and I didn't see you anywhere. I tried calling you Saturday. Where were you?"

"I know, Suzanne. I suck. I should have been here helping, but I just couldn't. I don't know what to do." He gave her a lame smile. "How was your date?"

"I don't want to talk about it." She avoided making eye contact as if she was afraid he'd read something in her eyes that she didn't want him to see. Having composed herself, she looked up with slightly glassy eyes. "Look, Clark, we need to stay focused. You don't have a lot of options. Major Underwood is going to call you today, and you need to be ready to tell him what you think."

"I know, but I can't think of a reason why he shouldn't give the information to the SJA."

"I can."

"Thank God, Suzanne. What'd you come up with?"

"It's not what you think." She paused as if gathering the courage to tell him. "You should tell Trip to contact Major Underwood, which would allow him, as defense counsel, to present the information to the convening authority."

Here we go again, Clark thought: the great Trip Stephens and all his money and his family and their influence. Would this guy ever be judged by his accomplishments, instead of his birth certificate? All that "congratulations" crap from Trip at the gas station—his bullshit flowed like a drainage ditch during Rainy Season.

"Hold on, Clark, I can tell exactly what you're thinking by that look on your face. You know—and I know—that Colonel Allen is in big trouble with the General because he was screwing Specialist Weeks."

"How did you know that?"

"The entire post knows it, Clark. Nobody says anything because he's the SJA. He and his wife have been having a tough time. Like a lot of wives down here, she hates Panama. This place is a male-chauvinist paradise. Weeks just twitched her tail at him one-too-many times."

"You're kidding me. You're saying it was common knowledge they were having an affair? I never suspected a thing."

"That's because you're a boy scout, Clark." Suzanne shook her head ever so slightly from side to side. "But the problem in front of us now is that we need to do the right thing. You and I both know that Colonel Allen is trying to get back into the General's good graces. And, the General is real happy that we got a conviction in a notorious case. Or should I say, 'you got a conviction'? You remember the dining-in, don't you?"

"Unfortunately," he groaned. They stared at each other for a long time, and then Clark said softly, "I'm going to look like an idiot."

Suzanne didn't let up; she made Mr. Bray look like a pushover. "I don't think Allen will give Underwood's report fair treatment. He'll think of a way to minimize its importance. He might even refuse to present it. And, you know that Underwood's report will be extremely important and that a man's life depends on it being considered properly."

"Why will it make a difference if we give it to Trip?" Clark asked, sounding like a kid who didn't want to face his punishment.

"Because Trip will present it in the best way possible for Gomez. Allen will try to bury it, if he comments on it at all. If Trip presents it well, General Kraus won't be able to ignore it. It'll be part of the record. And more than anything else, generals don't want to look silly. So just tell Trip to call Major Underwood. Our job is to do justice, remember?"

Clark knew she was right, but he dreaded what was going to happen when this news hit the General's desk.

"Let me think about it for a while."

"Okay, but you don't have a lot of time. You've either got to give it to Trip, or at least go tell Allen before he hears about it from Major Underwood."

Suzanne went back to her office, and Clark shut his door, stared out the window at the Canal, and tried to clear his head. He reviewed his behavior over the past few weeks. He'd cut corners and bent rules—all the while telling himself that it was for the greater good. But that wasn't how he'd been raised. His father would have never done things like that. And regardless of whether his father was looking down on him now, he wanted to live up to his good name.

Clark decided that he'd been enjoying the adulation too much and had failed to follow the advice of his favorite poet. He pulled a crumpled piece of paper from his desk drawer, on which he'd written the entire Kipling poem. He focused on a particular passage:

If you can meet with Triumph and Disaster

And treat those two impostors just the same;

His current "triumph" was indeed an imposter, and—if he was honest with himself—it was no "disaster" for him to do the right thing now. Suddenly, everything became clear.

He yelled loud enough for Suzanne to hear, "Okay, Suzanne. You're right. I'll do it."

CHAPTER THIRTY-NINE

FOR A LOT of reasons, Clark didn't want to tell Trip about the telephone call from Major Underwood. For starters, he knew he'd no longer be the "toast of the brigade." He'd be just another JAG weenie who couldn't get the job done. But there was a lot more to it than that. He'd accomplished something important. Not two years out of law school, the kid from Pemberton, Georgia, convicted someone of murder. Now, all that was going away.

He shuffled into into Suzanne's office and slumped into the chair across from her. "You know what really annoys me about all this?" She looked up from her work and raised her eyebrows, indicating that she was awaiting his answer. "Once again, Trip is going to come out on top through no effort of his own."

Suzanne sighed. "This isn't about Trip, Clark. It's not about you. It's not about me."

"I know. I know, but for once I'd like to see the guy have to work for something. You and I have worked hard for everything we've achieved in life, including the conviction of Raul Gomez. Trip just coasts through life. Everything is so easy for him—too easy."

"Face it, Clark: some people are born into luck. Get over it."

"Have you ever seen Trip work hard for anything? Does he

have a clue about how to sacrifice for someone else? Does he realize his clients are depending on him?"

"Didn't you tell me you weren't supposed to ask a lot of questions without waiting for the answer?"

Clark was too fired up for that mild rebuke to slow him down. "He acts like the world revolves around him."

"Come on, Clark. He's not that bad."

"Oh, I don't think he's evil. He's just been spoiled and catered to his whole life. That's his reality. And because of his family's prestige, everyone—including the SJA—gives him a pass."

"I thought you wanted to do the right thing," she reminded him.

"I do." Clark got up, walked to the window, and looked out at the Canal. "And I know you're right, Suzanne. I just hate having to be the delivery boy for Trip's latest bit of good fortune."

Clark turned and went back to his office, reflecting on what Suzanne had said. He plopped down in his desk chair. I know it's not about Trip. And it's not about me. It's about doing the right thing. He contemplated those thoughts for a few moments and then stood up, determined to finish the task. Heading for Trip's office, he stopped at Suzanne's doorway. "You're right, Suzanne. I'm going. Our job is to do justice."

She smiled and nodded.

Clark sat down across the desk from Trip. Judging from his expression, Trip had no idea why Clark had come to his office. Did it have something to do with what Clark had told him at the gas station about "getting ready for next week"?

"I need to tell you something." Clark paused, searching for the right words. Not finding them, he finally blurted out in exasperation, "You need to call Major Underwood."

"Underwood? For what?"

"You need to talk to him. He's had second thoughts about his testimony at trial."

"What? What are you saying?"

"I'm saying he's ready to serve up a slow one right across home plate, and you should be able to knock it out of the park. Talk to him and then file something with the convening authority in a way that he has to consider it when he does his post-trial review."

"Why are you doing this? Why didn't you say something about this when I saw you at the gas station on Saturday? Did Underwood just now call you?"

"I'm doing it because it's the right thing to do, Trip. I didn't say anything on Saturday, because I hadn't decided what to do at that point. This thing only came up on Friday afternoon."

"Have you told Colonel Allen?"

"No, I haven't. You can tell him if you want to." Clark didn't wait for Trip to say anything else. He just got up and left, leaving Trip with a blank look on his face.

When Clark passed Suzanne's office, she looked up from her desk and smiled. He passed by without a word, went into his office, and shut the door. Not wanting to think about what was going to happen next, he stared out the window in an effort to distract himself. A big, ugly, rusty freighter was passing through the Miraflores Locks, bound for the Atlantic. It looked like the type of ship used to bring Japanese cars to the East Coast of the United States. After watching it for a few minutes, Clark turned and faced the wall in front of his desk, on which he'd hung his diplomas from West Point and the Georgia Law School. He recalled how hard it had been to earn them and was reminded of something in the Cadet Prayer:

Encourage us in our endeavor to live above the common level of life. Make us to choose the harder right instead of the easier wrong, and never to be content with a half truth when the whole can be won.

In this case that "harder right" was damn hard. Clark had never faced anything like this.

After a couple of hours, Suzanne knocked on his door. "Okay, Boy Wonder, you've sulked long enough. You need to go talk to Colonel Allen."

"What am I going to say? That I blew it for not asking the doctors whether they had reviewed Lydia's medical records?" Suzanne's disgusted look was worthy of his mother.

"Stop whining and go do your job. Bad news doesn't get better with age." She turned on her heel and left.

As soon as Clark entered Colonel Allen's office, he could tell that Trip had already talked to him. Allen was annoyed, and he didn't ask Clark to take a seat as he usually did.

"So, when were you going to tell me that Trip has new evidence to present to the convening authority?"

"I just met with him a little while ago, sir."

"A little while ago?" Allen raised his eyebrows and looked at Clark over the top of his reading glasses. "Trip came down here almost two hours ago and said that he'd already met with you about this. What have you been doing since then?"

Clark tried to derail the interrogation. "Did he explain what Major Underwood is going to say in his report?"

"Yes," Allen scolded, now red-faced, "and it sounds like none of your doctors did their jobs, and you didn't do yours either." He took off his glasses and looked hard at Clark. "Didn't I tell you before that I want to know such things right away?" He rubbed his forehead and looked down at his desk. "This is not going to sit well with the General. He's tired of losing cases."

"We got a conviction, sir."

Allen looked up at Clark with a piercing stare. "And then Trip put forth an extra effort and took it away from you, didn't he?"

"It looks that way, sir." For a moment, Clark regretted not coming to Colonel Allen first, but then his boss didn't disappoint.

"If you had come to me with this information, I might have been able to address it in a way that would have preserved the conviction." Allen was on a roll, almost hyperventilating. "I'm sure Trip will make good use of Underwood's revised report. He has to, doesn't he? I mean… that's his job, isn't it?"

Was Allen actually hoping that Trip—his golden boy—might consider *not* using Underwood's revelation to its fullest so that Allen could continue his plan of redemption with General Kraus? If so, Colonel Allen was a fool. Trip was going to use the report. He would probably take it to General Kraus himself. He was going to claim victory, take a victory lap, and go back to Mississippi one day as the champion of the poor and oppressed.

Allen stopped talking and put his head in his hands. After a few moments of silence, he looked up. "Don't you know that you have to probe your witnesses about this sort of thing? Now, Trip is going to present Underwood's revised opinion in a way that is dispositive of the case."

"Yes, sir. That's regrettable." After staring at Allen for a few moments, he continued, "Sir, Major Underwood is an experienced witness and came highly recommended. I assumed he knew what he was doing."

"Assumed?" The word almost hissed out of Allen's mouth. "Don't you know that assumption is the mother of all fuck-ups?" Allen wasn't trying to be funny. He looked back at the papers on his desk. "That's all, Clark," he said, without looking up. "You can go." As Clark turned to walk out of his office, Allen added, "Oh, and by the way, I've put in a requisition for a major to be the Chief of Military Justice. I think it'll be approved. But, you can continue as trial counsel."

Clark trudged up the stairs to his office. All the clerks stared at him when he walked by. None of them dared say anything. He flopped into his chair and spun around to gaze out the window. Suzanne waited a few minutes before coming in.

"How'd it go?

"About like a root canal without Novocain," he mumbled without turning to look at her.

"What happened?"

He spun around. "Well, he's pissed, but we both knew that would happen. He told me I didn't do my job—as if he would know how to prepare a witness for trial. But the big news is that he's put in for a new Chief of Military Justice."

Suzanne clenched her jaw and frowned. After a few moments, her face softened. "I'm sorry, Clark," she said in her mother-sounding voice. "That's not fair."

"It's okay. I have no business being in this job anyway." He let out a sigh and then looked at her intently. "Would you mind covering things for me? I need a change of scenery."

Suzanne nodded. Clark smiled, picked up his empty brief-case, and walked out of the office, past the silent, staring clerks, and headed for what had become his home away from home.

CHAPTER FORTY

AS CLARK WALKED in the door of Mother's Inn, he was reminded of his first visit. Merle Haggard was booming from the jukebox, and a frustrated lieutenant was banging on the cigarette machine by the door—it must have kept both his money and the pack he was craving. The scent of the place was familiar—musty with a hint of popcorn, stale beer, and, of course, cigarettes. But it was a comfortable, undemanding place. Clark reflected for a moment about all the important things that had happened to him in this dump since he arrived in Panama a little over a year ago.

When his eyes adjusted from the sunshine to the dim light inside, he could see that it was almost deserted. There were just a few officers sitting around the room, munching on hamburgers and drinking cokes—not the rowdy crowd that would materialize in about an hour. He headed for Elmer's corner, which was vacant. He decided his friend wouldn't mind if he used his spot. On the wall behind the chair where Elmer normally sat was his adopted coat of arms: a large, full-color replica of a Ranger Tab over Airborne wings. The manager had put it there to properly appoint Elmer's throne.

By the time Elmer arrived around 5:30 p.m., a line of empty beer bottles was arrayed in front of Clark, and he was intently arranging them, so that all of the labels faced the same way.

"We've been busy, I see," Elmer said, with the sing-song voice of a kindergarten teacher.

Clark looked up to see Elmer grinning at him. "Yes, we have." Clark made a sweeping gesture toward his line of empties.

"May I join you?"

"Of course, Elmer. It's your fucking corner." Clark smiled as he slurred that line, and Elmer knew his friend was drunk.

"Listen, buddy, I heard about what happened."

"How'd you hear?"

"Remember. All those people in the personnel office are assigned to Headquarters Company. They may work for the colonel in charge of personnel, but they answer to me. One of them told me that Allen called the head of personnel, all hot under the collar, wanting to put in an expedited requisition for a major to be Chief of Military Justice. Since you've been a water walker the last couple of weeks, I decided I needed to find out what was going on. So, you wanna tell me?"

Clark leaned back in his chair, raised his eyebrows, and looked up at Elmer. "Major Underwood—you know, the pathologist from AFIP—well, he's changed his fucking mind. He says the evidence is clear that Lydia died of meningitis, not by being shaken." Clark let out a deep sigh and, in his best imitation of a sportscaster, continued. "And, the great Trip Stephens is going to step up to the plate and hit Major Underwood's revised report so deep into left field that the convening authority will fucking have to consider it before taking action on the record of trial." Elmer looked puzzled. "It means, Elmer, that the General will probably disapprove the finding of guilty in the Gomez case."

"But I thought you got a conviction." Elmer sat down and fidgeted as he searched for something positive to say. "So, fucking Underwood changed his fucking testimony. So what? You still have Gonzalez and Arias."

"Yeah, but Underwood's testimony was the cement that held eveything together."

"Well, maybe the General won't be convinced by Underwood's revised report. Maybe he'll approve the finding anyway." Elmer sipped his beer.

"Not unless he's willing to risk looking like a fool when the Army Court of Military Review reviews the case." Clark took a long swig of the fresh Balboa the waitress had just put in front of him. When she started to clear away his line of bottles, he said, "Leave those, please." She shrugged her shoulders and walked away. "Think about it, Elmer. If General Kraus is willing to look the other way when Allen was screwing Weeks, because he didn't want to be embarrassed by his SJA, then he sure as hell is not going to confirm Gomez's conviction and risk having the appellate court overturn it." Clark stopped and chugged the remainder of the Balboa. As carefully as he could, he placed the empty bottle in line with its brothers and adjusted it, so that its label was perfectly aligned with the others. "Besides," Clark continued, turning to look at Elmer with fierce eyes, "the man might actually be innocent."

The two men sat for a while, drinking beer, staring ahead, saying nothing. Finally, Elmer leaned back and said, "Well, Clark, here's how you gotta look at it: some days you're the bug, and some days you're the windshield."

Clark turned to look at Elmer, cocked his head, and squinted his eyes. "What in the hell is that supposed to mean?"

"I don't fuckin' know." Elmer shook his head and laughed as he took another swig. "It sounded appropriate." Then he turned and looked at Clark with his penetrating blue eyes. "Listen to me, my friend. Get over it." His eyes narrowed as he studied Clark's face. "You learned this shit in Ranger School, didn't you? Life is not fair. How many times did you hear that? Fucking Jimmy Carter said it. Didn't you see guys flunk patrols because somebody fell asleep? They couldn't control that crap in the dark of night on some mountain somewhere. But they flunked anyway. Shit happens. You did your job right. Underwood didn't. He's just like one of those guys who fell asleep. Unfortunately, you have to deal with the consequences. That's just the way it is." Elmer paused. "You know, FIDO."

"FIDO?" Clark looked at Elmer with a blank expression.

"Come on, Clark, you remember that: fuck it, drive on."

"Oh, yeah." Clark knew that Elmer was trying to help, but he was still angry with himself. His situation was not like Ranger School. He should have questioned his witnesses about whether they had examined Lydia's medical records and history. It *was* his fault. And, who knows what would have happened if he had questioned them? Maybe Gomez would have been convicted anyway, or maybe the doctors would have changed their minds. Who knows?

They sat in silence for several minutes. "Tell me something good, man," said Clark.

"I wish I could, buddy." Elmer paused and cleared his throat. "But, uh, you're not the only one who got bad news today."

"What? What did you say?"

"I said you're not the only one who got bad news today." Elmer's face was somber. "I got served with divorce papers from my wife."

"And you're upset about that?" Clark asked. Elmer stared straight ahead and said nothing. "I don't get it, Elmer. I thought you didn't want to be married to her anymore."

Elmer jerked up straight in his chair and turned to look at Clark. "Whatever gave you that idea?" There was hurt in his eyes. "She makes me crazy all right, but I still love her—and Sally, Jessica, and Amanda. They're my girls now." Elmer slumped over the table and looked down, dragging his finger in and around a puddle of condensation. "I know I do some crazy shit, Clark, but I didn't want it to come to this." He took a long swig, finished his beer, and motioned for the waitress to bring him another. When she arrived, he asked her to bring him a shot of Jack Daniels, too.

Over the next couple of hours, Clark switched to Coke, while Elmer consumed a lot more beer and several more shots of Jack Daniels. They talked about the Army, their wives, Ranger School, growing up. By 10:30 p.m., Elmer had gotten philosophical. "I guess it was inevitable, Clark. She had a crazy, hard life before we met, and I'm living a hard, crazy life now. For a marriage to work, a husband and wife need to see the same future." He paused for a swig. "We don't. She hates the Army, and I love it. It's my life. I think about my fellow soldiers…" The beer and the booze had made Elmer overly emotional; his voice waivered. "If I ever went into combat with them, I'd be more worried about them than I would be about myself. And they'd be more worried about me than they would be about themselves. That's what a team is." He leaned toward Clark and looked into his eyes. "Why can't marriage be that way? Why can't a man and a woman worry more about each other than they do about themselves?"

"The good ones do, Elmer. That's the way my mom and dad were."

Elmer sat back in his chair and blew out a stream of cigarette smoke. "Well then, you're a lucky sonofabitch," he slurred, looking straight ahead at nothing. He stared at the ashtray in front of him and crushed his cigarette as if it wouldn't go out. "My family wasn't like that. My father was an asshole. All he ever did when I was a kid was work. He cared more about his damn law firm than he did about his family." Elmer pushed out his lower lip and shook his head. "Never said two kind words to me." He stopped crushing the cigarette and looked at Clark. "And now he's dead."

"I'm sorry, man. That must have been tough." Clark searched for words. "You're right, Elmer: I am a lucky sonofabitch."

Although Elmer's observations about marriage made a lot of sense, Clark could see that his friend was getting pretty drunk and was in no condition to ride his motorcycle home. Clark motioned for the waitress, who could tell what was going on. She brought them two mugs of hot, black, stale coffee, placed them on the table, and began clearing away the brigade of empty beer bottles—this time, without protest from Clark or Elmer.

Elmer didn't look up as the waitress cleared the table, and he didn't comment on the arrival of the coffee. He just picked up a mug and starting sipping. "I'm just going to concentrate on being a good soldier. That's all I know how to do. That's all I'm good at."

"Well, you're a damn good soldier, Elmer." Clark took a big sip of coffee and coughed. "This stuff is definitely lifer juice, isn't it?"

"Yeah," said Elmer with a half-smile. "I drink it all day long." He took another big sip.

The two men sat together, but didn't say much—only an occasional grunt. It was as if all their energy had left them. The raucous lieutenants who normally hung around Elmer stayed at the other end of the room. They could tell that something was wrong: Elmer never drank coffee at Mother's Inn. By closing time, most of the other officers had left, taking the vitality of the place with them. Clark turned to Elmer. "Listen, why don't you and I get going? I feel like cooking some breakfast at my place, and I need some company."

Elmer scrunched his eyebrows. "Breakfast?"

"Yeah. Eggs, bacon. Hell, I'll even make some grits. I'm not gonna take 'no' for an answer."

A hint of Elmer's grin seemed to emerge. "Grits?" Clark nodded. "Okay, Counselor, but it's only 2300 hours. That's at least five hours before breakfast."

"Well, that's about all I know how to cook."

Clark went over to the bar to pay their tab, while Elmer went outside to lock his motorcycle under the porch. As the two men walked slowly to Clark's car, Elmer threw his arm around Clark's shoulder. "You're still the best damn lawyer we've ever had in Panama."

CHAPTER FORTY-ONE

ALTHOUGH CLARK PROBABLY shouldn't have driven home, Elmer was in worse shape—and certainly in no condition to ride his motorcycle.

They didn't talk during the drive to Clark's quarters. Clark reflected on what Elmer had said when he walked in. His first question had been about Clark's situation, not his own, even though he was clearly hurting over the demise of his marriage, too. It caused Clark to consider his own life, the priorities he'd established, and his character as a man and as a friend. He wasn't sure he would have done the same thing. Why hadn't he worried more about his friend than himself? As he drove along the dark road, his introspection got deeper. Was his career more important to him than Ellie? Would she think of him the way Elmer thought of his father: an asshole who worked all the time?

Elmer was a strange guy. He was obviously intelligent, but his behavior was often outrageous. There was even a rumor going around that he had punched out a Guardia National captain for no apparent reason. And why would a guy like Elmer ever have gone to Oral Roberts University? He certainly didn't walk the "straight and narrow." Maybe at one time he had—or at least had tried to. Why had he married a woman with whom he had nothing in common? And then he allowed himself to become emotionally attached to her daughters. Clark looked over at his friend in the passenger seat—head tilted back, mouth gaped open, snoring, and occasionally grunting like an old hog.

Despite his bizarre behavior, Elmer had been a good friend. When he helped Clark get home to see his father before he died, he did so without acting like it was a big deal; there was no hint of you-owe-me-for-this. Just one buddy taking care of another. And then, there was the time Elmer called him out about the old gardener to whom Clark had given money. Elmer was right: if Clark had really been helping the old man in the name of Jesus, then he wouldn't have said anything about it to anyone. Elmer was indeed a walking paradox, but more than anything, a good, good friend.

As they pulled into Clark's driveway, Elmer woke up with a snort. He looked at Clark and asked, "Was I snoring?"

"A little," Clark smiled.

To Clark's great relief, there were eggs and bacon in his refrigerator, and he quickly got to work.

"You look like one of them chefs at Waffle House," Elmer teased.

"I think those guys are 'cooks,' Elmer, not 'chefs.'" He poured Elmer a cup of coffee.

"Well, you might have another profession if this lawyer thing doesn't work out." He smiled and sipped the coffee. "Hey, this stuff is good."

They were both so hungry they downed everything in a few minutes. Although it was well after midnight, they continued to drink coffee. As the effects of their exploits earlier in the evening began to wear off, Elmer got philosophical again.

"You know, Clark, I know you're beating yourself up over the Gomez trial. But I don't think you should." Clark's eyes narrowed as he looked at him and sipped his coffee. "You gotta remember that even though you're a damn good lawyer, you've only tried two cases." Elmer stared at Clark for a few moments. "And you know and I know that experience is the best teacher." Elmer took a drink of coffee and then finished his point. "I bet you'll question the hell out of the witnesses when you prepare for your next trial. I pity them." He raised his eyebrows and grinned.

"You better believe it. Watkins told me the other day that experience is something you don't get until just *after* you need it."

"I knew that girl was smart. Here's the deal, Clark. If Darst had been here, he would've given you guidance. He would have seen that issue coming."

"Yeah. He does have a lot of experience. Have you heard anything else about him?"

"Just that the Army compassionately reassigned him to Fort Bliss. What are you gettin' at?"

"You remember that night when you and me and Jaime went downtown and got chased by that white truck?"

"Hell, yes, I remember it. It scared the shit out of me. You told Jaime that you thought it was Darst's truck, didn't you?"

"I started to, but then Jaime told me that Darst wasn't the subject of any investigation. They were focused on Weeks, and of course Allen was the one having an affair with her."

Elmer stared at Clark for a while, deep in thought. "I don't know, *compadre*. I think you should have told Jaime about the truck. But, at this point, it probably doesn't matter. If Darst was hooked up with Weeks and her drug guys, then she'll implicate him in her case. So, I guess I'd leave it alone."

Clark didn't say anything for a few moments and then changed the subject. "What do you think I should do about Carmen and Gomez? She'll never understand what happened if the General decides to set aside his conviction. She hates Gomez now that I convinced her he killed her little girl."

"Well, you gotta fix that, but I'd wait until the dust settles. If the General does set the conviction aside, then we'll get Jaime to help you. He can *habla* with her. And, he's pretty persuasive."

"Yeah. Good idea." Clark set down his mug and stood up. "You want me to take you home now?"

"Hell, no. I'll rack out on your couch. Set the alarm for 0430 hours, and you can take me home then. Unless you want to go to PT with me tomorrow." Elmer grinned slyly. "You remember how early that is, don't you?"

"Very funny. I'll be ready to take you home. You just make sure you're ready to go."

Elmer flopped down on the couch in the living room. "See you in the morning," he mumbled, his face in a pillow.

Clark got Ellie's Winnie-the-Poo quilt and draped it over Elmer, who was already snoring. The guy was a machine. He got by on almost no sleep, consumed large quantities of beer and booze, and yet was always in top physical condition. He'll go home tomorrow, take a shower, and be ready to lead PT at 6:00 a.m. Elmer thrived on all that rah-rah stuff—PT, field exercises, hard drinking at Mother's Inn. Clark smiled as he looked at his friend, snoring on his couch. He was the strangest person he'd ever met.

The next morning, Clark staggered into the dining room at 4:35 a.m. to find Elmer sitting at the table, sipping a cup of coffee.

"Ready to go, Counselor?" Elmer asked cheerfully in a voice that was a bit too loud for Clark's throbbing head.

"I'm ready to take you home, but that's about it."

Clark took Elmer to his quarters and then returned to get ready for work. He wasn't about to try to keep up with Elmer today on a three-mile run with the troops.

As he was taking a shower, it dawned on him that he hadn't tried to call Janelle in quite a while. By the time he finished getting ready, it was 6:30 a.m., 7:30 a.m. in Pemberton. Not too early to call.

"Hello." Her voice sounded strange. It had been weeks since they'd last spoken, and yet, she sounded downright perky.

"Hey. It's Bobby."

"What do you want?" The perkiness vanished, and her voice became flat, as if she was suddenly in a bad mood.

"I just wanted to know how you and Ellie are doing."

"We're fine."

"Did you get my letter?"

"Yeah, I got it. Congratulations on your trial." Same flat tone.

"Well, it kind of came unraveled."

"What do you mean?"

"It's not important. Listen, I want to know when you're coming back."

Silence.

"Are you still there?"

"Yes. I'm here."

"Well, when are you coming back?"

"I'm not."

"What do you mean you're not?"

"I mean I'm not comin' back, Bobby. I just can't do it anymore."

"Do what?"

"Live with you and the Army and movin' around all the time. I can't do it."

"But this is my life."

"That's just it, Bobby. It's your life, it's not mine."

"Are you telling me you didn't enjoy not having to work and having a maid?"

"There you go again with the maid. Lots of people in Panama had maids."

"Do you have one now?"

"No, and that's just fine. Listen, I gotta go. I have to take Daddy to the doctor."

"What's wrong with him?"

"He's sick, Bobby, as if you really care. I gotta go. Bye."

And that was it. He didn't even get a chance to ask her about
Ellie. What was going on? She used to listen to him. She used to
think he knew best. What did she mean about the Army being
his life, not hers? He sat down at the dining room table with a
mug of the coffee that Elmer had made. It was now so stale that
it qualified as lifer juice. He sipped it and thought about how
difficult it was to talk with Janelle now. She wasn't the girl he'd
grown up with. Carrying on a conversation was almost impossible. Maybe Suzanne was right. Maybe he and Janelle were just
too different to be married to each other. He got up, picked up
his briefcase, and left for work.

CHAPTER FORTY-TWO

TRIP SUBMITTED MAJOR Underwood's revised report to General Kraus, along with a request that the General disapprove the finding of guilty. The General summoned the SJA to brief him on the matter, and Allen made Clark come along. The two men waited silently in the General's outer office for more than a half hour after the scheduled time of their appointment. As the clock slowly ticked, Colonel Allen's right knee bounced up and down—a nervous chain-smoker in dire need of a cigarette. Finally, the General's secretary ushered them in.

"Good afternoon, sir," Allen said, as he approached General Kraus, who was seated behind a large wooden desk, wearing his boots and camouflage uniform. Flags and plaques were arrayed behind him, adding to the intimidating scene.

"Sit down," he said without looking up. Clark and Allen sat down in two wooden chairs in front of the desk. No one said anything as the General examined and filled out a form, which took him at least two minutes to complete. He folded the paper carefully, put it in an envelope, and licked the flap. It was only then that Clark noticed that it was an order for the Army and Air Force Exchange Service. Incredibly, the General had had them wait while he ordered something from the PX catalog—a clear indication of how little he thought of them. Kraus took off his glasses and leveled a somber gaze at Colonel Allen. "What do you have for me?"

"As you know, sir, one of Captain Clark's key witnesses, a Major Underwood…"

"I've read Captain Stephens's submission. What can you tell me about that?"

"Well, sir, these things happen occasionally. As you know, Captain Clark obtained a conviction of Specialist Raul Gomez for the charge of murder. And then…"

"Why wasn't this meningitis issue explored at the Article 32 Investigation?"

"Uh, Clark, can you shed some light on that?" Allen asked, turning to the former fair-haired boy.

Clark cleared his throat. "Yes, sir. Pursuant to common practice, we presented a minimum amount of evidence at the Article 32. The goal of that tactic was to avoid revealing our entire case to the defense prior to the trial. Consequently, Major Underwood didn't testify."

"Well, I suggest you deviate from 'common practice' in the future, Captain Clark. The Article 32 Officer should have all the facts before him prior to making his recommendation to me. Am I clear?"

"Yes, sir." The General was playing Monday-morning quarterback, of course, but Clark knew enough to keep his mouth shut.

At that point, Colonel Allen leaned forward, like an eager student in class. "I should point out, sir, that the defense counsel, Captain Stephens, is an experienced trial counsel." Clark cringed and bit his tongue.

"Indeed." General Kraus looked at Clark and then back at Allen. "Perhaps you should have brought in an experienced prosecutor from the States for such an important case."

"Yes, sir."

Kraus stared at Clark as if sizing him up, causing Clark to

have a flashback to Elmer's toast at the dining-in and the General's reaction. After a few moments of agonizing silence, General Kraus turned his focus back to Colonel Allen. "Is there anything else?"

"Just what's in my review, sir. I would like to point out…"

"Something in the review?"

"Yes sir."

"I'll read it. Anything else?"

"No, sir."

"You're dismissed."

Clark and Colonel Allen stood up. Allen saluted the General, and Clark—startled by his boss's sudden embrace of military formality—quickly followed suit. General Kraus barely looked up as he returned their salutes.

As they walked back to the JAG Office in silence, Clark thought about what Colonel Allen had just endured. He had been surprised by how professionally Allen had conducted the meeting with General Kraus. He hadn't tried to make excuses for the result, nor had he asked the General to order a rehearing of the case, which he could have done. But Clark didn't think the SJA or the General really cared about what had happened to Lydia Mendoza. They only cared about the result of the trial. And he wasn't convinced that Major Underwood's revised report was correct. It was still possible that a little girl's life had been brutally ended when it had barely begun, and yet Kraus and Allen seemed to be more concerned about how the matter would be perceived in Washington.

When they got back, Colonel Allen stopped in front of the liquor store before heading upstairs. "I need to pick up some items in here. But I wanted to tell you, Clark, that we'll soon be getting a major to be the Chief of Military Justice. You made a good effort, but you were in over your head. So, from now on, until the new major arrives, I want you to refer to yourself as the Acting Chief of Military Justice."

Clark had expected as much, but hearing it from Allen still stung.

Two days later—to no one's surprise—General Kraus disapproved the finding of guilty in the Gomez case.

At Elmer's suggestion, Jaime went with Clark to tell Carmen the bad news. Although Clark didn't understand what Jaime said to her in Spanish, it seemed that Carmen didn't grasp what he was saying either. That was no surprise to Clark. He was still in denial. It was hard for him to grasp what had happened. Of course, General Kraus's disapproval of the finding of guilty didn't mean that Gomez was innocent; it only meant that Underwood's revised report had cast doubt on the guilty verdict, and under the circumstances, Gomez couldn't be retried and had to be set free. Clark had done the right thing, but it didn't feel like it.

Several times, Jaime pointed to Clark and said *"hizo bien"*— his way of telling Carmen that Clark had done a good job trying the case. When she started to cry, Clark's stomach twisted into knots the way it had when he was preparing for the trial. As tears streamed down her face, she looked down at a large, gold crucifix that she was clutching in both hands and asked over and over, *"por qué? por qué?"* It broke Clark's heart to watch this young mother sob uncontrollably.

Losing his father was not like losing a child. Clark knew that. But his loss was so recent that he felt he understood what Carmen was feeling. She didn't understand the legal reasoning Jaime was trying to explain to her. She only knew that the General had said Raul Gomez was not guilty. Did that mean she could no longer blame him? And if she couldn't blame Raul, then whom could she blame? Whether it's because of cancer or violence or meningitis, losing someone you love leaves a hole in your heart. Clark knew that, because he had one. He wanted Carmen to have someone to blame, because when there's no one to blame, it's easy for a person to get angry at God.

Did Carmen's desolate cry of "*por qué*" mean that she'd lost her faith? Clark hoped not. He wanted to share with her what Judge O'Brien had said about how—in the end—God works things out the way they're supposed to be. But he couldn't speak Spanish well enough, and he didn't want to get into a big religious discussion with Jaime. It probably would not have comforted her anyway. Her loss was too fresh. So, he just sat there and watched her cry, while Jaime droned on in Spanish.

As they were leaving Carmen's apartment, Clark asked, "Do you think it would help Carmen if we brought her to the CID Office for a call with Major Underwood?"

"No, I don' thin' so, Capitain Clark. She pretty mad. An' I don' thin' tha' woul' help her un'erstan' wha' happen'."

"Is she mad at me?"

"No, she still ma' a' Raul. But she don' un'erstan' wha' happen' and why Raul i' free and why her baby died."

"Should I try to arrange a meeting for her with the chaplain?"

"I don' thin' so. The chaplain i' a nice guy an' all, bu' he don' speak Spanish. An', I thin' she jus' need some time. Le' time do the work."

"What about Raul? He's still her brother-in-law, and now, he's a free man."

"Tha' family will work i' ou', Capitain Clark. Dey pro'ly mad a' him 'cause he made a pass a' Carmen. An' dey may still thin' he killed Lydia. Bu', dey will work i' ou'. Don' worry 'bout i'."

Later that day, Elmer called Clark to inform him that, despite Colonel Allen's repeated requests, the brigade was not going to get a JAG major assigned anytime soon. Clark knew Elmer was trying to be thoughtful by keeping him apprised of those developments, but he no longer cared. He no longer wanted the job.

After word got out that General Kraus had disapproved

the finding of guilty in the Gomez case, Clark's celebrity status ended. No one at Mother's Inn bought him drinks anymore, and Elmer no longer sang his praises to congregations of lieutenants, although he did remain a good friend.

Now that the trial and its aftermath were behind him, Clark wanted to work on his marriage. He bought three calling cards from the PX and tried to call Janelle almost every night. No one answered. After the first few attempts, all he ever reached was an answering machine. The recording was of his father-in-law. "We ain't interested in buying nothing, but if you wanna leave a message, we might call you back."

Getting nowhere with calling, Clark turned to writing letters, which also went unanswered. Fortunately, his mother kept him up to date and reported that Janelle and Ellie looked fine and seemed to be travelling a lot. He decided to ask Colonel Allen if he could take a long leave. He wanted to go home to see if he could convince Janelle to return to Panama. Even if she refused, he would at least get to see Ellie. He couldn't stop thinking about her.

CHAPTER FORTY-THREE

ON A SUNNY Friday afternoon, a few months after the Gomez trial, Clark stopped by his mailbox and was surprised to find two letters addressed in a handwriting he didn't recognize. They were both postmarked "Lubbock, TX" and had been sent only one day apart. For several weeks, checking his mail had been a twice-a-day ritual. He stopped every afternoon on the way home and then again the following morning on his way to work, hoping for any sort of response from Janelle. None came. After a while, he began to worry that none ever would. To avoid becoming depressed twice a day, he began checking only once, usually on his way home. But even that routine was eventually eroded by disappointment. On this particular Friday afternoon, it had been three days since he'd last checked his box.

He decided not to read the letters right away. At home, he poured some Maker's Mark over ice, got one of the Cuban cigars that Elmer had given him as a condolence present, and headed for the terrace. The sun was below the horizon, and the sky was beautiful—an array of color no artist or photographer could ever hope to capture. Clark took it all in for a few minutes before deciding it was time to read the letters. After settling into the lounge chair and lighting his cigar, he opened the envelope with the earlier postmark. As he suspected, it was from Major Darst.

Dear Clark,

In case you haven't heard, I'm a civilian now—no more Major Darst. It's a long story, which I'll tell you one of these days. I've been meaning to write to you for some time, but today I received a letter that prompted me to write this one.

It was from a defense counsel representing Belinda Weeks. He said she was going to be tried at Fort Leonard Wood on drug charges. Needless to say, that was a big shock. He asked me to be a character witness for her. He also said he was trying to get her an administrative discharge in lieu of a court-martial. If the drug charges are serious, I can't imagine a convening authority agreeing to do that.

Is there something I don't know? I suspect that there must be, since she's not being tried in Panama. Did the SJA get it moved because she's a legal clerk? If you can't say, I understand. After all, I'm now a civilian, and I'm no longer your boss.

Belinda was always such a good soldier. It's hard to imagine that she's in so much trouble.

If there is some reason I shouldn't testify on behalf of Belinda, please let me know. If it's just that she got tangled up with drugs, then I don't care. She was always a good soldier for me. She's had a hard life. Her dad beat her and her mom. That's why her mom divorced him and moved back to Panama when Belinda was a little girl. Unfortunately, she grew up in the Panamanian culture, and as you know, there are things about it that are screwed up. It's hard to make ends meet honestly. So, I don't blame her for trying to help her family.

I wish we could have gone fishing more. I enjoyed talking to you about things. I laugh when I think about our conversation about women. I think we could have learned a lot from each other. I don't have any siblings, so it's just me and my mom, now. I don't have anyone to talk to about things.

Well, I'd better sign off. Write to me and let me know about Belinda. I won't help her if she did something terrible, but I will if it was just drugs or something stupid. Also, let me know how the Gomez trial turned out. I'm sure it was a tough one!

Regards,

Jake

Well, so much for Major Darst being a criminal. He would have no reason to write a letter like that if he was mixed up with Specialist Weeks. It sounded sincere, and it sure didn't sound like he knew about her affair with Colonel Allen. The truck that followed Clark and Elmer and Jaime that night must have belonged to someone else. Or, maybe Weeks had borrowed it from Major Darst. In any event, Clark wasn't going to think about that anymore.

After he finished the first letter, he was out of whiskey but still had plenty of cigar to smoke and another letter to read. Before opening the second envelope, he lay back in the lounge chair and stared up at the sky. Where was his life headed? Would he be able to reconcile with Janelle? Probably not. He wasn't used to failing. Even the most difficult challenges in his life had been no match for the sheer force of his determination.

But that wasn't working this time. His marriage was ending, and he had no idea how that would affect his role as a father. When would he be able to see Ellie? Would she even get to know him? Would she love him the way he had loved his father? He felt a cool breeze and went inside to get a jacket and a fresh drink. His cigar—resting on the edge of the table—was still glowing when he got back.

He sat down and tore into the second letter. It was also from Major Darst, although now he was just "Jake."

Dear Robert,

I guess that is your name, isn't it? Everyone always called you "Clark," and I knew that wasn't correct. But I followed everyone else. Following the crowd has sometimes been a failing of mine.

I decided that I owed you another letter. The one I wrote yesterday was too abrupt. I guess I'm just used to being your boss, Major Darst, instead of Jake, the guy you went fishing with. Well, anyway, I think I owe you at least this letter.

First, I want to thank you for being a professional. I know that I dumped a load on you when I left. I should have explained myself, but I couldn't. My family has been going through a horrible time.

As you know, a lot of family ranches and farms are being foreclosed upon. A few years ago, my dad came back to the family ranch after finishing his career in the Army. Everyone was always so proud of him because of his service in Korea and Vietnam. Suffice it to say, he was a much better soldier than he was a rancher. He borrowed too much money, bought too much equipment, and got in way over his head. Unfortunately, he was too proud to tell me about it until it was too late.

In the end, he couldn't bear the responsibility of losing a ranch that had been in our family for over a hundred years. He hanged himself in the barn. My mom found him. She's in bad shape emotionally. I don't think she'll ever get over it. I'm sure that image will never be erased from her memory. Dad always talked about being a descendent of one of the defenders of the Alamo. I guess he thought he had to live up to that, and when things didn't work out for him, he couldn't take it.

As I am sure you understand, I had no choice but to return home and help my mom. My dad's death so shocked our little community that people from all over the county and around Texas showed up to help. We were able to save the ranch, but of course I would have rather saved my dad.

Sometimes, being strong and independent is a good thing. But, it's not the only thing. Dad should have asked for help. He should have put all that Davey Crockett bullshit behind him.

I know that you lost your dad, too. So, you know what I'm going through right now. In my case, though, I can't even take comfort in the knowledge that it was God's will, because I don't think God causes suicide. I just hope He forgives those who commit it.

I've been thinking about the trouble that Belinda is in, and it got me to thinking about our discussion about perceptions. Do you remember that? I showed you the picture of the old lady and young lady. Well, anyway, what I was trying to say is that you need to focus on the fact that sometimes people see what they want to see. Reality is not always the same. I guess that's the case with Belinda and me. I wanted to see a professional soldier, not someone committing crimes under my nose.

So, I guess I need to qualify my advice—assuming you still want to hear it. As much as you should try to understand the other guy's

*point of view—and the way he sees things—you also need to be
aware that you might not be seeing things properly either. As a
prosecutor you must do your best to ensure that you're seeing things
correctly before drawing any conclusions. Otherwise, people could
get hurt or treated unfairly or both.*

*At the risk of sounding like an old guy, offering advice all the
time, let me share a couple of thoughts with you that I've been
considering since I got home.*

*You're a good prosecutor, and I think you have good instincts
about trying cases, so this should make sense to you: life is like a
trial. In a trial we have the evidence we have. We do the best we
can, and after that, it's up to the Big Guy. Life is the same way.
Do the best with what you have and don't worry about tomorrow.
If you've done your best, then worrying about things doesn't
accomplish anything. That said, a little stress is not a bad thing.
Martin Luther King, Jr. had a term for it: "creative tension." He
was talking about civil rights, of course, but I think it's applicable
to life in general, too.*

*The other thing is to always do things for the right reason.
Ulterior motives are a terrible guide. Say what you mean and
mean what you say, no matter what. You probably read some
books by C.S. Lewis when you were a cadet. Here's a quotation
from him that I've tried to live by:*

*"Courage is not simply one of the virtues, but the form of every
virtue at the testing point."*

*It's when you're in a tough spot that virtues matter. Being honest
when it's easy to be honest doesn't mean as much as being honest
when it's hard. That's when it counts. And, it's the same with*

every virtue, such as Duty, Honor, Country. Don't get me wrong.
I'm not saying I'm courageous. I wish I were. But, I've tried to be
virtuous. I think old C.S. knew what he was talking about.

I hope that our paths will cross again, Robert. And I hope that
you'll visit me in Texas sometime. I'm sure I'll be at this address, so
I'll be easy to find.

Yours in friendship,

Jake

How difficult it must have been for Jake. What a horrible situation he'd faced when he went home. It made Clark appreciate Darlene and Frank even more, knowing they were taking good care of his mother. He also thought about his cherished memory of that last visit with his father and how it compared to what Jake went through. Jake's second letter was a shocker, especially since it discussed something so sensitive and personal. It seemed that Jake thought a lot more of Clark as a friend than he had realized.

There was still a lot of cigar left to smoke—absolutely couldn't waste a bit of a Cuban—so Clark decided to stay on the terrace, watch the night sky unfold, and just think. Jake obviously didn't know about Colonel Allen's affair with Specialist Weeks, and Clark decided not to tell him. What good would it do? He was already concerned about the trouble Weeks was in and, at the same time, was disappointed in her. It just didn't seem right to tell him something that would only disappoint him further. Maybe he'd never find out.

The more Clark reflected on his experiences with Jake, the clearer it became that his former boss was a genuinely good man, sincerely interested in helping other people and searching for the best in them. Those disparaging comments Jake made about

Suzanne when they were fishing came before he'd had time to see that she's a capable lawyer with an accurate moral compass. And maybe his comment about "coon fishing" was just what he said it was: a joke. After all, Specialist Weeks is black, yet Jake appeared to be genuinely concerned about what was going to happen to her. And in his letter he'd quoted Martin Luther King, Jr. A racist wouldn't have done either of those things. Clark felt he'd been unfair to even suspect Jake was a racist. It made him realize he needed to learn to be more circumspect—to require more evidence—before drawing a conclusion about someone, especially such a negative conclusion. Just like Jake advised.

The stars began to appear in the night sky. Clark lay back on the lounge chair and looked up in the tree for John. He kept still and watched to see if the "monster"—as Janelle had described him—might peek from behind a palm frond. It had been a long time since he'd seen any sign of him and his sneer. The last time Clark had yelled at him and told him to go back to hell. Maybe he had.

Clark's thoughts returned to that last visit with his father. His dad knew he was dying, and yet, he wanted to tell Clark things he felt were important. In the wake of the Gomez trial, Clark decided he'd never again forget the importance of testing evidence and being careful about drawing conclusions. He began to think about the other things his father had told him that day. He remembered him saying that good and evil could reside in the same person. Although that was a tough concept to understand, he knew his father was right.

Now—this night—it was time to be honest with himself. He could try to justify his actions—telling himself it was because he was depressed, lonely, drunk—but there was no excuse for what he did that night at Club Iguana. And, as he recalled the events of the last few months, he realized he'd done other terrible things: listening in on private conversations; manipulating the SJA;

showing little respect or concern for Suzanne, who had tried so hard to help him. His behavior throughout the Gomez trial had been horrible. Judge O'Brien was right, and his criticism wasn't nearly as harsh as it could have been. Clark knew that Suzanne's advice about telling Trip to call Underwood was the right thing to do, and yet, he'd agonized over that decision. It should have been easy. He had to admit he'd allowed his ambition to turn him into a man he neither recognized nor respected. He had to admit he was one of those men his father was talking about—both good and evil resided in him.

He took the last draw on his Cuban and lowered the back of the lounge chair, so that it was flat, and he could look up at the stars. There were millions of them—far more than he'd ever been able to see back home. He knew there were deeper meanings to his father's lessons. He knew he would have to ponder them for a long time, just as his father had done. And then his thoughts turned to the many nights that he and his father had been outside under the stars—camping, fishing, or merely enjoying the beauty of God's creation in their own backyard.

He looked up at the stars and reflected on what a good man his father had been and how lucky he'd been to have him as his dad. Something came over him and whispered, "Goodnight, Dad." He got up and went inside, went to bed, and slept better than he had in a long time.

CHAPTER FORTY-FOUR

WHEN HE WALKED into the JAG Office on Monday morning, Clark could tell that something was stirring. Clerks were whispering to each other but stopped and looked up at him as if he'd caught them doing something wrong. Suzanne came out of her office and motioned for him to come quickly.

What's going on?" he asked as he walked into her office and shut the door.

"You don't know?"

"No, I just got here. What happened? Did somebody die?"

"Well, not exactly. You sure your buddy Elmer didn't tell you already?"

"Suzanne."

"Okay, okay. Allen is leaving." The smirk on her face meant there was more to the story.

"What?" For a moment, Clark was surprised. Then, his mind started racing. Maybe the prosecution of Specialist Weeks wasn't going according to plan, and Colonel Allen was being implicated.

"I just found out this morning. He's being reassigned to Fort Sheridan. And get this: his wife is leaving him."

"So what's with the clerks? They're all acting strange."

"Are you kidding? You can't keep a lid on this. I'm sure they know all about it."

"Is it because of the affair with Weeks?"

"No." She shook her head and smiled as she raised her eyebrows. "Apparently Allen and Colonel Bednar's wife were also more than cozy."

"What? Bednar's wife?"

"Oh yeah, she's a looker."

"So I've heard."

"And get this…" Suzanne was almost giddy. "Saturday night, Bednar found out about it and confronted Allen in the O-Club bar at Fort Amador. Allen was a little drunk and said something like 'yeah, what of it,' and then Bednar beat the crap out of him right there in the bar. Some other officers had to pull them apart. They took Allen to Gorgas. Had to get five stiches over his left eye. He's not even here today."

Clark was speechless. He stood there staring at Suzanne, who seemed to be enjoying Colonel Allen's misfortune a little too much. He'd seen some rowdy behavior at Fort Hood but never anything like this. Two lieutenant colonels in a fight in the O-Club? Is every male in Panama a serial philanderer? What was it about this place that made men forget who they were and how they had been raised?

Suzanne was fired up and on a roll. "You know what this means, don't you?" she asked eagerly.

"Well, it means Colonel Allen has ruined his life. What about his children?"

"They'll go with his wife. They *always* do," Suzanne said dismissively, apparently not realizing—or noticing—how that sounded to Clark, who winced as he heard the words. "No, Clark, it means that we're going to get a new SJA. They might drag their feet about getting a new major to be the Chief of Military Justice, but they have to send us a new SJA. Regulations require it."

"Good point. I wonder how fast that will happen."

"I bet it will be fast. That job is coveted by every newly promoted lieutenant colonel in the JAG Corps."

A smile emerged on Clark's face. "I think I'll quit calling myself the '*Acting* Chief of Military Justice'." Suzanne knew he no longer cared about having the job. His comment was just a dig at Colonel Allen.

"I would." She smiled, and he turned to leave. "Wait a minute, Clark." Now she was fretting her brow and looking down at her desk, as if pondering something. Without looking up, she said, "You know, I don't think you should take that leave you were planning."

"Why not?"

She looked up at him. "There's too much crap going on, Clark, and we have another trial term to prepare for, remember? You don't want to be gone when the new SJA shows up and asks about criminal law."

"But I already wrote Janelle and told her I was coming home."

"Did you say when?"

"Not exactly."

"Did she write back?"

"No."

"Listen, Clark, I know your marriage is important to you but so is your career. You haven't committed to a time to go home, so you aren't really breaking any plans. You'll just be going later."

"Yeah. Maybe. But I need to think about it." Clark knew Suzanne was looking out for him, but he also knew he needed to get home. He went to his office, sat in his chair, and stared out the window. Suzanne had been a good friend, even when he hadn't. And, if he went on leave and left her, she would have to brief General Kraus on the upcoming cases by herself. That would scare her to death. He decided to write Janelle, tell her what was going on, and let her know that he would like to visit the next month. Regardless of what he did, she would still think he had put his job ahead of his family. But he had no other choice. He couldn't desert Suzanne, and she was right about the new SJA.

For the rest of the week, Clark and Suzanne worked hard to prepare for the trial term, although none of the cases were as significant as the Gomez trial had been. They had a couple of cases involving aggravated assault and several dealing with the distribution of illegal drugs. Trip had another attorney assigned to him—probably because his win-loss record wasn't exactly stellar, so there were now two defense counsel and two prosecutors.

Clark continued Major Darst's practice of going to the CID Office and reviewing the cases with the CID agents while they were still being developed. It was an effective strategy. The evidence the agents assembled in their final reports was so compelling that, in five of the seven cases, Trip and his colleague asked Clark to enter into pretrial agreements (the term the military uses for plea bargains) with their clients. That left only two contested cases to try.

Clark asked Suzanne to handle both cases, since Trip had assigned them to his new guy. He was a Notre Dame graduate—a straight-arrow kid, fresh from the JAG School and full of enthusiasm but with no experience in the courtroom. This time, Suzanne was the veteran trial counsel, and she did an excellent job. She was thoroughly prepared and meticulously listed each element of each offense and lined up evidence to prove each one. Although she seemed a little nervous in the courtroom, she got two convictions and was justifiably proud of herself. She seemed to have conquered whatever it was that had prevented her from performing like that in the past, and Clark was happy for her.

On the Friday that they wrapped up the trial term, Clark took Suzanne to Mother's Inn to celebrate her victories. Although she didn't like the smell of the place or the raucous behavior of its patrons, she did like being included with "the guys." As they sat down, the company commander of one of the soldiers whom

Suzanne had prosecuted came over to their table, put a beer down in front of her, and said, "Thanks, Captain Watkins. This is for you. I'll be happy to buy you more if you want. You got rid of my biggest headache." She smiled, cheeks flushed, and just nodded her head. Clark felt good that she was getting the recognition she deserved, though it was clear she had no idea of how to handle it.

They'd been there for a while, and had more than a few empties lined up on the table in front of them, when Elmer walked in looking glum. Although he said hello, it was clear that he wasn't himself. He walked by without his typical bravado and sat down in his corner alone. Something was going on.

"I wonder what's wrong with Elmer?" Clark mused.

"Why don't you go talk to him?"

"You don't mind?"

"Naw," Suzanne said, shaking her head. "I need to get going anyway, before I've had too many. I sure as hell don't want to get a DUI." She had a smile on her face and a new air of confidence about her. It made Clark feel good. He knew that no matter how hard she tried, she would never be able to keep up with the guys on the morning runs, but she'd finally won their respect, and she deserved it.

"I got this tab," Clark said. "I insist."

Suzanne shook Clark's hand, which was a little strange—possibly the result of a couple of beers too many—and then turned and left.

CHAPTER FORTY-FIVE

"WHAT'S GOING ON, Elmer? You look like you lost your little black book." Clark's attempt at a joke failed to elicit even a grin.

"My career is over," he said, looking down at the table.

"What? What are you talking about, man? Whatever it is, it can't be that bad. FIDO, remember?"

Elmer downed a shot of Jack Daniels, which he'd ordered as soon as he sat down. He turned and looked hard at Clark. "I didn't get picked up for Command & General Staff College." His face bore a pained look that Clark had never seen. His eyes were red-rimmed.

Realizing his friend was hurting, Clark softened his tone. "When did you find that out?"

"Today. You know what this means, don't you?"

"It means you need to apply again."

"It means I'll be passed over for promotion to major. It means my Army career is shot to hell."

"No it doesn't, Elmer."

"Really? What would you fucking West Pointers know about being non-selected? You fuckers get selected for everything."

Elmer's comments stung, but Clark knew Elmer wasn't himself. Clark's expression must have betrayed what he was thinking because before he could say anything, Elmer continued, "I'm sorry, Clark. You don't deserve that. I'm just pissed. I didn't mean that shit about West Pointers." He looked at Clark to gauge whether his apology had been accepted. "It did sound a little envious, didn't it?" His grin returned.

"It ain't nothin' I ain't heard before, buddy. But listen to me, you need to apply again."

"That's just it, Clark. This is the second time I've applied. It means I'm not going, and I think I know why." Elmer paused as if he was trying to decide whether he should explain. "As a lieutenant, I got a bad Officer Evaluation Report from a tight-ass West Point captain, and it's haunting me to this day."

"No wonder we have a bad reputation."

"Aw, I probably deserved it." Elmer took a swig of beer. "I got caught screwing the wife of one of our sergeants."

"Damn, Elmer, that *is* pretty bad. Were you drunk or something?"

"No. And, you know what? I deserved worse than I got— at least the captain thought so." Elmer tried to rally. "She was fuckin' hot, though." Clark stared at him like a big brother. "I know. I know." Elmer realized his rally had failed. "That's why he gave me a shitty OER." Elmer stopped and stared down at the table. "I have a problem, Clark, and it's screwing up my life. Jaime's got his wife back, and I saw your leave request. You'll go home and make nice with your wife, and she'll be back down here with you in no time." Clark didn't respond. "I'm just a worthless piece of shit of a husband." Elmer looked at his wedding ring and twisted it around his finger, although it refused to come off. "I don't deserve her."

"Bullshit, Elmer. You're a good man and a good friend. You can fix whatever it is you're going through."

"Thanks, man. But I don't know." Elmer sighed and leaned back in his chair. After a few moments he turned to Clark with

490

the same pained look in his eyes. "I've got a problem, Clark. I know it, and I know I need help." He inhaled deeply and exhaled. "I'm gonna resign from the Army."

"What? You can't be serious, Elmer. The Army is your life."

"I am. And I'm going to go back to Columbus, Georgia, and I'm going to try to work things out with Tracey. She and the girls are already there." He lit a cigarette. Inhaled and exhaled. "She had every right to be mad at me. Even if she is a little trashy, she never really had a chance at life. I did, and I blew it. Well, I'm starting over as of today."

"Are you sure, Elmer? Your blood is OD Green. We need officers like you." Clark stared at his friend, but he wouldn't make eye contact. "Is there anything I can say to make you change your mind? Are you sure you want to be a civilian? What about all that stuff you said about how the Army is honest and genuine?"

"You remember that shit?" Elmer was grinning again.

"Every word."

"Well, it hasn't turned out that way for me, buddy." Elmer took a long drag on his cigarette and then crushed it out. "Look. I know you're trying to look out for me, Clark, but I know this is the best course of action for me. I screwed up big time. I screwed up my career, and I screwed up my marriage. I can't do anything about the first one, but I'm gonna fix the second one. And, I'm going to make my way in the world without looking back."

"Are you sure you're ready to be a civilian, Elmer? Nine to five. Living in a cubicle. Taking orders from some pussy piece-of-shit who hasn't done half the shit you've done."

"Language, Counselor, please."

"I'm serious, man."

"I know you are, Clark, but my mind is made up."

Clark took a drink of his beer and then leaned back in his chair, deciding what to say next. He sat up and studied Elmer, looking for any evidence that his arguments had caused—or might cause—Elmer to reconsider. There was nothing. Clark could tell that his friend's mind was made up. "You've been a great friend to me, Elmer."

"Here's to friendship." Elmer raised his Balboa.

"To friendship." Clark clinked his bottle with Elmer's. His eyes narrowed as he looked at his friend, and then he said slowly, "Look, if there is ever anything I can do for you, you gotta promise me you'll let me know."

"Absolutely. In fact, there is something you could do, Counselor." Clark sat up and looked at Elmer, waiting to see what he'd say next. His grin was back. "You can take me back to your place, fire up your grill, and give me one of those fancy cigars you smoke. I think I bought some of 'em. Anyway, I've got two steaks at home that are ready to be grilled, and you're a better cook than I am. Sound like a plan?"

"You got it, buddy."

On the way home, Clark stopped to pick up his mail, which included a letter from a law firm in his hometown. It wasn't from the firm of the lawyer helping his mother, so Clark was afraid he knew what was inside. He decided he wasn't going to open it or even think about it until after Elmer was gone, because at that moment his friend needed him.

Clark got home at the perfect time. The sun was setting, and the sky was beautiful. When Elmer arrived a few minutes later, they decided to smoke one cigar before dinner and one after. It was a great evening. When the steaks were grilling, the air was filled with a pleasing aroma that was the perfect complement to a magnificent sunset. They had a good meal, smoked another cigar, and philosophized about life, drinking bourbon until the wee hours of the morning.

Clark convinced Elmer to sleep on the couch again, because he was in no condition to drive, but when Clark awoke the next day, Elmer was gone. He'd left a note on the kitchen counter that said, simply, "Thanks for being my friend." Clark didn't want to contemplate life in Panama without Captain Elmer T. Jackson.

He sat around his quarters most of Saturday and read a little. Having failed to use Elmer's remedy of four aspirin and several glasses of water before bed, he was a bit hung over and, as a consequence, didn't feel like doing anything. He certainly didn't feel like reading what was in that envelope from the law firm.

Sunday morning came, and he decided to do something he hadn't done in a long time: he went to church. The "Protestant" service on post was pretty plain vanilla—designed, as it was, to appeal to Protestants of all denominations. Fortunately, they sang a few familiar hymns, which reminded Clark of home.

He went by The Happy Buddha after church, and they treated him like royalty. He was seated at a nice table in the front of the restaurant and his waiter kept coming by and asking if he needed anything. He didn't know whether it was because he was still the Chief of Military Justice or a frequent customer, atlhough he suspected it was the latter. It was no fun eating alone, so he ate quickly. He knew he needed to get on with reading the lawyer's letter.

As he drove home, he thought about Janelle and their life together. He decided Suzanne's assessment was correct: he and Janelle really weren't right for each other. She wanted to live in Pemberton and grow old there; he didn't. She wanted a quiet life; he wanted to accomplish something significant with his. They certainly didn't see the same future, as Elmer had said a husband and wife should. In fact, he didn't think she really cared about what future he had dreamed of. But if he was honest with himself, he had to admit that he hadn't given much thought to what future she had dreamed of either.

He decided to read the letter on the back terrace, which had become his favorite place in Panama. If—as he suspected—it was bad news, then at least he would learn of it while surrounded by natural beauty. He used a letter opener and carefully sliced open the envelope. It was from Janelle's lawyer. She was filing for a divorce, and if that wasn't bad enough, she was asking for sole custody of Ellie. Clark had reluctantly accepted the demise of their marriage. He knew Janelle had heard all those messages he'd left on her father's answering machine. Yet, she answered only one call—probably because she was expecting someone else—and she never answered any of his letters. He might have to accept the reality that there was no future for them as a couple, but he was resolved to fight her request for sole custody of Ellie. He and Janelle might not have been right for each other, but Ellie was part of him. She had a place in his heart that no one else could fill. He couldn't think clearly about what he needed to do. He could barely breathe. He put the letter back in its envelope. First thing on Monday he would take it to one of the legal assistance lawyers and get his advice.

He spent the rest of Sunday afternoon and evening on the terrace, drinking bourbon and smoking two Cuban cigars, which was at least one too many. He never saw John and assumed he was gone for good, just like Janelle. Although he hadn't eaten anything since lunch, he wasn't hungry and didn't feel like cooking anyway. When the stars came out, he decided to go to bed so he could sleep and forget about all the problems and issues that lay in front of him.

On Monday, he got to the office early and went straight to the Legal Assistance Office, which was on the opposite side of the building from the Criminal Law Section. Although he didn't have an appointment, no one stopped him when he knocked on the door of Captain Wilson, who had arrived in Panama only a couple of weeks before. He was a graduate of the University of Virginia School of Law. With that kind of education he was the best choice. Clark gave Wilson the letter and asked him for an appointment at the earliest opportunity. Captain Wilson was gracious and said to come back on Thursday afternoon.

Clark spent the next four days trying not to think about the divorce and the custody battle. What would Captain Wilson tell him? He and Suzanne worked on post-trial matters from the last trial term, and on Wednesday they both went to a farewell party for Elmer.

The party was at Mother's Inn, of course, and it was quite a bash. The place was packed, and the manager had even decorated with black and gold streamers—the colors of the Ranger Tab. Every attractive woman in the post headquarters was there, along with Elmer's usual collection of lieutenants and a number of other officers and sergeants. Jaime and Agent Robinson showed up, and General Kraus even made a brief appearance. When the General walked in, everyone got quiet. He walked over to Elmer, put his left hand on his shoulder, and grabbed his right hand. Clark heard him say, "We're going to miss you, Captain Jackson. I wish you the best."

The General didn't acknowledge Clark's presence, which was fine—it wasn't Clark's party, after all, and he'd made peace with himself about how the General had handled the Gomez case. Clark knew that he was a good lawyer, and he no longer cared what the General or the SJA thought about that subject.

After the General left, Elmer was again the center of everyone's attention. Although he was having a good time, he was not succumbing to the wiles of the beautiful Panamanian secretaries hovering around him. He was polite, of course, but—uncharacteristically—kept his distance from them. Clark smiled to himself. Either there was something special about Elmer that wasn't readily apparent to the male eye, or these ladies were looking for an American husband. Clark suspected the latter. A few days before, Elmer had explained his "course of action" to Clark, and now, like a good soldier, he was focused on accomplishing it.

Thursday afternoon finally came, and Clark went to his appointment in the Legal Assistance Office. Of course, by now Suzanne knew what was happening—either her sixth sense or her motherly instinct was that good—but she didn't ask Clark about it. She knew it was too painful for him to discuss.

Captain Wilson began rather officiously, "You know, Captain Clark, you can get a stay of these proceedings pursuant to the Soldiers' and Sailors' Civil Relief Act. You can't be forced to participate in legal proceedings in the United States while you are deployed overseas."

"Yeah, I know that, but I'm not sure that's what I want to do. I come from a small town in Georgia, and I know a lawyer there who can represent me. He has a good reputation with the judges, and I'm sure he'll look after my interests. I'm just concerned about her request for sole custody of our daughter."

"Well, you know, Captain Clark, judges have broad equitable powers in these matters. Why don't you send your lawyer this handout on the Soldiers' and Sailors' Civil Relief Act? He might want to request a stay in the proceeding until such time as you can return home for an extended period. He'll also have a better idea of how likely it is that a court would grant your wife's request for sole custody."

"I guess you're right. There's not much more to it than that, is there?" Captain Wilson shook his head. "I guess I just wanted to get another perspective on the matter," Clark sighed.

As Clark started to leave, Captain Wilson cleared his throat. "May I ask you a question?" He leaned across his desk with an eager look in his eyes. Clark nodded. "How can I get to be a trial counsel?"

"Well, the short answer is that you can ask the new SJA, although I don't anticipate anything opening up until Captain Watkins leaves. She'll be headed to the JAG Advanced Course next spring."

Wilson leaned back in his chair, clearly disappointed with that answer. Something within Clark prompted him to continue.

"Have you thought about why you want to be a trial counsel?" Wilson looked at Clark as if he'd asked him whether he really wanted to win the lottery. "Seriously, if you haven't thought about it, you should. It's not an easy job, but it is an important one. If you want it because you think it will put you in the limelight, then you're seeking it for the wrong reason. A prosecutor's job is to do justice. It's not just about winning cases with courtroom theatrics. It's about prosecuting those who should be prosecuted. And sometimes, that's not easy to discern."

Captain Wilson squinted his eyes and cocked his head. He clearly didn't understand what Clark was trying to tell him. "Look," Clark said, "come see me in six months. Captain Watkins will be heading back to the States around then." Wilson smiled, and Clark stood up to leave. "Thanks for taking a look at that for me."

"Oh, uh, no, Captain Clark. Thank you. I would really welcome the opportunity to learn from you."

"Make sure you think about what I said before you come to see me." Clark gave him a quick nod and went back to his office.

ABOUT THE AUTHOR

WILLIAM H. VENEMA is a Distinguished Graduate of the U.S. Military Academy at West Point. He also earned an MBA from Georgia State University and a JD from the University of Virginia School of Law. His legal career spans over thirty years and includes time in the U.S. Army Judge Advocate General's Corps, in law firms, and as in-house counsel in major corporations. He has written extensively on legal topics and published a book entitled *The Strategic Guide to Selling Your Software Company*. Prior to entering private practice, Bill served in the U.S. Army in Germany, Panama, and several stateside assignments. He is a graduate of the Army's Airborne and Ranger schools, as well as the Command and General Staff College. His author website is at: www.williamhvenema.com.